Jonathan,
I
Happy Chris
[signature]

Capital Sin

John Orchard

Grosvenor House
Publishing Limited

This book is published by
Grosvenor House Publishing Ltd
Link House
140 The Broadway, Tolworth, Surrey, KT6 7HT.
www.grosvenorhousepublishing.co.uk

This book is a work of fiction. Any resemblance to
people or events, past or present, is purely coincidental.

A CIP record for this book
is available from the British Library

ISBN 978-1-83615-015-2
eBook ISBN 978-1-83615-016-9

For Mum.

Acknowledgements

First and most importantly, Debbie, without whom none
of this would have happened, and our beautiful,
ever-expanding family for their unflagging support.

Thank you xx

I would like to particularly acknowledge the encouragement and
advice of Bondee, I wish you were here to see it published. The
challenging intellect, stimulation and friendship of George and
Morley who gave me so much, and Simon who doesn't realise
how much he does.

Susanne and Stuart, thank you for your unflagging efforts,
hugely appreciated. Further appreciation for professional input
from Mark Wilcox, Pete Coyle, Catherine Hammett, but especially
Gideon Roberton, (who writes the *Drake's War series* under the
pen name Gideon Saint) – huge thanks. To Nikki and Sally for
enduring the earliest draft; for my random pestering of Chris
Holder and Chris Smith plus Carol, Canadian Wendy and of
course, Julie from Grosvenor House Publishing.

To my other friends, and the strangers now friends, who over the
years have tolerated being alternatively bored and bombarded
with the demands of *'The Book'*......

Prologue

Sam's fear transcended all other emotions, so strong it powered her to yank the seatbelt painfully tight and squeeze even harder on the overhead handle as their Landcruiser careered chaotically through the rain forest. Violently bouncing over the uneven terrain, it slapped away the leathery palms that reached down from the jungle canopy. Marco's savage spinning of the steering wheel as he zig-zagged through the underbrush was the only thing keeping them out of their pursuers' reach.

'Get on the phone, call the emergency line,' Marco shouted over the roaring engine, crashing undergrowth, and bursts of gunfire. 'They're going to kill us.'

'Keep your foot down, we've got to outrun them,' Sam replied, her voice straining to sound more positive than she felt as gunfire ripped, like a scythe felling wheat, through the dense rainforest. Exhausted and bruised, she prayed for a clearing, a small path, anything that might give them a chance to distance themselves from the semi-automatic fire being unleashed by their relentless pursuers.

Bracing herself as best she could, she grabbed the cumbersome satellite phone and punched in the World Health Organisation's emergency number, praying one of their employer's operators would answer. They rammed a tree root as big as the car, splintering glass and buckling metal plates, which added to the discord and threw the passenger side wheel into a rut. Distracted by the phone, Sam already knew she had reacted too late, thrusting her feet forward just as her head slammed into the windscreen pillar. Nausea flooded her senses while blood, pouring from the wound on her temple, blurred her vision as she fumbled to retrieve the phone.

Could she hear it ringing? Yes, though barely audible amidst the racket of gunfire and engines as Marco sawed at the steering wheel to escape the rut. They were off again, underbrush clawing against the jeep as they picked up speed. It was impossible to tell what was happening on the other end of the line. The phone, slippery from blood and the suffocating humidity, jumped away from her ear with every jolt. There was no way to tell whether anyone had answered.

Shaken like a ragdoll, she clutched it with both hands and shouted, 'This is Samantha Forbes. I have proof that Sino Polymetallic is dumping cadmium into the Amazon.'

The Landcruiser lurched violently to the left smashing Marco into his door; Sam slammed against him but held onto the phone for dear life.

'Gallons of it every day,' she yelled. 'Kids dying all over the place, and now they're trying to kill us. They're shooting at us, they're insane, we...'

Marco lost his hold on the steering wheel after a stomach jolting contact with a fallen tree, regained it, and pushed the accelerator to the floor. The phone spilled from Sam's hands as she grasped for the handle, and for breath; she let the phone be.

They both exclaimed with relief as they broke out into a clearing and picked up speed through the tall grass. Marco turned to Sam for reassurance, tears running down his face. He turned his gaze towards the photograph he had stuck to the dashboard – his wife Margaretta, smiling with one arm around Chico, their first child, the other cradling her belly.

'We're not going to make it, are we, Sam?'

She scrambled for the phone again, yelling into the mouthpiece, 'Dear God, you've got to help us.'

*

The Landcruiser didn't explode when it compacted hard into the ravine floor, thirty metres below the jungle's edge. That mattered little, though, as by then Sam and Marco were already beyond the realm of the living. Their pursuers, Vinny and Raul, descended leisurely, their pace unhurried. There would be an autopsy, but their coroner had already been told what the verdict was.

Raul pulled Marco back by his hair and centred his photo on the gaping hole in his forehead.

'Dumb fuck oughta looked where he was headed,' Raul snorted, as he moved to kneel at Sam's feet, gently brushing away loose earth from her thighs to improve the picture's composition. Vinny watched him crouch down to frame the glimpse of her panties under her shorts, taking time to position her head at the right angle, with her bloodied hair spread out on the rock.

'You're a sick bastard, Raul.' Vinny's harsh features creased further. 'The Chinaman only wants one photo to prove she's dead, not a goddam portfolio.'

'It's art, my friend, its beauty lies in the eye of the beholder. And will you look at that Bluebird tattoo on her shoulder? That's a beauty, I'm having that as my screensaver.' Raul laughed, the small tattoo of a cross next to his left eye creasing into a star shape as he continued to capture the macabre scene with his mobile phone.

'It's twisted voyeurism, *my friend*. Go grab all their phones and laptops; we need to find out if they sent anything and, if so, who the hell it was to.'

Vinny turned with unemotive coolness, the jerrycan of gasoline in his hand felt weightless, as if it were an extension of his arm. With a fluid motion, he emptied the contents over Sam, Marco, and the Landcruiser, drenching all. The flammable vapours filled the air, mingling with the jungle's heavy humidity.

Both men scaled the ravine's steep sides with ease, hardly out of breath as they stood at the top. With a swift tug, Vinny pulled the tag on the red flare, igniting a vibrant crimson plume to billow against a bright blue sky. He launched the flare to sail in a downward arc towards the wreckage below. In an instant the jungle erupted, its inhabitants shaken by the explosion. A giant whoosh as the air was sucked in, fuelling a deep boom which echoed and bounced off the hard rock faces, applauded by the frantic flapping of a thousand wings.

Impatience oozed from Raul like a persistent fever. It wasn't the money itself; it was the pursuits it enabled.

'You gonna call the Chinaman now?' he enquired, his voice tinged with restlessness. 'He's gonna pay well for this one, eh?'

Vinny, aware of the delicate balance of their association with this particular client, replied with a cautious demeanour, 'Let's put some distance between us first.' His mind was always attuned to any potential risks.

'D'ya trust these guys, Vinny? This Chinaman and his four *associates*. We done dozens of hits fo' them now, and I ain't even thinking about that plane.'

Vinnie had never managed to completely forget about that plane, or its one hundred and thirty-eight innocent passengers. Nor the hundreds of children in Manaus, poisoned by the cadmium, and he wondered how much of the iceberg's tip he was looking at.

'That's a lot of time, Vinny. We cool with them? You know, with our identities an' all?' Raul was too desensitised to be scared; conflict and greed were his stimulants.

Vinnie saw a very different risk in being so deep with this client. 'He pays big, and he pays on time. I don't need to know any more.' Preoccupying himself with the sat phone's keypad to avoid further questioning, he dialled the number from memory, prudently never storing his clients' details. The call was answered promptly, the Chinaman's voice lusting to learn the outcome.

'Is it done?' he demanded.

'Yeah,' Vinny confirmed. 'It's all been taken care of.'

'Good.' No hint of appreciation. 'I'll make the transfer. There's something else I want you to do. The head of security for the zinc mine should never have let her get as close as she did. I want an example made. I want to send a message.'

'Sending messages like that is visible, so it comes at a price.'

'Just do it,' came the resolute reply. Vinnie knew the Chinaman had too much on them for him to refuse.

Chapter One

Ben lost himself in the bright Zurich morning as he gazed out of the conference room's tall windows. A plane, high up, invisible but for its vapour trail in the clear blue sky, drew a taut, white line behind it, signposting its direction on the edge of the earth's atmosphere. He cleared his mind and focussed on his opening lines. He knew that when he walked to the lectern, the audience of several dozen senior leaders from Global und Mercantil Bank would quieten. They did, and while he waited for them to get comfortable, he made eye contact with every person in the auditorium.

'Good morning. I'm Ben Mason, and for the next two days I'll be leading the team to take you through your leadership course. Over these two days, we will share with you some techniques of decision-making and leadership practices used in conflict environments and how you can apply these in your roles within the bank.'

Ben paused and listened for the questioning murmur that floated through the audience. The audience had been briefed on their military history, and the murmur always came when he mentioned conflict environments.

'Please feel free to ask questions as we go along. Anything you don't understand, or disagree with, just put your hand up.' Ben knew that to clear the air early it was essential to provoke the audience.

A hand was raised; it always was at this point. 'Yes, the lady next to that aisle.' Ben pointed. 'Can we get her a microphone please?'

'Herr Mason, do you honestly believe techniques and decisions made during a war can be applied to a Swiss bank in peace time? Also, how does an ex-soldier understand how we make decisions in our bank?'

Ben patiently listened as assent murmured through the audience. The questioner's voice sat closer to self-satisfaction than curiosity.

'It's a great question, thank you. For some years I was a director of one of your biggest competitors, so I know how a bank works. Before that I was in the army, so I know how that works. I've seen military decision-making more beneficially applied within banking than banking techniques being applied to the military.' Ben could see the questioner was halted by the implied criticism of her profession.

'Why?' The questioner was defensive now.

'Because the stakes are higher in a conflict, so your performance level must also be higher, or you can die. It's as simple as that. As a leader in GMB, the consequence of poor decision-making is a combination of lower profit or dented professional pride. They're important, but hardly fatal.'

The slightly chastened questioner mumbled a quiet 'thank you' and settled back in her seat.

No more hands were raised as Ben continued. 'First, it will help set the scene if you witness some real examples of decision-making in conflict environments. The following footage is reproduced under licence from the TV channel who included it in one of their documentaries. They made it using British soldiers' bodycams on a real patrol that I led in Helmand Province, southern Afghanistan, fifteen years ago. We've added videos and stills from soldiers' own mobile phones. They're more graphic and tell a deeper story than the broadcaster's. Some of the scenes you'll see may be distressing. I'm sorry about that, but to be clear, this is not a glorification of war. This is to set the scene for you for the next couple of days.

With that, Ben used the lectern's controls to dim the lights and lower the window blinds. The audio-visual equipment powered-up as a soundtrack began and took the senior leaders of GMB into a different and less comfortable world. For the next ten minutes, Ben and his practised team rotated to narrate and explain what was unfolding in between the stills, the bodycam feeds, and smartphone videos. The images had been taken by Ben's comrades on that patrol, then slickly edited to produce a gripping depiction of what decision-making in a Helmand conflict environment was like.

To the audience, Ben was providing an objective narration for their Leadership Development Course. In reality, he was reliving a difficult history: Ben Mason was playing the character Ben Mason, in a film about Ben Mason. For them, it was projected on a screen;

for Ben it was projected in his mind, and the scene on the huge screen was all too familiar to him.

*

The two camouflaged Jackal armoured vehicles bounced across Helmand's rough ground, kicking up sand for the scorching wind to spit in their faces. The vehicles' thick tyres bit into stone and sand, churning up a dust-funnel in their wake. Ben scanned the barren landscape beyond the village as he motioned the driver to slow. The other Jackal, ten metres to their left, slowed in time with them.

Ben knew that tearing in there with their own sandstorm wouldn't win any hearts or minds. Anyway, by now they'd have told the Taliban and the local War Lords, plus those getting rich from opium, or all three. Just depended on who was currently paying the best price for intel on British military movements. The arid heat pressed down remorselessly, sapping life from everything apart from the bloody flies, a fitting back-cloth to one of the most desperate places on earth.

He felt the usual awakening as they approached their destination, and his senses welcomed the familiar hit. *It's natural and necessary,* he reasoned. *Nothing I can do about it even if I wanted to.* Ben Mason knew his instincts and capabilities had kept him alive during two tours in Afghanistan. Otherwise, he would be as dead as so many of his colleagues. They had said it would be a straightforward patrol. They had said. The same *they* who decided to put thousands of boots on the ground, supposedly to handhold post-conflict Afghan reconstruction. Really? They said no detected Taliban activity, opium farmers, or their hired Jihadist fighters for miles around. Supposedly none of the dreaded Green Zones of irrigated wadis whose thick vegetation provided the cover much loved by Taliban fighters. Just an infinity of desolate sun-baked sand and rock.

Turning in his seat, Ben gave an enquiring thumbs-up to the other armoured vehicle. Wrapped tightly against the heat and the sand, he received a thumbs-up from his Corporal leading the other Jackal. Ben nodded in acknowledgement as he leaned towards the driver.

'Put her on top of that mound, Samsy.' He indicated a small rise thirty metres short of the nearest building. 'Point us away from the village. I want that 50 cal ready just in case,' referring to the fifty-millimetre-calibre heavy machinegun mounted on the Jackal's rear platform.

Four years ago, joining the Parachute Regiment had been Ben's salvation; his only option outside a young offenders' institution. But the last two years in Helmand had robbed him of any remaining naivety. Too many good people needlessly killed through a lack of accurate intel and inadequate equipment. Their patrol today was to offer 'compensation' for a villager allegedly injured by their regiment in a recent Taliban firefight. A village of four or five dozen people who were not just expecting them, but who should have been welcoming them. Yet there was not a soul in sight. Ben trusted his instincts more than he did the Army's intelligence.

The Jackal circled and easily gained the slight slope as it turned to face the way they had come. The other vehicle faced forward, towards the village. Its four infantrymen stood and stretched.

'Okay, boys. Ferret and Samsy, you're Bravo One. Stay here with the 50 cal and be ready to go in a hurry if we need to. Smudge, you're Bravo Two. Take your team and work parallel with us up the right side of these.' He pointed to the closest buildings.

'Bravo three,' informed Ben, with a half-glove thumb jabbing his own chest, 'we'll take that main track through the middle. Now remember, on your toes. They said this one will be as close as we'll ever get to a peacekeeping mission.' Ironic gallows humour carpeted every word.

Sand, the colour of burnt cream, puffed from under their boots as they jumped down, the hot wind hurrying to erase their footprints. Ben wondered if that was a metaphor for how long it would take to erase the impression made by the army of foreign soldiers occupying this land. Giving a thumbs-up to the two soldiers remaining with the vehicle, and slinging weapons in the familiar ready position, the two groups set off on their routes.

They picked up the vibe from Ben. No-one to be seen, no sound apart from goats bleating somewhere further up the track.

Just heat, dust, and the ever-present wind whistling past the built-in helmet microphones.

Ben had learned the hard way that the Taliban were an unconventional enemy. They had two distinct advantages over their better-equipped invaders: They placed a lower value on their own or the enemy's lives; and they chose the time and place to engage that enemy. This time, they chose to wait until the two teams were out of sight of the Land Rover, and of each other.

He heard the fast metallic clang-clang-clang of semi-automatic machine gun fire milliseconds after the first deadly rounds thudded into the stone walls next to them. Internal chaos, as his heart rate shot up and his stomach churned; being shot at was that extreme. Even when you're expecting it, an attack always comes as a surprise and is still the most frightening experience. Someone you've never met hates you so much they want to kill you for a reason you don't understand. Diving head-first into sand and stones means nothing when fear this strong grips you.

Ben forced himself to surface, to swim above the fear. He rode the rapid increase in his pulse, to control and direct it. Grasping to retain control, he knew it was not just a case of making the right decision, it was making it quickly and avoiding the wrong one. If you don't, you're dead. As simple as.

'Taff, you cock. Down, mate. Get down.' He yanked his friend hard by his webbing. 'And on your front, you knobhead.' As he pushed him hard onto the ground, he was angry that Taff's poor thinking could have got him killed. 'Right, Taff, that wadi,' he pointed, 'the gap in the broken wall, let 'em know you're fucking serious, mate.' Positive action was the best-known cure for panic, as Taff immediately started firing short bursts from his light machine gun into the gap.

'Wilksey, on your belly, through this hut, and three-round bursts into each of those there.' He indicated a group of huts at right angles to Taff's, from where he had seen tell-tale muzzle flashes.

Ben knew the secret for survival when you were fighting both fear and an enemy. Find cover, return fire, occupy your mind with positive action, and take responsibility. You'd then be too busy for negative thoughts or panic, even though you just wanted to bury your head in your hands and scream. Hoping it would all go away. It wouldn't unless you first faced and overcame the fear inside you. Then you could face the enemy. That is what Ben did.

More rounds raked the dusty ground around them, a long blast of continuous and random firing. Ben was focussed now, his breathing and thoughts under control, recognising the shooter had randomly sprayed all thirty rounds of his magazine in one anxious pull on the trigger. He now knew some parts of the attack force was poorly organised. No seasoned soldier, Taliban, or squaddie ever uses an entire magazine in one blast, unless he is an idiot or on drugs, which the Taliban sometimes were.

The walls of the single-storey building provided all the cover they needed for now. Their attackers had panicked and opened fire a few crucial moments before Ben's fireteam were stranded in open ground. It helped that Ben had chosen a route with good cover which he pressed hard into, the bleached stone walls providing sanctuary as the initial burst of fire abated. Ben gave short and clear instructions, quickly ensuring they had all angles covered as he radioed the other team.

'Bravo Two, sitrep!' he shouted over the renewed staccato of machine gun fire.

'It's a daylight-mugging, Sarge. We've got contact from the north, no casualties, returning fire.'

'Bravo One, sitrep,' Ben radioed to the armoured vehicles. 'Bravo One, are-you-reading-me?' Still no reply.

There never would be. The sniper had shot Ferret and Samsy just as the ambush started. A single second was all that had separated them as they stood manning their fifty cals, baking under a foreign sun.

'Bravo Two, we're pinned down. and Bravo One's unresponsive. I'm going back for them, and I need cover.'

'On it.' Smudger didn't need to elaborate as he directed his two reports to concentrate their firepower onto a small group of buildings below them. It had the desired effect. Ben's team were up and running back towards Bravo One and the Jackals.

'Oh shit.'

'You fuckin Tali bastards.'

Anger and despair gripped him. Despair for the reasons they were here; anger at being given intel that had completely miscalculated the degree of risk. Again. With accurate intel he would have planned a completely different approach or, more likely, not approached at all. He felt sick with the needless loss of life and more so as they were his men. He forced himself to rise above it. Again. He had to or they would all die.

Ben snapped into the present, just in time to stop his men crossing the last thirty metres of open ground to their vehicle. From the bloodied skulls of their two colleagues, barely attached to their bodies hanging limp over the side of the vehicles, he could see what had happened. A glistening crimson stream washed down the Jackal's door, already darkening to deep garnet as the life-giving fluid baked slowly in the sun. Ben was focussed again as he looked through the sight unit on his rifle.

'Both shot from the left. Possibly from slightly above. Our shooter is in that cluster of buildings there.' He pointed to a group of single-storey buildings set back thirty to forty metres to the left of their murdered colleagues. 'In fact, he's still on the roof terrace.' He continued to look through his scope. 'He's ducked down behind the top wall. Look on the roof, to the left of that dip in the wall, there's a drain hole. You can see a movement behind it.'

The two soldiers nodded as they also looked through their rifles' sights. Had it not been for Ben, they would have run out to their dead colleagues, all adrenalin-charged fury, and been shot.

'Yes, Sarge,' they echoed in unison.

'Bravo Two, what's your sitrep?'

'Mopping up. We got the guys who were pinning you down, then we outflanked our friends up here. Making our way back to you now. You rendezvous with Bravo One?'

'No. And it's not good mate, not good at all. The fucking Tali had a sniper on them, he was waiting for it all to kick off. He got Samsy and Ferret. It's another intel cluster.'

'Fuck. Where's the bastard now?'

'He's on a roof, sixty metres away. Retrace your route, veer left one hundred metres out. You'll see a group of buildings set out on their own, with a broken livestock enclosure to its right. Our shooter's on the roof terrace, but we don't know who else is around.'

'Roger. I'll ping you when we have it in sight.'

Ben sensed the movement behind him before he heard it, spinning and bringing his gun to the firing position in one swift movement. A small boy, with frightened brown eyes set in a soft face, stood shaking and looking at him from an open doorway less than ten paces away. Ben hated himself as he kept the boy's forehead in the crosshairs of his scope, but he had to. The boy's eyes, wide with fear, were magnified through Ben's rifle scope. Cruel experience had taught him that the Taliban did not discriminate when choosing their suicide vest couriers. Without moving his rifle, he slowly raised his left hand.

'Stop. Stop or I will fire.' He replaced his hand back onto the rifle's barrel. His right index finger increased its pressure on the trigger. He knew exactly how much pressure was needed to explode a ten-year-old's skull, and he hated being able to make that calculation.

The boy froze; so did Ben. Their hearts pounded at the same rate. Two strangers with only a desolate Afghan desert in common, and neither wanted to be there nor understood why Ben was. Probably only the boy would die, and before he would be old enough to understand why the foreigner had killed him. Ben didn't know what a 'soul' was, he knew his soul did not want him to kill the boy, but his head said, 'If he moves, squeeze the trigger.'

Ben aged a year every few seconds. *How can I care so much yet be capable of such cruelty? How can I?* Another unanswered lament. His brain won, he was focussed again, he was breathing, and he checked the pressure on his trigger finger. Then the boy moved, and through the scope the boy's magnified head disappeared.

The fat, brown fingers of his hysterical mother had grabbed him, and the pair fell sobbing into the dustbowl that was the front door of their home. Ben lowered his rifle. He was shaking. 'Fuck,' he murmured, as slowly a dozen villagers appeared from the semi-darkness of their homes while Ben's radio reported Smudger's news.

'Bravo Two in position. Movement on the roof but do not have a shot. There's two doors and an archway – all covered. You got the front? We're ready to go in.'

'Hold your position, Bravo Two, we've already lost two men. We've got a situation here, and they've got at least one sharpshooter up there, so hold your position. Just keep them pinned down until I'm with you.'

More nervous villagers appeared from seemingly nowhere. 'Keep 'em covered, boys, just in case,' he instructed his two reports.

'Anyone speak English?' Ben shouted to the group now of about thirty villagers.

'I,' came the guttural reply from a tall, willowy man in greying robes matching the greying beard that reached down to his chest. His stooped frame rested on bony hands that leant on an even bonier cane as he inclined forward. His skin was like cracked leather, with stubble protruding above the line of his beard, and withdrawn, sunken eyes.

'I speak Eng-lish.' His thickly accented pronunciation was hard to understand. The crowd parted as he shuffled forward, supported by a stick as crooked as him. 'Tariban, Tariban. They say kill us if we warn you.' He spread out long, calloused fingers in a begging motion. 'My son, my son. Tariban make him do. They make him do.' His hands pressed together, rising and falling in a praying motion.

Everyone flinched as gunfire crackled behind them. Ben hoped that he recognised the sound of a British Army light machine gun.

'Stay here and cover them. No-one leaves or moves from here. Got it?' Ben shouted firmly as the two paras nodded. He sprinted towards the gunfire. 'Bravo Two, was that you?' he shouted into the radio as he ran, hoping the roof sniper had not got another one.

'Yes, Boss. He's on his own and tried to make a run for it. Think we've winged him; either way he's pinned down. We're going in to finish the job.'

'Negative, Bravo Two, they're just kids set up by the Taliban. Hold your position until I get there.' Ben ran across the open ground.

He was almost too late. One of Smudger's reports had pulled the wounded shooter from the roof terrace and was pressing his gun against the head of a very frightened teenage boy.

'Do not fire your weapon, Private. I repeat, do not fire your weapon, and that's an order.'

Ben repeated the same order, as all three members of Bravo Two turned towards him. The red mist which shrouded them did not need to be visible for Ben to see its effect. Even his closest supporter, Corporal Smith, wrapped his morals within its folds.

'Sarge, he just murdered Samsy and Ferret. Shot 'em in cold blood. Our mates, Sarge.' Smudger started to lose it now. 'This fucking bastard just shot our fucking mates. We can't let him get away with it.' He shook with rage and tightened his finger around the trigger, just as a few dozen nervous looking villagers appeared around the corner.

Ben's two colleagues, unsuccessfully holding back the human tide, walked backwards in front of them. The mother of the ten-year-old boy from earlier was now down on her knees, screaming hysterically in Pashto. Anguish is a universal language, as she thumped her fists against her chest. She reached out her scrawny, rag-clad arms to him, then towards the shooter. Ben realised it was another of her sons, carrying out the Taliban's bidding under threat of death, of murdering his family. They'd given him a gun and press-ganged him into their service.

'Shoot the fucker.' This time it was Smudger who raised his gun and stared mutinously at Ben.

Chapter Two

Ben used the lectern's controls to gradually bring up the lights in GMB's spacious auditorium and conducted the large window blinds to retreat into their ceiling recesses. As light flooded into the auditorium, a man, so obviously out of place in a Swiss bank, emerged from the shadows at the back. He had seen all he needed to. Walking calmly to the car park, he made a call.

'It's me. Mason checks out, he appears to be solid. I'd say go ahead as planned. I didn't detect anything that says he knows this was orchestrated.'

'Good, thanks, Francois. I'll meet with him later today and see if we can get him on board.'

*

Ben was always intrigued to observe audiences' reactions at this point. A universal exhale, blinking against Zurich's bright morning sunlight as it flooded into the room. Gradually they came back into the present. Ben knew it was not just the bright sunlight that made them blink. They were all stunned by the intimacy of their submersion in war's brutality. Mainstream media's stage-managed reproduction was seldom close enough to show the real horror as it unfolded. Nonetheless, a tentative applause built. Civilised business protocol dictated you applauded at the end of a presentation, although many were unsure whether they should be doing so.

Helmand had been fifteen years ago, and Ben Mason was now a consultant running a two-day 'Leadership In A Crisis, or Crisis In A Leadership?' seminar for the senior leaders of GMB, one of the world's largest and most systemically important financial institutions.

The Helmand patrol had been the final straw in his crusade against the British Army for their inadequate intel, equipment, and strategy. But they only let you leave on their terms, and Ben had

11

been forced to sign an NDA – a legal contract that was effectively an indefinitely suspended sentence.

'You will shortly break out into your working groups, then we'll rotate you through the various modules. But before we do that, are there any questions?'

Ben pointed. 'Yes, the young man on that end of the row. Your question, please?'

'I've never read the Geneva Convention, but you can't just shoot prisoners. Your men's reaction almost implies it would be accepted if it can't be proved?'

'You're right, you cannot just shoot prisoners.' Ben paused. 'Simplistically, if war has been declared, you can legally shoot the enemy if they are a threat to your life. But literally, within a second, you must protect them if they cease to be a threat. For instance, by surrendering. In short, though, no, we did not shoot him. We took him back with us and handed him over to the ANA, the Afghan National Army, who processed him under their laws. The village elder was particularly pleased, as it was one of his four sons. Two had already been killed by the Taliban, so he was very happy with the outcome.'

Ben was accustomed to that question, and it benefited no-one to dwell on the legal complexities of armed conflict. None of these people would ever have to make the decisions he'd had to. Nor incur the rejection of their comrades for saving a prisoner's life while, simultaneously, attracting the disdain of their seniors for letting the incident happen in the first place.

'Herr Mason, which aspect of your version of leadership deals with assaulting a senior member of staff? Your boss, I believe?'

Eighty people's rapt attention creates an audible sound.

Ben tried hard not to pause. 'There's no particular aspect of leadership which directly covers that.' His smile hid much. 'But as you appear to be so interested in my personal life, I will tell you. I was a Director of Staunton Wier.'

They all knew Staunton Wier – an aggressive and profitable London-based competitor.

'I ran asset infrastructure mergers and acquisitions.'

The audience now knew who Ben was; Staunton was the market leader of this profitable sphere.

'My boss sent me to Zurich, to set up an office for the emerging Eastern European market. His criteria for choosing me was because, unknown to anyone, he was obsessed with my wife.'

Dissent rose from the audience.

'My wife worked at Staunton, that's where we met. We now know from text messages that my boss was fixated with her, and you would understand why if you had ever met her. I joined Staunton, and over some years we met, fell in love, and married. This did not sit well with him, so he created a reason for me to be transferred to Zurich. And while I was away, he sexually assaulted her. It happened on a group Away Day, and late in the evening, with some drink consumed, he groped my wife. No witnesses, her word against his. "It was a misunderstanding, a bit of fun that got out of hand" was his defence, so I confronted him. He smiled, said she had been drunk and had encouraged him.

'That was an insult to my wife, and me, so I punched him, and that put Staunton in an impossible position; they had to immediately fire me. Unlike my relationship with the British Army, I haven't signed a Non-Disclosure with Staunton, so I can tell you about it. To directly answer your question, I think we would want our leaders to brave enough to do the right thing, no matter what the circumstances. That is what we'll be talking about over the next two days. I hope that has answered your questions?'

The impulsive applause from the audience answered that question and won Ben many admirers. None more so than Claus Oppenheimer, the Chairman of GMB, who had stayed at the back, exactly where the stranger had stood earlier. Claus left and sought his secretary.

'Iris, can you find out if this leadership course has a wrap-up meeting. If it does, please move whatever is in my diary so I can attend. Thanks.'

Chapter Three

'Hello, Ben, I'm Claus Oppenheimer.'

Claus extended his hand, giving Ben time to evaluate him for the first time. Almost forty years between them, Claus' handshake was firmer than Ben had expected. An athletic frame supported an upright posture, rare for a man in his seventies. Only a few inches shorter than Ben, he had calm, blue grey eyes sitting steady in a healthy face. As they shook hands, Claus gave a barely perceptible shrug that said, *'I'm comfortable being Claus.'*

'You really do not need to introduce yourself, Mr. Oppenheimer. It's a pleasure to meet you.'

'Tell me, why such a dramatic role change, not to mention income reduction? Why didn't you try to find another role like the Staunton one?'

Ben noted how Claus smiled while he talked.

'It's a big risk to employ an ex-special forces soldier with a history of punching their boss. The person who gets that one wrong seriously damages their own career if something happened again. So, yes. I took a downgrade to take stock of my situation, and it's worked well, so far.'

'What would you say to working here, at GMB? We'd really like you to join us.' Neither man blinked as each searched the other's eyes.

'That's not what I was expecting you to say.' Ben laughed in response, trying to hide his surprise. 'I would be lying if I said I wasn't interested, but what job are you offering? I don't want to be a Leadership Developer all my life?'

'No, that would be a waste of your talents and GMB's money. I don't want you to do that either. I want you to recreate a team here to do exactly what you did so successfully at Staunton.'

Claus was not comfortable lying, but he knew he had no option. 'I want you to build a team here in Zurich, because I want to be close to this. We won't need to haggle about your conditions.

Shall we say the same package as Staunton?' Claus extended his hand towards Ben.

'Hold on, Claus. I haven't said I would do this yet, but if I did, I wouldn't expect the same package until I had produced the same results.'

Claus just smiled. 'OK, Ben, you write your business plan. Tell me what you need in order to build your team, and if you generate the same results, we'll pay you the same. Can we at least shake on that? And I'd like you to start straight away.'

'Blimey, Claus, you don't hang about, do you?' Ben smiled as he shook Claus' hand. 'I'll need to tie up a few loose ends with my current employers, but I'm sure they'll co-operate.'

'Oh, I'm sure they will, Ben. I'm sure they will.' Claus had already spoken with Ben's employers. *Not in a million years could you ever guess the business plan I have in mind,* thought Claus, behind his charming smile.

*

No-one could refuse an opportunity such as the one Claus had offered and, after the leadership course, Ben's employers organised an impromptu celebration in his honour. That it secured GMB as their client for some time to come was a bonus. A cause worthy of much celebration, which predictably resulted in Ben not even trying to catch his Friday night flight home. As a result, his employers insisted Ben stayed overnight in one of Zurich's best hotels – the Sonne Berg.

Unfortunately, they had a room available.

Chapter Four

The fog in Ben's head muffled the siren, smothering the shrill decibels before they scattered. The noise inside his head pulsed painfully, in time with his heartbeat, and growing louder as he regained his senses.

The explosion had ripped out the hotel's façade, tossing him like trash in a storm onto the second-floor landing in the process. An hour earlier he had been celebrating a new job; an instant earlier he had been in his room on the floor above; now he was on his back, looking up to where the upper floors used to be as he battled confusion. He lay next to the grand oak and bronze serpent of a staircase that spiralled skyward, up into the smoke. It was all that separated him from the inferno blazing below and into which he now stared.

Flames leapt from the twenty-metre chasm torn from the building's colonnaded front. Vibrant bolts of red and crimson brought to life the small statues in their alcoves, set into the stairs' curved wall, as Ben dug into his survival instincts to control the fear. The deafening noise, heat, and smoke allowed no respite, and he struggled to think clearly as death's spectre prowled. He'd seen men lose everything when that happened, overcome by the instinct to just run, often fatally. Panic is an undemanding mistress compared with the taskmaster of rational thinking.

Water sprayed from the ruptured pipes, showering him as he tried to take in the mayhem. The fire's energy pulsed through the wooden balustrade as he gripped the old beam to haul himself upright. He had been close to too many explosions, and the trauma did not become easier with familiarity; it became harder. Every time was a new battle to quell the fear that grew inside.

Ben pressed his back into the contour of the staircase's curved walls as he descended. Soaked by the sprinklers, the cool of the wall contrasted to the fire burning hot against his face. He was winning the fight to bring his breathing under control as he inched down the staircase, one tentative step at a time. The fire raged in the ground floor foyer, gaining momentum and billowing up to reach him. He choked as the black cloud enveloped him, folded him into its body, filled his lungs, and gouged his eyes. Tears streamed down his face as he looked up at the plumes of smoke escaping through the hole ripped from the Sonne Berg hotel's upper floors. Past where his room had been and out into the cold Zurich night sky. Almost obliterated while asleep in the world's safest city.

Ben's self-preservation mode was interrupted by the wheezing cough of another casualty. Alive but injured by the sounds of it, as he dropped below the thickening smoke to crawl across the wet marble landing. A body lay face down a short distance ahead, perilously close to the newly formed edge of the landing. Ben heard a thin, rasping cough, barely audible above the thundering bellow of the fire.

'Hold on, I'm coming,' he shouted above the fire's roar and the grind of metal against metal, as the crippled structure twisted in agony. Its ancient steelwork, damaged by the force of the blast, hopelessly defending against the inevitable.

'Hang on.' Each word raked his throat as the smoke tightened its grip; involuntarily he choked and convulsed as he stretched out his long frame until he met the familiar submission of a corpse. A cold and clammy hand, unresponsive. Hand-over-hand Ben dragged the slight form across the wet marble and away from the edge. Pulling the body closer, it reacted to the movement and coughed as poisonous smoke invaded its lungs.

'I can't wake him.' It was a woman, sobbing, her thin, lank hair plastered to a pale, scared face. 'My husband's still in our room and I can't wake him. You must save him.'

Although the fire's heat rolled over him, Ben shivered as long-buried memories resurrected themselves. The flames spiralled skyward from the hotel's lobby as he instinctively drew them both back further from the edge. Back towards the relative safety of the staircase, where the air close to the wet floor allowed brief relief. The woman used the respite to plead with Ben.

'The explosion, I can't wake him.'

Ben's instinct screamed at him to run and save himself. He'd been here before, though; he knew he couldn't walk away, his conscience said save her and her husband. Memories returned, anxiety flooded in, threatening to drown him. His senses said run; finally, he surfaced.

'I'll get him,' Ben shouted above the noise. 'Where is he?' She pointed a shaky finger back into the dense, clawing smoke.

'OK. Can you make it downstairs on your own?'

A feeble nod, but Ben could see the fear as her pleading eyes refused to let him go.

'I know you can make it on your own. Just keep close to the floor and you'll be fine. I'll get your husband,' he told her.

Ben squinted through half closed eyes, blinking away tears from the toxic fumes, and looked low across the hallway floor. Several metres away he could make out the open doorway to one of the grand suites. With his face skimming the cold marble, he crawled forward on his elbows, starting now to register the dozens of scratches on his body as he moved into a calmer and more measured frame of mind.

Pushing open the suite's heavy wooden doors, he pressed himself further into the floor. The doors' burnished brass furniture and polished surfaces reflected the flames prowling behind him. His body exhaled in gratitude when he found himself sliding over the relative comfort of the thick Chinese rugs gracing the Sonne Berg's exclusive grand suites.

Stay focussed, find the husband, and get the hell out of here. Repeating it over and over to himself, the distraction worked. He had learned to use it years ago when it had also been life and death.

Thick smoke made breathing and vision difficult, and with each breath the pain in his lungs reminded him that time was running out. He felt the heat from the fire below radiate through the oak-beamed floor and thick rugs. Fighting to retain the control he had gained, Ben concentrated on making a systematic, crawling circuit of the room. He buried his face into the expensive fabrics covering chairs and sofas, filtering the poisonous air through the heavy materials. The smoke's talons scored his throat and lungs, each cough causing a convulsion as the body's natural defence was to cough, again. His head felt about to burst as he blindly collided with furniture, forcing himself to ignore the pain accumulated from blind contact with broken ornaments previously adorning tables and shelves.

His tentative touch met a different object – cool and smooth, not sharp and broken. Ben thought he heard classical music. *A Brahm's lullaby?* He drew it close to his face, inviting the inevitable pain when he squinted through swollen eyelids to examine it. The blurred outline of a mobile phone appeared, and it was ringing.

Eyes closed against the feeling of gravel being ground into his eyes, he pressed the answer button and croaked hoarsely into the phone. 'Whose phone is this?'

A hysterical voice replied, shouting quickly in a language he did not understand.

He cut across the voice. 'I'm in the Sonne Berg Hotel. There's been an explosion, and the hotel's on fire. I'm trying to find someone, probably the owner of this phone, but I can't see anything. Can you tell me their name, yes or no? Anything other than yes, and I hang up.'

Straining his ears for a response, he was about to drop the phone when a female voice clearly announced, 'Claus Oppenheimer. My father's name is Claus Oppenheimer.'

Chapter Five

Ben had to repeat it in his mind several times. Was the man he had met for the first time today, his new boss, somewhere in the same poison-filled cauldron of the blazing Sonne Berg Hotel? Musty steam rose through the thick rug as the clock ticked down, and Ben tried to straighten his mind. *What was Claus Oppenheimer doing here?*

Ben inhaled and shouted Claus' name. The convulsion gripped his core as a faint and feeble voice whispered from above. His hand searched upwards into the dark haze, and a frail forearm tumbled down. As they connected, Ben pulled the limp and barely alive Claus Oppenheimer from his to-be deathbed where, ten minutes earlier, he had been knocked unconscious by the blast.

He could feel the inferno below, heating the floor, now almost too hot to touch; even a few seconds contact was painful. Ben dragged his pyjama-clad companion across the wet floor as wispy steam spiralled slowly upwards. The thin vapour raised the layer of toxic smog, making it possible to breathe and to drag the increasingly alert Claus.

'Wait, wait, where's Ingrid?' jabbered Claus. 'She's in here.'

Claus was hysterical now and dug his fingers into Ben's arm as he dragged him across the steaming floor.

'Your wife? She's downstairs. She was the one who sent me here to get you. Come on, we've got to get out of here.'

Claus, blood trickling from an enormous bruise on his forehead, became immovable when he recognised his saviour.

'Ben? Are you one of them? Have you come to torture me, to tell you everything, and then you'll kill me?' Claus incoherently demanded. 'I'm not going anywhere with you if you are with them,' he slurred.

Ben's instincts were to get to safety as quickly as possible and worry about anything else afterwards. *But who were 'they'? And why would 'they' want Oppenheimer killed?*

He gripped Claus by his pyjama jacket, drew him close, and in a voluble voice stated, 'I've no idea what you're on about. I'm getting out of here and not holding a bloody debate about it while running an increased risk of being cremated. You've taken a knock to your head, you're concussed, and not making any sense. Now, stay if you want, but I'm getting out of here.'

Even above the increasing roar of the fire, Ben's sentiment brooked no discussion. Claus' blue grey eyes blinked as they searched Ben's, then slowly he nodded his head, and something passed between them.

'Sorry, Ben.'

'No worries. Now put your hand on my back and don't take it off.'

A contrite Claus stumbled on meekly, leaning heavily on Ben as he led the way back out into the dense smoke.

'Ingrid. Her name is Ingrid,' Claus mumbled. 'She's a very persuasive woman. She proposed to me, you know.'

Ben wasn't sure, but he thought he heard Claus chuckle.

'We'll reminisce later. Right now, it's time for us to get out of here,' said Ben in an altogether calmer voice. With one hand guiding Claus, he continued, bent double, towards the doors of the suite and into the mayhem beyond.

Out on the landing, the fire's thunder was deafening. It was a testament to the engineers and architects of the Sonne Berg's centuries' old structure that it hadn't already collapsed, but Ben knew that was imminent. Through the combined effects of the explosion and the fire's heat, the floors above disintegrated. The uppermost levels closest to the explosion, and immediately above the fire, crumbled. Falling in upon themselves, they formed a huge crater, out of which rockets of flame roared skyward.

The sweeping staircase was a spiralling funnel of combustive energy, creating a vortex that dragged upwards much of the black, acrid fumes. It allowed Ben and Claus to stand, bent over, as they blindly staggered along the hallway, deeper into the hotel and away from the fire.

'Do you know how to get out of here?' Claus shouted above the noise.

21

'Not exactly. But this hallway goes only two ways and,' jerking his thumb behind them, 'we'll be fried in an instant that way.'

'I may know a way out. We've stayed here many times. If each floor has the same design, there'll be an emergency exit at the end of the next hallway on the left.'

Claus gave a knowing nod as the fire escape appeared exactly where he said it would be. Ben knew better. He tapped the door handle for a second, then held it for a few seconds longer.

'The handle's cold, which means there's no fire on the other side. But it's not all good news. I can feel cool air being dragged through the gaps around the doorframe; the fire this side is drawing it in to feed the fire which causes a vacuum the other side of the door. First hurdle is to open the door against that vacuum. Then, as soon as I open it, fresh oxygen will rush to this side, feeding that monster.'

Pointing to the cauldron steadily advancing towards them, Ben went on, 'When the fire realises there's fresh oxygen up here, it will come at us like a runaway train. Do you understand?'

Claus' wild-eyed stare told Ben he did, but he added a nod to confirm it.

'The fire will search high first of all. It'll burn the oxygen against the ceiling, then it'll come for us. Your pyjamas, your hair, your skin, it'll go for everything. So be ready. When I get the door open, get through and down as quick as you can. The door will be pulled shut by the pressure.'

'You good to go?' Ben recognised hesitation lurking in Claus' eyes, and he placed a hand on the man's shoulder. 'You're pretty brave for an old man, Oppenheimer, I'll give you that.'

Claus mumbled a weak, 'Thank you' as another part of the hotel crashed down behind them.

'OK, let's go.' Ben tucked Claus under his arm, crouched down and, turning the handle, pushed against the door. It held firm at first, until a sudden whoosh of cool air rolled over them, the door gave way, and they tumbled through. Although Ben had told Claus what to expect, the fury of a roaring, oxygen-hungry monster was unlike any noise heard in nature. In an instant Ben felt intense heat on the back of his head. A second later he smelt the sulphurous stench of burning hair as he shoved Claus down the first few steps. Then he spun on his back on the concrete floor and twisted, tearing skin against the rough surface, and slammed the door closed with his feet. The flames trapped on their side of the door snarled angrily at him. Then evaporated.

Any thoughts of recovery were loudly interrupted by the sound of several thousand tonnes of steel and concrete rising in a crescendo as the proud but crippled old building entered her final death throws.

Ben picked Claus up in a fireman's carry then launched himself down the fire escape, three steps at a time. The speed of their descent on the concrete steps, exacerbated by Claus' additional weight, tore at the soles of Ben's feet. His heart raced; his feet felt as if they were on fire. Down another flight. Five agonising bare-footed impacts, twisting on the half-way platform, then another bone-jarring five. Now taking the steps four at a time. They were in a race against time as heavy chunks of masonry tumbled from above. A direct hit would be fatal. Ben's free hand gripped the rail running down the centre of the staircase. Each painful step sent shock waves through him.

His high-speed descent carrying Claus tested every muscle to the extreme. Finally arriving at the ground floor, having taken the last flight in two giant strides, the force of the impact and their combined momentum collapsed him onto one knee.

In an instant Ben had gathered himself and was charging headlong across the last twenty metres of the bare concrete corridor towards the two exit doors. Driving his knees higher with every bound, he increased their momentum.

Masonry crashed down around them. They would not have enough time to stop and operate the exit's Push-Bar mechanism. The door on the right would be anchored top and bottom into the frame. The door on the left would only be fixed to the one on the right by the Push-Bar halfway up. Mustering all the energy he could, Ben tensed every sinew and dropped his free shoulder hard into the bar of the left-hand door.

Whatever testament to construction was owed to the original architects of the Sonne Berg, the same could not be said about the more recent architects of their fire escape doors. Ben's fight-or-flight fuelled momentum ripped out the locking mechanism of the now freely swinging left-hand door.

Unsure whether he had broken something, or everything, Claus' deadweight on his shoulder had sandwiched Ben's head against the door on impact. Blood now gushed, mixing with the sweat on his smoke-stained skin, and ran in rivulets down his shoulder and chest. Swaying unsteadily, he tried to take in the frenetic activity around him.

The earth throbbed with a deep percussion as a herd of diesel engines produced a discordant, dense wall of noise. Zurich's emergency services' shrill sirens shrieked in a higher key, to which the hundreds of emergency personnel frantically danced. Writhing pythons cavorted down Bahnhofstrasse; hundreds of metres of slithering, pulsating, circular grey canvas firehoses, stretched taut from the enormous pressure.

The activity paused momentarily to turn and look at Ben, dressed only in his boxer shorts, with the inert body of Claus over his shoulder. As he collapsed unconscious onto the dark wet floor, a dozen hands reached out to him.

Chapter Six

Ben regained consciousness on a stretcher in the back of an ambulance, wrapped in a silver recovery blanket, reflecting the bright ceiling lights and illuminating the interior. He raised an arm to shield his eyes, bringing with it an array of electric sensors, drips, and wires. A monitor displaying his vital signs was accompanied by the rhythmic soundtrack of a steady heart rate as he half raised his sore body onto his elbows, the action quickly reminding him of his painful exit. His guttural reaction, muted by the oxygen mask, attracted the attention of the ambulance's male nurse attendant who placed strong hands upon Ben's shoulders.

'Ah, we were wondering when you would re-join us, Herr Mason. Claus has been telling us how he found the way out of the building. You are both extremely brave and a little fortunate. It is a miracle not more people died in this attack.'

'Attack? It was an attack? Not a gas explosion or something?'

'No, Herr Mason, not a gas explosion. Gas explosions seldom take out an entire city block, nor occur on the fourth floor of a hotel. The Police believe it was a terrorist attack.'

Pre-occupied with survival, Ben had given little thought to what had caused the explosion, but terrorists in Zurich didn't sound right. Right now, though, nothing did other than he was alive. He lay back on the stretcher, slowly working his mind around his body. *What hurt? How badly?* Then sitting bolt upright, he pulled the mask from his face,

'Did you just say Oppenheimer found the way out of the building? Did he tell you that?' demanded a somewhat agitated Ben.

'Please calm yourself, Herr Mason. Herr Oppenheimer is just in the adjacent ambulance being attended to before being transferred to the hospital. You're both going there when the doctor has seen you. You were unconscious, so Herr Oppenheimer has given quite a full account of your escape. I know he and his family will be pleased to learn you are awake and alert.'

'Damn right I'm awake,' exclaimed Ben, irritated with Claus' version of events.

Chapter Seven

Ben did not recognise the lady striding confidently into his room in Corpus Christi Hospital. The nurse holding open the door gave a small nod, and the woman smiled to acknowledge the polite gesture then walked directly towards Ben. The tall lilies cradled in her arms were placed carefully on the bed as she took his hand and held it in both of hers.

Elegant with a serene smile and opal green eyes radiating warmth, she was dressed modestly but expensively in the best the purveyors of *haute couture* for ladies of considerable wealth and style could provide. Ben doubted he was the first person to be entranced by whoever she was. Her hair was expertly and recently coiffured, the perfume subtle, and her movements unhurried.

In fact, it was only when she spoke that Ben fully recognised who she was. It seemed an eternity ago, amid the volcanic chaos of the Sonne Berg's crumbling and enflamed second floor landing, that he had met Ingrid Oppenheimer.

'Thanks for the lilies, Frau Oppenheimer. I'm sorry, but I didn't recognise you with your clothes on.'

Ingrid's laugh was spontaneous; full enough to be genuine, but not short enough to be dismissive.

Tilting her head towards him, Ingrid Oppenheimer held Ben's hand to her cheek. 'Our family owes you a huge debt of gratitude, Mr. Mason, but please call me Ingrid. I hate the formality of Frau anything. And no more *"recognise you with your clothes on"* jokes, my husband may not approve.' Ingrid smiled with her eyes.

'Your husband nearly got himself left behind on a couple of occasions, Ingrid.'

'Aha, I see you have met the real Claus Oppenheimer.' She laughed, her face lighting up, her eyes electric, a passion and an energy shining through them from which Ben could see the Oppenheimer family were a formidable force. No ordinary pairing of husband and wife.

A thirty-year younger embodiment of Ingrid had followed her into the room and was extending her hand towards him. 'Hi Ben, I'm Stephanie Oppenheimer.'

A head taller than her mother, the intensity of her emerald eyes revealed the genetic connection. She had a wide, confident smile beneath high cheekbones, framed by shoulder-length auburn hair. Shaking her hand, Ben was surprised by how much he had underestimated the strength of her grip.

'We can't thank you enough for saving my father, and I'm sorry you were injured. I hope you're not in too much pain?'

Stephanie was indeed sorrier than Ben could ever have guessed; he had been in their plans, the Sonne Berg had not.

'The only pain I have is not being allowed out of this bed, and not knowing what happened or why? Do you know what the Police think?'

Stephanie's eyes momentarily flicked to her mother before replying cautiously, 'They're not saying anything at the moment, although a terrorist attack is the most likely explanation.'

'Terrorists?' Ben paused to study the body language of his two guests. 'I don't go with that. A terrorist cell, organised enough to source that much high explosive, would pick something strategic like the Parliament building or Zurich Airport, not a posh hotel.'

Ingrid returned Stephanie's glance before continuing. 'Then what other reasons could there be?'

'Whoever was responsible wanted to make a statement about themselves, about how powerful and ruthless they are.'

'Does this put you off working with my husband then?' Without realising it, Ingrid had just connected Claus to the explosion, or at least she had in Ben's mind.

'After last night I don't know, because now I don't know what the job is. Who were they trying to kill, Ingrid?'

Ingrid was too smart to show much, but she showed enough. He could see her carefully framing her next statement. Still holding his hand, she sat down on the edge of his bed as if suddenly tired. He noticed a slight change in how she held herself, her shoulders imperceptibly softened. Ben waited for her to speak.

27

'We don't know for certain.' Ingrid's eyes hid many truths, and there was resignation in her voice as Stephanie sat next to her, placing an arm around her mother's shoulders. Stephanie looked directly at Ben.

'Actually, Ben, we do know for certain. We know a group of four people want to kill my father to send a message, exactly as you just guessed.' Ben could see each word was a struggle. 'They would have succeeded if you hadn't saved him. You must understand how grateful we are for that.' He could see anger and strength in Stephanie's eyes, hear it in her voice.

'If you think the Sonne Berg explosion was attempted murder, why haven't you gone to the Police?'

'We have, but we have to be careful, this is so much bigger than you can ever imagine, and we don't know who to trust. We've spoken with Inspector Remy, a senior policeman who we know. We're not close, but he knows us well enough to know we're not excitable paranoiacs. Remy was already suspicious and had people looking into it. It will take some time to determine anything concrete.'

Before Stephanie could say anything more, Ingrid regained her composure. 'We're grateful to you for saving Claus, but we shouldn't involve you in this, Ben, it's not your battle.'

'It became my battle when they tried to blow me up, crush, and cremate me. I'd like to find the people who did this.' Ben hoped that would suffice, for now.

Ingrid still had hold of his hand. 'Ben, there is so much you do not understand; these monsters are some of the most dangerous people on the planet. They annihilate anyone who stands in their way, and no-one is safe from these people if they think you're their enemy. But if you did find them, what would you do?'

'Well, I'd hand them over to the authorities, of course.' Ben paused and looked at Stephanie. Neither needed to say anything. 'I want to find these people, and you can work with me if you want, but you'll need to tell me everything you know.' Ben's tone was flat, direct.

Mother and daughter said nothing. He knew they were trying to read each other's minds.

'Ben, there's more to this than you can ever imagine, and my husband should be the one who tells you. It's complex and dangerous. We're seeing him next, so I'll let him know what you've said.'

Ben was both relieved and disappointed when the young nurse in the crisp white uniform announced that Trauma Patients' visiting times were restricted. He was unsure as to which trauma the nurse was referring: that of escaping the Sonne Berg, or discovering your new boss was the target of a hit squad.

'We will leave you to rest now, Ben. I'll talk with Claus, and I know he'll want to come and see you. As you now understand this was a deliberate attack, you'll understand why we want to move the two of you to our summer home overlooking the lake. We'll all be safer there, and you'll understand more when you and Claus talk. Because of what's going on, the house is being reconstructed to make it more secure, which is why we were in the Hotel Sonne Berg.' Ingrid held his hand firmly. 'And thank you again for saving Claus, and yourself. This is not over yet. It won't be for a long time.'

'Goodbye, Ben.' Stephanie stopped herself from saying anything more. She would leave that to her father.

Ingrid and Stephanie were respectfully shepherded out of the room by the young nurse. From the deference she showed to his two guests, you would have thought minor royalty had been visiting.

*

'I think it's only fair Papa should tell him. That man is lying in a hospital bed because of us, Mamma. He deserves to know.'

'Claus wants to tell him, but we must recognise we're putting Ben in a lot of danger if we do. It's not just about being fair. It's also about protecting Ben.'

*

Late summer sun shone through the half open window, gently reflected from the white bed linen and light-grey walls. Ben closed his eyes to think and connected with the sounds of normal life drifting in. The muted rumble of distant traffic, a plane in the distance, presumably landing or taking off from Zurich Airport. The hospital had to be near a river, or possibly even the lake, as he could hear the deep rhythmic pendulum of a marine diesel engine. Faintly, the higher pitch of excited children's voices reminded him it was a Saturday – no school today.

Ben lay like that for some time. Turning over in his mind the events of the last thirty-six hours, he reflected on how life was never scripted but merely a sequence of unforeseen events that never ran according to any plan. He already had a pretty good idea who it was that had nearly killed him, and he knew what he was going to do. Before then, he needed a long chat with Claus Oppenheimer to hear from him more about the people who wanted him dead, and why.

The room's serenity, contrasted with the mayhem of Friday evening, were such opposing states that Ben had difficulty connecting them. They both seemed completely unreal when compared with his life before yesterday. Instead of the unscripted stay at the Sonne Berg on Friday evening, he would have flown back to London City Airport. He preferred flying into City Airport for a couple of reasons. One was logical; it was a small airport. Few planes landed at nine o'clock on a Friday evening, so there were no queues at customs and immigration. Immediately outside the terminal was the Docklands Light Railway, and ten minutes on the DLR saw Ben home.

The other reason he liked to fly into City Airport was a more emotional one. A few decades ago, that part of London had been home to the centuries' old, terraced houses of London's dockers and porters of the capital's famous and vibrant markets. The fruit, vegetables, fish, and meat markets, whose fresh produce arrived in the pre-dawn to be handled by the planet's oldest machines – man, and the occasional woman. Occupations since replaced by the computerised logistics and delivery systems of internationally travelled containers.

This was Ben's heritage. His typically large and extended east end of London family had lived and worked here. They had been born, married, drunk, fought, went off to, but not all returned from, the British Empire's various wars from here. Their memories were buried in the very ground where the Olympic Stadium now proudly stood. Ben had been born in East Ham, a few minutes' bus ride away, and he loved the feel of the whole place. It was a natural habitat for him, and where most of his oldest friends still lived. The people, their earthy priorities of family, friends, and life couldn't have been further away from high finance and murderous explosions in five-star hotels. But here he was in a Zurich hospital bed, recovering from exactly that.

Chapter Eight

'Mr. Mason. You need to wake up.'

With one large hand firmly rocking Ben's shoulder, the tall and rangy stranger woke him. 'Wake up, Ben, we have to leave.'

Startled, Ben sat up quickly in his bed. 'Who the fuck are you?'

Now fully alert, Ben viewed his visitor with some suspicion, recognising the type even though he had never seen him before. From the look, haircut, and penetrating eyes, Ben guessed ex-soldier. His posture confirmed the profile, and he appeared to have learned his English at the same school as the Oppenheimers.

'My name is Francois.' He offered a paw of a hand to Ben. 'I am a friend of Claus Oppenheimer, and I am here to take you to him. I am sorry, Mr. Mason, but we must go now.'

Ben wondered how long and deep he had slept, as he batted away the offered hand. 'I don't know you, mate, and I don't know any Claus Oppenheimer.'

Francois' craggy features conceded a weathered smile. 'Claus told me you wouldn't be compliant, but I wasn't expecting that answer.' He nodded. 'Claus said you would question whatever I suggested. He told me to prove my credentials by saying that it was he who led you both out of the Sonne Berg by finding the fire exit. He also told me that is like a private joke between you?'

Ben felt his ire rise. The revelation went some way towards proving who the stranger was, though.

'It may have been private, Francois, but the Sonne Berg wasn't much of a joke.'

'Yes, so I heard from Ingrid and my goddaughter, Stephanie.'

'You said we have to go. Go where? And why do we have to hurry?'

'We have to go now to the roof where there's a helicopter waiting for us.'

'A what? A helicopter? People don't leave hospital in helicopters. You'll need to explain some more before I go anywhere. Anyway,

I don't have any clothes. I've got my hospital dressing gown and that's all. You'll need to do better than this.'

Shrugging, Francois pulled his phone from his pocket and tapped a few keys. The phone's speaker crackled.

'Ja, hello?'

'Hi Ingrid, it's Francois. You were right, he wants more than just me asking him nicely.'

'OK. Hello, Ben, can you hear me?'

Ben cautiously confirmed that he could.

'This is Ingrid. Events have moved faster than we expected and I'm sorry, but we may have inadvertently put you in further danger. We believe the people responsible for the Sonne Berg attack are in your hospital now. They'll be trying to find Claus, and probably you.' Ingrid halted. 'According to Francois, who knows about these things, as far as they're concerned you're a loose end, and these people don't leave loose ends lying around. You and Claus need to leave the hospital immediately. Claus will explain why when you're on your way.'

Ingrid let the comment hang in the sterile air of Ben's hospital room. He didn't answer immediately.

'How do I know you're Ingrid? We've only spoken once.'

'We haven't. We've spoken twice. Once on the Sonne Berg's second floor landing on Friday night, and once an hour ago with Stephanie, in the room you're in now. And to prove who I am, I had my clothes on both times,' Ingrid stated emphatically. 'There's too much to explain in one phone call, as there isn't enough time, and we're concerned your association with us may have inadvertently put you in danger. That's why we want to get you out now, with Francois and Claus. I'm sorry, but Claus will explain more when you are on the helicopter or at the chalet.'

'Chalet?'

'Yes, we're all meeting at our chalet. Now please, Ben, you really need to go with Francois.' Ingrid Oppenheimer was not someone who pleaded, but the sincerity in her voice was evident.

'OK, Ingrid, we're on our way.'

*

Avoiding any awkward questions from medical staff, they were swallowed up by the press of arrivals for the afternoon visiting session, carried along with the human flow until taking one of the lifts to the upper floors. The lift's other passengers cast curious glances towards Ben. Head bandaged, an orange jumpsuit two sizes too small and battered, old trainers that Francois had brought from the helicopter.

Ben was preoccupied with processing the recent conversations with Francois and Ingrid. Given the events at the Sonne Berg, he had to believe what both had said. If the explosion had been a deliberate attempt to kill one of the financial world's most prominent figures, then the answer to why must be frightening.

As the lift announced their arrival onto the tenth floor, Francois held his finger on the Close Door button.

'I don't want you to freak out, but this is not a charade.' Francois reached behind his back and pulled a handgun from under his jacket. The familiarity of the object propelled Ben's mind back many years to a baking hot Afghan plain. He immediately transformed from being irritated by the pain in his feet, to a state where he was oblivious to it. Ben decided to defer any questions for the time being.

Francois held the gun for him to see. 'I'm not trying to frighten you, but neither am I playing games. We know they're in the hospital, that they're looking for Claus... and you.' Francois' matter-of-fact manner was in keeping with his character. *Ex-Special Ops, or something similar,* went through Ben's mind.

'It's OK. I was in the army for a few years and can recognise a P320 when I see one.' Ben referred to the GIG Sauer in Francois' hand.

'Thanks for telling me, although us old soldiers recognise each other, don't we? When we exit the lift, we'll take the outside fire escape to the roof. The chopper's arrival may have alerted them, or they may think it's just the Air Ambulance. Either way, if they're already on the roof they'll be covering the lift, so we'll take the stairs.' Again, the matter-of fact delivery.

Ben's mind was not in a Zurich hospital, it was in an Afghan desert; he was on high alert and in a killing mindset. His every movement bristled with supressed energy. The tenth floor was two floors below the roof and was empty as they exited the lift. Ben now saw an energy about Francois not evident before. Nothing you could specifically identify; it was like a film being played imperceptibly faster. Old habits die hard as Ben found himself adopting similar movements.

They continued their stealthy progress along the deserted corridors, now aware of the sound of their footsteps on the highly polished floor. How the soles of Francois' shoes emitted an audible squeak as he lifted each one. How the stark lighting of fluorescent tubes, four abreast behind diffusers spread across the brilliant white ceiling, emitted a dull static buzz – some louder than others. How each buzz was slightly different, and how the pitch changed as they approached, passed under, and then walked past. Aware now of sounds that he had not registered before Ingrid's and Francois' revelations, but which now crowded his mind, sending millions of signals each second to brain and body.

Crisp, fresh air invigorated Ben as they stepped outside and started to climb a spiral steel staircase to the roof. Eleven floors up and the brisk wind tugged earnestly at them as they climbed. The staircase's open structure provided no protection from the elements.

As Ben recorded the soft clunk of each footstep on the stair, he held on tightly to the rails on either side with both hands and avoided looking down. The wind snatched away the occasional sound of Francois' pistol grip as it bumped into the galvanised steel rail.

Just below the concrete balustrade ringing the hospital's roof, Francois raised his fist, locking his elbow into a right angle. Ben recognised the signal, automatically stopping as the familiar dry taste of anticipation returned after several years' absence. Francois made eye contact with Ben. Jabbing a finger in his own chest and pointing up towards the edge, he indicated he would go over first and alone. Ben gave a thumbs up and received a nod from Francois as he turned to climb the last few steps.

At that moment, a gun barrel appeared over the balustrade. The serious-faced man holding it appeared over the balustrade and levelled it at Francois' head.

'I could hear you tap-tapping that gun against the stairs a kilometre away, my friend. Were you ever a drummer in a band?'

'Fuck you, Christophe, and I will if you ever point a loaded gun at me again.' Ben concluded Francois' response was driven more by embarrassment than by anger.

He recognised Christophe as the ambulance attendant from the previous night's exit from the Sonne Berg.

'Nice to see you again, Herr Mason. Apart from your strange choice of clothes, you're looking a lot better than the last time we met.'

Christophe's laugh was truncated by the distinct voice of Claus Oppenheimer as he appeared over the balustrade next to him.

'Christophe, do you think we should send the improperly dressed Herr Mason to my tailors before allowing him up here?' He laughed more than spoke. 'A gentleman should be properly dressed at all times, don't you agree, Herr Mason?'

'On that basis, I should have refused to carry your sorry arse out of the Sonne Berg two nights ago until you changed out of those old pyjamas. But probably just as well for you that I didn't, eh?'

'*Touché*, Mr. Mason. An elegant riposte to our childish taunting.'

Ben wondered if Claus ever took anything seriously or whether it was his coping mechanism for serious situations. He didn't know, and for now it didn't really matter, as Claus was motioning for them both to come up and onto the roof.

*

The wind moaned as it weaved through the helicopter's long rotor blades while the two pilots engaged the turbines and started their whining prelude to lifting off. The four of them ran, crouched, below the rotors' increasing draft, then climbed the short steps, Christophe first, turning to pull each of them on board and then haul up the stairs. As they hurriedly took their seats, he gave a thumbs-up to the watching flight deck, and without hesitation they lifted off. Climbing fast, they banked away from the hospital and towards the Zurich See – the expansive glacial-water lake that stretched away southeast from the city.

Had Christophe remained on the roof at that point, he would have heard an even louder tap-tapping of several people quickly climbing the fire escape with guns in their hands.

Chapter Nine

The Airbus Dauphin may have been at the top end of executive helicopters, but it was still too loud for meaningful conversation. Claus motioned to Christophe to bring helmets for himself and Ben, and the energy-sapping din was soon replaced by the intimate serenity of the helmets' noise-cancelling audio system. The silence was eerie. Two metres away in the noisy interior he could see Claus' lips moving, while his voice whispered inside Ben's head with total clarity. Ben suppressed the urge to question Claus, as he knew he would shortly reveal much about the last few days' events.

'Ben, I must apologise for the way you've been treated and for the danger we may have placed you in. I'll explain everything, then I hope you will understand we had no realistic alternative.'

'Thanks, Claus, but first I'd like to understand exactly how much danger I'm in. And why a kill squad want you dead?'

'Very well. We are now certain the Sonne Berg was an attempt, by a group of four powerful people, to kill me. I'll explain them in a moment. They probably think you are an ally of mine because you saved me from the Sonne Berg. You and I know that you are only an ally in an employer-employee sense. However, as evidenced by the lengths to which they appear willing to go, they may not be too worried about such detail. We expect them to try again to kill me, and if they can get to you, it's likely they would kill you, too. I'm sorry, Ben, that's the simple truth.'

Even with the distraction of their buffeted craft and the two-metre gap between them, Ben sensed Claus' regret. It was in his face and in his body language as he leaned forward against his four-point harness.

'If these guys weren't targeting me before, they definitely will be now that I've left the hospital in a helicopter with you.'

'We realised that could be an unintended consequence. But the alternative was leaving you in hospital for an assassin to shoot you. Which would you prefer?'

'Neither, to be honest. But there's not much either of us can do about that now. I suggest you fill me in on why these four want to kill you.'

'I will compress into a few minutes what has taken decades to form. No matter how civilised we believe our species has become, basic human instincts are still part of our DNA.'

'I guessed it had to be serious for people to go to these lengths, but I love a good story, so let's crack on before they have another go at us.' Ben sat back in his seat, as the layers of the life he had created over the last dozen years were slowly peeled back, preparing himself to do whatever was necessary.

'I am trying to expose an organised group of four individuals, globally high-profile, publicly recognisable, who are responsible for embezzling countless billions of dollars over the last six or seven decades. These people control some of the world's largest financial institutions, and over that period they, and their predecessors, have killed thousands of people to preserve their personal wealth. They've established a web of financial sub-contractors, of which they're the beneficiaries, which revolves and recycles deals amongst themselves, milking their corporations in doing so.'

Claus now had Ben's attention.

'The original group of five was formed at the end of the Second World War by the world's most powerful financial and industrial figures at that time. They created the group with well-meaning intentions, to stabilise economies and societies to avoid another pan-global military conflict.'

'That's how the IMF and World Bank were formed.'

'Almost identical, but this group was formed covertly by five people who headed the world's largest financial institutions at that time, as opposed to twenty countries' governments. They believed they could deliver benefit more efficiently through direct interaction between each other, than the bureaucracy of public proclamation, hence why they have no name. And even though there's only four of them left, I call them the Five. For some decades, the original Five brought great benefit in enabling trade to rebuild a damaged planet. Over the years and decades, to sustain the Five's existence, the founders gradually handed down to their successors as they retired or died. But each subsequent succession corrupted the original aims until, seventy years later, their personal financial fulfilment became the objective.'

'I could understand why someone would want to kill them, but why do they want to kill you?'

'Early last year, one of the Five died. I now think she may have been killed by the others, I don't know. The remaining four approached me to take her place, because GMB, the bank I run, coordinates and syndicates the World Bank's medium-long infrastructure deals. Those are very profitable, and the Five wanted me to give them exclusivity. That is trillions of dollars of profitable infrastructure deals over many decades, and I just would not do it. There are always rumours doing the rounds of Old Boys' Networks scratching each other's backs, but their influence is negligible. The rumours around the Five, though, were too farfetched to be believed. They were mythical, like the Yeti or the Loch Ness monster, but no-one was keen to absolutely deny they existed. It's almost as if people were scared.

'I now know that even the most farfetched stories merely scratch the surface. They proceeded cautiously with me. They wanted to tempt and test me, but didn't want to reveal anything incriminating until they'd hooked me. Meanwhile, I discovered more about their activities. These four are some of the most powerful people in global finance, forming secret alliances with each other, guaranteeing self-serving benefit, and thereby mutual discretion. Threaten the pack and they'll turn on you. And that's what I did. I threatened the pack.'

'They're hardly being covert or secretive now. Why so public? What's changed?'

'Something has, though I'm not sure what. I still don't know enough about them, but it may be as simple as absolute power corrupting absolutely.'

'Why didn't you just anonymously deliver proof to the IMF or the authorities?'

'I don't have proof, that's the whole issue. They're trying to silence me before I can find some and take it to the authorities. On the few occasions we met, I only had hearsay and unprovable face-to-face discussions; nothing concrete. Psychopaths tend to be incredibly smart, and these individuals are that and more. I became suspicious and then reluctant, which was when they showed me what happens if you go against them. I'm sure you remember the Scandi-Air flight that mysteriously crashed into the Baltic Sea last year?'

'Of course. One of the worst peace-time airline disasters ever. Are you going to tell me they were responsible?'

'I wake up in a cold sweat when I recall this.' Claus sat back in his seat and blew out his cheeks before proceeding. 'At that time, they were talking to me about joining them, but I didn't like what I was discovering. I told them they should change – to use their wealth and influence to do good, or I would go to the authorities. That's when they started threatening me and my family. I didn't fully believe them and bluffed that I already had proof – which I didn't.

'Their self-appointed leader, Thomas Liang, told me to watch for Flight SCY893 in two days' time. The Swedish politicians were amongst the one hundred and thirty-eight unsuspecting passengers and crew on that flight. The politicians were returning from the World Economic Forum in Davos, having just refused permission for a North Sea oil development owned by a member of the Five. You know the rest of that story.'

'You're telling me they killed one hundred and thirty-eight people, including half the Swedish Cabinet, because someone wouldn't let them drill another oil well? That's insane.'

'It gets worse. Do you recall what happened next, with the replacement Scandinavian Government?'

'I remember there was a lot of controversy, but not the details.'

'Less than a month after they took office, the new Cabinet approved the drilling of the North Sea oil well. It threw a conservative country into turmoil. The key members of the replacement Government were suspected of taking bribes – nothing proven, but there seldom is with politicians in these circumstances – when several of them were suddenly found to be owners of ski lodges, Mediterranean-moored yachts, and more. Totally inconsistent with a Cabinet minister's income. I know for certain they were taking kickbacks from the Five, because Thomas Liang told me. And he told me all these things before they ever happened.' Claus sat back, emotionally drained.

'I'm so glad you're telling me this, although it is almost unbelievable.' Now it was Ben who leaned forward against his harness.

'Unbelievable, and still only the tip of their iceberg, Ben. Do you know what neodymium is? It's the world's most expensive rare earth element, and Burundi recently announced they have the largest reserves on the planet. This was suspiciously disclosed one week after the bloodiest coup in their history placed a military junta in the Imperial Palace, who coincidentally just granted a Chinese mining company exclusivity for all extractive rights. The company is controlled by Thomas Liang. I know that because he told me so, *before* the coup or the rare earth disclosure, which was the reason behind the coup. And that's just so far this year. I daren't imagine how many other deaths they're responsible for.'

'Claus, we've got to go to the authorities, the Police, the IMF. We've got to stop them.'

'They're a small army trying to kill me, and they've already killed thousands over the years. They told me this to parade their power and ambition, to frighten me into keeping silent. Do you also recall the reactions when Malawi was admitted to the OECD?' Claus threw up his arms in despair. 'The list is endless, as is their reach.'

Ben readjusted his plans, trying to take it all in.

'I don't have proof, and I don't know who I can trust. If they do succeed in killing me, will they stop there?' Their eye contact said both men knew the answer to that. 'I can't stop them on my own.'

'You're not on your own. You've got Ingrid, Stephanie, Francois, and Christophe the gun-toting ambulance man. And now you've got me.' Ben placed his hand on Claus' hand and nodded.

'Do you understand what you're getting involved with, Ben?'

'I think I've got the picture.'

You haven't, Claus whispered in his head. *You have no idea, but I hope I can help you when you do.*

I have. Ben whispered in his head. *You don't know what I know, but that doesn't matter now.*

*

'Five minutes to landing, Herr Oppenheimer.' The pilot's clear tones cut through any further thoughts or conversation.

'We'll have plenty of time to talk at the chalet with everyone.'

'Have we got a plan?'

'We did have, then the Sonne Berg happened.'

'Well then, it looks like the business plan you asked me to write will be somewhat different now.' For the first time since their meeting in GMB, Ben saw Claus smile with his mouth and his eyes. He extended his hand to Ben, and they shook hands.

'You didn't say where your chalet is?' Ben changed the subject as he looked out of the window to watch their descent.

'Verbier. We're landing in the chalet's garden in Verbier.'

As you do, thought Ben. *As you do.*

*

The late September sun cast long shadows across Verbier's rolling meadows, sloping upwards to nestle into the dense pine forests ascending the mountains. Higher up, early season snow shrouded the uppermost pines, a frosty icing setting the trees into frozen statues that would remain until next spring. Wearing a light white dusting and standing in expectation at the top of the lower slopes, the mid-station's roofs reflected the late afternoon's light. In a month's time, the upper slopes would be covered in the lustrous, thick white blanket that adorned the Alps each winter. A few weeks later would be the turn of the middle slopes, then the lower shortly after. Icing a mountain, as you would a cake, in reverse, and slower.

Ben got a good view of the chalet and the grounds as the helicopter slowed and started to turn, lining itself up for their descent directly into the chalet's garden. The new chalet was set on the higher part of the large plot, and it was huge, with an older and smaller chalet next door. Ben felt the downdraft bouncing back up to them, buffeting the craft and the smaller chalet, closest to their landing spot.

The smaller chalet was made of dark wooden planks, horizontally overlapped with a traditional wooden tiled roof, all warped by decades of harsh winter weather and summer sun. Ben doubted it had been built with the thought of big helicopters landing close by and wondered how much downdraft blew its way through the old timbers, just as he caught a glimpse of their neighbour dragging a bag inside before the helicopter landed.

I wouldn't be too happy either if I lived that close to a house that landed helicopters in its garden, thought Ben, as the pilot skilfully guided them to rest on a purposely flattened section of lawn.

Ben walked out, bent double, crouching beneath the reach of the rotors. The helicopter started to lift off before they had even reached the stone path leading to the chalet's back doors. The departing craft raised itself above the chalet, dipped its nose, and turned back in the direction of Zurich.

Late afternoon birdsong gradually replaced the turbulence as Ben stood and absorbed the quietness. Taller trees, the roofs of chalets higher up, and the west-facing slopes held the fading amber of the evening sun. He breathed in a lungful of crisp, fresh mountain air, invading his senses and spreading through him a sense of calm. *How wealthy are these Oppenheimers?* he wondered, as he noticed an old but still active two-person chairlift that lifted off from their garden. The age of the lift was evident by the old-fashioned wooden slat seats and a restraining bar the user had to raise and lower by themselves. No padded, heated seats and automatic systems here. *But no lift queues either when it's in your own garden,* he noted.

As they shared the large garden with the smaller chalet, Ben wondered if they also had to share the chairlift. He stood for a beat and studied the smaller chalet. No lights on inside, no smoke from the chimney, just darkness beyond the red-chequered curtains hanging at the windows.

'Ben, we're in the kitchen if you'd like to join us?' Francois interrupted his thoughts.

*

From the darkness behind the red chequered curtains, the mercenary held Ben in the crosshairs of his assault rifle. His finger rested comfortably on the trigger, ready if the inquisitive stranger walked towards the chalet. As Ben turned to go inside, he lowered the weapon.

'Who is he?'

'We don't know. He's not in our intel. Must work for them; some sort of assistant, we think. He was the one who carried Oppenheimer out of the Sonne Berg.'

'We'll find out soon enough. Is everyone here, and are they ready? Mission run-through in fifteen.'

Chapter Ten

The aromas of garlic, charcuterie, and baked bread carried on a platter of faint woodsmoke beckoned Ben into the spacious and modern kitchen. The interior had been finished in traditional Swiss-mountain style, with flagstone floors sweeping out to stone walls supporting the thick wooden beams of the upper floors. This was a ski chalet, but not of a class he had ever experienced.

'Ben, this is Mia Keller. She and her husband, Petre, take care of the chalet for Ingrid and Claus.' Christophe introduced an approachable, smiling woman in her sixties.

Her full but yellowing hair was tied back neatly with a red Alice band adorned with mountain flowers. Dressed traditionally in a blouse of thick white linen, underneath a black and red patterned dirndl, Mia earnestly wiped her hands on a long red apron betraying evidence of this afternoon's food preparation. She brushed away loose strands of hair with the back of her hand and extended a still floury hand to Ben.

'Welcome, Herr Mason. We have heard all about your heroics in the Sonne Berg.' Mia rubbed her hand over her eyes. Sniffing, she straightened and vigorously shook his hand. 'Thank you for saving Claus, but I don't understand. Who would want to do such an evil thing?' she implored, close to tears.

'I don't know either, Mia, but I'm glad we both got out alive. Is that a cheese fondue I can smell?' Ben relieved Mia of any further angst.

'Ja, my own special recipe, with a secret Schweitzer ingredient,' she excitedly exclaimed.

Widening his eyes in theatrical surprise, he held out his hands. 'Well, I look forward to trying to guess what that is.'

'I'll show you to your room, Ben, and I think someone's been busy clothes shopping for you.' Christophe took Ben up to the third floor. 'Ingrid and Stephanie will be here soon. We plan to eat when they arrive.'

The chalet's walls and floor spoke of their newness, sharing with him a hint of a sawn pinewood aroma as the two men walked towards his room. Family and group photographs smiled back at Ben from their frames hung on all sides of the corridor. Stephanie riding various sized ponies right up to full sized horses. Several of a group, standing in front of their horses, wearing Team Suisse bibs over their silks, with a huge gold trophy in the foreground. Accidentally beautiful mementos arranged on windowsills, and in a washed-out polaroid's fuzzy definition, youthful exuberance grinned happily at him. Novices holding skis far taller than them; a standard happy-family scene – mum, dad, and two kids posing on a ski slope.

Ben looked closer. He recognised a vigorously youthful Claus and Ingrid. Energy and confidence radiated from the couple in the old print, which was held within a thick, gilt frame and set conspicuously on a tall table at the corridor's end. A girl and a boy, he slightly taller, awkwardly squinting against bright sun and snow. Mum and dad proudly draping their arms around young shoulders. The young girl's defiant chin, the challenging angle of her head. Unmistakably Stephanie. But who was the boy? Ben waited at the photograph until Christophe noticed he had stopped.

'This is an old photo, Christophe.' Ben trod cautiously.

There was something about the way Christophe came back to where Ben stood, as if trying to tread quietly. He looked at the photograph when he spoke, not to Ben.

'Yes. Claus and Ingrid had a son. Stephanie's older brother, Adrian. He died nearly thirty years ago in a skiing accident.'

Christophe held the frame reverentially.

'Stephanie blamed his school. More exactly, she blamed the privilege of attending one of Switzerland's most exclusive private schools. She was at the same school and had seen Adrian's friends intimidate the teachers because, she said, their parents were influential, wealthy people. Adrian's friends bullied the teachers into letting them race down a notorious black piste for the last run of the day. The light was too flat for racing and, although no one saw exactly what happened, Adrian was near the front and had a bad fall. He broke his neck.'

'That must have been terrible for Ingrid and Claus, and Stephanie.' Ben could see the emotion gripping Christophe's face. 'That must be so tough to recover from.'

'Yes. Life around them changed for many years, as they each had to deal with their own grief, in their own way. Stephanie withdrew for a long time. She adored Adrian, he was her hero, and she rebelled in a big way. Adrian's school friends came to his funeral; Stephanie blamed them and she attacked them until we managed to pull her off. Spirited is an understatement. The school said they understood, wanted to keep it quiet, and would not expel her. But she continued to blame Adrian's friends and to pick fights with them at every opportunity. It was impossible for her to remain at the school, so Claus and Ingrid finally agreed to take her out. She then refused to go to another private school, and eventually they agreed to send her to a state school.'

'Poor Stephanie. Poor Claus and Ingrid. That must have been a tough period; maybe it still is.'

'It certainly formed Stephanie's views on life. You'll discover she places more importance on behaviour than wealth.'

They walked on to Ben's room with their own thoughts.

*

Ben reflected on the Oppenheimer family history as he explored his spacious accommodation. A holdall containing several changes of clothes had been placed on the bed. Also laid out amongst the assortment of toiletries and clean towels were a mobile phone, a chronometer watch, and a room key from a Hotel St Gallen in Zurich. Most curious was a business card of an Andrew Calvert, at the British Embassy in Berne, carrying a handwritten notation 'happy to arrange replacement Passport'. *Welcome Pack Oppenheimer-style,* he mused.

The distinctive percussion of a helicopter interrupted further thought. It reverberated throughout the chalet on its approach, landing as he had done in the garden; the Oppenheimer ladies completing the group. He somehow felt he knew them better now.

*

Ingrid stood quickly and crossed the large stone floor to meet him as he entered the kitchen, smiling with her eyes. He was becoming so comfortable with her that it felt as if he had known her for years. He searched for signs of buried grief but found only lightness and positivity.

'A fully dressed Ben Mason for the first time.' Her laugh carried him with her, as she performed the obligatory air-kiss, barely brushing each cheek. 'I always seem to be either thanking or apologising to you, but I'm glad you came, Ben. Maybe we can get to know each other better here. Come, sit next to me. I think you know everyone, apart from Seb.'

Ben had already noted the serious looking man on the other side of the kitchen who now raised his hand in acknowledgement. They nodded to each other, both arriving at the same conclusion as to their previous occupations, before the man returned to continue looking out of the chalet's rear doors. The distinctive bulge of a handgun was visible through his drab olive gilet. Ben had been so distracted with Ingrid that he had almost forgotten why they were all here; Seb's gun reminded him.

Mia stood by the range, with Claus, Francois, and Stephanie seated at the other end of the central island, in animated debate. They broke briefly to acknowledge Ben, then returned to their discussion.

'Petre is opening up the dining room and lighting the fire, so you can go there after supper while I clear up,' Mia reported to Ingrid and Claus, who had walked over to greet Ben.

'You have a fantastic chalet, and with your own chairlift in the garden? Never seen that before. How did that happen?' Ben enquired of the couple.

'The original chalet was Ingrid's parents'. They left it to us over thirty years ago, but that's the old one next door. The plot was so big that we built this chalet and kept the original one to keep the warring family factions separated at Christmas.' Claus laughed as Ingrid chided him.

'Who's using it now?' Ben enquired.

'No-one. It's all locked up. We won't open it for another two months.'

Across the divide, Ben's eye contact with Francois halted his discussion. Stephanie and Christophe followed his gaze towards Ben.

'I saw someone go inside as we circled to land.' The words were like a leaden blanket on the room.

'How sure are you?' Economy from Francois.

'One hundred per cent. Male, dark clothes, or at least dark trousers. He went through the door nearest the chairlift and was dragging a bulky bag. I saw his leg turn as the door closed.'

Francois stood up. 'Claus, take Ingrid, Mia, and Stephanie with you to the basement. Seb, go to the store and get the kit. Where's Petre? He should go with you. We've been through the drill, you know what to do. Ben, this is not your fight. Go with them while we check it out.'

Ben was more accustomed to making decisions in conflict, but he decided to do as Francois said. For now.

Claus grabbed Ingrid's hand as he hurriedly led the way through the hall and down the stairs into the basement. Seb jogged with them until coming to a keypad next to a tall door. Quickly tapping in a code, five high-pitched beeps echoed around the concrete basement. An alarm warning, and Ben realised why when Seb pushed the door fully open to reveal a large collection of rifles and handguns, all neatly arranged in illuminated racks, with dark green ammunition boxes below. Ben guessed it wasn't Seb's first visit to the gun store, as he had no hesitation in choosing certain weapons and ammunition.

'I can't defend Claus and the others without a gun, Seb.' Ben placed himself in the other man's path to reinforce his request.

Seb was cautious. 'Do you know how to handle one?'

'Yes, I do. And I'm familiar with most of those,' Ben added, nodding towards the cache of weapons.

'OK, so which would you chose for this work?'

'The SIG Sauer, nine mil, any day.'

Seb knew he didn't have time for a debate. 'Show me how the breach works.' He handed the gun to Ben.

Without breaking eye contact with Seb, Ben dismantled and reassembled the breach, double pumping the slide with a solitary 'all clear' click from the trigger on an empty chamber. Seb nodded as he handed him three full magazines. Ben knew he had now entered dangerous territory under his agreement with the British Army.

'Hope to see you later.' Then Seb was off towards the stairs, laden with kit for Francois and Christophe.

The weapon's familiarity sent a sensation up Ben's arm and into his soul, triggering long forgotten memories, but he felt calm and in control now. He turned the gun over to feel the cool metal against his palm, like a long-ago alcoholic holding a bottle, resisting the temptation to drink. Breaking his agreement with the army sat easily with his conscience. His exit had been complicated, Ben had refused to go quietly, so the army had reacted by making the NDA even more one-sided. Eventually he'd signed; it was his only way out. If he was ever arrested for a 'serious offence', though, it gave the army the ability to recall him to face a military court. There was a good chance his actions in the next fifteen minutes could constitute a 'serious offence'. He did not even need to be convicted; just being arrested was enough.

He tucked the gun into his waistband and addressed the four scared faces in front of him. 'Francois said that you'd all been through the drill. What was the plan from here?'

Claus responded. 'We go to the Safe Room, that's the old nuclear bunker – all properties had to have one. Ours is now split in two: one half is an activity room; the other's my wine cellar.' Claus talked quickly. *We each have our own coping mechanisms,* thought Ben.

He took Claus' arm, hurrying him along the corridor to the middle of the concrete wall where two huge steel doors stood out. Ben looked enquiringly at Claus, then leaned hard against the right-hand one, drawing out a mechanical whine from the hinges of the blast-resistant doors as they protested to six-months' lack of use. They filed silently through the gap and hurried across the first half of the basement. Necessity and demand had transformed it into a cinema and games room.

They came to the wine store where Claus carefully tapped in the code, opening the door to an Aladdin's cave for a wine connoisseur. Floor to ceiling, wall to wall, rack upon rack of bottles and wooden crates, with a tasting table and chairs at one end.

'I've been collecting wine for more than sixty years, Ben. There are wines in here which even most connoisseurs think have all been drunk years ago. It's almost like having another child to care for.' Claus absent-mindedly ran his fingers over the nearest bottles.

'Where's Petre?' Mia anxiously enquired as they filed into the wine store. She was answered by five blank expressions.

'I'm sure Francois has it covered, Mia. I'll call him.' Claus raised his phone to call.

'No. Don't. Francois will be concentrating on other issues right now. I'll get Petre,' Ben announced.

'I'll come with you.' Stephanie's emphatic tones drew everyone's attention. 'I know my way around the chalet, and I know Petre. You know neither, Ben.' She dared Ben to challenge her.

'If I'm right about the chalet next door, hell on earth is about to kick off, so it's best I go on my own.' Ben had learned not to blink when negotiating with Stephanie. They stared at each other until Ingrid broke the silence.

'Please be careful, Ben.' Using only her eyes, Ingrid implored Stephanie not to argue.

'He's bald, has a hook nose, and a pointy chin.' Stephanie's description of Petre was her way of conceding the argument without losing face.

'Thanks, I hope there won't be too many of those upstairs.' Ben smiled his appreciation.

Familiar feelings awoke from their long sleep as he closed the wine store door behind him. He automatically checked the SIG Sauer's safety was off as he jogged across the activity room, past the blast doors, and out into the basement corridor.

There were loud sounds above him, furniture being dragged into position, commands and acknowledgements. They'd be going through their prep before the off. *I'll be with you in a minute, boys.*

Reaching out his hand to push open the door to the stairs, he was assaulted with an almighty impact of energy he had not experienced for a dozen years. The door absorbed most of the blinding flash and thundering roar from the hallway above – an instantaneous transition from serenity to devastation. A violent ferocity debilitating anyone unlucky enough to be within tens of metres.

The door swung viciously towards him as a ferocious wave hammered him to the floor. His senses were stripped of any relativity, any connection with up or down, light or dark. Deafness and confusion coalesced, pummelling him in waves. Protectively dropping to the floor and burying his head in his hands, he lay prone, still gripping the gun. The first explosion was followed quickly by a series of smaller ones and a staccato of automatic gunfire. The combined energy tore at the door, smashing it against the wall until it hung in limp submission. It had saved Ben from the worst of the physical and sensory assault.

Instincts seldom roam too far, and in an instant he was up on his feet, charging through the distorted doorway and up the stairs, gun – and years of training – ready to deploy. The scene at the top was something out of a disaster movie. Thick, grey masonry dust blanketed everything like a pre-dawn sea fog, smoke hung dense and immovable in the air, deceiving the vision and deadening Francois' orders, commanding them from somewhere back in the cloud.

Ben inched his way forward, irresistibly drawn towards the conflict. Everything happened so fast. Automatic weapons furiously clattered, grenades exploded shattering windowpanes, splintering wood and glass. Explosions wrenched the ceiling sections from their strong timber beams, twisted ribbons of electrical cables formed tenuous connections to lights suspended in disarray, randomly flickering on and off as they swung back and forth, adding the effect of a black and white war movie to the macabre scene.

It was impossible to distinguish friend from foe, and the draft blowing through the bare window recesses swirled the smoke and played tricks with his mind. He heard a man scream in agony somewhere in the dust and smoke. An alarm bell added its clanging contribution as the sprinkler system was triggered by the explosions and heat. Still the shouting and shooting continued, automatic gunfire echoed off the hard surfaces. He heard Christophe call out and Francois answer. Ben shouted to Francois, there was silence at first, then anger.

'Get the fuck out of here!' Francois screamed. 'I'm not going to be responsible for you getting yourself killed. Get the hell out of here. Now.'

Peering round the corner, a gap in the smoke reminded him of man's destructive obsession with ballistics. No matter how many times he witnessed it, he was always amazed at how much blood could be shed in such a short space of time. Scarlet slashes decorated the walls and a confluence of deep ruby streams coalesced into small lakes in the floor's undulations.

One casualty had dragged itself halfway across the hallway with a fatal wound to a major artery, judging by the pool of red surrounding him. His final resting place was signposted by a ten-metre crimson causeway ploughed in blood-soaked trousers. A checkmark every few metres as the man had shifted from one elbow to the other before fluid loss, or another bullet, had drawn a veil over the futility.

A tropical monsoon sprayed from the sprinkler system, adding to the general un-worldliness of the scene, diluting and spreading the wash into small streams which traced the contours of the stone floor. All the time dancing shadows from the swinging lights gave life to stationary objects and lifeless bodies.

Although the chalet may have been unfamiliar to Ben, the scenes were not, as he rolled two casualties onto their backs. Even allowing for how death and fire can disfigure, he recognised neither of them. They were both attackers, and most of the survivors were Francois and company. The shooting died down; a not unusual mid-firefight lull, as Ben presumed everyone was taking stock and adapting plans.

Pumped with annoyance, Francois spat the words, 'Christophe, if you can see that idiot Englishman from where you are, shoot him.'

Christophe did indeed have a clear sight of Ben, although he understood Francois had no real intention of his command being carried out.

Ben had arrived at the doorway between the kitchen and the hall, which ran the length of the house. A swirling draft cleared the smoke enough to see that the walls on either side of the huge stone pillar of the central chimney breast no longer existed. The chimney breast faced into the dining room, which looked directly towards the smaller chalet next door. Ben's experience told him that whoever the assailants were, they had fired some type of rocket-propelled grenade into the dining room and straight into the chalet's most solid structure. The surrounding walls and ceiling had suffered worse than the massive chimney.

He called across the short distance, 'I've got two dead, can't see any others. I came to retrieve Petre. Do you know where he is?'

Christophe raised himself onto one knee and cautiously scanned the battlefield, throwing a comradely wink at Ben and motioning him to keep down. Ben nodded an acknowledgement at the exact moment two of the attackers ran out of the diminishing smoke to the right of Christophe.

Ben pivoted, levelled his gun, and with ruthless accuracy fired two rounds – one into each man's head, less than half a second apart.

Seb immediately rose from behind Christophe with a small cannon and fired it back into the smoke from where Christophe's attackers had come. The noise and energy drove into them like a train. Anything within the room from where Christophe's attacker had come was now obliterated. Such accurately applied violence is unimaginable unless you experience it.

"In the army for a few years" doesn't teach you that. Exactly which army, and where?' Francois' tone was notably calmer than his first outburst at Ben.

'British. One Para. Two tours of Afghanistan and one of Iraq. Now where's Petre?'

'Over here.'

Ben swivelled and aimed his gun at the direction of the voice. 'Come forward, slowly.'

A bald pate covered in masonry dust emerged out of the smoke and mayhem. Crawling over the wooden beams, he nodded from side to side as he shuffled on his elbows. The hook nose and funny chin of an extremely scared Petre Keller looked up bewildered. Ben grabbed him by the shirt and dragged him against the wall next to him.

Francois explained, 'You were right about the chalet next door. What you spotted enabled us to be prepared. They didn't expect us to counterattack even before they attacked, but they're regrouping now. They're well equipped and too many for us to hold off forever. It's difficult to defend against rocket-propelled grenades.

'Ben, this is bigger than we thought. You've got to get the Oppenheimers and the Kellers to safety on your own. Take Petre down, and we'll hold them for as long as we can. If he hasn't already, tell Claus to call Inspector Remy and the Federal Security guys. They'll contact the local police. And tell Claus to execute the plan we agreed. You'll have to lead them out.'

Ben gave a thumbs-up and retreated in the direction of the basement with a traumatised Petre in tow.

A thick, grey dust now carpeted the broad wooden steps down to the basement. Their shoes left distinct footprints as Ben led Petre down, while a double-hand grip held the SIG Sauer. The new layer of powder covering the corridor was undisturbed, so no-one had been down here since he'd left... not yet. The huge blast doors were still ajar as he cautiously peered around them. All quiet, he motioned for Petre to follow him, and they made their way across the activity room to the wine store.

He tapped the gun barrel three times. 'Claus, it's Ben. I've got Petre.'

Before Claus unlocked the wine store, Ben recognised the soft mechanical whine of the blast doors' hinges behind him. Someone was pushing them open. He spun, ducked, brought the P320 level, and fired. The attacker's head inside his balaclava was barely visible beyond the door's edge, but it was enough.

The powerful round connected, crumpling the attacker onto the tiled floor. In four strides Ben was over him, calmly putting another two rounds into his chest. The sound echoed loudly off the hard floor and walls.

Ben had his gun up, trained on the edge of the other blast door. A millisecond would be all that separated life from death for whoever next came round the door. No-one did.

Cautiously Ben approached and peered around it. Nothing, just three sets of footprints on the dusty stone floor – his, Petre's, and the dead attacker's. *He followed our footprints,* Ben chided himself, annoyed at his sloppiness.

He turned back and crossed the floor to the wine store, and to the horrified looks of Petre, Mia, Ingrid, Stephanie, and Claus.

Chapter Eleven

Ben did not try to explain; their expressions said it all.

'Francois says we have less than three minutes, Claus. You need to call an Inspector Remy? And you need tell us what the agreed plan is so we can execute it.'

Nobody moved. Nobody spoke.

'Claus.' Ben raised his voice, almost to a shout. 'You need to contact somebody called Remy.'

'Yes. Sorry. Inspector Remy. I've just called him.' Claus displayed classic stress indicators but slowly regained himself. 'I spoke with him just now and he's alerted the local police, they'll get here quicker. Remy is organising a helicopter with a force from the Federal Security Office. They'll take longer, but the local police will be here soon. We are to stay here and wait for them to arrive. I told them we don't think the attackers know where we are,' Claus added hesitantly.

'Staying here is not an option. Francois will hold them for as long as he can, but they're better equipped and there's more of them. We need to execute the escape plan Francois gave you, and very quickly. From here, it looks like we've walked into a dead end.' As Ben looked around the store, all he could see was scared people and wine bottles.

Claus regained his composure. 'Follow me. I'll show you.' He weaved through the racks 'A couple of years ago we created a tunnel between here and the small chalet so we wouldn't have to go outside. Here it is.'

One of the racks stood a metre away from the back wall. The space on the left was enough for someone to squeeze round it. Hidden by the dense arrangement of bottles and wooden cases, a narrow doorway had been built into the back wall.

'Where does it come out?'

'In the smaller chalet's basement, below the kitchen. The stairs go up from the basement to a larder at the back of the kitchen.'

'How likely is it they'll know about it?'

Claus shrugged. 'If they knew about it, they would have come through it by now. The stairs aren't obvious when you go into the larder as there's a dry food cupboard in front of them.'

'Let's hope you're right.' Ben cautiously turned the handle. Offering silent thanks to Swiss engineering, this door opened noiselessly. The tunnel was in darkness.

'There's a light on the left.' Claus' helpful advice arrived at the same time as sounds of dampened explosions and gunfire from above.

No concealed LED lighting here, just bare lamps on battens lined the seventy-metre walkway.

'If the attackers are as organised as Francois says, then they'll have left at least one in the small chalet as a control. He'll be coordinating the teams by radio and possibly bodycams. He'll be in the room with the best view of this chalet. Which one would that be?'

'The kitchen. It's also where this tunnel comes into.'

Another blast from above shook the bottles in their racks. Ben's charges exchanged nervous glances.

'Was there a plan beyond the tunnel?'

'Yes, we should take the chairlift in the garden. It's the other side of the smaller chalet from here. Turn right out of the kitchen, along the hall, and out the front door. Down a few steps and onto the chairlift, and the master key is under the control box. The control box is only so big,' Claus mimed the dimensions. 'Once the key's turned, you sit in the chair, push the blue button on the control box, and off you go. The next chair lines up behind. There's a built-in delay of ten seconds so you don't have a pile-up at the top. Hit the blue button and off you go.'

'Where does it take you to?'

'The Medran station. Even though it's early evening, there'll be dozens of people around. It's downhill mountain-bike season for a few more weeks, and Medran is a floodlit gathering point for them, by the dozen.'

'OK, this is what we'll do. I'll go first to clear the way.' Ben read their faces. They read the hidden intent.

'When it's safe, I'll call you through. The first pair, Ingrid and Stephanie, go quickly to the chairlift. Next pair, the Kellers.

As soon as the first chair has moved, get ready with the next one. Try not to expose yourselves or be out in the open for any longer than you need to. Get off at Medran and grab a lift operator, a pisteur, or any official you can find. Tell them what's happening, although they will have heard the fireworks upstairs by now. Find a crowd and stay in the middle of it until the Police arrive.'

There was another blast from upstairs and a crescendo of small arms fire. 'If that's loud here, it will be fatal upstairs. I'll call for you as soon as it's safe.' Ben disappeared into the tunnel.

*

Parts of Ben had not moved on in twelve years, and his mind was back inside an Afghan tunnel. This one was cooler, but the instincts and mindset were identical. He was grateful to be on his own as it allowed him to think clearly, to prepare himself for action. The others had crowded his mind with their horrified looks when he'd shot the attacker. For their sakes, he could not allow himself to be distracted, not even for a second.

He reached the other end of the tunnel and turned off the lights. They'd know he was here soon enough. Swiss engineering again obliged his silent aims, and the door in the smaller chalet opened into a century-old cellar. Through a small mesh vent high on the opposite wall, the fading day provided Ben with just enough light to navigate to the foot of the wooden stairs. A legacy aroma of cheeses and drying meats from long ago hung in the cold, still air.

Loud voices tumbled down from the kitchen above him. One voice was clearest, the other voices were distant – those were coming from a loudspeaker. *Keep talking, buddy. Trust me, it's best you don't hear me.*

Ben took a deep breath. The wooden stairs were solid and thick, but there was no avoiding their age; they looked a hundred years old. He knew they would take his weight, but the question was how much noise they would make. He placed his left hand on the handrail, pointed his gun at the door at the top, then gradually transferred his weight from the stone floor to the first step.

His ears were his most active organ, and he tensed in expectation of a silence-shattering creak, but none came.

He breathed easier, stabilised, then transferred his weight onto the next worn, seasoned wooden step. He stood still, tested the step. Anything loose? Any noise? No, continue. Step onto the next. Stop, that one's loose and will creak; step higher, onto the one above it. No, that one's been repaired. It won't break but it will make a noise, so step even higher. That one's loose as well. Step higher again; four steps above. He knew he was unstable and vulnerable as he stretched his legs over the one-and-a-half metre gap, angled uphill at forty-five degrees. He would be exposed as he couldn't hold the handrails and the gun. He had no option but to hold the gun in his mouth and use both hands to haul himself onto the furthest step. Would the handrails take his weight? Would the top step also creak? He knew the risk if he was heard.

Patiently he waited for the attacker controlling the assault from the kitchen to start talking again. Ben's teeth bit into the butt of the gun clamped tightly in his mouth. He could smell gunpowder residue, an epitaph to the man he'd just killed. A trickle of saliva carried the tang of dark metal down his already tense throat, and he fought the urge to cough. He couldn't clear his throat, not yet.

A last lungful of air, then heave. His muscles burned as his arms hauled a hundred kilos at forty-five degrees up the stairs. Even the veins in his neck stood out with the effort, while his hearing tuned in to the slightest squeak from the top step. Silence, apart from in his overworked mind. The step and handrails had held firm as he quickly freed one hand to point the gun towards the door. He held his breath and stood still. Control was still talking, too absorbed in orchestrating the murder of innocents to realise his own impending demise. Ben now stood with both feet on the stone floor of the kitchen's larder and relaxed his shoulders.

Breathe.

A dull green glow from the screens squeezed through the gap between the old door and its frame. Ben peered through the gap, his gun steady on the man's head. Impending retribution sharpened his senses as the Control sat, his back towards Ben, studying several screens and oblivious to Ben's presence. Each screen was divided into quarters, each one projecting live body-cam feeds from the battlefield next door. Some cameras transmitted stationary views of a ceiling or a wall – those would be the casualties. There were at least six active attackers left in the main chalet.

Slowly, Ben tried to open the door's locking lever. But it wouldn't budge; it was locked from the other side.

'Oppenheimer's in the basement.' Ben heard the clearly enunciated and clipped vowels of a South African accent boom out of the loudspeaker on the other side of the door. 'Ja, we have these pinned down. You two, the basement stairs are through there. We'll lay down cover. You go down there, and no survivors. Neutralise every single one.'

The loudspeaker's dynamic range could not cope with the sound of the gunfire unleashed by the attackers. Ben's heart raced with what he had heard.

He quickly weighed their options then turned and leaned his back against the door. He raised his knee till his thigh was held against his chest, tensed ankle and foot leaving one large shoe poised in the air. On the other side of the door, Control would not be transmitting while his comrades were talking.

Ben waited for the next announcement from the attackers in the chalet. All he could hear from the loudspeaker was the distorted sound of rapid gunfire. He waited. Foot poised. Then the South African's instructions yelled out from the loudspeaker and Ben drove his knee down and crashed the sole of his boot hard into the old door.

He had rehearsed his movements, his victim had not. An instant after Control had realised he wasn't alone, two deadly rounds found their mark as he turned.

Sprinting to the cellar, down the stairs, Ben threw on the light in the tunnel.

'Let's go, let's go. Come on. Let's go,' he called loudly.

*

'Control's not responding. Can't get any reply,' the South African shouted to his two colleagues taking cover behind the oak dining table, now lying on its side.

'It's either a comms failure, or someone's got to him. There are too many exits for us to cover. That means Oppenheimer could have got out of the basement. You two, get back to support Control, neutralise whoever's fucking with us, and find out how they got in. There could be a tunnel between the two chalets. If there is, go down it and take care of whoever's at the other end.'

Crawling on their elbows, holding weapons over their forearms, they exited through the hole ripped in the large chalet's dining room wall.

*

Ben repeated the instruction to move. Ingrid was the first one through the tunnel, followed immediately by Stephanie as she helped her mother.

'We've remembered the key is hanging in the kitchen and not under the control box,' Stephanie panted. 'Mamma knows where it is.'

'OK, can you get it and start the chairlift?'

'Yes.'

'Good, take the chair up and lose yourself in a crowd. I'll meet you up there. Where's Claus?'

'He's coming with the Kellers. You'll have to help Papa off at the top. The chair slows but it never quite stops.' As Stephanie nimbly made the steps leading up to the kitchen, the loudspeaker crackled with questions and orders shouted above the sound of gunfire.

Unplugging everything would confirm any suspicion of Control's demise. He decided instead to leave doubt in their minds that it could be a comms failure as he turned to go back down to the tunnel. After he had turned, one of the monitors showed a pair of red dots moving together out of the bottom of the other chalet's floorplan, heading towards him.

'Where's Claus?' Ben's anxious tone startled Mia as she led Petre out of the tunnel and into the stone-floored larder.

'I'm right here. Don't worry.' A slightly breathless Claus appeared through the narrow doorway behind them.

'Stephanie's chair will have left by the time you get down there, so get straight on the next one and set it off.' He helped Mia and Petre up the stairs. 'Claus, we'll be in the next one so let's go, come on.'

As Ben hurried the elderly group up the stairs and into the kitchen, Mia froze at the sight of the dead man slumped in a spreading pool of his own blood. Ben gently turned her shoulders away as he shepherded his flock through the dimly lit interior of the smaller chalet.

He changed from holding Mia's shoulder to holding the P320 as they emerged into the garden. The Afrikaner's order of *'No survivors. Neutralise every single one'* replayed itself in his mind. They were more vulnerable now that at any time, and his small group were not youngsters. It was dusk and, looking up, the line where the high mountains stopped and the dark purple sky began was barely visible, the way to the chairlift lit by the burning chalet. Now only single shots could be heard, muffled, not close, and no more explosions. *They must have retreated to the basement to fight it out from there,* Ben assumed.

Chapter Twelve

Yellow and orange flames reflected off the chairlift's thick steel cable, giving it the appearance of a huge, heavy-bellied snake. The snake draped itself over the chairlift's supporting pylons as it climbed the steep mountain, carrying beneath it the small, scared group fleeing for their lives as they disappeared up into the clouds of smoke from the chalet.

Ingrid and Stephanie's chair was now a dim blur in the distance as Ben guided the Kellers into theirs. Lowering the restraining bar onto their laps and pressing the blue button, he squeezed Mia's hand and smiled.

'You'll be fine, Mia. We'll be enjoying your secret fondue recipe another day.' Unsurprisingly, the Kellers were traumatised, blindly obeying Ben's instructions. Scared out of their minds and trembling, their vulnerability increased his anger.

'Don't forget Mia, when you get to the top, find the biggest group you can and stay in the middle of them.'

Mia and Petre looked blankly at him as the chair jerked forward when the arm caught the cable. The chair was suspended from the cable by a large, curved metal arm, and the whole apparatus sounded in need of servicing. Announcing the chair's departure were several loud grinding clunks, as it pendulumed backwards then forward, as it caught up with the cable's momentum. The old and cumbersome machinery complained loudly as it lifted the chair in a steep ascent.

'Our turn now.' Ben raised the restraining bar on the next chair and helped Claus into the cramped confines of the old chair. He hit the blue button. Nothing. He hit it again. Still nothing.

*

The two mercenaries peered cautiously through the smaller chalet's windows, past the red-chequered curtains, and into the dim interior beyond. Light from the flames behind them was enough for them to see their colleague slumped over the table in a dark pool.

'Whoever did him knows what they're doing.' One pointed towards his dead colleague.

'This place isn't very big. You go that way round, I'll go this and—' Audible above the sound of the fire burning seventy metres behind them, a loud, grinding clunk cut through the night air and interrupted the rest of his instruction.

Both nodded in recognition as they departed for their opposing routes around the chalet. Years of training and surviving warzones had taught them how to execute a kill order now that their enemy had given away their position. Claus was the main prize, but each member of his cohort carried a handsome bonus. A reflex action to double check their weapon's safety was off and that a round was chambered, they pulled their weapons tightly into their shoulders. Twisting from the waist, shoulder and gun, making efficient, sweeping arcs as they sighted along the gun's barrel. It was a practised routine, focussed on imminent engagement. Fingers held against the trigger, ready to be pulled the instant anything crossed their line of fire.

*

Ben hit the button again. Still nothing.

'Because it runs slowly, it allows ten seconds between chairs. It's to avoid a pile-up at the top when you get off,' Claus helpfully announced as he gently pushed the blue button, and the arm engaged the huge cable.

The same grinding metallic clunk rang out. The cable accelerated the chair to catch up with its own speed, swinging the chair through the air underneath it. They paused at the top of their arc before swinging back the other way, then stabilised to the cable's sedate progress.

Ben turned in his seat as the cable lifted them away from the smaller chalet, the approaching police and fire trucks' sirens now clearly audible.

'Never thought I would be so grateful to hear a police siren. But I am.' He slapped Claus on the leg. There was too little room in the cramped space of the old chair to do much else.

'Yes, we should offer thanks to Inspector Remy. It looks like they're just in time. They may be able to save some of the chalet, if we're lucky.' Claus smiled wryly, trying hard to control the shock and hide his fear. Their path took them nearer to the larger chalet, close enough to feel the fire's heat and smell the smoke.

Sharp cracks rang out as the sap in the huge pine timbers ignited and exploded. A series of sharper cracks rang out, and Ben immediately realised they were being shot at. Twisting as best he could in the confined space, he saw two dark figures next to the chairlift. They were barely visible in the shadow of the smaller chalet.

Ben looked for the muzzle flashes, like small fireflies, almost indiscernible, and returned fire as more rounds thudded into the chair and whizzed past them. All he could hear was a millisecond of supersonic zip as another round flew nearby. Ben knew he and Claus were sitting ducks and increased his rate of fire. More rounds flew past them, most smacked hard into the chair's metal framework above their heads. The ricochets screamed around them, sounding like excitable fireworks, but Ben stayed focussed. Three rounds of automatic fire; pause; another three; pause and click. The firing pin clicked on an empty breech.

Efficiently ejecting the empty magazine, Ben fitted a full one and continued firing. He knew their pursuers would work out how to operate the basic mechanics of the chairlift and would soon be following them up the mountain. In the darkness, he zeroed in on where he knew the cable would take each chair, eighty metres behind them. He aimed and fired into the darkness and shadows, hoping for a lucky hit.

'Fuck, that was close. You OK, Claus?'

'What? Yes. My God, that was the most frightening thing I've ever done,' replied a traumatised Claus. 'You appear to be making a habit of saving me, Ben. I'm not sure how to thank you.'

'We're not in the clear yet, so stay in the game, Claus. By the time they work out how to operate the chair, I reckon they'll be no more than twenty-five seconds behind us. Is there any way we can jam the cable or stop this thing at the top?'

'I don't see how. It's so old it doesn't have emergency stop buttons or anything.'

'What about the power? I could shoot the main fuse-box if there is one up here.'

'I don't know about those things, Ben. I'm sorry.'

Ben calculated whether twenty-five seconds was enough time to get Claus off, away from the chairlift, and to kill their pursuers. He knew it wasn't enough, but it was all he had.

'Wait. Yes. There is,' replied an excited Claus. 'There is. I remember it now, because when we had that heavy rain last spring, the control box leaked and tripped all the power.'

'Great. How far from when we get off?'

'Very close. On the other side of the top pylon. Five or six paces at the most from where we get off. There's something else I must tell you. It's about why I offered you a job.'

'We don't have time now. We'll talk later, but well remembered about the control box. We should be able to leave whoever's following us stuck out in the open, swinging from this cable.'

Ben checked the remaining rounds in his magazine and rehearsed his moves for their arrival. Twenty-five seconds to bundle Claus off, walk six paces, shoot out the box, kill the power. Send Claus to find the others, while he walked back down, in darkness, for overdue payback. Ben welcomed his plan.

As the chair slowly approached the Medran station, Ben scanned the onlookers gathered around the downhill bicycle pistes. Each floodlight spread a cone of bright light over the crowd below. He relaxed slightly when he was sure none were looking at him. Logically he knew they wouldn't have had time to get anyone up here ahead of him, but he knew not to trust logic in a conflict.

The chair rendered its familiar grinding complaint when the old machinery rotated around the enormous steel wheel above. He could see the control box.

'The bar's stuck. It won't budge.' Ben yanked at the bar, but it would not move. The confines of the old chair now felt smaller.

'You pull, and I'll try to lever it up using my arms on my thighs. Ready, one, two, three, go.'

It did not move. Not even a hint of flex from the over-engineered structure.

'What are we going to do?' Claus' elation of two minutes ago quickly turned to panic as the cable engaged on the horizontal wagon-wheel of a pulley above them. Slowly, the chair started to turn.

'I'm not sure.' Ben's tone said what he was thinking as he tried to force one leg up and out from under the bar, scraping his shin against the old wooden seat slats. He tried sawing his leg back and forth, but the chair was too small. With difficulty, he twisted his body to plant his foot on Claus' armrest and tried to pull up the bar up. It would not give. It was locked solid, with the bar resting on their laps and zero room to move.

'Do you think the ones shooting at us will be on the chairlift?' Claus calmly enquired.

'Yes.' No point in sugar-coating the inevitable.

They had turned through ninety degrees now.

'What can we do?'

Ben did not point out to Claus that he had asked the same question ten seconds ago. 'We're concentrating on the positives, Claus. We have the element of surprise, and in close-quarters conflict, that's worth loads. To us, it's worth one kill, possibly two.'

'How many do you think they are?'

'Two.'

Neither needed the Medran station's floodlights to see what the other was thinking. They heard each other clearly.

'OK. Tell me, what can I do?' Claus' understanding of their predicament helped Ben to plan.

'You can't do much. It's mainly down to me. You're on the side nearest to their chair, and we already know neither of us can move. So, as ridiculous as it sounds, I want you to duck down, present as small a target as possible, and turn towards me.'

'I suppose that is the best we can hope for?'

'Yes. The chances of surviving a body shot are far greater than a head shot. Sorry, Claus.'

In the fading light from the floodlights, Ben ran his hand over where the bar joined the supporting cradle. As he had expected, one of their attackers' rounds had jammed it where they joined.

They had turned through one hundred and eighty degrees now and were starting their descent, oblivious to the danger it was delivering them into. The steel snake slid down over the pylons, back the way they had come, ferrying them to pass within a few metres of armed murderers on their way up.

'I have faith in you, Ben. I feel confident for our chances with you here. But just in case, there's something I must tell you.'

Before Claus could say another word, Ben cut him dead. 'Claus, we're not going down the "just in case" route. It takes less than a second to kill two men. We have that one-second advantage because we'll see them before they see us. Think positive. OK?'

'OK, Ben. If you say so. When we get back to whatever's left of the chalet, there's something I need to tell you. It concerns you and why I offered you a job, and it's very important.'

'Claus. Enough now. We'll talk later. Right now I need to prepare.' Ben twisted Claus as much as his body and the confined space would allow, turning his head into Ben's side, nearly in his lap. Resting his hand on Claus' back, with some effort he avoided patting him.

Ben stared into the dark abyss of their descent. The featureless black space swirled as his focus dived deeper into the impenetrable mass, searching till his eyes itched for the merest glimpse of a shape that would identify his target. The other chair would pass to their left. Claus was on that side, but there was nothing Ben could do about that.

It was completely dark now. They had moved beyond the glow of Medran's floodlights and deeper into the forest. The cable sang as it stretched between the steel wheels on top of the pylons, chattering until they were released again, out into the blackness. The burning chalet cast an orange dome above the treetops, framing the pylons and the ascending chair behind with two unaware assassins clearly silhouetted against the inferno they had created. Too far away, but Ben and Claus had darkness behind them as he rehearsed his plan. He checked his safety was off, again, and waited patiently.

Ben could see they were near now as the two chairs closed on each other at twice the cable's speed. He whispered a warning to his new friend as he held the SIG in a double grip, forearms resting on Claus' bent back.

The chairs were closing fast now. Ben breathed deliberately but calmly, resisted the anxiety to shoot, and looked for a sign. He was looking for the tiniest change in body language of the nearest man that he knew would come. It would come the instant the man spotted Claus and Ben appearing out of the gloom. The tiniest, involuntary twitch of his head when he saw them. That would be the latest point at which Ben could guarantee to shoot first.

The nearest mercenary's head twitched towards them a millisecond before two rounds from Ben's gun violently snapped the same head backwards.

Ben quickly resighted on the surviving gunman, who had already locked eyes with Ben across the dark abyss. He saw surprise, but he also saw an experienced soldier callously pull his dead colleague in front of him, bring his gun round the side of the corpse, and fire blind at Ben and Claus. Unable to sight, most went wide. In an instant, the chairs were next to each other. Almost at point-blank range, Ben aimed and fired in rapid bursts.

The chairs quickly passed as Ben ducked lower and kept firing, pumping successive rounds into the back of the fast-disappearing chair. A sharp cry rang out from the surviving mercenary. One of Ben's rounds had found their mark. Wounded or killed, Ben didn't know, but the disappearing chair was no longer firing at them. The two chairs separated quickly, each swallowed into its own darkness.

'Hell. Yes. Come on!' Ben elatedly fist pumped the darkness. 'Come on, Claus, they're gone, and we got at least one-and-a-half of them. Yes.'

As soon as Ben drew Claus up, he recognised the inertia of a corpse. 'Claus. Claus.' Pulling him forward, his hand felt the sticky flow of warm fluid from Claus' back. Gently leaning the lifeless body against him, Ben didn't need daylight to feel the two wet patches on the older man's thick jumper, right behind his heart and lungs. A darkness was spreading, as two deep, glistening cavities merged into one amorphous, fatal black mass.

A futile reflex told him to check for a pulse, but there was not even the faintest trace. He gently eased Claus back in his seat and crossed his hands in his lap.

Ben held back hot fury. He didn't want that at the moment; he preferred cold sadness. But he understood the inevitable course his emotions would follow. Soon he would let anger in, and he would make a deal with it.

'Jesus. How do I explain this to Ingrid? To Stephanie? To anyone?' he cried out to the silent darkness as they glided the arial avenue cut through the forest. 'I don't want to meet them. I don't want, ever again, to tell another wife, or child, what has happened to their husband or father.'

Ben sat in silence and made a promise.

The chair lift lowered him towards a sea of blue and red flashing lights, while his mind crowded with thoughts of Claus, the Swiss Police, and the British Army. For the first time, he did not want to see Ingrid or Stephanie. *I hope they all got away from the lift and stayed up there, because I can't tell them how I wasn't able to defend Claus.*

Funnels of soot-laden smoke spiralled into the night sky as arcs of water doused the smouldering chalet, sending black steam hissing out from the charred wooden beams. Ambulances, fire trucks, and police cars crowded the chalets.

The blue lights jolted Ben from remorseful reflection. He'd just killed five, or possibly six, people and the Swiss Police would need to investigate him. Irrespective that he acted in self-defence, under the terms of his lopsided NDA, if the British Army ever found out that he was being questioned in connection with multiple murders, that would be enough for them to recall him. He could not run that risk. He was a decorated ex-Special Forces potential embarrassment who knew too much and was too willing to speak his mind. That made him a threat.

His only option was to ditch the gun and deny, deny, deny. The emergency services on the ground were too preoccupied with the chalet and the aftermath to have noticed him. He ejected the empty magazine, wiped down everything, tossed the gun one way, and the magazine the other. No-one shouted anything. The snows would cover it soon, and the forest here was so dense that maybe no-one would ever find it. Worry about that later and live to fight another day.

*

Ben saw Francois and Christophe in the middle of the crowd, and even the roar of the fire engines could not drown his shout. A dozen people looked up startled, as they threw themselves into unexpected action. Police officers drew side-arms, paramedics ran to grab stretchers, Francois and Christophe ran towards him. Christophe cut the power at the control box as they descended to within touching distance of the lawn. The cable juddered to a halt and several dozen people descended on the small patch of garden. Francois pushed the nearest away, others stepped back.

Ben met Francois' empty eyes. It was a look he had seen in too many faces. 'I'm sorry, Francois. One of their rounds jammed the machinery and we couldn't get off at the top, so it brought us back down.'

'We saw them firing at you. Saw them run to get on the chair, but we were pinned down ourselves and couldn't get to you. Where did it happen?' asked an emotionless Francois.

'On the way down,' Ben replied.

Francois nodded.

'It would have been very quick,' added Ben.

'But still dead.' Francois spoke in a flat tone without looking at Ben. Without looking at anything other than the bloodied and inert body of his lifelong friend.

As he carefully eased Claus back in his chair to study his face, Christophe and Ben deferred to Francois. No one spoke; even the fire seemed to quieten. Francois was silent, his face betraying no emotion at all, just a hint of tightening at the corners of his pursed lips. With expressionless eyes, impassive since emotion had vacated them, he slowly swept some loose strands of hair that had flopped down across Claus' closed eyes.

Carefully picking a few of the stray strands, he placed them neatly above Claus' forehead, smoothing them with his half-gloved hands, the gnarled and weathered knuckles in contrast to Claus' peaceful expression.

'Je suis vraiment désolé, mon ami, je vais te venger.' I am so sorry my friend, I will avenge you.

Ben welcomed the company.

They lowered the chair, and with help from a fire service crowbar, Francois, Christophe, and Ben carefully lifted Claus' body from the chairlift.

'Please place him in the coroner's wagon and be careful with him.' Inspector Remy had joined them as he gave instructions to the paramedics.

'Ben Mason? I'm Inspector Remy, and I am in charge of this investigation.'

Oh shit, thought Ben Mason.

Chapter Thirteen

'How well did you know Claus Oppenheimer, Mr. Mason?'

'He's one of the most famous people in global finance, Inspector.'

'Please answer the question, Mr. Mason. I asked how well you knew him?'

'Personally? I didn't know him that well. We'd only properly met a few days ago.'

'And how well do you know his family, or Francois, or Christoph?'

'Not very well, Inspector. I'd met Ingrid and Stephanie a couple of times.'

'So, a complete stranger, Francois, arrives unannounced in your hospital room. He convinces you to leave hospital, avoiding being discharged by a doctor, to go in a helicopter with him and Claus – someone whom you hardly know, but you do know some people tried to kill him and a few dozen other people the night before – to fly to a remote chalet, wearing only your hospital robes. I'd love to know what Francois said for you to agree to that?'

'He said Claus wanted to thank me.' Ben smiled the most honest smile he could manage. 'And when Claus Oppenheimer, who had offered me a job earlier that day, says he wants to thank you personally, I'm not likely to refuse, am I? I willingly accepted,' Ben lied fluently.

'In a dressing gown?'

'No. He gave me a pilot's jumpsuit.'

'Yes, so I saw from the hospital lift's CCTV. I also saw Francois show you the gun he was carrying. Did you ask him why he had a gun?'

'If you've got the CCTV, you'd be able to hear him,' Ben gambled.

'I want to hear it from you, not the audio.' Remy's face tightened a little.

Ben knew Remy didn't have the audio from inside the hospital's lift. 'I think it was just a bit of bravado. You know, boys and their toys and all that.'

Remy paused and considered Ben before continuing. 'And yet you still went with him?'

'I thought it wouldn't be a smart career move to decline an invitation from my new boss.'

'Phah.' An annoyed Remy waved his hand in the air. 'And what did Claus and you talk about on the flight?'

'We couldn't, it was too noisy.'

'No headsets? No built-in audio?'

Ben just shrugged.

*

The politicians wanted public visibility kept as low as possible until Remy could solve the puzzle of Claus Oppenheimer's death. Hence, Remy had gone for the low-key, no-witnesses interview in the smaller chalet's lounge.

Remy was a tough and seasoned member of the Civil Protection Sector, a department of Switzerland's Federal Office. His methods were old-school, but he produced results. In his forty years' service he had dealt with most character types, criminal and otherwise. But this Englishman was the most incomprehensible witness, suspect, he had ever interrogated. Remy knew Ben could easily claim self-defence for his actions but was instead claiming he was an innocent bystander. He was sure that discovering Ben's reasons for silence were connected to the recent attacks and deaths.

'You say you followed Claus through the tunnel from the basement to the other chalet?'

'Yes.'

'Before or after you shot the mercenary in the basement?'

'What mercenary?' *He's guessing,* thought Ben. *He can't know for certain I shot that guy.*

'In the basement, there was the aged Kellers, Claus, Ingrid, Stephanie, and you – a soldier with the British Army for four years.'

Remy raised his voice for effect. 'Which one of those do you think is most likely to have shot him?'

'I was trying to keep everyone safe and out of the way. When Petre joined us, we went through the tunnel and up the chairlift.'

'Which would be when you shot the guy in the other chalet's kitchen?'

'He was dead when we got there.'

'Oh, that's convenient.' Remy's sarcasm was thick. 'Then you took the chairlift. You can't get off at the top because the bar-release is jammed, so you had to come back down. Passing within a few metres of two experienced and armed hit men who were being paid to kill you. You say you were unarmed, and yet miraculously one of them dies from gunshot wounds and the other, from the blood we found, is wounded. And yet you say you didn't have a gun? Please explain by what divine intervention that happened.'

Ben felt his throat and chest tighten. 'They weren't expecting us to be coming back down. It was dark, and they didn't see us until we were level with them. Then they started firing. That must have been when they shot Claus. I was on the outside. I was just lucky.'

'You may be lucky, Mason, but you're also a bloody liar. And it still doesn't explain who shot the mercenary on the chairlift. Unless you're telling me that a dead man climbed onto the chairlift all by himself?'

'I have no idea, Inspector. I played dead all the way down. Maybe his comrade shot him by mistake?' Ben knew taunting would not help him, but the noose was tightening. He had to do something to disrupt Remy's rhythm.

'Don't fuck with me, Mason.' Remy was angry now. 'I can lock you up for years without a reason if I want to.' His face had reddened. 'And are you aware of Switzerland's laws for perjury or obstructing the course of justice? Or of the statutory sentence that will be passed? Or of just how ridiculous your whole story sounds?'

Ben silently agreed, but he just shrugged again. He was trying not to sweat.

'What did you do with the gun?'

'What gun?' Ben was unnerved when he saw Remy relax.

'You must have thrown it away on the chairlift.' Remy's eyes lit up. 'You could save us all a lot of unnecessary effort if you just told us where to look.' Ominously, Remy's voice raised half a pitch.

'I didn't have a gun to throw anywhere.' He was grasping now.

'And you'd be willing to swear to all of this under oath?'

'Sure.' Ben knew that word sounded crushed as he'd spoken it.

He wanted to justify to Remy everything that had happened. He wanted to tell him, but because of his exit NDA with the army, saying nothing was his only choice for now.

Further interrogation was halted by the arrival of another policeman, carrying Ben's holdall. He stepped close to Remy and whispered something. Remy nodded and took the bag.

'Mr Mason, your good fortune appears boundless. You room was not damaged, and the firemen have retrieved your luggage. Here. You look in need of a change of clothes. I suggest you use the cloakroom, through there.' Remy pointed to a door off to the side of the lounge. 'We have much more to discuss, so I have arranged for a Federal Services helicopter to take us both back to Zurich. We're going to a small airfield, Dubendorf, which is less than ten minutes from your hotel. I suggest you get changed now.' He handed over the holdall.

Ben selected fresh clothes and was relieved to be out of Remy's interrogative pummelling for ten minutes. He was surprised to see the inspector had waited for him when he came back into the room.

'You forgot to tell me what you and Claus spoke about before all the shooting started.'

'There's not a lot to tell.' Ben shook his head. 'We didn't really speak about much, or for long. Claus just wanted to thank me, so we had some food, chatted generally, and then it all kicked off.'

'You know I don't believe you, don't you? And you know there are so many reasons why I shouldn't believe you.'

The room was getting smaller. Ben shrugged again.

Remy gave a disappointed shake of his head before continuing. 'I think Claus expected whoever carried out the Sonne Berg bombing to attack him again. That's why he had his close friends, the ex-Special Forces pair of Francois, Christophe. and associates, come here. But why do they want to kill him?' Remy paced the floor.

The pacing halted abruptly as Remy spun to face Ben, pointing his finger with a triumphant expression. 'He told you, didn't he?' Remy's eyes lit up; an enlightened smile began to form.

Ben's room shrank even more, and the noose tightened.

'Claus told you why they wanted to kill him, and it was enough to make you fly here.' Remy's jubilation tried to overwhelm Ben.

'I don't know what you're talking about, Inspector. Claus wouldn't come here or bring his family here if he thought they would be attacked. So, it's logical to assume he didn't expect to be attacked, which is why he thought it was OK to ask me to come here.' Ben recovered some composure and forced his shoulders to loosen.

'You're no fool, Mason. You would have asked Claus why he was incarcerating himself with armed guards in a remote chalet. I am no fool, so don't expect me to believe you did not. The only plausible answer was that Claus told you why they wanted to kill him. That's the only reason that would have made you come here.' Remy glowed like a zealot discovering enlightenment.

Just as the noose tightened further around Ben's neck, Remy's phone rang. Irritated, he was about to cancel the call without answering, but hesitated. His finger hovered over the screen when he saw the caller's ID.

Even with Ben's lack of European languages, he could make out from the Suisse/German conversation that the caller's name was Ingrid. And if body language on a phone call was an indication of how important the caller was, then Remy was indicating this was an important caller. He replaced his phone and said nothing, although he was now glaring in a resigned attitude towards Ben.

'We'll continue this later, Mr. Mason. Oh, by the way, do you remember that man you shot?'

Ben had shot many. He gestured disinterest with a shrug.

'You must remember, on the chairlift? Not the one you killed, the other one?'

Ben remembered the eyes.

'The webcams captured him, limping with great difficulty, off the chairlift at Medran. Turns out that he's very famous, wanted by Interpol and a dozen police forces for murder and terrorist activities. He may be coming to find you. Would you like us to let you know when we find out where he is?'

Ben shrugged, hesitantly.

Chapter Fourteen

Under a perimeter of powerful arc lights, firemen doused the remaining pockets of heat. Serpents of steam hissed angrily at the water jets, disturbing their smouldering nests. Laden with soot, and with glowing embers for eyes, they gyrated up into the Verbier night sky. The previously sweet, clean mountain air was now thick with graphite and carbon. Forensics teams, clothed in protective white suits, worked methodically through the battlefield with the same body language as an undertaker; a practised oblivion to human suffering in order to get the job done. It looked like a film set projecting the horror of war by relating it to domestic reality. Because that is what it was.

Ben had taken himself outside and watched the helicopter carrying Ingrid, Stephanie, Francois, and Christophe depart. It was not just the cold air or the wind-chill from the downwash; everyone stood and shivered. Ingrid's loud, tearful denial and Stephanie's frantic cry marked the exact moment when they had identified Claus' body in the coroner's wagon. She and Stephanie were inconsolable. Ben wanted to say something, but when Ingrid went alone to sit in the smouldering rubble of their burned-out chalet, having just identified her dead husband, he thought it better to wait.

Francois had managed, with customary economy, to whisper, 'We don't know who we can trust. Say nothing. We've got your back.'

Mia and Petre Keller displayed classic post-trauma symptoms. They sat in shock and cried in bewilderment until the Police drove them home. One hell of a Saturday night.

Ben welcomed the solitude as he tried to reset his mind. Remy placed him to one side while he directed the initial crime scene investigation. They both knew Remy had the truth but not the proof. And that was crucial. Their next bout would come on the helicopter journey back to Zurich. Until then, every time they were close, Ben was bombarded with another well-thought-out question. *Let's hope the helicopter doesn't have those executive audio headsets,* he prayed.

Eventually Remy left the Police and Coroner to their processes as he ushered Ben onto the helicopter and into the seat opposite him. Officers from the Federal Security Service joined them, saying little and watching everything. Ben knew their silence and stares were all part of the game that Remy had no doubt told them to play. As a result, Ben acted the Grey Man in the game, where you become invisible, even when you're the only one in the room. And so the game continued, all the way back to Dubendorf airfield.

Ben's assumption that they would not be equipped with the same quality of audio helmets was correct. Remy competed unsuccessfully with the clatter of machinery and wind, but Ben cupped his hand to his ear and invariably asked him to repeat the question before shouting his reply. It was usually a question that required further unsuccessful shouting by Remy, who eventually waved him away. A shrug and a mouthed 'Too noisy' from Ben earned a long hard stare from Remy. Ben closed his eyes and tried to restore some sanity.

Their return flight to Zurich was not as comfortable as their outward one. It was the same model of helicopter but stripped down to the bare function of carrying military personnel. Ben was familiar with the cocoons of criss-crossed canvas straps, hung from tubular metal frames to form individual hammocks, and he welcomed the discomfort if it meant Remy stopped firing questions at him.

When they landed into the small Dubendorf airfield, the Security Service officers did not wait for any instructions and were out of their seats before the helicopter was even stationary. Steady rain, carried hard on a strong wind, crashed into the interior when the doors were flung back. Remy guided Ben by the elbow – *a bit too tightly*, he thought – down the steps to collect their luggage. A small coach approached, ready to transfer them to the terminal buildings.

As soon as they were on board, Remy continued the verbal body blows. 'You've been thinking all the way back, Mason. I could see that. I'll give you one last chance to tell me why you are so scared to admit you acted in self-defence when the terrorists attacked you.'

Ben knew that if Remy discovered that answer, he'd also discover he could hold Ben hostage to a military sentence. Remy's stooge, or a prison from where it would be impossible to execute his plans for the Five. He had no option; he had to say nothing.

'I've told you. I didn't have a gun or shoot anyone.'

'You're a fool if you think I am, Mason. Why didn't those two professional ex-soldiers on the chairlift riddle the two of you with bullets on your way down?' Remy continued to twist the knife.

'It was because you had a gun, and you shot them before they could shoot you, wasn't it?' Remy would not let go of this particular stick, and he hit Ben accurately with it. 'You had a gun, you shot them with it, and then you got rid of it.'

Remy drilled deeper and closer to the truth. 'What I don't know is why you won't admit that. It is the most straightforward case of self-defence I've ever seen. No jury would ever commit. In fact, the Police, and I speak as the Police, would never charge you. It can only mean you're more scared of something else. More frightening than the Sonne Berg and chalet attacks? Wow, that must be really scary. You'll remain my suspect until I find out what it is, and I cannot release a suspect, even if he appears to be a hero having saved many people's lives.'

Ben didn't need to reply. They both knew.

The transfer coach pulled up to the small terminal as a group of passengers from a commercial flight filed through the light drizzle into the building. Ben joined them in the hope it would stop Remy's questioning.

Remy walked silently with Ben through the building and towards the exit doors of the domestic terminal. Despite Ben's youthful brushes with the law, Remy's questioning preoccupied him as he placed his bag on the scanner's conveyor belt. Conflicting thoughts of how much truth to blend with fiction seized his mind.

Alarm sirens rang out all around, followed immediately by several armed members of the Civil Protection Sector tackling Ben to the floor.

'Down. Down on the floor. Armed Police, hands behind your head. Don't move.'

Ben's head swam when his face slammed into the cold, bare floor. Still dizzy from the blow, nausea swept over him as he tasted blood running from his nose into his throat, choking him. A boot swung viciously into his exposed ribs, followed by several to his back and head, the air driven from his lungs. He could feel himself losing consciousness when a knee or a boot, he couldn't tell, pressed hard into his neck. His vision swam, and he was now fighting for breath with his hands held painfully high up his back.

The X-ray scanner displayed the distinct outline of a SIG Sauer P320 inside Ben's holdall. Given the tension from the Sonne Berg attack, the gun had a paralysing effect on the few dozen passengers now lying prone and petrified on the terminal floor.

A boot was placed in the small of Ben's back as his hands were secured tightly behind him. Nothing could compare with the wave of dread that washed over him.

'Stay down. Do not move. I am an armed officer, and I will fire if necessary.'

The speed and aggression of the security officers may have surprised Ben. But that was nothing compared with the surprise at seeing the outline of the gun which three hours ago he had thrown deep into bushes on a dark mountain, two hundred kilometres away. Magically, this had found its way into his holdall. He recalled Remy's questioning back at the chalet. Not for the first time, he saw his life flash past him and ending up in a very bad place.

Face down on the floor, with a knee crushing his neck, he could hear Remy calmly thanking the security team staffing the exit door. Ben was rolled over onto his back to witness four officers whose guns were matter-of-factly pointing at him.

'Oh dear, Ben. You really should have cooperated with me. Now it looks like you are in a whole world of trouble.'

Yes, I am, thought Ben, as he explored his limited options. The security officers dragged Ben away from public view and into a windowless side room.

*

'Well, Ben, looks like you did have a gun after all? Not an offence in isolation, but you've now become a person of interest, so I can detain you indefinitely. Withholding evidence, obstruction, and perjury. Oh my.' Remy's faux surprise helped Ben understand so much more.

'And I'm betting your fingerprints are all over this weapon.' It was now secured inside the evidence bag Remy had produced from his pocket.

How convenient that Remy had one of those, thought Ben.

'My fingerprints won't be on the gun until you tell someone to put them there. And you know that very well, Inspector.'

'If your prints aren't on the gun, it's because you wiped them off before you threw it from the chairlift. And you know that very well, Mr. Mason.' Remy mimicked Ben's accent.

An understanding was forming between the two men as each played their hands.

'I bet we'll also find rounds, which match this gun, in all sorts of places, and even inside some of the bodies piled up in the morgue.' Remy smiled confidently.

'Only if you plant them there.' Ben's only weapon now was bluff, as he tried to rationalise that this was just the opposition piling on the pressure in a negotiation. But he knew it was more. Remy would not have realised he was now holding the key to Ben's military prison sentence. He knew his bluff could easily be called, so he chose the direct route.

'What do you want, Remy? You and I know that either you put that gun in my bag, or you arranged for it to be put there. So, let's cut to the chase, what is it you're after?'

Remy continued his charade with a display of righteousness. 'What do I want, Ben? I am a seeker of the truth, and maybe a degree of cooperation – from you – that's what interrogations are designed to achieve.'

'Bollocks, Remy. This isn't an official interrogation, because you haven't got a witness or a recorder in here, nor did you at the chalet. And, when I was changing at the chalet, you didn't collect my clothes in a sterile environment. All that lovely DNA compromised, and we both know nothing is admissible without any of those. I saw how you reacted when Ingrid phoned you earlier. She's powerful, and smart. So are you. So be smart and don't confuse me with someone who's scared or stupid.' Ben made unblinking eye contact throughout. 'Again, what is it you really want?'

'We want to know what and who Claus was involved with, and why someone was trying to kill him. It's as simple as that. And remember, I gave you a second chance with the gun. There are no more second chances. Tell us what we want, or you'll be arrested and charged on three counts. You decide.'

Ben did not reply immediately. He was performing his own calculation, weighing risk against reward – and that decision was easy. The more difficult decision was how much to leave out while making sound it credible. Ben decided the direct route was his best option.

'OK, Remy. I can't prove any of this, so don't ask me to.' Without proof, it couldn't be publicised, and nor could Ben's involvement. 'You'll just have to take our dead friend's word for it. Claus was killed because he wanted to expose a secret group of four powerful individuals, a globally organised crime group, but on a scale which is unbelievable and has been operating for decades. Also, they've murdered hundreds or even thousands of people who have stood in the way of their own personal gain.' Ben was pleased to see Remy physically react. He stared open-mouthed at Ben.

'That's not possible,' Remy managed eventually. 'We would know of them. Are these four people Swiss citizens?'

'You're thinking too narrow, Remy. You saw what they did at the Sonne Berg and the chalet. I suggest you think of abuse in the most extreme sense, and then you'll be getting close. Swiss citizens? I don't know but given the scale of what they appear capable of, I'd be thinking international rather than domestic.'

'Who are these people? Why didn't Claus come to the Police? Why did he feel he had to be the one to expose them?' Remy couldn't hide his uncertainty.

'They killed him before he could tell me who they were.' Claus had told Ben the name of their leader – Thomas Liang – but Ben had his own plans for Mr. Liang. 'They are the successors of a group that was formed many decades ago. Originally a group of five, one of them died a year or so ago, then Claus was approached to replace the one who died. He quickly discovered how murderously corrupt they were and threatened to blow the whistle on them. That's when they threatened him, and his family. He said he would expose them if they didn't change, so they killed him.'

'Killing someone as prominent as Claus is not something you could expect to do covertly. They'd know it would create a huge shitstorm. They must have a lot to protect. Did Claus give any indication?'

'Yes. More billions than you or I could count.'

Remy's surprise was evident. 'They must be prominent people themselves. They must be well known, oligarchs, dictators, public figures?'

'Presumably.'

'Did Claus say anything about the identity of these four men? Names, nationality, company names, anything?'

'No, he didn't say if they were men or women. Just that they were powerful and ruthless. But we now know that.' Ben felt a release, like a weight had been lifted.

'Did he say anything at all that might point to their identities?'

'He had just started to tell me when the chalet was attacked. After that we were fighting to survive.'

Ben knew their leader was Thomas Liang. He also knew he could find names of the attendees at the World Economic Forum in Davos. The murdered Swedish politicians on the Scandi-Air flight would be public, as would their schedule at the Forum. Then it was just a case of trawling press records to find the identity of the firm wanting to drill in the North Sea whose application had been rejected. That firm was run or owned by another member of the four. That was two out of the four, and he knew a very smart man who could recreate the other half of the jigsaw.

'It's like a plot for a movie. Internationally prominent people embezzling billions, employing assassins to kill other internationally prominent people, global swindling for decades. We're looking at the world's biggest ever organised crime group, if this is true.' Remy's look spoke loudly.

'I know it sounds incredible, Inspector, but this is exactly what Claus told me. A few hours ago, I was reacting exactly like you. I had the same thoughts as you have now. It is unbelievable, but it's credible. It has to be something on this scale to warrant the Sonne Berg and chalet attacks. You know I was in the British Army, so I can tell you that this was a professional and well-funded group.'

'Just to satisfy my curiosity, did you shoot the attackers in the basement, the smaller chalet, and the chairlift?'

'That's not the deal, Remy. You said you wanted to know why someone was trying to kill Claus. That's what we agreed, and that's all your getting.' Ben's emphatic tone was not faked. 'Do you want me to continue?'

'Please.'

Ben would accept any win now. No matter how small.

'Why didn't Claus come to us, the Police, with what he had discovered?'

'I asked him that. Claus said he didn't have any proof, but he did know they had senior people in the Police and Government.' It was an embellishment that Ben hoped would make Remy more cautious who he repeated this to.

'Do you know what Claus was planning to do next?'

'No.' Another half-truth. 'But as he had threatened to go to the IMF and the Police, I presume ultimately that's what he planned to do.'

'Why did he take you into his confidence and tell you these things?'

'He feared I was at risk because I had rescued him from the Sonne Berg. The bad guys might think I was part of his inner sanctum. I was not. I wasn't even an employee at that stage.' Just enough truth to make the story credible.

'Now your future employer is dead, what are your plans?'

'I'd like to go back to London, to my life, my old job, and to put all this behind me.' Not even a half truth.

'And I'd like you to be available for further questioning, so don't leave Zurich without my agreement. You understand that this conversation never took place, don't you, Mason? And that you can never reveal this conversation to anyone.' Remy fixed him with a threatening stare.

'Yes, of course, Inspector.' Another lie. *If this conversation never took place,* thought Ben, *then your instruction not to leave Zurich never took place, which is convenient as I think my plans will be taking me to many places far from Zurich.*

Ben had previous experience of the uneven relationship when your only option was to make a deal with the Police. The best an informant can hope for is, if they stay out of trouble and the Police never return to squeeze them for something else, then maybe they can avoid prison, retribution, or worse. *First objective is to walk away from this car-crash and deal with tomorrow when it arrives,* thought Ben.

'I will stay within the law,' Remy continued without any visible irony, 'and I will crush you in an instant if you step outside the law. Fortunately, again, for you, you appear to have the support of people whom I support. Right now, that is the only thing keeping you outside a prison cell.'

'I also want to stay within the law, Inspector. Always have done.' Ben did his best not to blink.

'Good, I'm glad to hear that. I would like your mobile number, and I want you to keep in frequent contact with me and to let me know if you remember or discover anything else. I can assure you I will keep in touch with you.' Remy's mouth smiled, but his eyes did not. 'Now I must become your taxi driver, Mr. Mason. I have been asked to make sure you get to your hotel without any further incident. I wonder if you can manage that?'

Chapter Fifteen

'We've been expecting you, Monsieur Mason.' Fabrice, the concierge, betrayed his regional French heritage, pronouncing Ben's last name as *Masson*. Bowing slightly from the waist while slowly nodding his head, he went on, '*Je suis* Fabrice,' pronounced *Fab*reeze. 'We are honoured to welcome you to the Hotel St Gallen. May I take your bag?'

The overt obsequiousness of the concierge was welcome relief after the ride with Inspector Remy. 'No, thank you, Fabrice. I can manage. Where do I check in?'

'Oh non, Monsieur Mason. We do not have a "check-in" at the St. Gallen. It is more like staying at a friend's *petit manoir* when they are away. You just tell us what you want, and we arrange it.'

'OK, I need to get to Berne, possibly first thing tomorrow. What's the best way to do that? By train? Hiring a car?'

'I believe you're going to Berne to obtain a replacement passport, *oui*? And from Monsieur Calvert?'

Fabrice's knowledge intrigued Ben, but his disdainful treatment of Calvert's name intrigued him more. 'I am, and I'm guessing your preparedness is linked with the Oppenheimers?'

Ben noted Fabrice's confident facade slip. His voice wavered. 'We still find it so hard to believe. Dear Claus of all people. We cannot understand why. The Sonne Berg, then Verbier. All the shooting and killing. I'm sure you know far more than you can say, Monsieur Mason, but no-one in all of Switzerland can understand why this happened.' Fabrice was frantically wringing his hands, and his voice cracked as he sniffed.

Embarrassed, he fished a handkerchief from his pocket and looked up to Ben through tear-dampened eyes. 'Monsieur Mason, please forgive me, but Claus was a shining light of compassion and understanding to me. I loved him and would have done anything for him, although I am not a brave man. I feel helpless about what has happened.'

'It's OK, Fabrice. I didn't know him as well as you did, but I know what you're saying. He was a remarkable man, and I wish I'd known him better.'

'*Oui*, a remarkable man, Monsieur, and a remarkable family. Ingrid told us you would be seeing Calvert.'

'I don't know why I'm surprised that you know that, Fabrice, but yes, I'm hoping to get a replacement passport from the British Embassy, and I'm told this Andrew Calvert has offered to arrange one for me.'

'It is best to go by helicopter. There is a company we have used frequently. It is late now, and you probably need to rest, but I can contact them. I will organise a car and a helicopter for first thing tomorrow. The car will drive you two minutes to a private helipad a few kilometres along the ridge, and you will be in Calvert's office within an hour.'

'An hour? How fast does this helicopter go?' Ben jokingly added, 'Does it land in the British Embassy's back garden?'

'I don't know exactly, although I believe it to be more than two hundred miles an hour. As regards landing, although I have not done it myself, I believe the British Embassy have an arrangement with a tennis club near them.'

Fabrice paused and placed a hand on Ben's forearm while he gathered himself.

'Wait. The helicopter, I know exactly how long it takes because Calvert used it to come here to meet Claus.' Fabrice's eyes had dried, and Ben noticed the concierge's hesitancy had been replaced with determination as they searched Ben's face.

'Andrew Calvert used to come here by helicopter to meet Claus? Were they friends?'

'Non! He was never a friend of Claus. He used to show off that he'd left his office "only fifty-five jolly fast minutes ago",' Fabrice mimicked. 'Once he came to meet some of Claus' business partners, but he came to see Claus several times and always to argue and threaten him.'

'Seriously? I can't imagine anyone bullying and threatening Claus Oppenheimer. Especially not a senior member of a British Embassy. How do you know this? How can you be so certain he wasn't a friend of Claus?' Ben leaned back, sceptically regarding Fabrice.

'Everyone heard them, as they were on the terrasse. Calvert is so arrogant and loud that it was difficult not to hear them. But anyway, I have replayed many times the CCTV from the terrasse – there are two cameras – and you can hear it clearly. I can tell you, they were not friends.'

'When was this, Fabrice?'

'The worst was maybe two weeks ago. You can hear him shouting and threatening Claus, telling him he had to stop, but I don't know what he was referring to. Telling him it "wouldn't just be him",' Fabrice mimicked an upper-class English accent again, 'and that he "should think of Ingrid and Stephanie". I am such a coward. I should have done something. I should have said something.'

'You're not a coward, Fabrice. You *are* doing something, you're telling me. That's taking a brave risk and I respect you for that.'

Fabrice straightened at the compliment and put his handkerchief away. 'I think it would put us both in danger if you repeat this to anyone. I don't know why. I have CCTV of two men arguing, which doesn't prove anything. But I don't trust Calvert, and I don't think Claus did either. I know I can trust you because Ingrid called to say I was to treat you like a member of their family. That's good enough for me.'

Fabrice pushed back his shoulders, holding his head higher as he jutted out a rebellious chin. Ben was not sure how many filters to apply to his revelations.

'Do you know what the argument was about?'

'No, not entirely. But it had to be something very important, because I've never seen Claus so angry.'

'Thanks, Fabrice, this is interesting, although I'm not sure what it tells us. For now, I'll call Calvert, find out if he's able to see me in the morning, and let's see what happens from there.'

Chapter Sixteen

He turned over Andrew Calvert's business card in his hand and pondered what sort of reception he would receive from British officialdom. *Admit nothing and keep a low profile, again,* thought Ben. At least it would tell him whether they knew anything from the Swiss authorities about the shootings at the chalet.

As expected from the Charges d'Affaires of the British Embassy, the card was beautifully embossed, with the United Kingdom's emblematic lion and unicorn arranged either side of the shield and crown of the kingdom. Spoiling it somewhat was the hand-written, broad ink sweeps, 'PTO' scrawled across Andrew Calvert's name and the many letters after it. On the card's reverse was a nine-digit number suffixed with 'PERSONAL' and underlined.

Ben dialled it from the mobile phone he'd been given, storing the number in its memory.

The response drawled in a haughty English accent, 'Calvert.'

'Sorry it's so late, Mr. Calvert, my name is Ben Mason.'

'I rather presumed it would be you when it said Caller ID Unknown. I don't get many of those on this phone.' All enunciated in precise, rounded vowels. A window into Calvert's path through the English public-school system, probably rounded off with a very good regiment and a top university.

'I presume you got this number from my card. The one I sent to Hilda to give to you? And that you probably need a new passport?'

'Yes, to all three.' Ben was building upon Fabrice's view of Calvert with every word the man uttered.

'You'll need to pop in to see me then? Jolly good. We can have a chat. I've a number of questions I'd like to put to you.'

Alarm bells started to ring in Ben's mind. He had doubted Calvert's offer of help had been entirely charitable. Now he knew.

'I'd appreciate that, Mr. Calvert, but it's a weekend. Is the Embassy open?'

'Not to the general public, obviously. Skeleton staff for emergencies, and these are challenging circumstances, so I think we can make an exception in your case, don't you?'

'I'm very grateful, Mr. Calvert, thank you. I'm happy to answer any of your questions.' Both men took turns to lie. 'I need a replacement passport and I have absolutely no ID. It was all destroyed in the Sonne Berg Hotel. I don't even have so much as a credit card. Will that be a problem?'

'Not a problem at all. We're online to the London Passport Office and can issue a replacement from here. All it needs is a few signatures, I'll witness them, snap a few photos, and Bingo! A brand-new British passport. Just remember not to smile, eh?'

'I don't think that'll be a problem. There hasn't been a whole lot to smile about recently.'

'No, there hasn't, has there? I hear you've been through quite a lot, and the Verbier business is just dreadful. Just doesn't make sense. I was rather hoping you could shed some light on what happened, as you were right in the middle of both events?'

Ben's alarm bells rang a little louder. 'I'll give you all the help I can, but I've got more questions than I have answers myself.' He knew this sounded weak.

'Let's chat more when you're here, Ben. You sound quite chipper, so if you're up to coming here tomorrow morning? Tell Fabrice to organise transport for about nine am, if that's OK. You'll be here around ten, and when I hear you landing at the tennis club, I'll pop the kettle on. Never thought the cutbacks would extend to one having to make one's own cuppa, but we've all got to make sacrifices, eh?'

'Perfect. See you tomorrow then.'

*

Andrew Calvert, the Charges d'Affaires of the British Embassy in Berne, searched his mobile phone's contacts then clicked the dial icon next to the unnamed number.

'Yes,' came the sharp and accented response.

'Mason will be here tomorrow morning. He knows something, but he's not saying what. I'll change that. Our Mr. Mason is just an ex-squaddie with history, he won't be a problem.'

'I hope not, Calvert. You know what I want. Succeed and you will be rewarded. Let's not discuss what happens if you fail.' Then in a honeyed tone, the voice added, 'You do know DNA is forensically detectable for such a long time, don't you, Andrew? And that the Police haven't closed their files on that poor girl's murder? A shocking business, wasn't it? Those innocent sex games can become so dangerous, can't they?' The call ended.

Calvert was visibly shaking with anger and fear in equal measure.

*

The journey by road from the St. Gallen Hotel in Zurich to the British Embassy in Berne takes about two hours. A few seconds after the helicopter's downdraft had bent the trees and shrubs surrounding the small helipad inside-out, Ben knew the journey would be considerably quicker. Fabrice's arrangements had worked out exactly as he'd said they would. His car was outside the St. Gallen ten minutes after he had finished his breakfast; the drive to the private helipad took five minutes; and there the sleekest-looking helicopter Ben had ever seen was warming up and ready to go. Red and white livery contrasting reflective-black windows finishing off the whole Executive feel.

An informal safety briefing, help with his four-point harness, donning headphones, and they were ready to take off. The three thousand horsepower torqued the huge rotor blades and very soon they were lifting off from the close-cropped grass platform. Early morning dew from the grass was sent spiralling out by the force of the downwash, the spray resembling waves crashing onto rocks in a storm and sounding like a million angry wasps.

They banked hard to the right as soon as they were above the treeline and accelerated quickly up to their cruising speed.

To Ben three hundred kilometres an hour felt even faster due to their relatively low altitude above the densely wooded, rolling hilltops. Flying in an arrow straight line took them over the sparsely populated west bank of the Zurich See and into the countryside beyond. At their height and speed, the patchwork quilt of small fields merged, like an impressionist painting, into a blur of a hundred different shades and textures of green. The colours of each east-facing slope of the rolling terrain was bathed in the rays of a warm morning sun behind them. Their shadow danced across the hills and fields in front of them like a wraith escaping its pursuers.

Thirty minutes later and they started banking to the right, scrubbing off speed for their landing into the Kirkenfeld tennis club. Predictably, there was a car waiting in front of the clubhouse for the short journey to the British Embassy.

*

The two men were of similar height and build. Andrew Calvert was a tall, athletic man in his mid-fifties. He was wearing a tailored, cream linen suit with hardly a crease in the material, highly polished brown brogues, and a cornflower blue open-necked shirt. He had tucked a blue handkerchief into his breast pocket. With a long, narrow face, a defined jawline and a strong neck, he carried no excess weight. His erect frame was accentuated by broad shoulders, probably a function of some decades rowing, Ben presumed. Unblinking hazel eyes that hid a thousand lies crinkled into a welcoming and too practised smile when he shook Ben's hand. *Definitely a rower*, thought Ben, returning the trial of strength on equal terms.

Calvert's office overlooked a small courtyard ringed with mature lime trees, through which the mid-morning sun sent shafts of sunshine. Andrew Calvert's urbane, last century charm contrasted with the large plasma screens covering the walls as Ben tried to work out where the covert audio-visual devices were hidden. They'd be there, he was certain of that.

'I really appreciate all your help, Mr. Calvert.'

'I'm hoping we can help each other, Ben.' Calvert's forced-suave rhetoric defined him. 'Considering my long and fulfilling relationship with Claus and Ingrid, and your short but intense association with them, why, we're nearly family.' Andrew Calvert plucked a raffish smile from his library.

'Earl Grey OK? Excellent.' He continued without asking or waiting for a reply. 'Now I want to hear all about your escapades in the Sonne Berg, and the dreadful events at the chalet. Poor Claus. Poor Ingrid. I've written to her, of course, and will leave it a few days before trying to speak with her. Ingrid's a trooper and she'll be putting on a brave face, but it must be a huge shock when somebody murders your innocent husband.' Calvert emphasised the last few words and fixed Ben with unblinking eyes. Every one of his words and actions added credibility to Fabrice's warnings.

Ben underplayed everything that had happened and gave Calvert a Remy-Lite version of events, selectively recounting a few events from the Sonne Berg, fewer still from the attack on the chalet, and certainly no mention of him firing guns. Unlike Remy, who had been genuinely shocked, Calvert was not, and even made a poor job of pretending he was.

'My dear chap, what an extraordinary story. An innocent British citizen visiting one of the world's most peaceful countries and you're conscripted into someone else's war. How on earth did you avoid all the shooting?' Calvert see-sawed between sarcasm and scepticism while staring fixedly at Ben, looking for the smallest tell-tale sign.

'With difficulty,' Ben returned with equal insincerity. 'I wouldn't want to be in the middle of all that. Scares me just to think of what it would have been like.'

'Scares you? That's an intriguing response from someone who was decorated for bravery in Iraq. Two tours in Afghanistan and one in Iraq, in One Para?' Calvert's empty eyes never blinked.

Although he had been expecting Calvert to know he had been in the army, it made Ben uneasy. He found himself agreeing with Fabrice's opinions.

'Confidentially, old boy, what's really fascinating is that we may be able to help the Swiss Police with the identity of the gunman who shot the terrorists on the chairlift.' Calvert leaned back comfortably into his chair.

Ben faked interest to cover the shock. 'Oh really?'

'As luck would have it, one of our techies has managed to retrieve a copy of Verbier's ski-cams. Our chap contacted the Verbier Tourism Office and managed to get hold of the ones looking down from Medran, towards the chalet. It was getting dark, so it's a bit grainy, and they can't make a positive identification at the moment. But that's where our tech boffins come into their own.' Calvert sank more comfortably into his chair and steepled his fingers. 'They have this amazing gizmo called Predictive Pixelation. More Earl Grey?'

Ben declined.

'It predicts the missing pieces from a hundred million human faces in its database. Anyway, they're running it through their app right now and reckon they could have an identifiable picture within a day or so. Fascinating, eh?' Calvert's tone left no doubt as to the underlying message.

'Yes, fascinating.' Ben didn't trust himself to say anything else.

Calvert's large hand gently punched Ben's knee. 'Yes. Quite fascinating, isn't it?' The boyish enthusiasm was too deliberate, too thin. 'The point is, we're bound by convention to hand that over to the Swiss chaps when it's fully developed. It's an unwritten law of how we friendly nations behave in an ally's country. Even more so if the perpetrator turns out to be one of our citizens.'

While Calvert let his last point hang in the still air, Ben silently thanked Fabrice for his warning.

'Sounds very promising for you, Andrew. But all it will produce is an indistinct image of someone acting in self-defence. Why is that such a big deal?' Ben tested Calvert.

'Well. Let's just pretend the "someone" is a person who has something to lose. That would be a big deal, don't you think?' Calvert leaned towards him.

Ben shrugged his shoulders and said nothing. Was Calvert bluffing or guessing? How far away were the webcams when he'd shot the attackers? Did this pixelation thing work, or even exist? Too many imponderables to consider.

'OK, let's pivot this concept.' Calvert prowled with the confidence of a predator closing on a kill. 'Slightly nuanced this, but bear with me. Let's just say someone had information which was of value to HMG. And let's just say HMG is quite keen to better understand any threat to our financial stability, national security, and all that good stuff.' Again, Calvert's over-quizzical eyebrow. 'HMG would appreciate any information that person could provide. If there were to be an undertaking to provide that and any future information exclusively to HMG, via me, then that would also be favourably viewed.'

'What's your definition of favourably viewed?' Ben knew his negotiating position was weak.

'Hypothetically, if the information is helpful, we may find that the predictive pixelation gizmo doesn't actually predict anything. At all. There would be nothing to give our Swiss friends.' Calvert's carrot.

'Equally, if the information is not helpful, then the pixelation gizmo will probably produce some startling results.' Calvert's stick.

Ben's corner now felt even smaller than it had with Remy. 'All a bit too clever for me, Andrew, but I'm happy to tell you what I know, if that's of use to our government.'

'Tell me what you know, Ben, then we can let our government decide.'

Ben read danger into every one of Calvert's words and actions. He knew governments couldn't afford to be saints nor angels; they had a job to do, and it got dirty at times. But would they treat a person's freedom like a commodity, purely for information that could become public in a few months or weeks? *Unlikely,* Ben concluded, which meant saying as little as possible.

'Well, I really don't know very much. Claus was heavily concussed when I rescued him from the Sonne Berg.'

'How did you come to do that? To rescue him? Are you his bodyguard, or working for him or something?'

Ben's laugh was genuine. 'No, nothing like that. I'm just a management consultant. It was pure coincidence. I was staying at the same hotel as him, and in the chaos of trying to escape a burning hotel I found Claus unconscious in a corridor. I picked him up and carried him out with me. When I picked him up, he rambled some rubbish about people he was doing business with trying to kill him. Then he passed out, and that was that.'

From Calvert's non-plussed reaction, Ben sensed the fraction of truth he had woven into his story was maybe enough.

'And Claus said nothing more? Even heavily concussed, it's a weird statement to make without some connection to the truth, don't you think?'

'That's exactly what I thought.' Ben fluently agreed with Calvert's incorrect opinion. 'The next day he invited me to their chalet, saying he wanted to thank me for saving his life, but also to talk to me about the possibility of starting a new team at his bank. Obviously I went along.' Ben's faked elation was disarming.

'Surely, even if you were there to discuss this job offer, both of you would have talked about what happened at the Sonne Berg? You must have asked him about his concussed accusations in the Sonne Berg, of people trying to kill him?' Calvert was not as sure of himself now.

'For sure, it was the first thing I asked him. We talked a lot about the fire at the hotel, how terrifying it was, and how we managed to escape. Those are war stories you tell your grandchildren. But when the head of GMB Bank is thanking me for saving his life and offering me a seriously well-paid job, the last thing I'd do is to remind him he was a rambling idiot less than twenty-four hours before. Not a chance.' Ben laughed his way through the last few words.

'I see.' Although Calvert probably did not. 'And at the chalet, when you were under attack, Claus still said nothing? Even when he knew they would kill him?'

'In a firefight, all you're concentrating on is trying to stay alive. I was shepherding five mainly old and scared people out of a burning chalet and onto a chairlift. There was no time for any discussions on anything apart from surviving.'

'Claus never mentioned any names? Anything about the companies they ran, their nationalities, how they met, or why they wanted to kill him?'

Too specific, thought Ben, *I never said they ran any companies, nor that they were foreign nationals, nor that they had met.*

Calvert clearly wasn't asking questions to gain information. He already knew more than Ben and was asking questions to find out how much Ben knew.

'You're suggesting there's actually a group of foreigners, who are running companies, trying to kill him? That's a bit far-fetched, isn't it?' Ben made sure he did not overplay the role of surprised innocent, while Calvert's body-language shouted a realisation that he had overstepped the mark.

'Well. No. I mean, I don't know. I was just following on from what you had said, Ben. You're right, it's far too farfetched.'

Ben knew he now had to put the pressure back on Calvert. 'I hope that was helpful to you and HMG. I'm sorry I can't tell you any more than that, because that's all that Claus told me.'

Calvert's recent uncertainty turned malevolent. 'It's a start, Ben. But we need a lot more. I understand you are currently in favour with Ingrid. Given what she's doing for you, she must trust you. We would like you to use that trust to find out as much as you can about what Claus told Ingrid about this group of associates and report it back to me. Don't really much care how you do it, or what that costs you – that's up to you to come to terms with. But we want you to find out whether the Oppenheimers or their friends are intending to do anything ill-advised.' Again the trademark eyebrow. 'We will be in touch to see if you discover anything further. More tea?' concluded an emotionless Calvert.

Ben's expression revealed nothing, but he felt like a piece of meat. *Andrew Calvert thinks he now owns my soul because of this Predictive Pixel thing. Be careful what you wish for Mr Charges d'Affaires,* ran through Ben's mind.

'Well, as there's not much more to add, I suggest we get your mugshot done, run off your passport, and send you on your way, Mr. Mason. You've got all my contact details, so you've got no excuses for not staying in touch.' Calvert selected another transparent grin from his catalogue.

Chapter Seventeen

Calvert recognised the fake caller ID as he answered his mobile. No-one could trace it back to Thomas Liang.

'Mason's just left,' Calvert informed him.

'Yes. I know.'

Calvert couldn't believe they had surveillance inside a British Embassy. Could they? Calvert was unsure.

'Does Oppenheimer's family know enough to go to the authorities?'

'I'm not sure. Oppenheimer told Mason something that was important enough to convince him to discharge himself from hospital and jump on a helicopter to Verbier, so that has to be substantial. Even so, he has no proof and is saying he doesn't know if the family are planning anything. I'm sure he has been told more than he is admitting, but I have a couple of ways to change that.'

'Make sure you do. And what did he say when you asked him where he was going with the passport you so kindly bent Her Majesty's Passport Office rules to give him? Please tell me you asked him.'

A hesitant Calvert stuttered, 'I didn't ask him, but the passport offer was the only way I could get him to come here. To me. To find out what he knew.'

Liang hung up and the line went dead.

Calvert's knuckles bled, but he kept on punching the desk. At that moment, it was the only outlet for his frustration. He would go out later, when it was dark and quiet, to find another avenue. When Liang had cleaned up after that game-gone-wrong with the little Chinese whore, he'd shown his gratitude, he'd repaid the debt. But he hadn't realised Liang's idea of payback was that it was never paid back, that it was infinite.

He'd assumed his tip-off about Claus going to the chalet would have secured some credit with Liang. Then he'd gone the extra yard, coming up with the suggestion about the smaller chalet being empty at this time of year. Instead, though, it had given Liang more leverage over him.

If Mason delivered any proof, he wouldn't merely hand it over for free to Thomas Liang. No. Southeast Asia's fleshpots were calling him. From there, and without his position at the British Embassy, he could blackmail Liang and buy immunity for his perversions. And an endless supply of little Chinese whores.

Chapter Eighteen

As soon as the Mercedes dropped Ben in front of the tennis club, the helicopter's rotors started spinning slowly in anticipation. Even at that distance he could feel the power of the engines as the turbines started their ground-thumping build-up. It was midday on a Sunday and many of the tennis club's members had turned up to play for a few hours in the perfect late summer temperature. They stood silent and curious as Ben took the helicopter's short steps in two strides, seconds before the huge rotors defied gravity and tore six tonnes of helicopter vertically. In just a few seconds it was above the height of Bern's tallest buildings.

Ben looked down on the fast-diminishing forms of Kirkenfeld tennis club until they resembled small dots against the red-brown clay. The pilot banked steeply to the right, and even before they were level, had accelerated to skirt around the southern side of the Swiss capital's residential boundaries.

Relieved to have escaped Calvert's questioning, Ben weighed up the contrasting threats of Remy and Calvert. Both wanted to be the first and only game in town when it came to finding out more about the Five. Although it was unfair and borderline-legal, he knew Remy was just doing his job. Ben had been squeezed before by the Police; he knew that ultimately Remy wouldn't risk public scrutiny of his fabricated evidence at trial. It was unfair, but he understood it was just a very tough negotiating tactic.

Calvert, though, was a nasty bastard. He wouldn't hesitate to push Ben under the bus. He'd fabricate evidence, avoid getting his hands dirty by handing it over to the Swiss authorities, and take credit for doing so. It wasn't the normal behaviour of a British Embassy's Charges d'Affaires unless they had an ulterior motive. *I need to level the playing field with Calvert,* he concluded, and started to put together a plan in which Fabrice played a key role. Even if his new friend did not realise it yet.

The pilot interrupted his thoughts. 'Slightly longer on the way back, sir. Flight plan changed, so we can drop you at Schindellegi.'

'What's at Schindellegi? Why aren't we returning to Zurich?' Ben shouted above the noise.

'I'm informed that you have received a message on your phone, sir?' Without waiting for a reply, the pilot turned back to his controls, leaving Ben to read his text.

It was a text from Stephanie.

Hi Ben, hope U got new passport OK? Could you meet Mamma and I @ St. Johann kirch, Rapperswil-Jona. Pls? Car will drop you at station, take tram across Zurichsee. St. Johann is top of hill. will explain when U get here. C U then, S.

Ben replied that he would meet them, but what he could not see was Stephanie's next text conversation with Ingrid. '*Mamma, we have to tell Ben that none of this is an accident. We should tell him what Papa didn't. S xx.*'

Ingrid replied. '*I know, but not now, please. It's been less than 48 hours. I want to protect Ben; we don't know what he would do with information like that. It could be very dangerous for him. Let's wait, for now. XX.*'

*

Ben had always known what his objective was. But what he didn't know was what role the Oppenheimers would play in helping him achieve that. Stefanie's latest text, though, might be a start to answering that.

He immersed himself in providing answers to questions about the recent past, present, and future. He had his own plans for the remaining four of the Five. Meanwhile, how to stop Remy digging too deep into his background? What was the unstable Calvert's real motivation? What were the Oppenheimers planning? And how much of that could he safely feed to appease Remy and Calvert?

Half an hour passed very quickly until they touched down at their destination on one of the Hofmann Flying School's landing pads near Schindellegi. Unsurprisingly, there was a car waiting to take him the few kilometres to the Wollerau tram station on the south-west side of the Zurich See.

Trams in Switzerland hold the same position as a bike in France or a car in America. Each is a foundation-block of their society's structure and, being Swiss, their trams are efficient, clean, and run precisely to the timetable.

Ben bought his ticket and took a forward-facing window seat, trying unsuccessfully to admire the view as the tram crept over the road and tram causeway bridging the south-west of the huge lake with its south-east neighbour. Thirty kilometres an hour felt like walking pace after the three hundred-plus of his previous transport. He abandoned admiring the scenery and instead put the finishing touches to his plan while he called Fabrice.

'Hi Fabrice, it's Ben. I think you're right about Calvert. I also think he was involved in Claus' death.'

'Putain de bâtard.' Fabrice spat his opinion with uncharacteristic anger. 'From the first time I meet him, I knew he could not to be trusted. I wish I had been braver for Claus.'

'It's not too late. If you want to do something for Claus? Now's your chance, if you're up for it.'

'Oh yes, most definitely. I feel angry enough now to do anything.'

'Good. I'm working on a plan, and your part is to retrieve everything from the St. Gallen's CCTV system that has even a glimpse of Calvert on it. Can you do that without anyone knowing?'

'Yes, for sure. I have all the access permissions for our CCTV. I will do that straight away. What else is in our plan?'

'It may be best that you don't know, Fabrice. It's not entirely legal, and we are dealing with very dangerous people. I'll contact you in a few days' time, but in the meantime, don't mention this to anyone.'

'*Certainement,* Monsieur Masson.' Ben had an image of Fabrice all but saluting as he spoke.

Spotting the huge spire of St. Johann's church perched on the hill overlooking the southern tip of the Zurich See was simple. Climbing the steep hill up to it was less so, and Ben was reminded that his body had not fully recovered from the exertions of the previous few days.

106

Apart from the occasional wedding or funeral, he hadn't spent much time in church, but he recognised wealth when it so stridently announced its presence. St. Johann's was nothing like its bucolic British countryside equivalents. Vibrant painted frescos burst forth from the massive column-heads supporting the hand-carved wooden ceiling, providing a celestial canopy for the absent congregation. Padding for knees and seat on each individual position softened the ritualised penance of kneeling and sitting on hard wood. This was certainly not an impoverished religious sanctuary. Although lacking any explicit signs, the unseen hand of the Oppenheimer family was evident everywhere.

Ben strolled contemplatively down the broad nave towards the main altar, behind which the huge stained-glass triptych stole a broad spectrum of light from the bright day outside. The mellow hue of the stone mullions dividing the three pictures glowed a soft gold, bathing the altar in a pastoral warm gossamer. Enrapt with this peaceful ambience, Ben was oblivious to the stooped figure slowly shuffling up the nave, not fully registering the customary old-lady-in-a-church figure as she drew next to him and whispered, 'You should visit the presbytery, young man.'

Processing took a few seconds, due to its unexpectedness. He turned to engage with her, but she was already gone, shuffling back along the nave and out of the arched doorway. The handful of tourists and parishioners sharing the solitude of St. Johann's appeared not to have registered anything.

Ben made his way to the large oak doors off to the right, behind a side altar, and through which he knew would be the presbytery. Tentatively pushing open the heavy wood and iron portal, he stepped into the room normally reserved as the private domain of the clergy. There was no clergy, as he had expected, but he did not expect to be greeted by the group of people who turned towards him: Ingrid, Stephanie, Francois, Christophe, and two other people he had never met.

Ingrid's eyes were a poor hiding place for the weight she carried. Clasping Ben's hands in hers, she forced a thin smile.

'Oh Ben, I am so pleased you came. I knew you would. Claus said you would.' Ingrid closed her eyes and exhaled for some seconds.

Even through closed eyes, the pain was evident as she struggled to continue an obviously prepared script. The energy and passion Ben had noticed when they first met was still there, but now Ingrid was fighting a losing battle with every emotion.

'It may appear callous to be this pragmatic so soon after Claus,' her voice tailed off. 'But we all have our way of dealing with grief, so please allow me mine, and let me explain. Claus knew this day would come. We tried to enjoy our short time and to prepare ourselves, but it's never enough, is it?'

Ben was not sure he fully understood, nor was he confident of the best response, other than to keep it as brief as possible and to let Ingrid continue. 'No, Ingrid. It never is.'

'You see, Claus feared this could happen. We underestimated how far they would go, and we now know it was inevitable with their power. He knew there were risks standing up against them, but that doesn't make it right. Does it, Ben? But now, we know we must continue what he started, to find the proof we need. Will you help us, Ben, will you please? For Claus?'

Tears were now flowing freely down Ingrid's cheeks as her script descended into a sobbing plea, and the veins on her hands stood out as she gripped Ben's hand more tightly. The poise with which she had so elegantly held herself when they met in the hospital, started to sag as her voice faded. Ingrid's defences were crumbling under an avalanche of deep emotions.

Stephanie stepped forward and quickly wrapped a protective arm around her mother. 'What Mamma is saying, Ben, is that we will not let my father's murder be in vain. We now know about the Five, his stand against them, and why they murdered him. We are his family and his friends, and we will bring all of them to face justice. I would give my life to achieve that. You do not have the same motives as us, so you can walk away now if you want. But we hope, I hope, that you won't. Please will you help us, Ben?'

He had no intention of walking away.

'I am so sorry for what happened to Claus. He must leave a huge gap in your lives. and I wish I'd known him better. I have my own reasons, which are partly for Claus, but also because they're murderous greedy bastards who tried to kill me twice. Being blown up and shot at is a bit of an incentive, so I'm in.' *That would do for now,* Ben reasoned to himself.

Ingrid had not let go of his hand nor looked anywhere other than directly into his eyes. Now she lowered her forehead into his chest, emotion wracking her body. 'Thank you, Ben. My husband liked and trusted you. Had you known him, you would understand such sentiments were not given out easily by Claus Oppenheimer.'

Ingrid took a minute to compose herself then reverted to more of her natural character and took control of the room.

'How rude of me, Ben. I haven't introduced you to everyone. This is Hilda Kaerle. Hilda and her parents have been friends of ours for many years, and we've known her all her life. She is the most capable person you'll ever meet and could run an entire continent if she wanted to. Hildy will organise everything, from hotels to helicopters, as she has been doing already.'

Hilda Kaerle's intelligent and open brown eyes simultaneously welcomed and challenged. Soft freckles decorating the cheeks around her eyes added to her appeal and understated her age. She'd probably played the elder-sister role to Stephanie but could pass for the same age, effortlessly combining a ballet dancer's posture with athletic energy. *Not a person to be underestimated,* he concluded.

'Hi Ben, I hear everything went OK this morning and the St. Gallen is in order? Fabrice fusses a bit, but he said you seemed happy with it.' Hilda spoke with the faintest hint of American.

'Yes, like clockwork, thank you. I can't believe I went from the hotel, to Bern, to here, and picked up a passport on the way in under two hours. Opening the Embassy on a Sunday, bringing in staff to process a passport in record time, and all just for an unfortunate like me. Andrew Calvert must have been a great friend of Claus?'

He was shaking the tree, and now he watched to see what fell from it. Out of shot, a glance was exchanged between Stephanie and Ingrid. There was an imperceptible movement at the corners of Hilda's mouth – an ironic smile, perhaps, but no indication behind her eyes. And a stiffening in Francois.

Ben nodded; Fabrice's instincts had been accurate. He'd suspected there would be something, but at the moment he didn't know how the pieces fitted together.

'Thank you, but I can't claim credit for the passport. Somewhat out of the blue, Andrew Calvert contacted Ingrid and offered to take care of you personally.' *I bet he did,* thought Ben, as he reflected further on the blunt threat Calvert was using to coerce him.

Ingrid introduced the remaining member of the group. 'And this is Felix Hochstrasse. Felix is our family lawyer, as was his father before him. Felix makes sure I don't do anything silly.' Ingrid smiled while she affectionately patted Felix's arm.

He was somewhat shorter than Ben, maybe five foot ten, not made to look any taller by a polished dome of a scalp. A narrow face tapered from dark, suspicious eyebrows to an angular chin. Ben shook his hand and recorded that when Felix smiled, only his eyes joined in. His mouth tried to, but it came out as half smile-half snarl, and the closest natural material to Felix was probably teak.

Felix spoke with a heavy Swiss accent when he explained the obvious, 'My client, Frau Oppenheimer, has suggested I proffer my opinion as to a possible strategy. These are no-one else's thoughts but my own.'

Ben realised Felix was protecting Ingrid and the others under client/attorney privilege by speaking on their behalf.

'The objective is to obtain proof of the Five's activities, sufficient for the IMF and any interested nations' authorities to prosecute them. Claus provided me, under privilege, with certain information about the Five, of which now only four remain. We know they have scheduled a video call for five days' time, Friday afternoon European time. We believe this is their regular weekly call, and notwithstanding the events at the chalet,' Felix paused, lowering his head and his voice ever so slightly before continuing, 'that they will hold the call as planned. This will be conducted on-line from their respective locations, using their single-purpose tablets – these open a secure portal through which they can communicate with only the other members of the Five.

Uniquely designed with a processor and no hard drive, there's no record of anything. The video call is in a virtual room; if anything other than their custom-built tablets is detected, it immediately collapses the room. Bottom line: to obtain the proof, we need to hack an encrypted, virtual, and secure, live unrecorded video call without being detected, and to steal what may or may not be incriminating evidence.'

A dismal silence fell over the room. Felix didn't pull his punches. He had eloquently summarised the impossibility of the situation.

Ben broke the silence. 'Daunting, but it may not be impossible.'

Felix's sceptical expression led the general murmur of disbelief in the room.

Ignoring it, Ben continued, 'Who are the four players, and do we know where they'll be for the call?'

Felix raised an eyebrow while looking at Ben, then replied, 'Uwe Mueller, CEO of Euro Bank; he'll be in Monte Carlo for the Annual Grand Masters' Baccarat Tournament. Brad Towner, Executive Chairman of The Central Bank of the Americas and Canada; in his New York office. Bianca Sabitini, CEO of BBF Ltd, one of the world's largest fund managers; in her London office. And Thomas Liang, Chairman of ASEAN Ex-Im, the centuries-old and world's largest trading and commodities company; he will be in his apartment on Peak Heights in Hong Kong.' Felix folded his arms and leant back in his chair.

He had just listed four of the world's most recognisable leaders in global finance, so Claus had not overstated the danger to world stability that this represented. It would make the global financial crisis seem like a storm in a small teacup by comparison.

Ben made eye contact with everyone, except Felix. 'I know it's a cliché, but a chain really is only as strong as its weakest link. I'm sure you're right, their on-line VC will be secure, their comms are encrypted, but they still have to connect with each other and they'll do that over the internet via a WiFi connection. That is their weak link.'

Hesitant expressions looked back at Ben. It was Ingrid who quietened the shaking heads. 'Go on, Ben.'

'There are devices which can capture the radio waves sent from a device to a router. The data you transfer to a Wi-Fi router is simply radio waves. Once a radio wave is in the air, anyone who is on that frequency can capture it. That's how a million people can all listen to the same radio station at the same time. So, let's not try to hack the secure virtual rooms or customised tablets. Instead, just capture their radio waves transmitted from the tablet to the router.' Ben sat back and folded his arms.

'I'm presuming these devices would be very small, portable devices?' Felix threw out his next obstacle. Are you saying they're capable of capturing *all* the data sent to and from the router?'

'No. We only capture data sent from the tablet *to* the router. That is a fraction of the total data transmitted, and it's the only piece we're interested in.'

'But you would just capture encrypted dots and dashes. Meaningless unless viewed through one of their tablets.' Felix hadn't uncrossed his arms.

'Ingrid, do you have Claus' tablet?'

'Yes. I do.' Ingrid's quick and positive response surprised them. 'And I wrote down his passwords for him.' Her eyes closed again as painful memories suffixed her support of Ben's plan.

'But if they detect Claus' tablet has joined their virtual room, it will collapse.' It was hard to know whether Felix was overly cautious or objectionable.

'No, Felix. Our tablet doesn't *join* their call. No-one *joins* their call. We just capture their radio waves transmitted from their tablets to the router, using the devices I described. Then, after we've captured those encrypted dots and dashes, we pass them through Claus' tablet, which has the same encryption/decryption programme as theirs, to decode them. That converts it into something viewable and readable. When we've converted it, we send it to the IMF or do whatever we want with it.'

'Are you sure this is legal?' Felix's eyebrows narrowed, and he lowered his head to question Ben.

'I never said it was legal. You're the lawyer, you go worry about that. I know they exist, and they work.'

'I like practical solutions.' Stephanie's strong voice held the room. 'And Felix, I know you have our best interests in mind, but with my father lying in a Zurich morgue right now, I couldn't give a fuck about legality.' Her body language echoed her sincerity.

Before Felix could give any more legal advice, Ingrid contributed, 'Let's not get bogged down with legal detail. For now, we have the beginnings of a plan; a feasible plan. Do you know where we can get these devices from, Ben? And do they have a name?'

'They're called Passive Data Capture, PDCs for short. And yes, I know someone who can supply and sort out all the technical kit. For cash.' Ben took some small pleasure in seeing Felix wince when he mentioned cash.

The mood in the room changed noticeably as Ben went on to explain how, through his old friend Danny Mullen, he knew of such a device. As well as being one of Ben's oldest friends, Danny was an IT geek who split his time between flirting with women or flirting with the wrong side of the UK's data and privacy laws, snooping for a broad client base whose interests ranged from industrial espionage to gathering divorce evidence.

'But that means we would need to place one of these in the homes and offices of each of the remaining four by this Friday afternoon. They're spread around the world, so that's a lot of logistics.' Felix pursued his due diligence.

'It is, but a real room is a lot easier to break into than a virtual room, and they don't collapse when you enter them. All I'm saying is that at some point they will have to send data via the internet, and that's when we intercept it.' Ben continued to overcome each of Felix's objections.

'As regards logistics,' Hilda chimed, 'we have friends in all those places who would help us. But the question is, who will plant these devices?'

'I will.' The speed of Stephanie's reply surprised everyone other than Ben. 'I absolutely insist on being a part of bringing these bastards down. I don't have the experience Francois and Christophe have, but I do know my way around London, Monte Carlo, New York, and Hong Kong, so that makes me the ideal candidate.'

'You cannot go,' Francois and Ingrid shouted in unison.

'This is dangerous, high-level espionage being conducted in the very homes and offices of psychopaths,' Francois warned.' These men and woman are responsible for hundreds, thousands of deaths. For your father's death. You only know your way around these places because you've viewed them from inside a limousine, a five-star hotel, or restaurant. You don't know how to live below the radar in these places, to blend in, to see and not be seen, and how to defend yourself against a dozen different types of threat. They will try to kill you, and you might have to kill to defend yourself. Could you do that?' Francois was sternly emphatic.

Stephanie glowered at her godfather. She knew Francois was right, but that wasn't the point.

'I can.' Ben's stony-flat vocal intimated a deeper determination. 'Rightly or wrongly, I've been trained to do all of those. I've also worked in two of their offices, and in Hong Kong. I don't know Monte Carlo, but I want to get back at these bastards as much as anyone, so I'll go.' His body language as he sat back drew a line under any further discussion.

'I know Monte Carlo and stayed in the Hotel de Paris many times. We could go as a team.' Stephanie's eye contact with Ben pleaded loudly.

He saw that Stephanie was a force of nature when, for the next fifteen minutes, she successfully defended herself against Francois, Ingrid, and Hilda. Even though they were just trying to protect her, she won by never taking a backward step and launching a constant barrage of logical arguments to defeat their emotional ones. Reluctantly, Ingrid and Francois agreed she should go with Ben. When that was agreed, they sat down and made their plan.

Chapter Nineteen

Ben connected with the unmistakable aroma of quality leather. A leather goods shop or a shoemaker's smells of leather, but not the smile-forming, caramel and soft-spice comfort blanket that wrapped itself around him as he sank into his armchair on the Embraer Phenom jet. That was the subliminal message the private jet delivered. Every surface gleamed, while polished walnut competed for depth with the luxurious carpet running the length of the six-person cabin. The deep pile underfoot tapered into seamless joins with the leather wallpaper encasing the entire inside of the fuselage.

Ben reclined his seat as the footrest sympathetically elevated to support his crossed ankles. 'Definitely the speediest boarding I've ever had,' he commented.

'You're better off never getting used to what money can do. Most wealth corrupts; a fair-weather friend who only loves you when you're winning. People who don't have money look at people who do and dream of a life without drudgery or work, but they don't see how it corrupts the person. You can't enjoy wealth and privilege unless you accept the responsibility and danger they bring.' Stephanie's voice trailed off as she stared out of the window.

Ben said nothing, deciding to leave her with her thoughts for now. There would be time enough for those conversations later. He didn't know her yet and he didn't want to rock the boat for no good reason.

The female co-pilot's gentle enquiry over the inter-cabin PA interrupted his thoughts. 'If you're strapped in and ready to go, we can take off whenever you want.' She had turned round to face back down the aisle towards Ben and Stephanie.

Ben had never been asked by a pilot for his permission to take-off. It was a first, and while he savoured the informality of the experience, Stephanie cut in, 'We're good to go, thank you. What's our ETA into Biggin Hill?'

'Eleven ten local time, ma'am. Weather's fine and we've missed the rush hour, so shouldn't be any problems with our routing. When we clear Zurich control and reach our cruising altitude, we'll be back to commence the in-flight service. You can get this morning's news and entertainment on your screens. Just tap that recessed silver button by your elbow.'

Oppenheimer-Class travel could lull you into relaxing too much, and Ben was keen to get on and plan the days ahead.

'I texted Danny Mullen to say we'd be with him by half twelve. Told him about your father. He'd read about the Sonne Berg and the chalet, but it didn't make the front pages over there. I went light on detail other than to say it was very important to you and me. He won't need or want to know any more than that.'

'Nothing will stop me from bringing down these bastards. You know that, don't you? I'm not just avenging my father, I'm going to destroy them, their corporations, anyone who had anything to do with them. I'm bringing the whole shit-pile down.' Stephanie's eyes burned like a fanatic. The warmth had gone, and an uncharacteristic edge had entered her speech.

'I understand, and I feel the same way,' Ben replied. 'But let's face facts, you're a complete novice in this espionage game. I'm no secret agent, and we're crazy if we think we'll become experts overnight, so I'm keeping my feet firmly on the ground. I don't even know for certain how we'll get the PDCs planted, then pray we can capture something and get it to the right people in the IMF. Let's be realistic and get comfortable with that. Trying to bury some of the biggest financial corporations on the planet is maybe a step too far.'

Stephanie made a dismissive sound in her throat but didn't respond. She didn't need to. Her expression said it all.

*

The countryside flashed past under the Embraer's tinted windows as they made their approach into Biggin Hill. Early summer's lush green fields had transitioned into a burnished cream and straw quilt after Kent's farmers had gathered their harvests. Dotted from above with deep green pockets of the ancient forests that covered much of this part of southern England.

If Ben liked the Embraer's speedy boarding, he loved the speed of disembarking even more, walking a hundred yards from the private jet to the waiting car. It was a far cry from the misery inflicted upon the millions of passengers on scheduled flights trudging through the world's major airports.

Ben preferred to drive, and they would need a car, so Hilda had arranged one exactly as he had requested. He had replied tongue-in-cheek to Hilda's question of which car he wanted 'an unbadged RS4 please'. And here it was, less than 24 hours later. Four hundred and fifty horse-power, V Six twin-turbo, all-wheel Quattro drive, and unless you were a petrol-head, you would never guess what lurked beneath the bodywork until you started it. When the hedgerows of Kent opened into the arterial roads of south London, he found himself agreeing with Ingrid's description of Hilda's ability to run an entire continent.

*

The meeting in St. Johann's church had achieved many things. It had aligned the group with a common and obvious purpose – to destroy the remaining members of the Five – but also the beginnings of a plan as to how they would achieve that. Each person had contributed something of themselves to their plan. Francois and Christophe, decades of covert military experience and contacts in the shadows; Ingrid, knowledge of the Five and powerful contacts; Hilda, just kept on delivering; Hochstrasse, an ability to bend legal-light. *What a testament to Claus*, reflected Ben, plus Ingrid throwing considerable Oppenheimer wealth behind the whole operation.

They decided London would be their proving ground and where they would bring Danny Mullen into the plan. Ben had worked in the same building in Canary Wharf as BBF. This was where Bianca Sabitini, its CEO, would join the Five's conference call, and where they hoped to plant the first of the four PDCs.

*

'Danny's arrived.' advised Ben.

'Where?' questioned Stephanie, after some seconds had passed without anyone coming into the Kings Arms.

'The unnecessarily loud exhaust you heard a minute ago. Well, that'll be Danny. He'll be parking his car in the most ostentatious place possible. A lover of fast cars and even faster women, although the cars always last longer than the women, so don't be taken in by his boyish charms.'

'You look like shit, mate. Nothing new there then.' Danny Mullen loudly laughed his way through the greeting and embrace with a natural, open smile. A wiry frame, one inch shorter than Ben, and offering a permanently grinning, angular face set beneath a pair of enquiring blue eyes that never stopped searching. Danny's energy was obvious from his body language; never still for a second. His medium-length fair hair exaggerated his perpetually moving head and was rounded off with the broadest Cockney accent Stephanie had ever heard.

'And I hear you're still driving big cars to make up for physical shortcomings in other areas,' laughed Ben in reply. 'I'm guessing that noise a few minutes ago was you and a new toy? What've you got now?'

'A Quattroporte.'

'A what?' Ben replied, while Stephanie gave him a questioning look.

'It's Italian for Fucking Noisy Maserati.'

'Gotcha, now let me introduce Stephanie.'

'Oh shit, sorry about the language, darlin'. I got a bit carried away with myself there. Haven't seen this tosser in ages. How you doin?' That was the closest Danny Mullen would get to apologising for swearing as he offered his hand to Stephanie.

'I'm doing OK, thanks, Danny. Tell me, have you got the V6 or the V8?'

Danny's startled look spoke louder than he did. 'The V8. If it's a Quattroporte, then there is only one engine.'

'The V8 is awesome, but don't you find there's a touch of turbo-lag up to about three thousand? After that it's a monster.'

Danny's facial expression spoke for him. 'Blimey, Ben, you've got a live one here.' Danny Mullen's normal measuring process was visual assessment, followed by how willing they were to have sex with him. Seldom did a female go immediately into the star chamber, and never on automotive knowledge. Stephanie had broken the mould.

Ben noticed how easily Stephanie identified and dealt with Danny's tactile manner without offending him. Ben's phone pinged to announce a message arriving. He left them to chat while he read and answered Fabrice's message.

I've retrieved all the CCTV recordings of Calvert with Claus. Also, Calvert with a lady and gentlemen, associates of Claus. Fabrice.

Ben replied.

That's great, Fabrice, thnx. Pls forward vids to me. Thnx. Ben.

'Dan, thanks for coming over. Since we spoke, our timeframe's become much tighter. First, though, can you explain to us how these PDCs work? Then Stephanie and I have got to place one of these in four different locations: London, Monte Carlo, New York, and Hong Kong. We've got five days to do that so they can record a video conference call this coming Friday night.'

Danny threw back his head and laughed, every facial feature stretched naturally to fit a broad smile. 'Nothing's ever straightforward with you, is it?' He shook his head. 'You'll be collecting a lot of air-miles mate.'

A still grinning Danny took from his pocket what looked like a white plastic matchbox. 'OK, now pay attention, children, and if anyone asks you where you got it from, you didn't get it from me. Right?' When he was being serious, Danny suffixed most sentences in that way.

The smiling Danny was replaced by a serious and focussed Danny, as he ran them through the PDC's basic operations.

'Pull out this little plastic tab to connect the battery to power it up. Then it just sits and collects radio waves. Simple as that. It can store up to one gig of compressed data, so that's a few hours on a video conference call depending on definition quality. More than enough. It's white because most people don't notice white stuff.'

'How long will the battery last?' Stephanie was quick to pick up a potential problem.

'Up to ten days, and that's normally enough to do its job.' Danny's expression saved further explanation as Ben and Stephanie nodded. 'These are single use devices, right? Turn it on, put it near a router, and it'll pick up RF waves going to the router. You ain't gotta do nothing. When's it's happy and working, it'll ping me to confirm that it's receiving data. These little batteries are fickle, mate. Some last for weeks, some don't.' Danny gave a small shrug. 'But if the battery's low it'll ping me, then you have twenty-four hours before it goes to sleep. It doesn't have much of a range, so ideally it needs to be within a metre of the router. I've put double-sided tape on the back, so it's quick and easy to pop it somewhere it shouldn't be without too much attention.'

'How do we retrieve the data?' Ben enquired.

'It's not powerful enough to send anything, so you have to retrieve it yourselves using Bluetooth, or you can go back into the room and just pick it up. But I'm guessing that may be too risky, right?' Danny's enquiring look drew no response from either of them. 'You download data from it using your phone's Bluetooth, but to be certain it's got enough battery left, you should do this within, say, five days of starting it. And you know you gotta be close to retrieve using Bluetooth, right?' They both nodded. 'Then we take the data captured by the four PDCs, editing everything together in a timeline, just like cutting and splicing four videos, and there's your blockbuster movie. Takes time and you need the right kit, but I've got all that.'

'The retrieval range is very tight,' Ben informed him. 'But let's take this one step at a time: get them in place first, then worry about retrieving later. Now, Dan, including all the editing and delivering to us a complete film of the video conference, how much? And I'm talking Mates' Rates here; we're not a multinational corporation.'

'Seeing as you're one of my best mates, even though I hardly ever see you these days, and,' he turned towards Stephanie, 'because you understand why Italian cars must be noisy, the four PDCs and all the editing would normally run to £10k, right? But to you, five in cash.'

'How much?' exclaimed a surprised Ben before Stephanie interrupted.

'Five is fine, Danny. How do you want that? Shall we say half now and half when you hand over the film?'

'No thanks, Steph. I'll take it all up front if you don't mind. It's not about trust. It's about you two being around to pay me after your Mission Impossibly the maddest thing I've ever heard of. Just in case, right?' An apologetic smile suffixed Danny's difficult statement.

Stephanie nodded in agreement. 'That's fine, Danny. You'll need our mobile numbers to message us when you receive those pings to say they've got data and battery.'

'Sure, no worries.'

'Dan, we need you to throw in something else. We – most likely me – need to get into One Canada Square, the 44th floor to be precise, and I need to do so either tonight or tomorrow at the latest. Sorry it's a squeeze, but we're not setting the timetable on any of this. Do you know anyone who can help? For cash obviously.'

'You don't want much, do you? Tell you what. You order me the lasagne and a spritzer, and I'll make a phone call. I'll be back in a jiffy.' And with that Danny was up, had dialled a number, and was talking into his mobile before he'd reached the pub's door.

'I like him. How long have you known each other?'

'Since we were two years old. Our families were neighbours, and we went to every school together, apart from when Danny was expelled for stealing a teacher's car and driving it in a banger race at Romford Stadium. You should have seen this old Austin Allegro. It limped out of the stadium with both axels and chassis so bent, it looked like something a clown would drive in a circus ring. All it needed was square wheels and a flower that squirted water, possibly the funniest thing I've ever seen. Poor old Danny was expelled and spent three months in a Young Offender's Institution for it. But he says it was worth it for the memories it created.'

Stephanie smiled with him. 'We can trust him?'

'With your life, my life, and everyone's life. He won't let us down and is as resourceful on the wrong side of the law as Hilda is on the right side.'

Danny arrived the same time as the food. 'Sorted. Do you remember a big, nasty bloke called Andy Taylor? He tried to beat me to a pulp because I went out with his sister?'

'No,' Ben shook his head. 'He wanted to beat you to a pulp because you were engaged to his sister, and he saw Lucy Shelby coming out of your place early one morning with a big smile on her face.'

'Whatever. Anyway, Fat Andy – as he's still known – is now a really good mate of mine as it goes, and he runs most of London Office Cleaning Limited. They, as luck would have it, have a contract for some of One Canada Square. Just checked with him, and his patch includes BBF on all seven of their floors. He's risking his job, and he knows that as it's you it's gotta be something big, so he wants a monkey. I said sweet, right? If we can sort that, he'll get you on tonight's shift.' Danny eagerly tucked into his lasagne.

'He wants a monkey?' asked a bewildered Stephanie.

'It's slang for five hundred quid. He wants five hundred pounds to get Ben into BBF tonight as part of their Albanian night crew. Brush up on your Albanian, son, it's gonna be a long night.' Danny took a mouthful of his spritzer, nearly choking with laughter.

Chapter Twenty

Fat Andy had worked hard to earn his moniker and must have weighed around twenty-five stone, nudging one hundred and sixty kilos. A huge, bulbous head was set directly onto his shoulders without a neck, and eyes set deep into the folds of flesh above his cheeks. His huge arms hung on equally huge shoulders, out at his sides, and he had to rock his weight from side to side to start walking. *What the hell happened to you?* wondered Ben.

'Andy, you haven't changed a bit.' Ben smiled as he clasped his old friend's hand.

'Fuck off, you flash git.' Andy Taylor pseudo-snarled in response as he shook Ben's hand. 'Never did like you.' He continued the pretence. 'And that ain't gonna change now. You got my monkey?'

'Yeah, here you go.' Ben slipped it into Andy's huge paw.

'You're working with a bloke called Zamir. He's got a team of eight. He grunts, farts, and smokes in Albanian. His crew is starting on the forty-third and then the forty-fourth. This never happened, right? And don't fuckup, or I'll sit on you and that little wanker Mullen till you turn blue.' Ben thought Andy winked at him, but he couldn't be sure as his eyelids were set an inch behind his cheeks. And Andy Taylor was not known for his outwardly smiling nature.

Ben found Zamir cleaning the toilets on the forty-third floor. Zamir had the darkest eyes he'd ever seen, matching the darkest stubble he had ever seen, and his bare, powerful forearms the unsurprisingly darkest hairs he'd ever seen. Zamir showed him what to do and left him to it.

He quickly discovered the whole crew had nationality in common, plus probably false work permits. They mainly only spoke – or in Zamir's case grunted – in Albanian as they worked their way around BBF's enormous trading room. He noticed the Albanian women were delegated the job of emptying bins, dusting, and wiping down desk and cabinet tops with sprays and cloths, whereas the men operated the floor-buffers or the industrial vacuum cleaners in between standing around having animated discussions.

Ben was teamed up with a guy called Tomaz, who spoke reasonable English. Tomaz talked about his magnificent and large herd of goats back in Albania; Ben also lied, saying he was an actor between acting roles.

They made their way to the forty-fourth floor which housed BBF's Executive offices. Andy Taylor must have spoken to Zamir to organise the rota so that Tomaz and Ben were given the C Suite offices to clean. They made their way through the various offices, wiping, dusting, emptying, and vacuuming.

When they reached Bianca Sabitini's office, everything took on a different meaning for Ben. This woman would have been part of a discussion that cold-bloodedly decided to murder Claus and anyone unlucky enough to be near him, which included Ben, in the same way she would about the bank altering its interest rates. Probably with a skinny latte in one hand while looking at the Asian market's opening prices. All to protect herself and further her ability to accumulate wealth when she already had more than she could ever spend.

Ben wanted her to be here now. He wanted to shake her violently by the shoulders, make her confront her greed, and admit what she had done. He would never hit a woman, but he knew he could make an exception in her case.

Tomaz's voice broke through his reverie. 'Hey, dream man, you gonna work or what?'

'Sorry, Tomaz, I always have a sugar-low at some point when working nights. I tell you what, you fancy a coffee? There's a 24/7 cafe in the first basement. I'll pay if you go get them?' It was not the normal offering of an office cleaner, and one which Tomaz was quick to accept as Ben handed over a handful of pound coins.

'Double espresso for me, please, and whatever you want for yourself. And grab a couple of chocolate bars, yeah?'

Ben wanted Tomaz gone for as long as possible so he could find the Wi-Fi router and position the PDC. The trouble with modern, high spec offices is that all the non-aesthetics are kept out of sight, hidden under floors, behind walls, or within the suspended ceiling recess. Ben searched frantically for several minutes but he still hadn't located the router when Tomaz proudly paraded back into the room carrying two coffees and two chocolate bars.

'Oh great, Tomaz, *falemenderit*.' Ben had picked up a little Albanian in the last few hours.

'Ska perse,' replied Tomaz, as they sat on the edge of Bianca Sabitini's desk. He took out his phone. 'I studied IT after goat-herding. Goats don't pay as well as IT, so I went to college in Tirana. When I worked in these offices before, I hacked their Wi-Fi so I could download music without paying the data charge. You won't tell Zamir, will you?'

Ben couldn't believe his luck. *A bloody Albanian goat herder is showing me how to hack into the Wi-Fi of the world's largest fund manager. Hilarious.*

'No, of course I won't tell Zamir a thing, if you share their password with me.'

'OK.' Tomaz sent him the link. 'They have very good IT here, it's 5G; all these companies have it. The best signal I get is over here, near the window.' Tomaz walked towards the floor-to-ceiling glass wall that provided a grandstand panorama over Canary Wharf.

Ben looked down to see the oxbow of the River Thames curving around the Isle of Dogs, with the illuminated Greenwich Observatory a couple of miles away. He waited until Tomaz was preoccupied with his phone before he slipped the PDC from his pocket and removed the small plastic strip to engage the battery. Using the double-sided tape, he stuck it to next to where Bianca Sabitini would be reading financial market data in a few hours' time. The white, matt finish of the PDC blended in perfectly with the same white plastic of her console. Even a close inspection wouldn't show it as out of place.

A few seconds later, Ben's phone chimed with an incoming message from Danny. The PDC he'd just fixed to her monitor had pinged him to say that it was happily capturing data.

Ben felt lifted by his first step towards retribution for Claus and for the two attempts on his own life. *The fightback has begun, Mrs. Sabitini, and we're coming for you.*

As Ben and Tomaz worked their way through their shift on the forty-fourth floor, they had ringside seats to dawn's prelude. The undersides of the high cirrus clouds captured and reflected deep crimson rays from the unseen sun, waiting beyond the earth's horizon. The pavements, still wet from overnight rain, reflected the pre-dawn sky in puddles of blue, crimson, and mauve – a meteorological red carpet for the coming day.

As loud Albanian was the only language being spoken in the lift as they descended, Ben took the time to reply to Danny's message.

'Thnx. One down n three to go. Let me know if you get battery warning etc. Random question. If I gave you a CCTV video of people talking, can you copy someone's voice, change the words, and make it sound like them saying something else? Thnx. Ben

*

Ben was keen to tell Stephanie about the night's events. Exiting One Cabot Square – the iconic, pyramid-topped monolith of London's decentralised financial hub – he ran the half mile to their pre-agreed meeting place.

'If you're hungry, I know a great place for an early breakfast.' He sank into the enveloping seats of the sporty Audi, where Stephanie sat behind the wheel drumming agitated fingers.

'Breakfast second, update first. How did it go? Danny texted to say it's working, but how did you hide it?' Stephanie jabbered in excitement.

'Whoa, slow down.' Ben waved his hands in a downward motion. 'You drive, we'll get some breakfast, and I'll tell you all about it. You do know how to drive a manual, don't you?' He sensed their relationship was forming and wanted to carefully move it along. Banter among competitive souls would oil those wheels.

Turning towards Ben, her eyes challenged him over the top of her sunglasses as she took the car's four hundred and fifty impatient horses to fever pitch. 'Let's see if I can drive, shall we?' All four tyres screamed under protest as, at nearly maximum revs, she expertly slipped the clutch to maintain engine speed and the burnt-rubber smoke now billowing from each wheel.

Catapulted back against his seat, Ben caught a glimpse of the twenty-five-tonne waste disposal truck as it hurtled towards them. The huge truck was only metres from crushing them against the granite walls of the neighbouring building. A few metres from the dark and murky waters of the Blackwall Basin dock, into which they undoubtedly would then have been dumped, Stephanie's electric movement, and the freak split-second timing, meant the truck only managed to clip the car's rear. But the combination of being clipped by twenty-five-tonnes travelling fast, plus the car's own forward momentum, sent their car into a spin with all four tyres pluming clouds of rubber smoke. Without panicking or slowing, Stephanie smoothly corrected with deft hand and footwork. Tyres still smoking, they straightened and screamed up the still deserted street.

'What the fuck!' they exclaimed in unison, as the car slid to an inelegant halt, lying diagonally across the street. They rocked back into their seats then looked at each other, speechless and dazed as the smoke took time to clear in the still air.

Ben looked back at the destroyed waste truck embedded into the stone wall. Its shattered front windscreen hung over the now smouldering engine compartment, with its crippled wheels buckled underneath where it had mounted the tall kerbstones at high speed. The driver could not be seen behind the exploded airbag, but his blood could. Slashes of red recorded where the side impact, from the last-minute swerve, had smashed his skull against the cab interior or building wall. It mattered little which immovable object the soft bone of his skull had met. The result would have been the same.

Their minds were working overtime to comprehend the near-fatal destruction, when a Black Range Rover roared out of the destroyed vehicle's smoke, like a charging lion. Its front grille snarled and raised as it accelerated hard and up the street towards them.

'Go, go, go!' shouted Ben, as Stephanie floored the Audi, red-lining through the gears for optimal acceleration.

'Who the fuck are they?' screamed an understandably anxious Stephanie.

'I'm betting it'll have something to do with the Five, and they mean business.'

Stephanie launched the Audi into a perfectly held four-wheel drift through a tight right-hand bend at nearly fifty miles an hour. Beautifully balancing power with drift, so they were still at maximum torque as they exited the turn, the front wheels fought hard for grip against the sheer power being applied. This was no adrenalin-fuelled piece of beginner's luck. *This is class,* thought Ben, as he gripped the left-hand door handle

In a clinical and swift ballet of coordination, Stephanie pulled hard on the handbrake, locking up the rear wheels, then steered into the next turn, downed the handbrake, changed down, and floored the throttle as she engaged the punished clutch again. Transmitting balanced power, they hurtled out of yet another fast corner.

The Range Rover was fast but not as nimble as the powerful Audi. It had dropped back as it emerged from the last corner, when a burst of automatic gunfire shattered the Audi's back window, showering them with pebbles of toughened glass.

'You have to trust me and do exactly as I say,' Ben bellowed above the sound of the screaming engine and gunfire, while Stephanie competently threaded their way round another tight corner.

'Go right, then three hundred metres up it looks like a dead end, but isn't. At the end there's a left, then a very, very sharp, narrow turning on your right. It goes into a pedestrian precinct and then across a walkway over the dock. Hopefully we're narrow enough to get between the bollards, but that insane Range Rover won't.'

Stephanie was wide-eyed in concentration as the Audi climbed to eighty miles an hour in a street two foot wider than the car. They flashed past the Victorian brickwork rear walls of old warehouses, now converted into millionaires' flats and apartments.

If anyone steps out of these doorways to see what the commotion is, they'll be dead, thought Ben, as Stephanie changed up and the needle touched one hundred mph.

The Range Rover struggled through the tighter bends and dropped further back, but the long straight allowed a clear line of sight for the passenger with the automatic weapon. The urgent staccato clack, clack, clack reverberated in the narrow street, the medium calibre automatic rounds smashing into the walls next to the frantic Audi. Masonry and brick rained down as the dust mingled with the smell of overheated oil and straining machinery, as Stephanie squeezed out every ounce of power from the game engine.

Rounds tore into the car's rear panels; one punched a spider's web pattern onto the front windscreen, just as the left-hand corner neared. Stephanie was going too fast for the corner. Locking up all four wheels in a cloud of smoke, she dramatically over-corrected for the immediate and sharp right-hander Ben had warned of, but the second corner was now too tight to take at this speed. The car slammed hard into the left-hand wall, covering them in broken glass and chunks of the building's stone cladding.

'Shit!' shouted Ben, above the noise of unstoppable-metal meeting immovable granite of the precinct walkway.

'Sorry,' exclaimed a shaken Stephanie. They came to an immediate and painful halt, recoiling against the seatbelts. A cloud of masonry dust threaded its way through steam and smoke seeping from a football-sized crease in the car's bonnet.

'We're good. Let's go, let's go,' Ben encouraged, as he turned towards Stephanie. She had frozen. Eyes and mouth wide open, teeth clenched, her fists white from her grip on the steering wheel.

'Steph, you're doing great, you've got this. Come on, let's go.' Ben gently shook her nearest hand. 'Come on, let's go.'

Stephanie snapped back into action, grunting with determination as she re-engaged first gear. And in an instant they were hurtling down the empty retail precinct. Ambivalent pigeons scattered amid flurries of feathers as one or two had not noticed the unusual danger in time.

'There's the walkway over the dock.' Ben pointed, as they sped over the smooth tiles in front of still empty coffee-shops and restaurants. Thankfully, the tight turns and Stephanie's driving skills had taken them out of sight and gunfire range of the Range

Rover as they charged towards the humped pedestrian bridge spanning a seventy-metre stretch of the old commodities' dock. At its mid-point, two bollards had been strategically placed to deter anything with more than two wheels. Ben's hope had been misplaced; they were too wide for the gap. Only by an inch or so, but still too wide.

'You just gotta floor it, Steph.' Ben pushed deeper into his seat, bracing his feet against the floor.

Stephanie accelerated flat-out into the gap. The Audi checked on first contact as the car's wings shrieked in protest and absorbed the initial impact. The car's abused door trims and mirrors shattered into many pieces, as the car jumped and their momentum carried them through... just.

Ben and Stephanie sprang back in their seats as they accelerated out of the gap, almost as much as they had slammed forward upon first impact with the bollards.

'Left along the dock, there, then right after that building.' Ben pointed their way out to the main road and free from their pursuers. The Range Rover had halted on the precinct a few hundred yards back, at the beginning of the pedestrian bridge. The driver had realised it was far too wide to navigate the same gap, even if the gap had now been widened by the physics of Stephanie's driving.

Three men jumped out of the Range Rover, trying to obscure the weapons they were carrying, and stared in their direction. One of the men walked in front of the others. Although more than one hundred yards away, Ben saw him limp heavily as he walked around the car to stare after the fast-departing Audi.

Chapter Twenty-One

'We've got to get rid of this, it's too conspicuous.' Ben was referring to their car, of which every piece of metal, plastic or glass was damaged beyond repair. 'There's an empty office block due for demolition about half a mile away. We'll dump it there, walk, and then grab a cab. We've got to get away from here, as it'll be crawling with Old Bill any minute.'

Ben paused when he realised Stephanie wasn't listening. She'd pulled the car over, bumped the kerb, and now sat stationary, lank hair hanging over her face, sweat sticking it to her skin. Tension was evident in her hands and neck, knuckles white on the steering wheel.

Metal grated against metal as Ben pushed with his feet to get his door open and came round to repeat the process with the driver's door. Steam hissed from something broken under the bonnet, the smell of heat carrying the smell of burning everything as the engine's metal components groaned and tinkled as they licked their wounds.

Ben spoke softly as he reached across and carefully unclipped Stephanie's seatbelt. 'It's OK, Steph, you beat them, they're gone now. Come on, you need to get out. I'll drive.'

Helping her climb out of the ruined vehicle, she vomited loudly as soon as she stood up.

'It's shock, Steph, everyone goes through it, but it'll pass. You did brilliantly. You saved us, really you did.'

'Fuck.' She managed a groggy, one word reply as she wiped her mouth with the back of her hand.

Ben settled her into the passenger seat and drove slowly to the derelict building site where they abandoned the wrecked Audi. They walked a few blocks before hailing a black cab, directing it to Smithfield Market – London's famous old meat market. The market's vibrant, early opening cafes were quite accustomed to the workers co-breakfasting with dishevelled all-night revellers. But the pair presented a curious sight: dusty fragments of masonry and glass in their hair and on their clothing, set against smoke-tinged complexions, as they did their best to ignore the curious looks from the porters. *Amongst this audience it should be easy to detect the arrival of Range Rovers and international hitmen*, thought Ben.

'Were you that scared, the first time someone tried to kill you?' Several cups of strong tea with a full English breakfast had revived them both, as Stephanie relaxed and questioned Ben across their breakfast table.

'I'm petrified every time someone tries to kill me, but you get better at handling it. You develop a sixth sense. You panic less, you think more clearly, and are able to act better, so it's more likely you'll kill them than the other way around.' Given what they'd been through, Ben knew Stephanie wouldn't want the sugar-coated answer.

Through clear eyes, Stephanie nodded. 'I wasn't freaked out at the time. It's after. That's when it's most real. When it's most frightening.'

'That's right, but it'll pass. Talking about it, like now, helps you to heal.'

'Thanks for helping me. I froze a couple of times, didn't I?'

'You did, once. But as I said, it's the same for everyone, and you picked yourself up immediately, and you saved us with your driving. Where did you learn that?'

Stephanie blushed. 'I didn't spend all my time being a good little girl in the Swiss finishing school that you envisage. In fact, I spent very little time there at all, and I was probably more badly behaved at school than you were.' Her voice was regaining its self-assurance.

'Well, whoever was the bigger baddie at school, it was time well spent, because your driving certainly saved us this morning.'

Stephanie raised her cup of tea to acknowledge the compliment. 'Moving on, how the hell did they find us? Our passports weren't checked when we got on or off the plane and Hilda said we didn't appear on the passenger manifest, so how did they know we'd be here?' Stephanie's voice was hushed as he leaned over their breakfast table.

'The only people who knew were the Zurich crowd, plus Danny and Andy.' Ben let the words hang in the air as they studied each other.

She fixed him with a steady expression. 'I've known the Zurich crowd, as you call them, since before I was born; one of them is my mother for Christ's sake. I would stake my life that neither Hilda, Francois, Christophe, nor Felix would have been careless enough to let a single word slip to anyone.' Stephanie pushed her empty plate away and pulled the café's metal and plastic chair forward. Her direct intonation challenged Ben to defend his friends.

'There's absolutely no way Danny or Andy would let slip anything. Not a bloody chance. You'd have to kill them before they'd say anything. And even then, they wouldn't say anything.' Ben paused for a beat. 'OK, look. The simplest answer is that no-one told anyone anything nor let anything slip. The remaining four of the Five worked it out for themselves; it's not rocket science. If I were them, I would expect some form of retaliation, and there's only four places to do that. London's the nearest.

'So, what will they do now? Do you think they know our plan?'

'I don't know, but we must assume they've worked out that we will try to get at them. I doubt they've guessed our plan is to place PDCs in each office to eavesdrop on them, but Andy Taylor will be able to tell us.'

'Why him?' enquired Stephanie.

'If they know I was in Bianca Sabitini's office with last night's cleaning crew, they could only have found out from Andy. So, if he's in a hospital or a morgue, then they know our plan. If he isn't, then they don't. I'll get Danny to call him just in case they have his mobile and can trace the incoming calls.'

'OK. I'll brief Mamma, she can tell Hilda and the others. To really get ahead of them we should go straight to Biggin Hill airport now and have the plane take us directly to Monte Carlo for PDC number two. I brought the passports and PDCs with me.' Stephanie produced their passports and patted her gilet pocket containing the precious IT gadgets. 'Clothes and money we take care of when we get to Monte Carlo.'

Ben hailed one of London's abundant black cabs, who was delighted for an early morning fare all the way to Biggin Hill. On the way, he called Danny.

'Dan, it's Ben.'

'Thank Christ for that,' exclaimed a relieved Danny. 'You won't believe the media feeds coming through. Headlining on mainstream as well. MPs posting about it, breakfast TV interrupted schedules to show it. I just knew it was you even before I recognised your car, but the media and the Old Bill are all over it, mate. Can't move round here for Anti-Terror, Drug Squad, TV crews, and police cars chasing all over the bloody place. It's mad, right?

'The buildings you went racing past, their CCTV feeds have been leaked online. The Old Bill aren't happy, saying it's evidence and all that, but what can you do? It's like a flippin' Bond movie. Camera feeds show those geezers in the Range Rover shooting at you. You've got some serious gangsters after you, you know that, right? You OK?'

'Yeah, yeah, we're fine. Steph's a bit shaken up but she's good.'

'Steph was with you?'

'Steph was driving, and I tell you she can drive.' Ben exhaled in admiration.

'She was driving? That's mad, like. I just assumed it was you. That's hard-core, mate. Old Bill thinks it's drugs. Rival gangs, county lines being crossed on and all that. They say they can't find either of the cars or the waste truck that crashed into a building – the driver's missing from that, but he left half his brains behind, so he probably doesn't really care where he is.'

'Yeah, it was full-on. Thanks for the text that the PDC's working. I need you to do something for me. I need you to get hold of Fat Andy and—'

Danny interrupted him. 'I've just spoken with him. He called me, he saw it on a feed and wanted to know if that was you in the Audi. He said he'd always known you were mad and not to ask him for any more favours. Secretly I think he thought it was cool though. Where are you now?'

'The less you know, the better.'

'Sweet. Before you go, your question about voice dubbing. Yeah, I can do that. There's some kit I use. It's from the film industry, if you can believe it, and it's called Implied Voice Synthesisation. A word to the wise, though, it's inadmissible as evidence, and you are playing with fire, right? The victim knows he's been completely stitched, and victims usually have a good idea who stitched them. So be very careful, my son.'

'I will, Dan, don't worry. But the stakes are getting higher all the time, and we have to have our own plan of attack.'

*

'Looks like they have no idea about the PDCs or that I was in Sabitini's office,' Ben informed Stephanie after the co-pilot had returned to the small jet's flight deck to prepare for take off from Biggin Hill. 'Thankfully Andy isn't in a morgue or a hospital. When Danny called him, he was his usual rude self.'

'Which means they don't know our plans, but we know they will be expecting us to get at Sabitini, hence the Range Rover gang waiting for us.'

'Yes, which means we should expect them to be waiting for us at all the other places.' Ben looked for nervousness but saw none.

'I'm glad your friend was OK. Mamma is not so happy. She thinks we're in too deep and insisted that Francois accompany us in Monte Carlo to be our guardian angel if you like. I think it's rather sweet that my godfather cares that much for me. It's also quite useful he's ex-special forces,' Stephanie pondered ironically.

*

Ringed by the foothills of the Alps on three sides, the sprawling city of Nice tumbles into the Mediterranean over bleached rocks. A sandspit, squeezed out by humanity to the city's southwest, hosts the Cote d'Azur's airport, penetrating the Mediterranean if not sitting within it. Most flights approach from the sea, providing those in a window seat with the most stunning scenery any final approach could wish for. A gentle onshore breeze whips up parallel lines of soapy foam atop turquoise waves that race towards the rocky shore. The approach is low enough to watch people lounging on boats, windsurfing, or just being on the water.

The Embraer glided gracefully onto the baking runway and taxied to the VIP and private plane arrivals area, tucked away from prying paparazzi eyes behind two aircraft hangars. Francois had enlisted the assistance of an ex-comrade at the National Gendarmerie to ensure French immigration officials were conveniently absent, as was the passenger manifest. Ben and Stephanie were led from their plane directly to a private waiting room containing a stern-faced Francois and a smiling Hilda, who spontaneously hugged Stephanie.

'Your mother and I are very worried, Stephanie—' But before Francois could continue, Stephanie showed she was better prepared.

'Tell me something I don't know, Oncle.' Her voice was dominant, using the familiar term of endearment she had grown up using for her godfather. 'I can't say I enjoyed being in a life-or-death car chase with my father's murderers shooting at us. You of all people knew it would be like this. You've seen enough armed action to know exactly what we were letting ourselves in for, so please don't lecture me. We knew this would be the reality when we agreed to avenge my father.' She delivered her gentle tirade without drawing breath or blinking.

'Maybe, but she's your mother, and that doesn't stop her from being upset.'

'Mamma is upset because the Five killed the rock of her life, my father. That's the cause of her unhappiness, and that's what we're doing something about. So, if you've come here as Mamma's messenger to try to dissuade me, you can't. You can help me and my father's memory by helping keep us safe and guiding us how to stay hidden.'

Poor old Francois, observed Ben. *Started badly and got worse. Never stood a chance with Stephanie on a mission.*

'*Bonjour, mesdames et messieurs,* we are ready to depart,' interrupted the designer sun-glassed, male model posing as their pilot. Behind the darkened lenses, he paid most attention to

Stephanie. He was all crisp-white, short sleeved shirt with a little too much gold trim on his epaulettes for Ben's liking.

The helicopter ride from Nice Airport to Monte Carlo on a sunny late September afternoon is a wonder of the modern world. Riding low and fast over the rugged coastline's breath-taking scenery, the azure coast's waves crash spectacularly onto irregular rock formations framing the white sandy coves dotted along the coastline. Each cove the premises of a single, white-sailed yacht, moored there, it appeared, purely for the purposes of their visual pleasure.

The sensational marine tapestry competed for optical favour with intimate views of some of Europe's most exclusive villas, protected all around by the naturally jagged terrain, plus obligatory security precautions. The view of these properties from only a hundred metres provided a personal peepshow into the lives of the rich and famous, even if played on fast-forward as the helicopter sped past at one hundred kilometres an hour.

The helicopter's downwash broiled the sea as they crept ever closer to the yellow painted 'H' on the quayside helipad. Less than five minutes later they sat comfortably in the customary black Mercedes, cruising effortlessly upwards through the snaking succession of hairpins to Saint Michel, with Monte Carlo laid out below them. Air conditioning and double glazing isolated them from the blazing afternoon sun bleaching the mountain.

'We're effectively untraceable here,' announced Hilda, after the chauffeur had deposited their few bags into the cool of the entrance hallway and departed.

They stood in the spacious atrium of an old French Colonial villa. Its thick stone floors, dark wooden stairs and doors were fringed on its external walls by covered verandas, promoting a gentle breeze throughout, countering the solar gain. Lustrous deep purple bougainvillea vines tumbled haphazardly down the pillars and balustrades, providing extra defence against the sun and enhancing the evening air with a hint of their aroma. Built into the steep hillside overlooking Monte Carlo more than a hundred years ago, its elevated vista over the Principality was dominated by the shimmering blue canvas behind.

'Only Ingrid and Felix know we are even in the country, and this apartment is owned by a nameplate on the wall of a solicitor's office in Panama. Nothing is traceable to anyone, especially not to the Oppenheimers.' She let the others take it in before proceeding. 'Stephanie and Ben, your rooms are upstairs at the front, and you'll find a selection of clothes and accessories in them.'

'You both look like you could do with a shower and freshening up. Shall we say half an hour, and then we'll have a videocall with Ingrid and Felix,' added Francois.

Ben turned the tap to its maximum, encouraging the freezing cold needles to stab him hard as they bounced from his neck and shoulders. He hung his head, holding onto the shower head in one hand, letting the sensation massage life back into mind and soul. The game had only just begun, and he knew some pieces were out of position; trouble was, he didn't know which ones.

With fresh clothes and mind, Ben stepped out onto the shaded terrace. The eaves' spines stretched out their limbs above him, like a Ferris wheel on its side, absorbing the heat and shading them. The tranquillity of Monte Carlo's early evening drew a deep honeyed pastel from the stone buildings below. It was a serene and calm image, coupled with the opulence of their fourth-floor eyrie from which he surveyed the scene. All in stark contrast to why he was there and at odds with their adrenalin-fuelled, murderously narrow escape that morning.

The shutters of the room next to him squealed from unaccustomed use as Stephanie emerged onto the terrace to join him. She smiled when she saw Ben. Her grace as she walked directly towards him only added more weight to the paradox of their situation. He leaned with his forearms on the balustrade.

'Feeling better?'

'Yes. But only after I'd sat and shivered in the shower for ten minutes.' She laughed nervously. 'I've never been as scared as I was this morning.'

'There are few things scarier than someone trying to kill you. But it's our advantage now, as they've lost the element of surprise. And they don't know where we are.'

'Let's hope so. I'm not sure we'll be as lucky next time.' A nervous laugh made her shiver in the warm afternoon sun as, unconsciously, she hugged herself. 'We can't back out now, can we?' She turned towards Ben for the answer.

'No.' He sensed Stephanie needed truth, no matter how brutal. 'They'll be after us until we end it.'

'Yeah, I know that now.' Stephanie also leant against the balustrade. 'Well, we'd better see this through then.'

'Yes. We had.' Ben offered a reassuring smile as they made their way into the villa and the video conference.

*

Felix's polished dome reflected his energy, bobbing from side to side on the plasma-screen. The video call was in progress as they entered the lounge. 'Thankfully you appear to be physically unharmed after this morning's excitement, but how do you feel?'

'It all happened so fast that I didn't have time to be scared. It's frightening if I think about it, so I'm trying not to. We were round the next corner, into the next street, or jumping on the plane, before we really had time think about anything. Now, I just want to get on and finish what we started.' Ben knew why Stephanie was projecting a brave image.

'Hilda showed me the CCTV images from the net. It's a hundred times more frightening than a disaster movie because it was you they were shooting at.' Ingrid paused to catch her breath. 'We've discussed that already so let's move on. It's been a long day for both of you, and I'm sorry, but it is about to get even longer. Felix will explain.' Ingrid slumped back into her chair as he spoke.

'Uwe Mueller checked into his suite at the Hotel de Paris this afternoon. He comes here every year to play in the Grand Masters' Baccarat Tournament at the Casino.' Again, Felix did the talking, as he had done in St. Johann's church. 'The tournament starts with tomorrow evening's reception and runs through to Friday lunchtime. We know Mueller is due to check out on Saturday, so he'll be in his suite for Friday afternoon's videocall with the others at 15:00 Monte Carlo time. Unfortunately, time is even tighter than we thought if we want to get all the PDCs in place for that call. I'll let Hilda explain.'

'Ben, you worked all through last night and have had quite a busy day so far, but you must plant the Uwe Mueller PDC tonight. Then early tomorrow morning you fly to New York for their midday and plant the New York PDC tomorrow night, Tuesday. Then you need to catch a plane to Hong Kong a few hours later.'

Hopeful eyes turned to Stephanie and Ben as Hilda continued. 'The only way the connections work is to fly around the world to the west. Your two am Wednesday morning direct flight from JFK crosses the International Date Line and lands in Hong Kong at seven am on Thursday morning. You then have one shot to plant the final PDC in Liang's apartment, on Thursday night, the night before the call. I'm sorry it's so tight, but we don't have any options if we are to have all four PDCs in place for Friday evening. They've got to be planted at opposite ends of the earth, in just a few days, and the planet is a big place. It's that simple.'

Ben interrupted the silence. 'OK, that's tight, but the longer we take, the more chance they have of finding us, so we'd better just get on with it. The tight timeframe makes some logistics decisions for us. The key lesson I learned when getting the PDC in place last night is that we need to know exactly where each router is before we go into that room. The pinch-point is how little time we have in each of these rooms. So, provided we can find out where those routers are before we go in, the timing shouldn't be a problem.' Ben was aware of his breathing.

'I will ask Christophe to help there.' The video conference software projected the serene features of Ingrid onto the screen. 'Hotel de Paris has just famously completed a three-year refurbishment. They would have had to submit to at least the DDE, the *Department Directorates pour Équipment*, and make their plans publicly available. I will ask Christophe to check but they should be available online.'

'If Christophe can find out before I go in, it's the difference between spending one or twenty minutes in there. And that's an eternity,' a thankful Ben encouraged.

'I'll get on it right away. And I'll start making enquiries with our New York and Hong Kong friends about what information they can find out about the places there,' she added. 'But in the meantime, what do you need for this evening?'

'I need a floor plan and Mueller's room number; I need a laptop with fast internet access; I need to know when Mueller leaves his suite this evening; and I need some food. And with Stephanie's help, we'll shortly have a small shopping list of the kit we'll need.'

'Food has been delivered, so I'll go get that ready now. This screen,' said Hilda, pointing to the one projecting Felix, 'is wired straight into a fibre optic feed, so it's very quick. Anything else?'

'Yes,' interrupted the gentle image of Ingrid. 'I want none of you to take any unnecessary risks.'

'OK, Mamma, will do. I promise.' Stephanie seldom lied to her mother, but...

Chapter Twenty-Two

As if to scratch his leg, Francois bent down to adjust the fastening around his calf. It secured ten inches of serrated commando knife in a small sheath against his leg. The hooks and loops of the Velcro needed to exactly overlap, which they now did. While he was there, he tapped the steel blade – it was an old habit; the weight against his leg told him it was still in place. A Ruger57 pistol in an under-arm holster completed his arsenal for the night. He brushed his upper arm against the holster as he replaced the small coffee cup back onto its saucer on the marble top of the Café de Paris' circular table, opposite Uwe Mueller's hotel. A burner mobile protruded from the folds of yesterday's *Le Monde* next to his cup and saucer, just enough for him to see if someone should send him a message.

He sipped his coffee, his eyes never leaving the hotel's entrance.

It never ceases to amaze me, thought Francois, *why tourists are so stupid. They spend so much time and money idolising people who don't give a shit about them.* He made this observation over his second espresso of the evening, studying the small flock of human sheep grazing on celebrity sightings in front of the triangle formed by the Hotel de Paris, the Café de Paris, and Monte Carlo's famous Casino, grouped together at the Casino end of a paved precinct in the middle of this vibrant human anomaly.

He knew very well what drew tourists to Monte Carlo; it was the same thing that drew the inhabitants. It was the inhabitants themselves, and their curious social mores. They came to see the human freak show; obscene, not always legal, tax-lite wealth paraded as ostentatiously as possible. Rich and old in symbiosis with young and beautiful, a trading arrangement between compliant parties and as old as the species itself. Each was obsessed with having what the other had. Be that wealth or power from one, and youth, physical perfection, or surgical enhancements from the other. One of the most anthropologically fascinating places on earth, Francois despised it.

He acknowledged that tonight, though, the irritating tourists did serve one especially useful purpose. Their clamour rendered him invisible, a temporary conscript into the people-watching tourist tribe, which suited him fine. Using a practised eye for the best field of vision, he had deliberately chosen this table, one row back from the small, paved area and the entrance of the Hotel de Paris beyond, waiting for Mueller to appear. These celebrity-and-wealth-obsessed fools wouldn't realise that one of the richest men on the planet, a famously unknown murdering sociopath, would shortly walk through the middle of them without anyone noticing. *Morons,* he grumbled to himself.

*

Ben ran the woven black polypropylene rope through his hands; it weighed almost nothing. He coiled it round his bunched fists and jerked it tight with a satisfying snap as the doubled ropes slapped against each other, its flexibility and strength evident. He spun the knurled screw gates on the carabiners next, they locked tightly, then he continued to check the package's contents against his order: eighty metres of Pro-Lite climbing rope, carabiners, a sling harness, head torch, belay device, jewellers' gloves, and a pair of black lace-up climbing shoes.

'You'll never get past the foyer without a reservation in the Grill Room. They're accustomed to credible-looking tourists trying to blag their way into that culinary inner sanctum. They will stop you, very politely check your reservation, and kick you out when it's discovered that you don't have one. Anyway, your credibility will already be questionable – don't forget you'll be wearing slippers. That'll be noticed.' Stephanie knew she was being unreasonable.

'They're black lace-up climbing shoes, no-one will notice. People don't look at other people's feet,' Ben reasoned, without success.

'I can assure you, the people in the Hotel de Paris notice everything and they most certainly do look at peoples' feet.

The only way you'll get into the Grill Room escalator without a reservation is for us to walk in there like we go there every night. I will create a distraction at precisely the right moment, allowing you to slip away unnoticed.'

'Are you sure you'll be able to distract them?'

'I'm sure.' Stephanie's body language concurred.

*

Uwe Mueller's suite enjoyed a prominent position on the Mediterranean side of the hotel and was only one floor below the exclusive Grill Room on the top floor. From the internet and Stephanie's accurate recall, they had devised a method for Ben to get onto the Grill Room balcony, to abseil from there to Mueller's suite, and then his exit, abseiling forty metres in the dark without disturbing the other guests on the lower floors. Getting onto the top floor balcony, though, involved Ben climbing out of the toilet window, crossing the roof, and dropping down out of site, onto the restaurant's balcony. In the meantime, they needed a dress-rehearsal.

'Now let's see what your disguise looks like.'

Stephanie and Hilda struggled to contain their amusement when Ben stood up and held his jacket out from his sides. The only way to hide eighty metres of nylon half-rope on his body was to wind it around his torso, until all eighty metres was wrapped around him, then putting on his over-sized shirt and jacket. This created a look-alike Michelin Man, which prompted the obvious joke that it was, after all, a Michelin-starred restaurant.

'Oh Ben, you look great. It's almost worth being shot at to see this. Well, maybe not, but you do look funny. *Merci*.'

Ben's mobile, announcing a text from Francois, interrupted the merriment. '*Uwe Mueller just left hotel, entering casino. Am following n will txt when he looks like he's coming back.*'

They had sixty minutes.

The mood changed immediately, and within minutes Ben and Stephanie were on the way to the Hotel de Paris and round two of PDC planting.

'Hilda, could you chase Christophe for the exact location of that router, please? It's really important.'

'OK, will do. Good luck.' Hilda closed the villa's heavy front doors after them.

An explosion of multi-coloured lilies, a metre tall, chased long-necked birds of paradise away from a flower arrangement cascading with every colour, texture, and shape Mother Nature ever conceived. The Hotel de Paris' foyer was spacious, even for a five-star hotel, but the arrangement dominated the space, flowing over the edges of its supporting table, of which only the sturdy legs were visible beneath its floral skirt. It looked to Ben like a firework display in freeze-frame as they entered the foyer, the century-old revolving doors clapping softly as they walked through.

Ben entered the foyer in the shadow of Stephanie's visual fanfare and maintained the same relativity across the polished white marble expanse. He was struggling to remain unobtrusive with an eighty-metre coiled torso inside an oversized dinner jacket.

Stephanie glanced behind her, winked, and immediately found something extra. Long legs strode longer, stiletto heels clicking with a flamenco dancer's retort on the tiled floor as she tossed her hair and seduced every man with smouldering eye contact. Taking an arrow-straight line across the middle of the foyer to the restaurant's exclusive lift, every eye followed her. Nearing the concierge's desk, her clutch bag spilled from her grasp – their pre-arranged signal. Ten paces behind, Ben dialled Stephanie's phone from the one held in his pocket, just as the enraptured concierge staff fought with each other for the favour of retrieving her bag's spilled contents.

'In whose name is the reservation please, madam?'

Stephanie held up a slender but polite hand while she raised her phone, pretentiously shrieking into her mobile. 'Caroline, darling! All OK for this evening? I've just arrived at the Grill Room. What?' – pause – 'NO!' – pause – 'Albert's not with me. I thought he was coming with Stephanie and Charlene.'

Monte Carlo is the people-watching capital of the world, and now the entire Principality was watching. Even without the attention which she had already attracted, her phone call let it slip that she was having dinner with the reigning prince of Monaco, his wife, and his two sisters, the Princesses Stephanie and Caroline.

'What do you mean "our plans have changed"? Oh really,' volume and octave level raised as she continued, 'I thought we'd agreed on the Grill Room.' – pause – 'OK, I'll jump in a taxi now and see you there. *Ciao, ciao, bella.*' And with a few air-kisses, Stephanie smiled, confident that every eye was still trained on her while Ben had slipped inside the Grill Room elevator and was on his way to the top floor.

With a touch more sashaying than she had used on the way in, Stephanie now carried every eye with her on her way back out and into one of the taxis permanently queuing in front of the hotel. Before the driver had even pulled away, Ben was secured inside the seventh-floor toilet cubicle, next to the only window of the Grill Room's *Hommes* facilities.

*

Ben soon discovered the difficulties of unwinding eighty metres of rope in a toilet cubicle. In between other patrons' visits, he made repeated and deliberate loops, with the nylon going behind his crooked elbow to the gap between thumb and forefinger, while keeping them up in the air to ensure nothing spilt out under the door to be seen by other users of the facilities. Leaving the door unlocked, but closed, he hung the three looped coils outside the window, climbed onto the small windowsill, and squeezed himself through the narrow opening. It was a tight fit, and he was breathing hard before he was standing on the outside windowsill with his forearms above his head, resting on the edge of the huge domed roof.

As quietly as he could manage, he lifted the coiled loops onto the roof, pulled himself up, and made his way around the lower edge, noiselessly sliding the toes of one soft, black climbing shoe after the other as he shuffled around the edge. He stopped every few metres and reached back for the three coiled loops, carefully lifting each one and, reaching forward, silently placing them a few metres forward. The roof's domed shape meant the slightest noise on the outside would echo loudly inside.

Heat pulsed from the thick lead covering, and it was getting hotter the further he shuffled to the south-facing side, releasing the sun's latent energy back into the warm night and scorching his palms. Ben inched his way around the narrow perimeter, balancing on his toes and leaning forward on palms and fingertips. His legs trembled with the exertion as he again reached back for the coils, lifting the first and second, placing them forward, and reaching back for the third.

Ben sensed the movement before it happened, instinctively pressing his upper body flat, his cheek hard into the hot lead roof as it started to move, rotating on its central axis, taking him with it. The Grill Room's huge domed roof was made of two giant half-domes, split down the middle, with powerful motors which allowed it to be opened to the stars when the weather and a majority of diners agreed. Ben was stuck like a fly in a spider's web as the half-dome rotated and the crevasse opened.

Aromas, light and noise spilled upwards, carried on a rising tide of diners' excitement, just as Ben noticed the last of the rope coils moving away from him on the other half-dome. Quickly pushing himself up onto his toes, legs straightened, he shot out his arm. His index finger made the smallest of contacts with one of the coil's loops, hooking it and hoisting it skyward as it slid down his finger. His palm eagerly collected more of the coil and snatched it into his shoulder as he lay breathing heavily, waiting for an observant diner's exclamation. None came. He lay, clutching his precious coils, as the roof slowly rotated him towards his goal.

Ben sat, like a gargoyle on a cathedral spire, squatting on his haunches on the roof's extreme edge, allowing his aching legs and breathing to recover as he absorbed the Monte Carlo night. A warm coastal breeze carried up to him the chatter of people dining and the sharp timpani of cutlery on crockery. A shrill whistle forty metres below cut through the night as one of the concierge staff called another taxi onto the rank. It was Monte Carlo's busiest time of the day for people movement; everyone had somewhere to be.

The vainglorious growl and bark of high-performance car engines bounced off the stone buildings until they escaped into the inky sky, engines made to satisfy ego more than for mechanical necessity. It was a nightly catwalk of automotive wealth; who had the most to spend on a car whose potential performance none of them would unlock for more than a few hundred metres?

Chapter Twenty-Three

Ben went over the plan he and Stephanie had devised at the villa. Jump softly onto the balcony two metres below, not far from several dozen people having dinner, hope no-one saw him hiding in the shadows, hope he could remember how to secure the rope with a Quick-Release Hitch, pray there was something strong enough he could secure it to, abseil down one floor without disturbing anyone, hope they'd got the right balcony, pick the lock or force entry – if not, smash a window and make it look like a burglary – find the router, hide PDC nearby, get out without leaving any DNA, abseil forty metres down in the dark, avoiding any guard dogs, un-hitch rope, ditch the gear, and head back to the villa without being spotted… hopefully. Ben draped the coils over his shoulder and squatted onto his haunches. He needed to check to see if Christophe had discovered the PDF's location on the refurbishment plans.

*

The scarred visage of the shorter of the Casino's two uniformed security guards grimaced more than smiled. 'Monsieur.' He held out a thick arm, pointing Francois towards the rear of the Casino. *'S'il vous plaît.'*

'Me? Why?' Francois did his best to feign the innocent tourist.

'We need to ask you a few questions. Please don't make us force you,' the scarred visage replied, while the other taller and equally gnarled uniform had a hold on Francois' upper arm that he knew would end badly if he tried to resist.

'Pas de problème.' With fake compliance, Francois walked with his two companions through the Casino's thronging crowds, all too absorbed in the excitement of losing their money in a dozen different ways to notice his abduction. Francois tried to work out why him? Did the Five have facial recognition kit in the Casino? How did they know they were in Monte Carlo anyway?

Francois decided that for the time being, politeness was the optimal strategy. He was more perturbed at losing sight of Uwe Mueller, who was losing money so fast he'd be leaving the Casino sooner than expected. Being taken into a small, windowless room, adjacent to one projecting dozens of CCTV images of the casino tables, also perturbed him.

'What seems to be the problem, *mon ami?*' enquired Francois. He knew it would soon be too late to warn Ben if Uwe Mueller were to return to his suite.

'I'm not your *"ami"*. I want to know what you're doing in this Casino. We've been watching you on CCTV and you haven't played a single table, not even a slot machine. You haven't accepted a drink offered to you, either. We know because we sent some of our most persuasive waitresses to offer you several.' Shorter gnarled features leaned, self-satisfied, back into his chair, his hands behind his head.

'I don't gamble, but I like watching others lose.'

Both security guards laughed. 'He bet,' shorter nodded towards his colleague, 'that you'd say that. All the flaky pervs do. But we think you're here to tail this man.' The security guard tapped a CCTV screen and brought up a monochrome image of Uwe Mueller seated at the high stakes roulette table.

Francois ran through his options: killing them both now would take only a few seconds, but how long before their bodies were found? A minute? Two or three at the most, then what? CCTV would show him coming in here with them and leaving alone, his face all over Monte Carlo's security networks, and possibly derailing the mission. No, he would have to take the harder route. Be nice to people you don't want to be nice to. It didn't mean he had to tell the truth, though.

Just when Francois thought he had a plan, the video feed showed Uwe Mueller throw his last chip to the croupier and leave his seat. He had lost and was leaving the Casino. Francois took several breaths.

'I'm impressed with your security. I am even more impressed with how well you guys picked me out. I really am. I'm in that game, so I can recognise a professional outfit when I see one.' Francois knew Mueller leaving meant he had to gamble.

'We're all in the same game, so you'll understand I can't break client confidentialities, but you're right, I am following that guy. Can't tell you who he is, but I can tell you he has put his wife into hospital half a dozen times. Last time it was for two weeks, after he poured boiling water over her legs. Time before that she had to have her spleen removed because of the beating he gave her. The wife's shit scared of him, backs down from pressing charges whenever it goes to court.'

'I say the bitch deserved it.' The taller, gnarled uniform-wearer finally spoke, his shorter colleague nodding in stoney-faced agreement.

'He's beat up his kids, too,' Francois continued. 'The eldest, a daughter, had to have plastic surgery on her face. She's engaged me to follow him because he's having two affairs that she knows of. Wants me to get evidence, and the family have agreed that if I do, they will all go together to court and nail the bastard.'

'Yeah, so what? How do we know you're not bullshitting?' The shorter, gnarled uniform picked up his colleague's theme.

Francois dropped his shoulders in fake submission. When he sat upright again, his left hand held the murderously serrated commando knife. He stared at the CCTV monitor showing Uwe Mueller's empty seat. It burned like a branding iron into his conscience as he ran through his limited options and prepared himself.

As if to signify really getting down to business, the uniformed guards took off their jackets and rolled up their sleeves then sat down at the table, revealing as they did instantly recognisable emblems tattooed on their muscular forearms. The inscription *'Honneur et Fidélité'* was inked in deep blue under the famous flamed insignia of the French Foreign Legion.

Francois tucked the knife back under his thigh and rolled up his shirt sleeves. He had the same tattoo, but his contained the subtle addition of five vertical lines, signifying the rank of Major in the French Foreign Legion. There were a couple of ways to reach the rank of Major, but all required fourteen years' very hard graft in one of the world's legendarily toughest regiments.

Had a bomb gone off in the room, the impact would not have been greater.

Immediately both security guards sprang to their feet and saluted the still seated Francois. 'Major, we had no idea. Profound apologies. I don't know what to say,' the shorter uniform burbled.

'*Pas de problème,*' Francois took a perverted delight in repeating, '*mon ami*' after a pause. 'You were only doing your jobs. And doing them very well.' The two uniforms' expressions were like schoolchildren being praised by an indulgent teacher.

'It really is not a problem, but it is urgent that I resume my surveillance of that guy,' Francois stated, pointing at the screen showing Mueller's vacant chair and disguising his anxiety.

'Do you want us to apprehend him?' enquired the two uniforms.

'No, don't do anything. It would ruin all my work,' Francois quickly responded. 'But I really must go now. *Merci, mes amis.*' After returning their salutes, he shook their hands, rolled up his jacket, now containing his knife, and hastily left.

Chapter Twenty-Four

Ben's legs started to feel numb from squatting on his haunches. He stood and flexed them, stretching them in readiness for Christoph's text and the Go. He had worked out his route to Mueller's suite and checked his messages, hoping for one from Hilda or Christophe while he waited. Instead, there was one from Remy.

'Coroner has extracted bullets from Verbier bodies. Running a match with your gun. Thought you'd be interested? Anything new on the Five/Four? All the best, Remy'

'You bastard!' Ben said out loud to no-one. *He's planted those there, and now he's trying to fit me up for a crime he knows I didn't commit.* Ben remembered his agreement to deliver anything he discovered about the Five to Remy before anyone else.

The next text was from Andrew Calvert.

'Ben, an update on the pixelation process. Nothing definitive yet, but boffins working hard on it. Look forward to learning of your progress. All the best. A

'And you're a total bastard,' he said out loud, again to no-one.

Struggling to devise a plan which avoided both possible custodial sentences, he looked to the next message. Still nothing from Christophe or Hilda, this one was from Fabrice. Attached were two videos from the St. Gallen Hotel's CCTV drives. He played the first one: Calvert and Claus sitting at a table on the hotel's terrace. The unmistakable sonorously over-stressed vowels of Andrew Calvert booming forth from beneath his ever-present Panama hat, broadcast upon the Monte Carlo evening.

'Whether you're right or wrong, you've got no proof, and without proof you'll look like a stupid old fool.'

Claus could be clearly seen and heard. *'I know enough, Calvert. I know what the Five are doing is illegal and a massive abuse of power. For pity's sake, it's damaging millions of people's lives.'*

'Little people's lives, Claus. They're just little people. Only misguided do-gooders give a shit about little people. Politicians pretend to, in order to get votes; rich people pretend to, in order to appear woke. But at the end of the day, no-one really gives a damn. It's a dog-eat-dog world and Thomas Liang is the biggest and nastiest dog in this small world. If you don't stop, God only knows what he'll do to Ingrid and the oh-so-fragrant Stephanie.'

At that point, Claus exploded in fury, reaching hopelessly for Calvert across the small table. Calvert provoked it and was expecting it, leant back casually, out of range, as crockery and glasses were sent flying. Ben saw Fabrice rush in. The video ended after a few more acrimonious seconds, leaving Ben staring at the frozen last frame: Claus snarling angrily at a grinning Calvert.

He then played Fabrice's second video, taken a few months before the first. Calvert again, on the same terrace, but this time everyone was happy including a man and a woman – the instantly recognisable Bianca Sabitini, CEO of BBF Ltd, and Brad Towner, CEO Central Bank of the Americas and Canada. They must have held a meeting of the Five in Zurich before Claus threatened to expose them. It was a convivial scene, early evening cocktails on the hotel's terrace, with much chatting and polite conversation. There was no arguing in this video, and again Calvert's voluble tones were the most distinct.

Ben forwarded both attachments to Danny with a request. *'That voice dubbing thing, can you make the loud English bloke say the following...?'* Ben remembered Danny's words of caution, but now they were in too deep.

His second message was to Francois to check Mueller was still in the Casino, as he was about to go into his room to start his search for the router. He was slightly surprised when, after a few minutes, the only reply he had received was from Hilda to say Christophe was still trying to find the architect's drawings. Silence from Francois.

Having worked through the previous night, followed by today's energy-hungry activities, Ben's mind began to wander. He decided he had no option but to get on with it, as he peered over the edge of the Grill Room roof. Had he looked down at that point, he might have changed his mind, as he would have seen Uwe Mueller emerge from the Casino and make his bad-tempered way across the road towards his hotel.

*

Ben squatted on the edge of his perch to reduce his overall height, the front half of his soft climbing shoes hung over the edge as he gradually fell forward, dropping the two metres and landing softly on the terrace below. Flexed ankles, knees and hips absorbed the impact as he melded into the shadows and held his breath. He waited for the shout, someone to gasp in horror, but no one noticed anything. The balmy evening meant the restaurant's floor-to-ceiling, wall-to-wall sliding glass doors were slid half-open allowing the elevated noise levels of late dinner conversation to wash over him as he crouched in the shadows. He knew anyone looking hard enough would see him, but no-one looks out into the darkness at half past ten at night when they're having dinner in The Grill Room.

The veranda was fringed by a stone balustrade just over a metre high, low enough for seated diners to see over but high enough to stop drunk diners falling over it. He lay down on the artificial grass surface carpeting the veranda and tied a quick-release knot in one end of the rope. These knots were used in mountaineering when you want to release the rope tied at the top, after you had descended it.

Using one of the balustrade's posts as an anchor, he secured the hitch first time. Tugging hard on one of the standing ends to the rope, it held firm. Continuing to hold it in his hand, he quietly straddled the balustrade and lowered the ropes down beyond the suite, one floor below. Legs braced against the balustrade base, he nimbly pushed himself away into the dark night and swung his arm out to free the rope. He controlled his descent to land gently on Uwe Meuller's balustrade and stood stationary, only the sound of the blood drumming in his ears as his senses took a moment to readjusted themselves when he heard the most welcome noise of all.

Silence.

No alarm from the diners above and no-one rushing out from their rooms below. He stepped down soundlessly onto the balcony and crouched, removing the rope from its belay and moved towards the dimmed lights, diffused through the mesh under-curtains. It was the master bedroom, and even through the hazy material he could see that turn-down had been performed on Uwe Mueller's suite.

He froze.

His phone pinged loudly, signalling an incoming text and instantly reminding him he had not set his phone to silent. Quickly pulling his phone from his pocket he read Hilda's welcome message. *Lounge, wall nearest sea, small, recessed cabinet, push to open. H.* Relieved that Christophe had found the router's exact position, he set his phone to silent and replaced it in his pocket.

Had that taken one second longer, he would have seen an incoming text from Francois. *Exit IMMEDIATELY. Mueller returning to hotel.*

But his phone was now on silent and in his pocket.

He moved cautiously along the balcony to the left, away from the master bedroom and towards the sliding glass panels of the sitting room. He could see the cabinet Hilda had referred to, tantalisingly close on the other side of the glass, only centimetres away. He tried the handles, but there was no movement at all in the brand-new mechanism. The hotel's refurbishment had upgraded the specifications for everything, including these doors.

Ben tried to lift it, again there was only fractional movement at best. He moved to the door on the far side of the sitting room, the second bedroom. *Christ, how big is this place?* he wondered. Same exercise; same result. Back to the master bedroom, same result, zero movement whether he pulled, pushed, or lifted. He realised now that his only option was Plan B – use a carabiner to break the glass of the second bedroom, which was less likely to be noticed until tomorrow's maid service, and steal something to make it look like a bungled robbery.

Suddenly bright light flooded over him from the sitting room, bathing the balcony and the master bedroom through the door to the sitting room.

The only part of Ben Mason that was moving at that moment was his heart, pumping furiously. He was as still as a statue, apart from his eyes, which swivelled towards the sitting room's sliding glass doors half a metre from him, and which were slowly opening. He had mere seconds to take advantage of the slight noise, quickly swivelling and flattening his back against the glass of the master bedroom as Uwe Mueller stepped out and onto the balcony.

The man was within touching distance and Ben could smell him; the odour of old cologne, stale body odour, and alcohol, a cloud that lagged behind him like flies around a dead body.

Ben knew he was the only one with the element of surprise, his body taut in expectation as Uwe Mueller shuffled wearily to the balcony railing and took out his phone. *What will I do if he looks left and sees my ropes?* thought Ben. *Could I throw him off the balcony? I could convince myself it was self-defence. Hell, I'm not even here. Could I make it look like he slipped? Unlikely,* he corrected himself, *that rail's too high. Suicide? Possible, but implausible,* he reminded himself. The other thought in his mind at that point was how the hell this had happened.

Uwe Mueller turned slowly and reached into his pocket. Ben tensed, ready to spring forward, but Mueller reached into his other pocket and turned away again. Slowly Mueller brought a fat cigar up to his lips, bit off the tail, and spat it over the edge. Then, cupping his hands more out of habit than necessity, he struck a match. The orange flare lit up the podgy and saggy features of an old man, exaggerated, looking like the villain in a pantomime.

Mueller coughed when he first inhaled, and he spat the product out into the night, to follow the cigar tail down into the darkness. Settling himself into one of the comfortable balcony chairs, he crossed his feet at the ankle onto a low table in front of him, the wicker chair groaning in submission. Only the glow of his cigar, like a tracer-bullet, signalled his physical geography.

The sweet aroma of an expensive cigar invaded Ben's senses. He was astonished at the absurdity of how pleasant it smelt; the cigar of a man who, three times, had sent a kill squad for him and the people he cared for. *How messed-up is that?* he asked himself, as he settled in for a long wait.

He was winning the internal battle to relax, fighting to overcome irrational thoughts that Mueller could hear him breathe. After a minute, he was in control. He knew he could overpower Mueller; he was behind him and in relative darkness. Provided Mueller just retraced his route back into the sitting room, Ben would remain undiscovered. If not, he had decided he would make it look like a bungled robbery. Knock Mueller unconscious, steal something valuable to make it look like a robbery, plant the PDC, and get back down the rope. That was his plan.

While he waited, he pieced together recent events. Taking great care to shield the faint glow from his phone's screen, he noiselessly drew his mobile from his pocket and was thankful that he'd done so. Francois had called and texted twice. Receiving no reply, he'd called Hilda and Stephanie, which kicked off a flurry of calls and texts.

The last one from Francois implied he would single-handedly storm the Hotel de Paris if he didn't get a reply. Ben joined all of them into one group, texting: *Am OK. on balcony w UM... he unaware. Hv plan.*

'Who's that?' Uwe Mueller loudly demanded.

Not for the first time that day, Ben's heart stopped, pausing in sympathy so that it too could listen while Ben adopted his default statue pose.

Mueller repeated his question, louder this time. 'I said, who is that?'

Suddenly Ben realised Mueller was talking into his mobile. Distracted by his texting, Ben had not heard Mueller's phone vibrating to announce an incoming call; no doubt- he would have had his phone on vibrate when he was in the Casino. Now the man was up, out of his chair, and speaking loudly in German with his caller. The only words Ben recognised were *Thomas Liang,* which Mueller slowly, sarcastically snarled.

With the phone still in his hand, Ben deftly dialled Stephanie's speed dial, silently thanking Hilda for her foresight in pre-programming their burners. He muted the phone's loudspeaker and held the phone, microphone-forward, towards the agitated Mueller, who was now shaking an immovable balcony rail as he continued his fractious conversation.

Ben knew Stephanie would have realised what he was doing. She would now be listening and following Mueller's conversation. Although a non-German speaker, it was clear to Ben this was not an amicable discussion, nor was it short.

Holding out the phone in his left hand, his right hand was now near the fully open sitting room sliding door. Ben carefully removed the PDC from his jacket pocket and removed the plastic battery tab to power-up with his right hand, cautiously exploring the inside of the open doorway behind him. He had to squat in the darkness, holding one hand forward, the other one backward, performing their different functions.

He probed with his fingers behind him until he found the small cabinet Hilda's text had mentioned. His third attempt pushing blindly against anything that felt like a small door eventually produced a satisfying 'click' as the small door sprung open. Moving his hand carefully inside, he imagined what it looked like if he were standing in front of it in daylight, as opposed to his current contorted thief-in-the-night pose.

There appeared to be ample room on the inside roof of the cabinet. So, applying pressure, he introduced the PDC to its new home. Caressing the cabinet door closed, he straightened and switched the phone to his right arm, as the strain on his left was causing tremors.

Then he remembered to breathe.

If measured by volume and word-speed, the infuriated phone call appeared to have exhausted both caller and called. Mueller was spitting single worded sentences now. 'Ja' pause, 'Ja' longer pause, 'Ja', and with a last emphatic and guttural 'Phaa', he signed off.

Mueller threw his phone onto the chair in which, a few minutes earlier, he had been comfortably ensconced. Obviously exasperated, he sank his head onto his forearms, his wrists limply hanging over the railing. Motionless, but for the sound of a shallow rasping as he panted, his body sagged like a wet canvas sail.

He grunted as he slowly raised himself, drawing one last lungful of smoke from the cigar before he bad-temperedly threw it over the rail.

Ben followed its glowing arc as it tumbled into the darkness. He knew Mueller would now leave the balcony and walk directly past him, the moment of greatest danger. He was old and tired, and Ben was ready to leverage the element of surprise with a blizzard of punches, if necessary. *Should be over quickly,* he speculated.

As Mueller turned away from the rail and towards his suite, Ben saw the man's eyes were red from tension. *From what? The call? Murdering Claus? Or just being a complete global bastard?* Ben didn't know, nor did he really care. As he drew close, Ben coiled.

Mueller passed, head and shoulders stooped in resignation, without the merest glance left or right, and entered the sitting room, bad-temperedly slamming the sliding door so hard that it bounced back from its bracket. He had to turn around to try again, but this time with less force. After a while, the lights in the sitting room went out.

Ben repositioned himself in front of the now empty sitting room and watched a slow-moving Uwe Mueller close his bedroom curtains. Within five minutes, Ben could hear the snoring of a tired old man as he held himself on the other side of the rail. He felt his phone vibrate, it was Danny confirming that PDC number two had checked in.

He retrieved the knotted line and rethreaded it back through his belay. Throwing the ropes out behind him, he again launched himself out into the darkness. He wanted to fly, he felt like shouting in elation, he wanted to spread his arms and defy gravity, so strong was the sense of release. The stress of the last hour was stored in his muscles and it wanted somewhere to explode. He bounced his way soundlessly down the hotel's wall, flinging himself away from the building, using his arm to tension the cable through the belay, soft feet with ankles and knees flexing to absorb the energy. He landed in between the floors in a perfect coordination of releasing his belay line and pushing hard again, out into the black night.

The darkness raced up towards him as he neatly controlled his descent into the hotel's garden. His feet sank onto the soft lawn, creating slack in the rope to free it from the belay and carabiners. Taking the other rope in his hand, he stepped backwards, looked up, and pulled the rope hard. A few years' lack of practice, but he saw the quick release hitch forty metres above him unravel and corkscrew downwards with a touch more noise than he had wanted. There was a drawn-out dull whump as it randomly braided itself, ploughing into a haphazard pyramid at his feet.

Distracted by his tumbling escape route, he did not notice the man whose strong hand clamped itself over his mouth and the crook of an equally strong forearm held him in a stranglehold around his neck. Unable to move, he knew that shortly he would be unable to breathe as he sensed the power in his assailant. A low growl of a voice pressed itself close to his ear.

'Christophe was right at the Verbier chalet, you are a surprisingly capable man, Herr. Mason.' Francois loosened his grip on a startled Ben Mason.

'Bloody hell, you're lucky, Francois. A few moments ago you could have had a fat German banker land on your head if he hadn't decided to go to bed,' a relieved Ben informed him.

'Ssshh. Not so loud. Grab the rope, and we can talk as we walk. Well done up there. Let's get out of here, and you can fill me in with the details.'

*

To the uninformed observer, you would have thought Ben's return to the villa was that of the conquering hero. If the tension had been difficult for Stephanie and Hilda when Francois had gone dark, it had become unbearable when they learned Mueller was returning early and Francois couldn't warn Ben. Their relief was evident.

'To the longest day. Ever.' Stephanie raised her glass in response. 'And to your brainwave idea of enabling me to hear Mueller's call. Very smart.'

'Two down and two to go.' Ben raised his glass.

'To Ben,' added Hilda. 'An impressive day. Francois said he thought you were a reckless idiot in the Verbier chalet. Then you saved Christophe's life, and he realised you knew what you were doing. Tonight, he gave us a running commentary as you were abseiling down from Mueller's suite. He said you reminded him of a younger version of himself.' Hilda smiled mischievously.

Francois' default expression did not alter. *'Je te salue.'* He was a man of few words; Ben raised his glass in response.

After Francois and Ben pieced together the chronology of their respective evenings, Stephanie provided an interpretation of Mueller's heated phone call.

'Thomas Liang called Mueller. I could hear what Mueller said, although he was slurring a lot and Liang's voice was a bit muffled. But it was interesting Mueller insisted on speaking in German. He didn't try to disguise his dislike of Liang. They must be panicking, because Mueller said they shouldn't be holding incriminating discussions on an open line; they should wait until this Friday's video call. What was really encouraging is that they don't know we planted a PDC in Sabitini's office.'

'They don't know I was in Sabitini's office?' enquired a surprised Ben.

'No. They thought we were scoping out her building to do something, but they don't think that we've done anything yet.'

'That's good. It means they don't know about Andy Taylor's involvement, and they don't know the PDCs exist, so they won't be looking for them.'

'Mueller and Sabitini think the car chase and shooting will have scared us off; Towner and Liang don't. That means they'll set traps. A tethered goat trap is what Liang called it, to lure us in and, well, try to kill us, I suppose…' Stephanie's voice trailed off before picking up.

'Why do you think Mueller doesn't like Liang?' Ben asked.

'It was Liang's idea to attack the Sonne Berg and the chalet. The others tried to dissuade him, but he ignored them. Mueller told Liang that he had lost it, gone rogue, and was screwing it up for all of them. He mentioned Papa's murder.' Stephanie paused and blinked a few times before continuing.

'Uwe said they had all made more money than they could ever spend and said he wanted out. Liang was furious. He shouted so loud at Uwe I could even hear him through Ben's phone. Liang sounds like a text-book psychopath, and insatiably greedy; Mueller sounds weak and hates Liang talking down to him, calling him a naive fool at one point. Liang told him he'd use every single resource to cleanse themselves of "Oppenheimer's spoiled brat" and an "out-of-work banker". Their words, not mine,' Stephanie mocked.

'I've been called worse,' Ben added.

'Apparently I've met Uwe Mueller, and maybe a couple of times,' continued Stephanie. 'When I was much younger, he and my father were friends. Mueller was key to introducing Papa to the Five when a previous member died. I didn't know anything about that, but Mueller said they had gone too far in killing my father. Liang just laughed at him.' A reflective silence settled over the room.

'To Ben.' Hilda broke the sombrous mood, raising her glass, grateful for the interruption, and the others joined in.

Francois moderated their advancing enthusiasm. 'The element of surprise, and intelligence about the enemy, are our most powerful weapons. But we must remember intelligence cuts two ways: on the one hand, it's positive to know our intel is ahead of theirs; but, on the other hand, we've just discovered they are arming-up with professional ex-soldiers to kill you two.' He wanted to drive home his point. 'So far, you've been good and a bit lucky. But from here on, you'll be outnumbered by professional killers who do this for a living. We should not underestimate the danger. It'll help balance the numbers if I come with you to New York.'

Stephanie nodded and quickly added, 'I think you're right to keep our feet on the ground, Oncle. But you, and they, would be making a grave error of judgement if you think I won't see this through.' She looked across at Ben who nodded in agreement.

'Let's hope we can continue to be lucky, eh?' Ben chorused.

Chapter Twenty-Five

They landed into a frenetically busy JFK shortly before eleven am, Tuesday. Exiting the baggage hall, they were greeted with a sign reading 'Big Apple Town Cars Welcomes... Hilda.

'The unseen hand of Miss Kearle strikes again,' Stephanie remarked.

Not advertising their names had been Hilda's idea, but the car had been at Francois' insistence.

'A helicopter is quicker and more comfortable than the Long Island Expressway, but you have to produce your passport for a helicopter flight, and that increases the odds on them finding us. Helicopters have been known to fall out of the sky, even in New York.' They had all agreed with Francois' suggestion of the Town Car option.

The Versailles Hotel was an exclusive, boutique establishment set into a narrow side street just off Water Street, at the very bottom of Manhattan Island. Apart from quality and privacy, its key benefit today was being able to access it through the underground car park. This meant their Lincoln Continental Town Car drove past the street-level entrance and straight down into the car park, from where they took the elevator up to the reception area.

Francois presented a Swiss passport in the name of Marc Barrault and asked them to confirm that the room charge had already been settled. It had, courtesy of a bank account Hilda had access to.

'The Five may have known the instant we took off from Nice. If they know we're in New York, they won't know where, but they'll be looking for us. I doubt they'll find us here, because Monsieur Marc Barrault was only issued with his passport a few days ago – courtesy of our friends back home.'

Francois was talking with them in the lounge area of their suite. 'We must work on the basis that they have access to the Police database and probably also the FBI and CIA's. They'll use those agencies and AI to access a thousand CCTVs and use a facial recognition programme to track us down, so we've got to stay ahead of them. They'll be looking for us, which means our job is to make it as difficult as possible for them to capture any recognisable images. Baseball caps, dark glasses, and turned-up collars are today's fashion tips for remaining inconspicuous.'

*

'I've got a reply,' Ben announced. 'It's from an old mate of mine, Sean Gryzbowski, from back in the day when we both ran trading desks at Central Bank of the Americas and Canada, Towner's bank. I texted him after we'd landed to say let's meet. Gryzbo knows everything and loves to talk, so I thought I might pick up some soft intel about CBAC.'

Gryzbo was the product of an Irish mother and a Polish father. A typical New York trader with the broadest Brooklyn accent ever, he still worked for the Central Bank of the Americas and Canada –the bank of which Brad Towner was the CEO.

'I'll read it to you: *"Hey buddy, nice surprise! Happy to meet but can only make a quickie. Security insane. Coming n going all monitored, will explain when meet. 30 mins KRoast coffee, OK? Gryzbo".*'

'That confirms it,' Francois observed. 'That's the extra muscle Liang told Mueller about in the phone call. We'll have to be even more careful now. Ben, you should meet your friend and find out as much as you can. I'll be your back-up, just in case. While we're doing that, Stephanie, can you update Hilda and Ingrid about the increased security at the bank? And see if they have any ideas. OK, first stop is buying baseball caps and sunglasses.'

Using the car park exit again, the two men made their way up to street level.

'Were you given much undercover training by the British Army?' Francois enquired.

'Not really. I was with One Para, more Special Ops than spying. Why?'

'Because I can see you've almost stopped breathing a couple of times.' Francois smiled as he said it.

Ben smiled with him. 'I guess you're right. It's been a few years since I saw action.'

'Where were you then?' Francois carefully enquired.

'Helmand.'

'Was it as bad as they say?'

'It was. And you're right, I'm seeing every person as a potential assassin. Crazy, huh?'

'Actually, no. Not really. One of these people,' Francois cast out an arm, 'will be an assassin, and maybe more than one. I feel the same, but I try not to waste energy worrying about things I can't change. Direct that energy into being even more careful, take no unnecessary chances, that sort of thing. They may not know whether you are in Monte Carlo, Hong Kong, or New York, or even if we are in none of those places, so the odds are all with us.'

Ten minutes later they exited a drugstore fully equipped with 'NY' logoed baseball caps and large sunglasses. Anonymity assured they blended seamlessly into the ambivalent tapestry of tourists and casually dressed office workers of lower Manhattan. A combination of Francois' words, and feeling that he was less conspicuous in the cap and glasses, helped Ben to walk easier.

They split up as they got closer to the coffee bar. Francois took up a position from where he could watch the bar's entrance. Ben crossed the road, his paranoia increasing with each step. *Had they discovered they used to work together? Could they have got to Gryzbo?* He worked for Towner's bank, so they could have pressured him or threatened his family.

Ben's mobile buzzed to announce an incoming message. It was from Calvert; Ben was almost grateful for the interruption, until he read it.

'Ben, you appear to have forgotten to update me. Would be a good idea to do so. BTW, some colleagues of mine from the British Police have a statement from an informant. A few years ago, your friend Danny Mullen may have unwisely used this informant to copy plans from a British Navy shipyard? I'm no legal expert but that might just be treason. Would be a good idea for you to give me an update. Many thanks. AC

*

'Good to see you, Buddy.' The stocky Sean Grzybowski grabbed his old friend in a bear hug.

'Good to see you, mate.' Ben returned the hug on autopilot, most of his mind overcome with hate for Andrew Calvert.

'So, what's this? I heard you was a management consultant or some crap. What the fuck, Bro, consultant? We's natural-born killers, man.' Sean's stocky head and shoulders shook as he laughed.

Ben tried to focus, but Calvert's text had detonated his mind. He stuttered his way through an incoherent recap about his job as a consultant, but left out any reference to Claus offering him a job, or his murder. Any mention in the New York press wouldn't have made the sports or the US markets pages, so if it didn't affect his narrow world, it was unlikely Sean would have noticed. Starting to regain some composure, Ben enquired what the current vibe was inside the world's largest Central Bank.

'Shit, man, place's gone crazy just this week. We got ex-marines taking over the security. No-one knows what's happening.'

'Ex-marines, Gryzbo? Come on, you ain't got vets being security for a bank that doesn't deal in cash.' Ben knew the best way to draw out his old colleague was to challenge his story.

'Man, I'm not joking.' Gryzbo bit, defending his version of events. 'We got mother-fucking vets checking your goddam passes when we go in. I ain't shitting ya.'

'Aw, come on. Who says they are? And why would the Central Bank of Americas and Canada use the ex-armed forces just to check on your lunchtimes?'

'These guys are for real. Couple of them trying to make out with the girls on the desk, and they spinning them some shit over drinks. Guy shows his scars, tells them about Desert Storm, Afghanistan, Black-Ops, and all that. Man, I'm telling you, they the real deal, armed and everything.'

'But why?' probed Ben.

'Beats the shit outta me, but some weird stuff's going down. You know these guys,' Gryzbo used his standard description for all management within the bank. 'They don't know shit, so who knows.'

They chatted a while longer about the glory days and laughed at each other's war stories as if hearing them for the first time, but Ben knew there was little more to be gained. So, after promises of getting together next time either of them was in the other's town, they went their separate ways.

After his old friend had left, Ben found a quiet table and re-read Calvert's message. It was as much a shock as the first reading. *Calvert, you are a conniving, devious, nasty bastard,* he concluded. *How did you find out Danny and I are friends? But more sinister, how did you dig up this stuff about naval shipyards?*

Ben replied to Calvert's message.

Ran out of battery. Am getting closer, can't say now but you'll like.

Then he sent another to Danny.

'*How R U getting on with that voice dubbing thing?*'

He decided against passing on Calvert's naked threat until he had some weapons of his own; Calvert would want him and Danny to become anxious.

Ben was building a plan to deal with Calvert, as he started to devise a way out of his precarious position. Fifteen minutes later, he had the outline of a plan – light on detail and long on risk.

Back at the hotel, he broke Sean's news to the others on the video call. He decided not to tell them about Calvert's message until he knew more himself.

'I used to work in their building, and before Sean told me of the extra security, I did have a plan for getting into the bank. It was risky, but doable. That risk has now multiplied.' Ben was speaking to the laptop transmitting the video conference to Hilda, Felix, and Ingrid.

'Sean said it's tighter than Fort Knox and no-one can get near the C Suite floor. They've cut back visitors to just the essential, super-important ones, so I need to become one of those visitors.'

'I'm intrigued, Ben. How exactly will you manage that?' enquired the ever-sceptical Felix.

'I'm going to become Marc Barrault. Hilda's going to build Marc Barrault's back story. Then Towner's guys are going to ask

Hilda if Marc could possibly meet them, and they are going to invite me into Towner's office.'

'They will, will they?' It was Hilda's turn now to be bemused.

'Yes, and to do that you need to become an overnight expert in the dark web, Hilda.' Ben then outlined his plan.

Chapter Twenty-Six

'Mom, there's a Fox News outside broadcast, and another van in front of our gates saying they want to talk to you.' Brad and Mary-Lou Towner's 17-year-old daughter Jessica was shouting to her mother as she walked with three friends towards their tennis court. They had just come from their pool, on the ocean side of the Towner's Hamptons' mansion, to play a few sets in the cool of the late afternoon.

'Don't open the gates, honey, these people are always fishing for something,' a rueful Mary-Lou called back, as the buzzer for the gate sounded throughout their Southampton Beach summer home.

'Ramirez, tell them we don't do random interviews,' she called to their on-property manager-cum-gardener.

Mary-Lou watched as Ramirez held a short conversation via the intercom with the driver of the other van. The gardener turned towards Mary-Lou, slowly removing his sunhat, and gave a submissive shrug as he opened the gates to admit two large, black anonymous vans.

'What the hell are you doing, Ramirez? Who are these people?' beseeched an agitated Mary-Lou, as the two unmarked vans advanced sedately down the curved driveway, cutting a neat curve through the mansion's manicured lawns.

'Mom, CNN and NBC are here as well. What the fuck?' screamed an unnerved Jessica.

'Jess. I've told you before about your swearing.' Snapped a confused and worried, Mrs. Towner. She watched as the first of the two black vans slowed to a respectful halt in front of her and a taciturn, apologetic figure in a dark suit stepped soundlessly from the front passenger door. He presented a stooped and deferential posture, like a *maître de* accepting a gratuity with false reluctance. His interlinked fingers empty, but held as if not, weighed heavily in front of him.

'We are so sorry for your sad loss, Mrs. Towner. We know what a shock this must be for you, but I can assure you Brompton's are renowned for their sensitivity at these times. I appreciate there is a lot to take in, but you need only one undertaker, not two.' He swept his arm back to gesture towards the rival undertaker's black van.

'What? What are you talking about? You're undertakers? What sad loss? Who's died?' screamed an almost out of control Mary-Lou Towner.

'Mum, what the fuck? Ramirez let another van in. Who's died? What's he goddam talking about? Mum, what's going on?' screamed her completely freaked-out daughter.

'Jess, go inside now,' Mary-Lou shouted at her daughter. Turning to the dark-suited sycophant, she demanded, 'Exactly who do you think has died?'

The dark suit now realised this would not be a normal home collection of the deceased.

'We, and them as well,' he stuttered, trying to share the blame with the rival undertaker, 'received the official instruction from the coroner that your husband had passed away this afternoon. We were to come immediately.' He cringed in expectation of the impending verbal assault and the ensuing attack upon the good reputation of Brompton's. 'We have processes to check these things to avoid, er, mistakes.' His frame appeared to deflate. 'The coroner confirmed a sad but genuine passing, and our fee was even paid immediately. That is unusual.' A light bulb glowed in the recesses of his addled brain.

Mary-Lou's onslaught was interrupted by the arrival of Ramirez.

'Mrs. Towner, there's another one outside, and the TV people wanna know if you'll give a comment? They said Mr. Towner's here and he's dead, but I didn't think he was here. I told them that, but they say he's died.'

'Mom, quick. Dad's on the phone!' Jessica shrieked hysterically from the house.

Chapter Twenty-Seven

'Tell me that's not the most blatant death threat you've ever come across,' an irate Brad Towner bellowed at Vincent Stabilo – Vinny. His new Head of Security.

'And don't goddam tell me "Don't worry, Mr. Towner, we got this covered",' mimicked Brad Towner. 'Because you ain't got shit covered, sonny.' He bellowed again.

'And in case you've forgotten,' Towner continued with the same anxiety and volume, 'those guys were inside my property, where my wife and family could have been murdered.'

Vinny knew the duped undertakers posed no threat to Brad Towner's family, but the message was clear enough. He counted the pulses in the veins surfacing on Towner's forehead.

'Mr. Towner, we were appointed by Thomas Liang to protect you. I'm sorry this scared your family, but no-one said anything about protecting your family. We can get another squad to come in to do that, and I know emotions are running high here, but we must remain calm and not do anything rash.'

'Don't talk to me about calm.' Brad Towner's raw emotion bellowed even louder. 'I want another squad out to my house, pronto. I want a small fucking army; I want the meanest sonsofbitches, and I want them now.' He empathised his point by jabbing his index finger into Vinny's chest.

'And if you can't do it, I want some other motherfucker who can.' Towner's bulging eyes told of the emotional drain of having his family paralysed by fear following various undertakers and news broadcasters visiting his wife to inform her of his death.

Brad Towner was the most successful person Brad Towner knew, living his own extreme version of the American Dream. One of the most recognisable faces in global finance – and in his opinion – he was charismatic, powerful, and respected. His philanthropy was legendary, even though he, like the other members of the Five, had woven such a labyrinth web of offshore firms and corporations that even he struggled to keep track of where his hidden billions were. He wished he could reveal to the world how clever he had been in structuring such a network of entities whose sole purpose was to act as a monetary drip-tray to his brilliant financial engineering. Hiding in plain view – that was him. It spoke to how smart he was, fooling all the people all the time.

'Be careful what you wish for, Mr. Towner, but if you're serious that you really want the meanest sonsofbitches, I can get you the meanest. Is that what you're telling me?' advised a calm but irritated Vincent Stabilo. An average of a thousand bucks a day each, plus expenses, for a cushy protection number like this bought you a lot. And it just about covered overweight, panicky bankers jabbing fingers into his chest. But only just.

'This will cost, and we'll have to go to some edgy places, as these guys don't advertise in Yellow Pages. We'll put the word out there on the dark web, but half of them are psychos, and the other half make the psychos look sane.'

'I don't care what it costs. Just do it and do it now.' Brad Towner would pay the price, although at that point he had no idea how much it would cost him.

*

'I love it when a plan comes together.' A self-satisfied Hilda was on a call with Francois, reading aloud the forum which had just been created on the dark web, called I-2-I, 'Invisible to Invisible'. A network accessible only through the dark web, it could not be tracked due to the layered encryption system.

'It appears Mr. Towner's hired help hasn't wasted much time in getting the word out on the dark web. It's amazing what you can find on there. I've been offered everything from wholesale drug shipments and weapons to bank account passwords. Because nothing's traceable, Towner's goons have provided an explicit job description, so I think we now need to tempt them with Ben's fairy-tale CV,' quipped a very self-satisfied Hilda.

'How did Ben know that Towner would go to the dark web to increase his security?'

'He didn't know, not for certain, but it was Towner's most likely option. Towner doesn't want legitimate security contractors for a job like this. He wants people who'd shoot first, with no thought for the consequences if the price is high enough. Something always happens if you shake the tree hard enough.'

'Whatever, it was still an amazing plan, and between you and Ben, you've not so much shaken the tree as you've blown-up the entire forest.' Francois nodded in appreciation.

'Thanks, and now for the next Act in the play.' Hilda's fingers danced across her keyboard as she turned back to her laptop.

*

Over two thousand miles away, in a darkened apartment a few miles south of Los Angeles, a notification pinged on the bank of monitors. It told the gamer that his Bitcoin account had just been credited with the equivalent of $2,000. So, the mysterious dark web contact with the equally weird request was for real; cool. He exited his on-line addiction, *Apocalypse Maker, the Final Theatre*. He'd annihilated most of the other players at the highest level anyway, and this new contract gave him a bigger rush.

He was good, he knew he was, but even he was surprised he could get past the US Department of Homeland Security's firewalls so easily. Good money for an hour's hacking and, risking a prison sentence longer than his age, he duly delivered. He was all set, he just needed to be told when. He re-entered *Apocalypse Maker* while he waited.

Chapter Twenty-Eight

Broadway is the anomaly of New York's north-south running avenues. The oldest and longest, continuing south through the Bronx for another eighteen miles, christened with a name and not a number further differentiating it. On this famous corridor, at the very south of Manhattan Island, stands the towering glass and steel monolith of Four Prudential Plaza – Brad Towner's building, where his eight-sixth floor office looked down on most of the other skyscrapers between him and the Hudson River on New York's west side.

To his right was the towering monument of One World Trade Centre, and the 9/11 Memorial Gardens. *Lest we ever forget,* he reminded himself every day, as he looked westward to the fading light of the day.

That fool Thomas Liang. I told him we should have eliminated Oppenheimer's widow and her cohort, Brad thought angrily. *We've got too much to lose, and they've got nothing to lose; only a fool picks a fight with someone who has nothing to lose. I told him from the get-go that we needed more firepower. Go big or go home, that's what we say. Mary-Lou knows that shit like this happens with my job, she'll get over it, but it's not good and it scared the crap out of the kids. Very not good.*

It was late on Tuesday evening, and Towner was making a final determination from the shortlist of CVs that had passed Vinny's review. Vinny had been right; his guys had only been hired to protect Towner and not his family. Today's events showed how misguided Thomas' thinking had been. He would not be making the same mistakes – especially not when his family were involved.

Remembering his Head of Security's words earlier that day, 'half of them are psychos and the other half make those look sane', he turned his attention to the CVs and there was one which stood out.

Marc Barrault. Security Consultant. British Parachute Regiment, SAS, Afghanistan, Iraq, Desert Storm One and Two;

liaison – Brad loved that word –with US Navy Seals and Mossad. The impressive list went on, painting a picture in Towner's mind of the perfect solution. References witnessed a modern-warfare-warrior. In his eyes, a hero of achieving the result without being distracted by any of the detail. His kind of guy.

'Vinny, this guy Barrault, when can we see him?' a slightly calmer Towner barked into his intercom. Vinny's contract included being on-call 24/7, so he was getting used to his boss' workaholic model.

'I thought you might like this guy, so I already reached out through the dark web. Turns out he's currently in Washington, which is interesting. He transits back tomorrow through New York for a couple of meetings. He said he could make an hour available early tomorrow morning.'

Chapter Twenty-Nine

Ben knew he had to control his emotions, as well as his breathing. The cover story Hilda had created on his CV contained enough true facts for him to bluff credibly. It had too many holes, though, if they did some proper digging, but Ben was gambling they didn't have the time to do that. Thankfully, he was right. Too late now to worry about that as he took a deep breath and looked out from Brad Towner's eighty-sixth floor eyrie.

It was early on Wednesday morning and the glacial blue, late summer sky over New York stretched taut to the far horizon. So far that he was certain he could see the Delaware River and Pennsylvania beyond. Ben silently thanked the distracting panorama, because he had just shaken hands with the man who had ordered Claus' murder, and he was still struggling with the urge to break his neck.

'Great view, huh, Marc?'

It took Ben a moment to recognise that Brad Towner was addressing him using his *nom du guerre*. 'Oh, yeah. Great view, Mr. Towner. The world at your feet and all that.'

'Marc, I'm really glad you could make room in your schedule to meet. You got many meetings downtown?'

'Some, Mr. Towner. There's many God-fearing folk in these increasingly unruly times who appreciate the type of strategic consultancy we can provide.'

'Come on, Marc, between us guys, it's not strategic consultation, is it? You mean protection; you stop the bad guys, any which way.' Brad Towner winked at Ben across his desk. 'You're like the hired guns in the old Wild West, yeah?' Towner wasn't able to hide his enthusiasm.

'We see our offering as a little more subtle than that, Mr. Towner. There are others out there who are just a gun-for-hire, but that's not us. We like to think our model is a little more cerebral. Old-school methods which embrace technology, if you will.'

'I'll be honest, Marc, after reading your CV, I was expecting someone a little older. You've seen a lot of action, and you're still in your thirties?' Towner talked with his hands, finishing in a small shrug, his palms up.

'I'm comfortable with conflict, Mr. Towner. It's never kept me awake, and I joined the Paras in my mid-teens.' Ben fixed him with his steadiest stare. 'If age is a problem for you, we have more than enough on our books already.' Ben placed his hands on the arms of his chair, very slightly shifting his weight forward, as if to stand.

'No, no. Please. I'm OK with that. I like old school. Liked it when we made the rules.' Towner's voice trailed off under Ben's unchanged stare.

I like this guy, thought Brad Towner. *Granite tough, thinks on his feet, and doesn't agree with me just to win the business.*

Any further thoughts were noisily interrupted as a thousand sirens and alarms went off throughout the entire eighty-seven floors of Prudential Plaza.

*

Two thousand miles away in a darkened apartment a few miles south of Los Angeles, the gamer knew the alarms were ringing. He never normally got out of bed this early, but two thousand bucks in Bitcoin for an hour's work was reason enough. The mysterious web contact wanted him to deliver at exactly eight o'clock eastern time. That's when he had hacked the US Department for Homeland Security and triggered a Level One Threat – Immediate Evacuation Drill on Four Prudential Plaza. It was the protocol to warn of an imminent terrorist attack on any skyscraper on American soil.

The gamer smiled. 'Sweet,' he mumbled to himself, as he resumed the virtual mayhem in the next level of *Apocalypse Maker.*

*

The worried faces of Brad Towner's PA Shelia and her secretary appeared around the door to Towner's office. 'Mr. Towner, I'm sorry, I wasn't told about this one. I don't think this is a drill. They say we must get out the building now.' Part statement and part question.

A fire marshal appeared behind Shelia. 'You must leave immediately and follow the Emergency Fire Marshals' exit instructions.' Mike Pearson read anxiously from a script on his company-issue phone, 'Do not take any excess personal belongings with you. Move immediately to Southwest staircase fourteen, and make your way down. Anyone needing Special Assistance should make their way to Facilities Elevator 2 in the Central Section. Y'all need to put in the code, 1776#, and to follow the Fire Marshal's instruction. Y'all gotta leave immediately.' Mike Pearson replaced his phone, then straightened his shoulders, his high-visibility jacket, and his cap in a self-important manner.

Mike Pearson was a recently recruited junior analyst at the Central Bank of the Americas and Canada, CBAC. The new guy was always given the unpopular job of 'Emergency Fire Marshal' which, along with his name, is what his badge said when he charged into Brad Towner's office.

'Go. Go, Shelia. We'll be right behind you.' A ruffled Brad Towner ushered them out.

'OK, buddy.' Towner held up his hand to jittery part-time Fire Marshal Pearson. 'We're coming now.'

Turning to Ben, he spluttered, 'Goddam it, I don't need this now, Marc. Real sorry, but we gotta take this seriously. It might not be a drill; it might be real, because I always get the inside straight when it's a drill. I go into the bathroom in my office and Shelia tells them I've already left, and they never know. This time, no heads up, so it could be for real.'

Ben could see uncertainty creeping into the edges of Brad Towner's previously arrogant demeanour. He heard a tightening in Towner's voice as he guided him out of his office to join the fast-flowing human tide sweeping down the main office concourse towards the southwest corner and Staircase 14.

Little respect was given to rank or title in the melee. One of the four richest and most dangerous people on the planet was jostled and elbowed exactly the same as the most junior clerk.

The human press increased as the mass squeezed through a pinch-point at the first set of doors. Ben sensed order and deference diminish, the collective panic rising as he knew it would. He chose this point to leverage Towner's arrogance and fear to ambush him.

'Shit!' exclaimed Ben. 'I've left my lap-top in your office. I've got to go back.' He forced himself against a closed doorway.

'No. Wait. You can't, we're not allowed to.' Real fear now gripped Towner.

'Mr. Towner, there's top secret US Government data on that hard drive. I'm committing a felony if I lose that laptop. There is no discussion, I have to go back.'

Brad Towner's self-generated fear meant that he was never going to offer much resistance as he compliantly surrendered to the human wave carrying him along. Especially when the alternative was to return with this lunatic for some secrets which would probably be vaporised if this was a real attack.

Ben held tight to the doorway, presenting as little resistance as possible to the mass, shouting over them, 'I'll catch you down there. We'd like to work with you. I'll be in touch.'

Scared eyes and a weak nod from Towner signalled his desperation to get as far away as quickly as possible.

Ben rode the physical contact as he aggressively turned to crash against the oncoming wave of bodies, colliding into parts of strangers which in other circumstances would be considered an offence. It was exhausting and constant, and he did not know how long it would take them to discover the alarm was a hoax.

After ten minutes of full impact, shoving aside flailing arms and legs, stepping two forward and one back, the crowd started to thin out. The disbelievers and the few who never placed the same amount of importance on these events as maybe they should, slowly made their way past him, probably taking their time to make last calls to loved ones. *Fair enough,* thought Ben, *it's what I would do if I were them.* They realised that running was pointless, as they would come to a crawl in less than a hundred metres anyway.

He could hear the clamour of the lower floors' alarms in the background, muted by layers of concrete and skyscraper infrastructure. He briefly thought of the thousands of people injured, frightened, and probably psychologically damaged as a result.

'Oh dear, Hilda. Look at what we've done. Do the ends justify the means? I doubt too many people in this building would agree they do,' he mused as he arrived back at Brad Towner's office.

Retrieving his bulky briefcase from the blind-side of Towner's desk, Ben removed Danny Mullen's third PDC and pulled up the architect's plan on the laptop. The drawings showed exactly where the router was hidden as he traced his finger along the west side of the eighty-sixth floor to where a bundle of ethernet cables met at a network panel. He looked up at the ceiling; the router was located inside the cavity somewhere above Brad Towner's enormous desk.

Ben was the only person in Four Prudential Plaza who knew that eventually all its occupants would safely return to their desks. He noted the position of everything before carefully moving aside papers, keyboard, and the strategically positioned happy-Towner-family photographs. Wiping the sole of each shoe to remove anything that could leave a trace of his footprint, he stepped up onto the desk.

The ceiling above was the standard all-office fare of light, decorative tiles resting on cross-members, making removal a simple task. The third tile he pushed up revealed a gleaming white Wi-Fi router, its green LED lights blinking reassuringly to indicate it was streaming data. 'You beauty,' he murmured to himself, as he removed the PDC's plastic tab to start the device and carefully placed it inside the ceiling cavity.

Ben made his way through the labyrinth of storerooms and filing rooms to the Central Section and the Facilities Management elevator for those needing Special Assistance. Exactly as Mike Pearson, Emergency Fire Marshal, had informed him, this elevator was for those requiring Special Assistance. But Ben already knew that, because he had worked here many years ago.

He set the briefcase on the concrete floor of the lift lobby and opened it, removing the pair of collapsible hospital crutches and the plastic ankle-fracture protective boot, then extended the crutches to their full size. He took off his right shoe and, using the black Velcro straps, secured that foot inside the plastic boot. Placing his not-needed shoe in the briefcase, he inserted his arms into the crutches and tapped into the escalator's keypad the code that Pearson had given him. Hardly a random choice of numbers – the year of America's independence – he pressed the call button.

While he waited, he looked down through the narrow vertical windows to the Prudential Plaza, eighty-six floors below. Thousands of tiny specs streamed out and away from the building, like ants escaping boiling water. The lift announced its arrival with a discordant ping, as the doors ground open on worn wheels and runners. Two mobility scooter users reversed further back into the cavernous elevator to allow him in.

'There's never a good time, but when you're in the john.' Ben shrugged, and left the unfinished statement hanging while, favouring his left leg, he leaned heavily on the crutches to propel himself forwards. To emphasise his injury, he threw in a grimace with an accompanying grunt for good measure, as he pivoted to face the closing doors. 'Yeah. It's never a good time.'

Ben heard his phone's alert. That would be Danny confirming the IP address had received its ping from the recently activated PDC. Three down, one to go. Hong Kong, here we come.

Chapter Thirty

'I used to fly this route a lot, and it always caused the same fogginess. My body clock would be telling me it was five o'clock in the evening in New York of the day we took off, whereas it was actually six o'clock in the morning, Hong Kong time, on the next day. Now it's enemy territory, Thomas Liang's back yard, so we've got to ramp up our game and be extra aware.' Ben was making small talk as they landed into Hong Kong.

'I wonder what New York is like after the faked terrorist alert. That place will be reeling for some time. We can catch it on the news.'

'The authorities must have worked out that it was a fake or they'd have grounded this flight and everything else. By now, the DHS will have realised they were hacked, but they won't publicise that.' Ben suggested, 'Washington will spin it to say that the only way to have a truly proper test is for everyone to believe it is a real one.'

'You could well be right. "Our Public Agencies Being Ever Vigilant" will be the spin. Guaranteed some will believe it.'

Ben and Stephanie were being studiously polite to each other after their fractious bickering in the first few hours of their flight from New York to Hong Kong. Before exhaustion had drained them of energy, they had run dry of ideas on how they could break into Thomas Liang's super-secure apartment to plant the last PDC. Stephanie's intractable demand to be the one who planted the final PDC, in the home of the man most responsible for her father's death, had drizzled petrol into the furnace.

'Francois was right, we're lucky amateurs living on borrowed time. We know almost nothing about Liang or his movements, so we need a better plan than just hoping we get lucky.' Ben was trying to present a reasoned approach to their thinking. It received a better response than many hours ago – before they had managed to get some sleep.

'I know, but whatever plan we decide, whenever we do, I want to be the one who executes it. Liang is the bastard, out of all these bastards, that I most want to nail,' responded a weary but unrepentant Stephanie.

A ping from her phone announced an incoming message, ending further discussion. They had just touched down smoothly at Chek Lap Kok, more familiarly known as Hong Kong International Airport – just two of over seventy million passengers who use the airport each year. The inevitably long taxi to their stand at the Midfield Terminal was an opportunity to change the discussion topic.

Stephanie read her message. 'Mamma wants me to call her. She says she just wants to hear about New York, but really, she's worried about me. I'll call as soon as we're in a car.'

'Your mum's met Liang. If it's not too raw, ask her if she's ever noticed any weaknesses or character traits. He's bound to be covering up loads of them. It may throw up something.'

Not completely reconciled from their previous argument, Stephanie shrugged and texted the question to her mother. Minutes later, a second ping announced Ingrid's response.

Ben knew immediately the reply had changed Stephanie.

'I think the expression you British use is *Bingo*.' They were waiting for the seat belt sign to be turned off to allow them to disembark.

Ben acknowledged to himself that one of his weaknesses was an inability to hold a grudge for very long if the other person didn't either.

'I've just worked out how I can get to Liang. I'm not even going to try. Instead, I'm going to get Liang to come to me.' Sticking out her chin, she subconsciously spoke in the first person.

'I literally cannot wait.' Ben suppressed some cynicism. 'Does it involve sending signals saying you were "available" after you "bump" into him when you were "accidentally" in the men's toilet, as you suggested last night?' Ben was referring to one of Stephanie's wilder ideas from earlier in the flight.

'That was a ridiculous idea.' Stephanie was too engaged with her new plan to rise to the bait. 'I was just problem-solving then. This idea will absolutely work, I know it will. Here, read Mamma's text.'

Ben duly read Ingrid's text on the question of Liang's weaknesses. *'To list his character traits and weaknesses would take too long; like a child, Liang wants whatever everyone else has, he covets others' material possessions, and is jealous of their achievements. It's what drives him. He's paranoid, a sociopath, and a narcissist. He considered himself superior to your father, and he was jealous of your father's ability to speak many languages and, of course, envious of his cave.'*

'Why was he jealous of your father's cave?' questioned a bewildered Ben.

'No. It's spelt c-a-v-e but it's pronounced *carve*. It means cellar, or wine cellar to be more exact. Papa collected wine for decades. He's got several amazing cellars, from which he would occasionally present Liang with a rare bottle.'

With trademark confidence, Stephanie was certain about her idea, daring Ben to wrest it from her. 'I'll fill in the detail later, but first we need to bait the hook.' She took him by the arm and propelled them out of the plane's first class cabin door.

*

What Stephanie did not show Ben was her previous text exchange with her mother.

'Mamma, another PDC in place, courtesy of Ben taking risks on our behalf. More reason why I think we should tell him. xx'

'I want to, but I also want to protect him. Can you guarantee he won't endanger himself, or us, if we tell him? xx'

'No, you know I can't. xx'

'Let's get the last PDC in place, capture the data, and then tell him. OK? Xx'

'OK. Xx'

*

Conspicuous consumerism is woven into the fabric of the Asian and southeast-Asian psyche. In Hong Kong, Communist China's beating heart of capitalism, your speed through an airport's processes is a direct reflection of how much you are willing to pay. Hilda's hidden but detectable presence was evident when they were met at the end of the airbridge by their uniformed VIP Courier, plucked from the thronging masses and chaperoned through the VIP and Diplomats' channels, straight to the door of their waiting limousine. As they sped along the six-lane Lantau Highway towards the world's most famous trading centre, they held a conference call with Hilda, Ingrid, and Francois. Ben was always amazed by Hilda's calmness, irrespective of the bizarre shopping lists she received.

The first of many outrageous deliveries arrived shortly after they had checked into their thirty-fourth floor suite at the discreet Pinnacle Apartments. Wealth buys you many things and here it bought anonymity with Hilda's online check-in and a discreet entrance through the underground car park. Stephanie's shopping spree, courtesy of Hilda, was soon unpacked in their two-bedroomed suite overlooking Victoria Harbour and Kowloon beyond.

*

'The wine merchant's place is only half a mile from here, so it's easier to walk than cab. But in these heels,' Stephanie kicked up one leg behind her and caught the Christian Louboutin stiletto in her hand, 'it'll be a difficult walk.'

'Are they strictly necessary? Heels that high?' Ben could not completely hide his doubts.

'Yes. They are absolutely necessary. It's all part of painting a picture in the other person's mind. In this case, it's one of Hong Kong's top wine merchants, Alban Fauchere. What else could I wear with this dress?'

Ben had to admit the sleeveless white Valentino cried out for an equal partner, but it already had one in Stephanie Oppenheimer. The famous Italian designer must have had her in mind when he created this masterpiece while the sheer fabric used light like fresh snow reflects a midday mountain sun.

'His shop is on a small street off Queens Road Central. That means it'll be crammed with locals all the way there, so you'll need to walk directly in front of me. You know what some locals, mainly women, think about tall, female Westerners? They don't like it at all.'

Although Ben had worked in Hong Kong for many years and he was taller than Stephanie even in her heels, he had never experienced what Stephanie was describing. To him, being tall was an advantage; being tall, white, and male, even more so. He'd never had difficulty walking anywhere, and hadn't even had to think about it. Now he found himself ploughing a path through the crowded Queens Road, walking closely in front of Stephanie to stop the locals from deliberately bumping into her. The occasional loud murmuring of 'Too tall, too tall' directed at Stephanie accompanying the bumping. She placed her hand over Ben's shoulder, pulling herself close to him.

The crowds thinned as they entered the small side street, and Ben tucked himself into a suitable doorway. He watched from a discreet distance as Stephanie entered 'Viniculture Globale', an unassuming, small premises squeezed between an electrical exporter and a laundry. It was accessed through an equally unassuming front door, complete with a small, old-fashioned bell on a spiral spring, that chimed to report your arrival or departure.

In fluent Italian, Stephanie – now transformed into Gina Ricci, in a jet-black wig, dark sunglasses, and bright-red lipstick – gently enquired, 'Good afternoon, I need to speak urgently with Signor Fauchere. Is he available?'

A smoker's growl replied in shaky Italian, 'I am Signor Fauchere, Signorina. How can I help?' Alain Fauchere's slight frame came slowly to attention, dragged upwards by shifty eyes as they profiled his latest customer. Unhealthy dark spots of saggy skin told of more late-night tasting of his products than was necessary for his profession.

'Oh, I do apologise, Signor Fauchere. I am in such a state of panic,' said the perfectly calm and elegant Gina Ricci in flawless Italian. 'Would it be easier for you if we spoke in French, or even German or Spanish?'

'*Français c'est preferable,*' the relieved Monsieur Fauchere responded. 'Do you speak all those other languages, by the way?' Fauchere's brow furrowed as he tried to assess his latest customer.

'*Oui*, Monsieur Fauchere. My name is Gina Ricci,' purred Stephanie, now in a deliberate Parisian lilt. 'And you were recommended to me as one of the most capable wine merchants in Hong Kong. I do hope so, as I have been the victim of a terrible theft today.'

'Oh, *madame*.' Fauchere's bulbous nose twitched in profitable expectation. 'This sounds terrible, please tell me, how can I help?'

'Well, Monsieur Fauchere, I'm in Hong Kong as the sole representative of a family who are selling a most unique wine collection. I shipped with me four sample bottles, all of which have been stolen somewhere between Zurich and Hong Kong Airport. For insurance purposes, I had to detail their values on the manifest, and I suspect the temptation was too great.' Gina's embroidered handkerchief dabbed at a non-existent tear, pausing for theatrical effect.

'This is terrible, Madame Ricci. May I ask which wines have been stolen?'

'Only a few of us would ever appreciate how terrible a crime this is, Monsieur Fauchere. I chose the wines myself – one champagne, a white, a red, and a Sauterne – to best illustrate the breadth of this important collection.'

'And I'm sure it did, Madame, but I was enquiring specifically which wines have been stolen, and of which vintage?' Alain Fauchere's greed was difficult to contain when he sensed a weak member of the herd.

'There was a Dom Perignon sixty-one, a 2007 Leflaive Batard Montrachet, a Vosne Romanee Grand Cru 1945, and a d'Yquem 1932. The VR still has many years ahead of it, but it would be a fascinating tasting.'

Stephanie allowed her bombshell all the time it wanted to fully explode.

It was exploding fully in the virtual bank account of Monsieur Fauchere, who was not sure he had heard correctly.

'Madame, most people have never heard of these wines, let alone be able to taste even one of them.'

'*Oui*, Monsieur Fauchere. You see my problem?' Gina Ricci dabbed the other eye this time.

'Yes, madame, I do. But please call me Alain.'

'I will, thank you, Alain. And please call me Gina.' Stephanie extended an elegant hand, palm down, for the eager Alain to air-kiss. 'The absolutely impossible task is that I need to replace those four wines and by six o'clock this evening, when I am meeting the first of my two potential buyers of the entire collection. Both Chinese, as you would expect, and each trying to outbid the other for the cave.' She used the familiar French way to describe a wine collection.

'Gina, I think I may be able to help. I need to talk with a few of my customers first of all. But even if I could get hold of any of these wines, they would be extremely expensive.'

'Their replacement cost is not totally irrelevant, although it will be partly offset by insurance. The reason I would pay such a price is because the whole collection is so unique, it is valued in excess of five million Euros. These four bottles were to be tasters, literally, to reflect the uniqueness of the collection.'

'Yes, yes, I see. But you understand I need to be certain—'

Gina Ricci placed her hand lightly on Fauchere's forearm to mute the excitable wine merchant. 'At this late hour, Alain, I would pay almost anything, but reasonably would expect to pay fifty thousand Euros for all four. Maybe more if I could get identical vintages.'

Fauchere was used to dealing in expensive wines and knew a few of his customers held these wines in his cellars. He knew he could buy replacements for less than half the price Gina was willing to pay, generating a tidy profit, but he also knew he would have to ask the owners' permission for the sake of his reputation.

'Madam Ricci, the world of wine at the level you are describing is exceedingly small. I would need to know the name of the collection these came from to convince my customers of its provenance, or they may be disinclined to engage in a discussion.' Fauchere sub-consciously rubbed his hands together – a sign which did not go unnoticed by Stephanie, nor that he was lying.

'I can't reveal the name. It is extremely sensitive, as it follows the recent death of the owner.'

Fauchere, now in full-on sycophant mode, simpered, 'I do understand, really, but I have to insist, Gina. I don't think I can convince my clients unless they know with whom they are dealing and, who knows, they could be potential buyers for you if your two buyers fall through.'

If a weasel could run a wine store, then that is you, thought Stephanie. She was delighted she'd got Fauchere chasing her.

'OK, Alain, you win,' sighed a mock-weary Gina Ricci. 'But you must only use this information to get me the four bottles. Agreed?'

'*Mais oui. Certainement,* Gina,' lied the weasel.

'The collection was owned by a Herr Claus Oppenheimer until his untimely death a week ago.'

Stephanie could see the Dollar, Euro, and Renminbi signs spinning around inside Alain Fauchere's head. One of Hong Kong's most avid wine collectors was Thomas Liang who, when buying from Fauchere in the past, had bragged of the one occasion he had visited Claus' cellar. Although last mentioned some years ago, Alain Fauchere did not forget valuable information like that.

'Gina, your secret is safe with me. Can I suggest you give me a few hours to make some calls, and I'll get back to you? Do you have a number on which I can reach you?'

Stephanie obliged, and even before the small bell on the door had announced her departure, Fauchere was already retrieving Thomas Liang's personal mobile number. He knew trying to speak with Liang would be futile. Instead, he texted him.

'I have exclusive access to Claus Oppenheimer's cellar. Several customers interested, are you?'

Even Fauchere was surprised at the speed with which Thomas Liang responded. The excitable wine merchant waxed lyrical to Thomas Liang about the strikingly beautiful Italian Signorina who appeared to speak every Romantic language and to know as much about wines as he did. He was expecting Liang to say he wanted to charge an extortionate price for the four bottles.

He was not, however, expecting Liang to say, 'Do you have CCTV?'

'Yes, why?'

'Send me the film of her.' He hung up.

While he pondered the fascinating behaviour of multi-billionaires, Fauchere retrieved the CCTV footage and sent it to Liang. Again, Liang replied instantly.

'Call her. Tell her I won't sell her the replacement wines; I will buy the whole collection for six million, and the deal has to be done over dinner tonight. Tell her, Lotus Garden, eight o'clock. And Fauchere, you get five per cent if she agrees.' He hung up again.

Alain wasn't sure quite what Gina Ricci had to agree to for him to receive five percent, but he knew there was no point in seeking clarification from Thomas Liang. He dialled Gina's Italian mobile number.

Chapter Thirty-One

'He's a murdering, perverted psycho who treats women as sex objects. He'll have you killed without hesitation if he discovers you're not Gina Ricci, or spots the tiniest inconsistency in your story. Wearing that dress sends all the wrong signals.'

They were all connected on a video call in which Francois was expressing his view of Stephanie's plan.

'No, Oncle. Wearing this dress sends exactly the right signals.' Stephanie raised her voice to the same level as Francois. 'I want Liang to think with his balls and not his brains. I'm not playing him; I'm playing his ego, because it's huge and obvious. I want him so lost in anticipation of his fantasy fulfilment that he doesn't look too deeply into today's events and how conveniently they fell into place for us. I want him to think I'm gagging for it because that is the only way I'll get into his goddam apartment.'

Ben felt like applauding. *She's not just playing a role in this plan; she is the bloody plan,* he thought to himself. *Her conviction reduces the risk, but can she keep it up for another seven hours?*

Francois and Ingrid had been trying for some time to convince Stephanie, now the stunning Gina Ricci in red Versace, that this plan was too dangerous. The contrast of Versace's unnatural creation with Stephanie's totally natural appearance was a paradox few would ever have to worry about. Ingenious application of materials and design drew out from Stephanie's form more than Ben had given thought to before. Flame-red lipstick echoed shade and texture, sunglasses which earlier had masked tell-tale emerald green eyes were now replaced with brooding, dark-brown contact lenses, more in keeping with her wig of lustrous, shoulder-length black hair. If legend was correct and the lines of Enzo Ferrari's exquisite creations were an imitation of the female form, he would have needed only one model from which to draw inspiration.

'Stephanie, we all understand the underlying motives of that man, but we don't need to become like him.' Ingrid could not bring herself to use Thomas Liang's name, and was obviously fearful of the danger her only daughter could be placing herself in. 'Ben, you're closer to this than anyone, do you think it's too dangerous?'

Ben noted how inclusive Ingrid became when presented with difficult decision-making. Nonetheless, he had hoped she would ask this question.

'It's very high risk, and I recognise all the reasons why she shouldn't do it.' He maintained eye contact, especially with Ingrid. 'Francois is correct when he calls this the most dangerous plan we've ever attempted.'

On the screen, Francois sat back more comfortably in his chair, while Stephanie shot Ben a hostile look.

He continued, 'But we don't have an alternative. We're in their crosshairs, and they're coming to kill us, all of us, whatever we do. And, when we say "the most dangerous plan", let's put that in context. We're talking about a plan to retaliate against your husband's murderers, Ingrid. People who indiscriminately killed and maimed innocents in the Sonne Berg explosion, executed an all-out assault on the chalet, chased us through London firing assault rifles, and who have contracted professional hitmen to kill us. In that context, is any plan too dangerous?'

By the time Ben paused, Francois and Stephanie had swapped body language. Ben had suspected all along that Ingrid knew the right answer, she was just too astute to be its champion.

'You're probably right, Ben,' she concluded. 'He's right, Francois. We're in too deep. These are not normal circumstances, and what we are trying to do is not normal either.'

Francois was still concerned about his goddaughter. 'Yes, I know. I know we all signed up to it and it's been successful so far, but it is still very dangerous. We should remember that and minimise unnecessary risks. And Stephanie, do not hesitate to bail if you have to. Ben, I've sent a couple of things over for you. Just stuff you're familiar with.'

Ben knew better than to enquire publicly what Francois meant. Hilda's short timeframe miracles continued, whether that was a full abseiling kit in Monaco, dark web mayhem in New York, or the intuition to identify Thomas Liang's wine merchant. Intelligently applied intuition was what other people describe as being 'lucky', and it was amazing how 'lucky' Hilda could be.

Now Stephanie's plan was rolling, and she was off to dinner with the man who had orchestrated her father's murder.

*

The Lotus Garden is known locally as The Tycoon's Canteen because of the prices, the wine list, and the difficulty in getting a table. Thomas Liang had never found it difficult to get a table, and this evening was no exception.

Stephanie arrived early. She knew a man like Thomas Liang wanted you to arrive early and wait patiently for him so that he could vaunt his seniority by arriving late. This was straight after she told Ben he was being over-protective, insisting on driving her to the restaurant himself, but secretly she liked that he was. Although they had enabled apps on their phones to track each other, she knew Ben would be tracking her every move, following from the restaurant, and be near Liang's apartment building. She felt as prepared as she could be, given the circumstances.

The swarm of overly attentive waiters, the maître de, and sommelier announced Thomas Liang's arrival. Observing his behaviour amongst the fawning audience, Stephanie profiled him as a self-absorbed, pugnacious little man, with a charmless expression that had probably never seen a reason to be otherwise. It told her a lot, as she forced herself into her character for the evening while waiting attentively.

Their table was set on a raised dais encircled with ceiling-hung, blood-red satin drapes, which could be discreetly drawn if required. Stephanie chose the exact moment Liang stepped up to step down. Genetics and Monsieur Lebouton's invaluable footwear ensured she was still taller. Albeit a hair's breadth, but it was enough. The point was not lost on anyone, as Stephanie gracefully extended a compliant hand.

'Signorina Ricci, such a pleasure.' Liang salaciously drooled while his stubby fingers shook only the fingertips of Stephanie's offered hand. She'd won the first round and reminded herself to breathe while trying to contain the fear his deep-set, narrow eyes threatened to invoke.

Continuing to hold the tip of Stephanie's fingers, Liang stood, unblinking, as he unashamedly ran his eyes up and down her body, lingering occasionally as if surveying an article he was thinking of buying. His undisguised sexual objectification of her was unnerving. Although her outward poise disguised her true emotions, as fear built inside her, she had to break the spell to stop it overpowering her.

'I hope you don't mind, Mr. Liang,' she spoke louder than necessary, 'but they had only one bottle of the 2011 Screaming Eagle Sauvignon Blanc left, so I ordered it.' Stephanie's default position of retaliating before she was attacked proved to be her saviour again. Returning Liang's unblinking stare, she dared him to disagree with choosing one of the world's most expensive white wines.

'The eleven? Why the eleven?' Liang challenged. His eyes briefly engaged hers before resuming their journey over her body.

'As I was discussing with Xavier here,' Stephanie indicated towards the Sommelier who had glued himself to them, 'the eleven has now attained its true potential. High summer temperatures allowed the winemaker to blend more of the upper blocks, carrying greater fruit weight, and the mouthfeel is so satisfying.'

Gina's body language and rhythm subtly mimed her description. Repeating it in perfect Spanish, as Xavier nervously nodded in agreement, she provocatively swirled a thousand dollars' worth of the pale-straw liquid in her glass. Raising it slightly towards Thomas Liang in a half-salute, she smiled demurely.

'Is this true, Xavier?' Without even a glance at the Sommelier, his boundless arrogance continued to undress Gina, 'Why did you not mention this to me before?'

'To be honest, Mr. Liang, I had forgotten, but the Signorina is right,' stuttered the petrified Sommelier. He decided honesty and contrition were preferable to losing face with one of his employer's biggest spenders.

Liang gave a short laugh, but not because it was funny. He was laughing at someone's embarrassment, their misfortune, caused in part by the fear he imparted.

Stephanie realised Liang's laugh was his version of sneering; he thought himself better than that person. She felt some satisfaction that she'd cast Gina Ricci perfectly. Liang was infatuated with her character, a woman who had won emphatically in his favourite subject. It was clear the Sommelier feared him, and Stephanie saw Liang feed on that fear. It made him want more; he liked exercising power more than power itself.

Is that the real reason you had my father killed? she wondered. *Because he challenged your insecurities; your reason to accumulate power and wealth, because you need those to hide behind?* Stephanie used anger to maintain her focus while ensuring dinner proceeded exactly as each of them had planned, even if their respective plans had contradictory conclusions.

She made sure Liang drank as heavily from the glass as he did from the Gina Ricci inspired expectations, freely pouring equal measures of each. Correctly guessing the picture Liang had in mind, she made sure Gina filled the canvas as precisely as if Liang had commissioned it himself. Morphing into the pliable, submissive object who possessed everything he coveted – educated, erudite, languages, with sexual innuendo oozing from every pore, but most importantly, that he controlled her.

Winning the sobriety contest was key to Stephanie's plan, which she easily managed courtesy of age and enzymes being on her side, as a couple more equally expensive bottles followed the first. Liang's overly tactile contact beneath the table was just another cost Gina was happy to bear, because it meant she was winning.

'I do apologise, Gina.' His body language said he did not. 'I find you quite stimulating.' Liang was starting to slur, needing to separate each syllable of the final word.

Gina advanced his thinking with an encouraging smile. 'We shouldn't forget why we are here, should we?' But Liang was already miles ahead of her.

'Certainly.' Liang lisped as he paused. 'Not.'

'What would you suggest then, Thomas?' Gina lowered her eyes, and her voice.

'We should conclude our discussion in a more convivial environment, at my penthouse.' Liang was not seeking consent as he rose unsteadily.

*

Peak Heights Apartments sits on the highest inhabited point of Hong Kong Island, looking to the north and west over Belcher Bay, Victoria Harbour, and the southern part of the Chinese mainland. Real estate here is amongst the most expensive in the world, and anything on the Peak is a multiple of those prices. A billionaire's domain and, unless accompanied by a resident, entry is an impossible process. If that resident is Thomas Liang, it is as straightforward as dismissing your butler by shouting drunkenly at him and open-handedly hitting him around the head. Which is precisely what he did.

Stephanie was alone with her father's murderer. No longer feeling vulnerable, she felt confident and in control. She had more than levelled the playing field through alcohol and advertising her availability. The thought repulsed her so much it was indescribable; only the thought of revenge sustained her.

'Now. Before we get down to the most important piece of tonight's business…' slurred the red-cheeked Liang as he ran his fingers through Gina's wig. Stephanie's heart missed several beats. The wig held, but for how long? Taking a deep breath, she reached for his hand, selected his middle finger, put it deep into her mouth and sucked it. Liang was overcome, she wondered if she had gone too far.

'…I must make myself more presentable.' Liang stood, unsteady and breathing heavily from the exertion. 'While I do that, why don't you help us to a small drink? A small one, Gina. We want to enjoy our, um, negotiation, eh?' His smile resembled a snake before it devoured its prey.

Stephanie had to fight back the fear and anxiety that rose from the pit of her stomach, and she retaliated by returning his wink. As Liang left the room, she moved fast.

Directing the energy from her anger and disgust, she quickly selected the best red wine she could find from the floor to-ceiling wine cooler, then retrieved a small sachet from her clutch-bag. The white powder carried a very faint chemical smell, nothing that a robust red couldn't overpower. She had been worried it might not, but Hilda's over-the-counter-medications recipe, combined with the alcohol Gina had administered, would take care of Thomas Liang. Most of a bottle of red wine was generously splashed into two bowl glasses as she shook the sachet's contents into one, swirling the glass vigorously to dissolve the powdered cocktail.

Liang, now draped in a loosely tied silk robe, lay lazily on one of the enormous settees in the living room as she carried the glasses through. Behind the carefully arranged mask, hatred strengthened her resolve. Slowly, she forced herself to relax, softening her rictus grin into a warm smile.

'No. No. We can't follow this evening's amazing wine with cheap shit like that,' Liang shouted angrily. 'Throw them away. You and I are destined for greater rewards than that, Gina. I have a one hundred and fifty-year old Cognac waiting for just such a night as tonight. Tip that rubbish away at once.'

Stephanie panicked; she had used her only sachet. If she threw away the wine now, her plan would fail and a conscious Liang would demand she delivered what she had spent all evening promising. She would rather die. *And how real a prospect would that shortly become?* Gina's light started to flicker, replaced by a panicking Stephanie struggling to maintain her composure after hours of acting.

She remembered Ben would be nearby. *Can I get hold of him?* she wondered anxiously. *If I did, how would he get into the building, let alone get up to the Penthouse in the private lift? What about the butler or the security he must have close by?*

*

Nine years earlier, and Ben's six-month secondment in Hong Kong with HKBC had introduced him to the business district, the bars, restaurants, and clubs clustered mainly within a half mile of the coastline. He'd run and cycled up many of the peaks and hills which were the backdrop to the shoreline's skyscrapers and container cranes. Familiar location, different emotions. Now it was a jet-black night, and he was looking through a sparse copse of trees at Peak Heights towering above him. They'd gone over the plan repeatedly, recognising the dangers and, as far as possible, devised strategies to negate them. But that didn't lessen his anxiety. Stephanie was playing a fatal game of Double Dare with the man responsible for hundreds of deaths, including her father's.

He recalled her bravado in their ironic conversation when he'd driven them to the restaurant. *'I'll drink heavily with my father's killer so that he'll invite me back to his apartment for sex. That's where I'll drug him, plant the PDC, and escape from a building bristling with high security.'*

She was a natural actress with a daring and infectious character, but that was just to cover her fear. They were both desperate to finish this, a shared goal which brought them together. Ben's reasons were parallel although his instincts to protect her were starting to override his other senses.

Driving up to Peak Heights, he had scoped out the area while she and Liang were still in the restaurant, twice cruising slowly past the Peak Heights tower, fully covering all perspectives and escape routes. He parked and, keeping out of sight, walked around the building for two hours, partly to be sure, partly to occupy his wandering mind. His transformation to viewing everything through a soldier's lens had been automatic; his training making instinctive assessments of escape routes and fields-of-fire before deciding there was nothing more he could do. Other than wait. A lot of emotional energy had been used trying to stop his imagination from running wild; it was now in the lap of the gods, or more accurately, Stephanie Oppenheimer.

It was too soon to think of an extraction plan; she'd only been in Liang's penthouse for seventeen minutes, he'd been counting, although to Ben it felt like hours. Encouragingly, Liang's exit from his chauffeured car spoke loudly that Stephanie's plan to drown him in alcohol was working. The recollection helped, but distraction was the key. He knew he'd done everything he could, but to avoid making a rash decision which could endanger her he needed to think of something other than her. With difficulty, he started to consider how to deal with the lesser of the many evils currently stalking him, Remy? Or Calvert? And their respective latest threats. Reluctantly, he knew it was best for now to turn his attention towards that as he opened his messages. Danny's was first, replying to Ben's enquiry.

'*All voice-overs completed exactly as you asked and even his mother wouldn't know it's not him. A cautionary note, this is like juggling Semtex over a bonfire, blindfolded... Be very careful. D.*

Calvert's message increased the pressure.

'*Can't hold off police n Special Branch from visiting your friend much longer – U need to deliver something n very soon. AC*

Ben knew he had to reply with something. '*Will have something for you in 24 hrs.*' One way or the other, he reasoned to himself. One way or the other.

The black and charcoal-grey steel of the compact Heckler & Koch P7 felt reassuring as it lay in his open hand. *How had Francois managed to get it to him? Or was it more Hilda magic?* Either way, Francois' throwaway comment at the end of the last video call had delivered a surprising result. Even when these had been the tools of his trade, and he had used his tools well, the contrast between size and lethality would always intrigue him. The split-second dividing kill or be killed – it all boiled down to that very simple, binary outcome. He knew for certain he would use it again to defend Stephanie. But at that point, he had no idea how near to danger Stephanie actually was.

*

'Come on, Gina,' Liang shouted drunkenly, followed by something insistent and annoyed in Chinese as he waved at her to throw the wine away. 'Get rid of that crap and let's have the proper stuff.' Liang was becoming more agitated.

200

Stephanie knew Gina had to put on the performance of her life. Literally.

Gina stood in front of Thomas, legs astride, drawing taut insinuation from Versace's creation. She arched her neck, tipping her face upwards, her lips gently parted, and slowly ran long, sensual fingers down her throat. Lazily she toyed her fingers into her bronzed and full cleavage. She now had Liang's attention again.

'Oh Thomas, I love the taste in my mouth and as it slowly trickles down my throat. Let me have my way first of all, then we can see about what you want.' Gina purred the last few words as she playfully toyed with the loose silk tie holding his robe. With pouting lips, she handed him his glass.

She saw the effect she was having on Liang.

'Come, Thomas, show me your amazing view from on top of the world.' Gina forced a naughty giggle from somewhere that Stephanie could never have, as she led him by the hand, out onto the broad terrace a mile above sea level. Stephanie made certain they took their glasses with them. Some full-body-contact flirting from Gina, appropriate awestruck giggling, a half-dozen Gina-encouraged mouthfuls, and shortly after he finally drained his glass, he was swaying and fighting to keep his eyes open.

'Shall we go inside and lie down, Thomas.'

Kicking off her shoes to avoid a turned ankle, Stephanie helped her father's murderer stagger across the broad terrace. Letting him crash stupefied, face-down onto the thick polar-bear rugs surrounding one of the ceiling-hung fireplaces was not deliberate, although it helped to confirm his unconscious state.

She collapsed into a chair, panting hard. The alcohol hadn't helped but she lay back and smiled self-satisfied. Tentatively nudging him with her foot, the billionaire murderer lay on the rug below her, as vulnerable as any of his victims had ever been. She prodded harder to make sure he wasn't faking it. No reaction. Just to be sure, she stood up, swung her leg and kicked him hard in his copious stomach. The only sound was a small amount of air being forced out of his mouth from the physical force of the kick.

'That's from my father, and there'll be more to come.' She went in search of the router.

Liang's private study was a proxy of the man. More than fifty square metres of floor-to-ceiling, wall-to-wall glass, looking down upon the little people of Hong Kong. Onto their homes, offices, and the innumerable container cranes perforating the shoreline. In the middle of his huge glass desk was one of the Five's custom-built tablets, ready and waiting for tomorrow night's call.

Stephanie saw it as a symbol of the Five, their means of communicating a million illegal activities. They'd plotted murders, possibly her father's, on these devices. For the briefest of moments she was tempted to destroy it, to smash it over the comatose Liang's head, but she knew that would merely temporarily inconvenience the Five, and it could ruin everything they had worked for. Instead, she directed her energies to find the router, discovering it quickly amongst the usual high-tech trappings of the wealthy. Just off the desk, on a glass shelf book-ended with Tombstones, the awards commemorating Liang's landmark deals. Unsurprisingly, it was emblazoned with his name or that of the world's largest trading company he ran.

She pulled out the plastic strip and started the small device on its quest for radio waves. The white plastic time-bomb blended in with the other white smart-speakers and smart-everything.

Stepping back from the window, she studied her reflection in the huge expanse of glass. An over-tightened spring inside started to unwind, every fibrous strand of muscle massaging itself looser. She felt her shape changing, she realised stress had been holding her shoulders high with a knot in her stomach. Everything was now releasing, the blood flowing freely around her body, coursing into parts that had been pushed to the back of her mind while obsessed with carrying out the plan.

She thought about Ben while looking at her reflection. She stood sideways, lifting her chin and straightening an elegant neck, holding her head tall above tanned, lean shoulders, admiring how her poise accentuated the size and shape of her breasts. She smoothed her hands down her form, across an already flat stomach, down to her waist to the tops of her thighs, feeling the heat as she did so.

I've known him for less than a week, and it feels like we've been together for years. The only man I've slept with and, well, just slept with, she smiled thinking about the overnight plane journeys. She knew then that of all her many suitors, ennobled, titled, wealthy, 'good family', and all that, Ben had cared more for her and her family than all the others put together. *How many times has he put his life on the line, for me? And how have we Oppenheimers treated him? Poorly. That has to change,* she promised herself.

She knew he would be waiting for her somewhere nearby. The thought provoked another anticipatory surge and she felt happy for the first time in many weeks. Since planting the last of the PDCs, something had let go inside her. When she pulled out her phone to text, she noticed there were four messages from Ben. His texts said he was in a small park opposite the building. It was a sightseeing point on the edge of the mountain, behind the trees. *How romantic,* she smiled as she texted. *'Mission accomplished. On my way now. xx'*

Were two kisses too obvious? she wondered? *Emphatically yes,* she decided.

They had achieved the impossible. In six days crammed with adrenalin, emotion, and little sleep, not to mention circumnavigating the globe, they had planted the four PDCs. All they had to do now was wait for the remaining four members of the Five to incriminate themselves in twenty-four hours' time. Compared with planting them, retrieval would be easy. As was compiling the proof for the IMF.

Grabbing her bag, she hurried from Liang's apartment, briefly checking he was still sleeping. Loud snoring evidenced he was. Joyously punching the lift's call button, she decided that as the mission had been successfully completed, she could let her hair down – literally. As the lift doors slid open, she gratefully pulled off Gina's black wig and shook out her own auburn locks.

'God, that's itchy.' She spoke loudly as she shook out twelve hours compressed under Gina's wig. It made her look like she'd had an electric shock. She laughed at her reflection in the lift's silver and gold-flecked mirrored walls.

'If I look like a tramp, maybe I'll act like one.' She rearranged parts of several thousand dollars of Versace to enhance their visual impact. The lift's swift descent nearly caught her off-guard, depositing her quickly onto the ground floor, and she hastily replaced Gina's wig, tucking up several loose strands of her own hair just before the doors opened.

Although it was the early hours of the morning, two liveried attendants manned the front desk. Peak Heights was a 24/7, three hundred and sixty-five days of every year, controlled environment. They bowed deferentially and in unison as Stephanie strode confidently across the spacious atrium. Christian Louboutin stilettos resonated their sharp retort against another polished marble flooring, attracting the same attention.

Out from the climate-controlled atmosphere and into the humid night, she saw as much as she sensed Ben through the thin foliage shielding the sightseeing area from view. She smelled the honeysuckle and jasmine as they cascaded through her heightened senses. Her skin was on fire, and she started to walk quicker, her pulse increasing. She could see Ben now, jogging urgently towards her, getting quicker now. She heard his footsteps through the grass quicken, then just as quickly stop, as Ben's phone sounded an alert. They had their arms around each other.

'Don't you dare answer it.' Stephanie had her palm against his cheek and was leaning her lips towards his.

'Shit!' Ben exclaimed loudly.

'What? What's happened?'

'The PDC you just planted is OK, but Danny's just received an automated message from the New York PDC. It's a low battery warning. He says we have less than twenty-four hours to get to Towner's office and download whatever it's captured before it goes into sleep mode. We've got to get to New York… now.'

Chapter Thirty-Two

'We've got to have your best guess, Dan.' Ben was talking to them all on a video call less than an hour later. Hilda had put it together, with Ingrid and Francois also on the call. 'Realistically, how long have we got?'

'Twenty-four hours max, probably less. It's difficult to say exactly, as none of them have ever failed before. It could be a faulty signal but you just can't take that chance. Bloody Chinese. Sorry, mate.'

'It's not your fault, Dan, shit happens. But can you complete the picture, the film, without the New York data?'

'Provided you can retrieve the data from the other three PDCs, I can complete *a* picture, but not *the* entire picture. It'll be a picture of what the other three are saying. You won't have any video output from the New York bloke. I'm playing catch-up with your mission here, but I guess that means you won't have any proof that NY bloke is one of the bad guys, right?'

'Yes, that's right. Which means he'll be free to come after us. That makes us the number one enemy of a billionaire psychopath.' Stephanie summarised what they all now knew.

'OK. It's two-thirty am here in Hong Kong, and the video conference takes place in sixteen-and-a-half hours. Let's be positive and say the battery in New York lasts that long, then I have to get into Towner's office as soon as possible after the video call, retrieve the data using Bluetooth, or physically retrieve the PDC. Hilda, how soon can you get me there?' Ben mapped out the practicalities.

'Before you answer that, Hilda,' Francois cut in. 'Ben, the last time you were in Towner's office, it coincided with one of America's biggest terrorist incidents since nine-eleven. Towner's well connected, and by now he may know it was a hoax and not an unauthorised evac drill. The question is, does he know it was just to enable you to plant the PDC? Or worse still, as a result of that, he's discovered you're not Marc Barrault.'

For a while, everyone disappeared into their own rabbit hole, each making their own projections of probability and outcomes.

'Francois is right. We need to be certain before you go back in, otherwise well, otherwise…' Stephanie didn't finish the sentence.

Ben knew the dangers. 'That PDC's battery is dying, so we're short on options. Homeland Security are never going to admit their systems were hacked and the hacker set off a hoax alarm. They'll pretend it was real and that they made it even more real by not giving their usual advanced warning to Fire Departments and building managers. There's absolutely nothing connecting it to Marc Barrault. We'll just have to take the chance.'

'You mean *you*; you're taking that chance Ben, not *we*. And I don't think that's fair on Ben.' Stephanie's tone and change in body language was noted by Ingrid. 'I'm coming with you.' Stephanie's eyes drilled into him.

Ben felt Ingrid and Francois watching closely. 'OK, we can argue later about who's taking risks, the point is that without Towner's data we can't nail him, and I am the only one who can get into his office. Simple as that. Don't worry, it'll be fine.' Ben laid his hand on Stephanie's as they sat in front of the laptop. 'Now, Hilda the miracle-worker, how will you get us to New York in nineteen hours? I don't think anything flies in that direction until the afternoon. Do we have to go round the world in the other direction?'

'I've been looking while you've been updating us. Give me five minutes to finalise it, but I'm chartering a Gulfstream. Talk amongst yourselves for just a few minutes.' Hilda was immersed in another screen, finalising the transaction.

'Francois, I've just sent you a list of a few things I'll need for when I meet Towner. They'll be familiar to you, could you source them for me please? Now I need to contact Towner, pretend that I've been in the States ever since our last meeting, and see if he can meet me midday tomorrow, NY time. While I do that, Dan, can you get hold of Andy Taylor, find out how much he wants for downloading the Bluetooth data from Sabatini's PDC?'

'Sure, will do. But following my last convo with him, we know he'll be expensive.'

Hilda did not wait for anyone to comment. 'OK, all done. We got lucky. A Gulfstream G600 will be on its way from Macau to Hong Kong within an hour. It's standing there dormant while its owner goes gambling and whoring in Macau for a week. Their rep will meet you in the private charter lounge of Chek Lap Kok Airport. The plane will be fully fuelled, has two pilots, two cabin crew, and is fully tech spec'd, so we can video and call while you're in the air. You'll need to refuel in Honolulu, already paid for, which will take one hour, and they'll arrange that en route. Your ETA into Teterboro private airport is ten thirty local time tomorrow.'

'You are amazing, Hilda.' Ingrid spoke for them all. 'Where's Teterboro?'

'New Jersey. By the time you land, I'll have arranged ground transport. At that time of morning, it'll take less than an hour to get downtown.'

'Let's work on the basis that I retrieve either the data or the PDC itself.' Ben was careful not to make eye contact with anyone; they all knew what the second option would involve. 'We've then got to come back here to retrieve from Liang before that battery also runs out. Thoughts on that small issue, Hilda?'

'I'm looking into that and will have an answer for you in a while.'

'Thanks, Hilda. As we've all got tasks to perform and we've got a plane to catch, I suggest we video call from the plane when we're airborne.' And with that, Ben ended the call.

Chapter Thirty-Three

Emma, the Gulfstream's flight attendant, didn't need anyone to tell her. She knew. She'd been sick two out of the last three mornings, and she was never sick. She was late, and she was never late, always within a couple of days, three at the most, not three weeks as she was now. IVF had nearly broken them financially and emotionally, and this third round had been especially traumatic for both of them. Neither said it, but both knew it had been make-or-break for them.

Now, though, it all seemed worthwhile. All the symptoms told her that now was the time to tell Jill she was carrying her baby; they were going to start their family, their new life together.

She'd do it when she got back from this trip, sneak a look at Jill's diary, work out when she had a good gap between shifts, maybe surprise her with a dinner at that Thai restaurant she liked so much. *She loved surprises,* Emma smiled as she hugged herself. *Boy or a girl?* she wondered. *It's going to be a boy.* She knew, she just knew.

*

Ben assumed it was no accident that every person they meet when chartering the world's most expensive private jet, was genetically perfect. Ben and Stephanie were shown more deference by more beautiful people in the few hundred metres from their chauffeured car to the gleaming jet's steps than he had received in a hundred commercial flights. The Gulfstream itself was an enclave of luxury at an impossible level, even before you considered that the primary reason for its existence was not luxury, but to fly you from A to B.

'Welcome on board, Mr. and Mrs. Smith. I'm Emma, your flight attendant.' Unable to stop smiling, Emma over-shook Ben and Stephanie's hands. 'Please, let me show you your home-from-home for the next eighteen hours. This G is divided into three living areas: we have the dining area here, the conference through there, and the bedroom beyond.'

Projecting a practised and engaging smile, with no detectable pause she moved on. 'To the front, we have the galley. We prepare all meals from scratch and cook them on board, so just let us know what you'd like. And to the rear we have the bathroom, complete with walk-in shower and bath.'

They both nodded, trying to take it all in. 'We'll need to make some calls and a video conference while we're flying. Can you set that up for us, please?'

'Of course. The conference room is fully equipped to host those. Now if you could take your seats, I'll let the captain know we're ready for take-off.'

*

An hour later, and they regathered the same group on a video call.

Hilda spoke first. 'Danny texted me; he's still talking with Fat Andy. Says he won't move off one thousand pounds to retrieve the data. I've said that's fine, and I've transferred two thousand to Danny's account to cover any incidentals. He'll join us as soon as he can.'

Ben knew how that conversation would have gone.

Ben was next. 'I spoke with Towner. He's very keen to resume our meeting and wasn't fazed by the evacuation at all. The conspiracy theories about that get crazier every day. The wildest is that it was a Russian cyber-attack, a trial-run on the Department of Homeland Security before they hack the CIA and FBI. The House is preparing a Bill to allow the US to respond; Russia denies it, which of course is a confirmation of guilt to the conspiracists. If it were a plot in a book, no-one would believe it. Towner has agreed to meet at midday tomorrow. Fingers crossed the battery lasts until then, and I'll do the retrieval by Bluetooth while I'm there.'

Hilda confirmed that Christophe had booked a table for this evening in the Grill Room of the Hotel de Paris, a short walk at some point during dinner to the balcony's edge and easy retrieval.

'Won't that look a bit odd, a single man, dining on his own in a restaurant like that? Surely that will attract unnecessary attention?' Francois nearly smiled but didn't.

'Yes, good point, Francois. Which is why I've suggested that Hilda accompany Christophe for that very reason,' interjected Ingrid, showing no surprise at the tryst revelation.

'How are we doing on the return flight, Hilda?' Ben moved them on before any of the others had a chance to ask any further questions.

'I saw an opportunity, and I took it. When I asked the Gulfstream crew whether I should contact the owner directly to get a quote for the return flight, he was very evasive. Then he let slip they had priced that into the outward flight, because the owner doesn't know they are chartering his plane and crew behind his back. Since discovering that, I've renegotiated the deal – provided I make a donation to an offshore account, which I have done, and of which I presume the crew are all beneficiaries. They'll file their flight plan, and you two are anonymous. The plane is listed as crew only on both legs, and they'll stay at Teterboro until you're ready to fly back. But for US Visa reasons, it has to be within twenty-four hours. Same route, same refuel, no passenger manifest.'

'Well done, Hilda.' It was Francois' turn to contribute. 'Ben, all arranged as you requested. It will be waiting when you arrive.'

'Thanks, Francois. Before we go, now that the PDCs are all planted, there's something I need to tell you.' Ben had everyone's attention.

'Inspector Remy and Andrew Calvert are blackmailing me.' He paused for their reactions. 'They're acting separately, and neither knows about the other, but they've each threatened to reveal fabricated evidence to the authorities which would secure convictions against me, and separately against Danny. To save myself, I've got to hand over to each of them all the information we collect on these four. They've both threatened to reveal their evidence if I tell anyone they're blackmailing me.'

'Oh Ben—' Stephanie started to speak, but Ingrid immediately took control.

'Stephanie. Let Ben finish. Let's not forget there's a lot happened. Ben, carry on. We understand, although had you told us earlier, none of us would have said anything outside of this group.'

Stephanie looked hard at Ingrid on the screen. Her mother looked right back, tight-lipped, an imperceptibly small movement of her head from side to side. Stephanie nodded. Both then turned their attention to Ben.

'No offence, but I wasn't sure who was on whose side. Until Remy and Calvert sprung their surprises, I thought they'd be on our side, old family friends and all that. Also, I want to nail the bastards who got Claus, and I knew that if I told you it might have added that extra bit of pressure which made us decide not to go through with planting the PDCs. I didn't want that to happen – all that loss of life would have been in vain.'

He turned to a worried looking Stephanie. 'Sorry, Steph, I wanted to tell you and came close to telling you so many times. I did it to protect you, and you, Ingrid. I didn't want to put any more on you; you both had enough to deal with.' Ben did not elaborate. They were all silent. Only Ingrid spoke.

'Ben, I'm sorry you're in trouble again because you're trying to help us. But why are they doing this? What can they gain?'

'Remy's an old-school copper. He's doing it because he's being pressured by his bosses, who are being pressed by politicians, for results, for arrests, to produce a culprit for the biggest attack ever on Swiss sovereignty. And Remy has no leads, apart from me. Calvert is doing it because he's Liang's puppet. He's working for the Five, and is probably being well paid to do so.'

'What have you told them so far, Ben?' Ingrid's clear thinking enabled her to ask the first question.

'Nothing, I fluffed-up what they already knew and promised to share anything new with them.

'What evidence could they manufacture against you?'

'Remy planted a gun in my bag so that they could arrest me when it set off the X-Ray machine at the airport. It was the gun I had used to shoot the man who killed Claus.' He paused, avoiding eye contact with anyone. 'I threw away the gun on the chairlift. Somehow, they managed to find it, and now bullets from it have miraculously appeared in some of the corpses in Zurich's morgue. Remy knows it's a game and that it's bullshit evidence which would never secure a conviction. But, technically, it's a murder charge. Calvert on the other hand, has used Verbier's webcams to falsify an image of me shooting someone from the chairlift. That's also an attempted murder charge if anyone wanted to pursue it.'

'I don't understand. That's straightforward self-defence, and you were returning fire towards hired killers, wanted by Interpol, who were shooting at you and killed Claus. No court would ever convict.' Francois held his hands in the air.

'You're right, Francois. Almost certainly I wouldn't be charged, and if I was, I would be acquitted on the grounds of self-defence. However, for me that's not the problem. The problem is that twelve years ago, in order for me to leave the British Army, I had to sign an NDA skewed strongly in favour of the Army. Within this lopsided agreement is a catch-all condition whereby if I'm held, in any jurisdiction, for a serious offence – irrespective of guilt, or whether or not I'm charged, and even if it never gets to court – the Army can drag me back to serve a sentence in one of their prisons. It's risk mitigation. Ex-soldiers like me are a liability, more prone to offend, easy prey for the tabloids to finance their many addictions by becoming "whistleblowers", revealing the military's numerous shortcomings. It's not Russia; they can't lock us up and throw away the keys. They want ex-soldiers like me just to fade away, out of the spotlight, away from public anything. Then there's less chance we'll be talking about failings which the Army don't want the public finding out about.'

'I've heard of exits like this, the British Army isn't the only one. Most other countries struggle with similar conflicts.' It was probably the longest speech Ben had heard Francois make.

Ben continued. 'To play it straight, like a normal citizen, is simply too big a risk for me to take. I cannot admit to having a gun and shooting six or more people and not expect the Police to go through due process, which includes holding me while they investigate. And if the Army found out – Calvert could screw me by telling them – that's all it would take for them to incarcerate me. Like you, Remy is also confused as to why I won't admit to a self-defence incident, which is why he's fabricating evidence to pressure me. It's all bullshit, isn't it?' He sat back, and Stephanie placed a hand on his.

'Okay, first things first. Leave Remy to me.' Francois picked up the thread. 'I can calm him down. I've got more over him than he realises. I don't think he's bad either, but he's got a job to do. What about Danny and Calvert, what's happening there?'

'It would be great if you could get Remy off my back, Francois, thanks. With Calvert, it's different. He's conjured-up an informant who is willing to testify Danny got some confidential naval plans and sold them. That would convict Danny of treason. That's a tough gig. Danny doesn't know about this yet, so leave it to me to tell him. I wanted to get something on Calvert before I ruined Danny's day.'

'And you kept this all to yourself so we could plant the PDCs to avenge my father?'

'Yes. I didn't want you, or any of you, to worry even more about this crap and let it distract us. I blame Claus for being so bloody likeable.' Ben sought to lighten the moment.

Ingrid and Stephanie exchanged glances.

'Calvert is a different proposition.' Ingrid explained. 'Claus always said he was Liang's local puppet. If he is the Five's puppet, that makes him as dangerous as them, possibly even more so if he's trying to impress Liang.'

'Provided you still trust me,' Ben tried to look at each of them in the room and on the video call, 'then leave Calvert to me. I've now got something on him, and he's definitely picked the wrong battle with me.'

'Ben, I'm not sure we can expect you to ever forgive us for what we've dragged you into. We really thought we were doing it for all the right reasons.' There was something different about Ingrid as she spoke; something Ben noticed but couldn't put his finger on.

Hilda and Francois chimed in agreement with Ingrid, who continued. 'I too am very worried about Calvert. He's unhinged and dangerous, and he's got Liang behind him. You can't take them on just by yourself.'

'Don't worry, Ingrid. I know how to deal with him, but we have to capture the data from the PDCs first.'

'Okay, Ben, if you're sure, but please be extra careful. You've put yourself on the line so many times already. Well, as Hilda said, tomorrow will be a long one,' concluded Ingrid.

The call had only just finished when Ben turned to Stephanie. 'I wanted to—'

'Don't say anything.' She stood and walked to the door leading to the main cabin. She locked it, turned, paused, and engaged his eyes before walking slowly back to him. Then she reached out a hand, which Ben took as he followed her through the other door.

Chapter Thirty-Four

Uwe Mueller's daughter had chosen the ringtone for his phone. It was a modern, electronic dance riff, and he quite liked it. When it woke him in his Hotel de Paris bedroom and he discovered it was Thomas Liang calling, he hated it.

'What the hell do you want? It's one o'clock in the morning,' snapped an annoyed Mueller.

'My dear Uwe, I am so sorry,' lied a not-sorry Thomas Liang. 'I'm calling you to let you know that you've been breached, as have I, and as have Bianca Sabitini and Brad Towner. Say good morning to Uwe, everyone.' Bianca Sabitini, at midnight in London, and Brad Towner, at seven pm in New York, sheepishly mumbled their greetings to their co-members.

Mueller quickly woke up. 'What? How have we been breached?'

'I've no idea how each of you has been breached, you'll have to find out for yourselves, but I can guarantee that you have. I've just sent you all a photograph of a small device they have planted, and you need to find them. I found mine,' Liang bragged. 'It was planted by Oppenheimer's brat. She conned her way into my apartment, if you can believe it, but celebrated too early by removing her wig when she was in the lift.

'She was spotted by my security on the elevator's CCTV, who checked it with our security contractors. In an instant they came back with her identity – Stephanie Raphael DeLouise Oppenheimer. Complete amateurs.' Liang's irritation was evident to the others. 'I've had my tech people look at it. It's very basic and simply catches signals sent to a WiFi router. You need to look near the router you will be using for tonight's video-conference call.'

'What was Stephanie Oppenheimer, of all people, doing in your apartment in the first place?'

'Fucking hell, Uwe, what does that matter? She conned her way in.' Liang's calmness was cracking. 'What matters now is that none of you do anything stupid, Uwe.' No-one spoke, everyone understood.

'To repeat, nothing stupid or out of the ordinary. First, you need to locate this device. Then you leave it in place.' Surprise murmurings from the other three.

'Yes. You leave it in place. My plan is to draw them out. I'll make them expose themselves so we can find out what they know, what evidence they have, what measures we need to take. We will proceed with the video call tonight as planned, but as we now know they'll be recording us, we put on a show for them. My EA will circulate an agenda, and we'll talk about world peace, and how to feed the starving millions, and crap like that.' Liang's voice was becoming strained.

'You all need to increase your security arrangements, because my IT people tell me they'll need to return after the call to retrieve what's on these devices. Maybe within a day or two. They will need to be near to it when they do, possibly in the same room. You will capture and then deal with any and all who come to retrieve these devices. Is that clear?'

Thomas' demeanour left them in no doubt as to the repercussions if they failed to deliver. 'I suggest you immediately go wherever you need to and find these devices. I expect a call back from all of you within the hour to advise that you have succeeded. Are there any questions?'

'Yeah.' Brad Towner's arrogant drawl bullied its way onto the line, 'Evidence gathered in this way is inadmissible in a court of law. I think we all know what they were really hoping to gain from our video call – some incriminating falsehoods with which to blackmail us.'

Towner continued his ironic creed. 'We've dealt with Claus, so he cannot have been the one to advise them on this misadventure. Since none of us four did, the only other person who could have done so is the recently widowed Frau Oppenheimer.' He paused, malevolence stalking in his shadow. 'If that is so, have you given any consideration as to how best to resolve this?'

The calculatingly dangerous Towner left the unasked question hanging. Even though it was a voice and not a video call, each of them knew that no-one was moving, awaiting Thomas Liang's response.

'A very good point, Brad, and one I have considered. Uwe, you know the Oppenheimers quite well, don't you?' The atmosphere thickened; Uwe's chest tightened. 'I recall you were vocal in your defence of Oppenheimer because you knew him; "he was almost a friend", I think you said.' Uwe felt the tip of Liang's verbal scalpel press against his heart. 'Is she a threat? If so, how do you propose we deal with that threat?'

Uwe mumbled something incomprehensible. Horrified by the direction of Towner and Liang's thinking, he knew he was the Five's weakest link, and he knew how Thomas dealt with weak links.

'Do you think Ingrid is our problem, Uwe?'

Trauma and paralysing fear devoured Mueller's defences. Despite his air-conditioned room, sweat soaked his bedsheets and collected in small pools in the folds of his skin as he sat, hunched, his head bowed down, and he started to gently sob.

'I-I don't know, Thomas. She's old and must be very upset after poor Claus. I doubt she could plan something like this. They must have had professionals, like the people we hire. This is not the work of an old lady.' Mueller gained a little strength from pushing back against Liang. He finished stronger than he had started but knew he was still in danger.

'You may be right, Uwe. We shall see but, if she is a problem, you'll have to deal with her.' Then breezily to all of them, he added, 'Excellent. I look forward to talking with you all in one hour's time.' And Thomas Liang ended the call.

The weight of guilt crushed Uwe Mueller's mind. He knew that sleep would not be visiting him anytime soon as he shuffled, broken, to seek solace from his minibar.

*

Ten minutes later, Thomas Liang answered Brad Towner's phone call.

'We found it, and we know who, when, and how it was planted. And get this, I can tell you to the minute when he'll be coming back to retrieve it,' cried a jubilant Brad Towner, as he went on to explain about Ben disguised as Marc Barrault, and the faked terror alert two days prior. After the hoaxed evacuation of Four Prudential Plaza, the building's facilities management and tenants had spent the next twenty-four hours wrestling with the Department of Homeland Security in acrimonious finger-pointing.

'A fake CV, guy calling himself Marc Barrault, applied for a job. Bullshitted his way past security, set off the alarm system, and planted the damn thing. Meeting hadn't finished by the time the alarm went off, so the guy's agreed to come back in tomorrow. Pretext he's giving us is to finish the meeting, but he's coming back to download that device thing. We'll be locked-and-loaded with a good old-fashioned welcoming committee for him,' boomed a very punchy Brad Towner.

'Good work, Brad. I have total confidence that you will deliver a satisfactory conclusion. I wish I could have as much confidence in Uwe, don't you?' And Liang hung up.

*

Bianca Sabitini was the next to call. 'I found it, Thomas. I didn't want to attract attention, so I came to the office on my own. It's two am, and when I got here, the cleaners were making their rounds. One of them told me there was an English guy who worked with them for just one night, and on that night, he cleaned in my office. That was three nights ago – just before those extra security lunatics you arranged spotted the Oppenheimer daughter and her banker friend. That's when those cowboys you employed, instead of quietly and unobtrusively taking them off somewhere to deal with them, left Canary Wharf looking like a war zone.'

'We are in a war, Bianca, and the first casualty of war is innocence. The extraordinary rewards we enjoy justify taking extraordinary measures,' Thomas responded firmly.

'The first casualty of war is actually truth, Thomas. And, as Cicero said, "In times of war the law falls silent." Well, if we are in a war as you call it, the law here certainly did not fall silent.

We've had all our staff interviewed, increased security, police crawling all over the place. You've attracted too much attention to us. Again.' Bianca replied equally as firmly.

Thomas Liang was struggling to recover from the previous night and was in no mood to compete in a pointless game of who had the best philosopher's quotes.

'Just make sure you capture and deal appropriately and quietly with whoever comes to retrieve the data on that device, Bianca.'

'I have some Belarussian associates who are slightly more subtle and efficient than your cowboys.'

'Good.' And Thomas Liang hung up.

*

The phone rang. Uwe Mueller's number appeared on the screen, and at first Liang thought the encrypted line had a bad connection until the voice on the other end cleared its throat.

'I found that little white thing.' Uwe Mueller slurred his words so much that, with his guttural German pronunciation, Liang could hardly understand what he was saying.

'Uwe, it is important you put it back where you found it. You must leave the device where you found it, put it back, and then I will take care of everything else.'

Uwe Mueller was too drunk to read anything into the last sentence. He hung up and collapsed onto his bed, exhausted by alcohol and emotions.

After he finished the call with Mueller, Thomas Liang made another encrypted call to an untraceable number.

'Da,' came the short reply.

'I need something taken care of,' Thomas Liang continued. 'I want to make a point; this one needs to look like an execution.'

'Depending on circumstances, an execution instead of an accident can be expensive.'

'Cost is not an issue. I'll send you the details.' Thomas Liang hung up, looking at his hand that had held the phone. It glistened with sweat in Hong Kong's mid-morning sun.

The stakes are increasing, thought Thomas Liang.

Chapter Thirty-Five

'Nice call, everyone. There were moments during that when even I was believing my own bullshit.' It was one minute after their Friday night video call, complete with its fake script, and Thomas Liang was in celebratory mood.

'We have to be remorseless with the Kill Plan.' Liang's words were deliberately chosen. 'When you have your foot on your enemy's throat, you do not take it off until you have finished them. You all know what you have to do. I know you will not fail me.' Liang, the self-imposed leader, imposed his will even further.

'Be vigilant. We have to find everyone who is working against us and eradicate them all.' He slammed his balled fist down onto his glass desk. 'When you have them, use whatever means necessary to extract everything, and when you have that, you must call me. I shall not be sleeping until this is done and we are free of them.'

Even if the other three recognised the necessity of the strategy, to varying degrees of reluctance or agreement, they were wondering how it had come to this. Especially Uwe Mueller.

*

Warily, Marc Barrault placed his briefcase into the X-Ray scanner on the ground floor reception of 4 Prudential Plaza. It was midday, Saturday, quiet without the weekday hordes, but there was still enough activity, and legacy paranoia from last week's evacuation, for a fully staffed security team. He carefully folded his suit jacket and placed it into the tray behind his briefcase.

Two hours ago, he and Stephanie had landed anonymously into Teterboro Airport's private terminal. An hour's ride in a Town Car and they were in lower Manhattan. For their rendezvous point, Ben had chosen an open space near the Holland tunnel, with a good field of vision plus good escape routes and a complex road system to lose a tail, if that were necessary. In the centre was an ornamental fountain framed with benches, crammed with high-rise-apartment dwellers lunching in the late summer sun or lazing on the grass. Stephanie would walk through it every half hour, keep herself within five minutes fast walk at all times, and await Ben's call.

As he had predicted, even though tensions were still high following last week's hoax evacuation, an office building's scanner was still nowhere near as good as the ones used in airports. His briefcase and jacket's normal contents arose no suspicion with the scanner operative. Not so for him, as the metal detector archway emitted an excited beeping as he walked through jacket-less.

With a wry smile, and exhaling a sigh of predictability, he held up his hands in mock surrender. Rolling back his left shirt sleeve, he revealed a wicked looking, twenty-five-centimetre scar running the length of his muscled forearm. The scar was bordered on either side with healed puncture marks, from where a painful and mechanical force was used to close the once gaping wound after the long metal pin had been inserted.

'Happens every time. Bit of a pain, but I've got used to it.' He clenched and unclenched his hand, lifting his arm up and around to show he was not hiding anything, and leaving his forearm with its horrendous scar on full view for further inspection.

'D'ya mind if I ask where you got that?' enquired the archway operator.

'Helmand,' replied a stony-faced Ben. 'Hurts less now. Not a physical hurt, if you know what I mean?'

He did, as evidenced by the respectful way the operator touched an index finger to the peak of his cap as he waved Ben through. The set-jawed and stony-faced Ben nodded in appreciation as he collected his briefcase and headed to the main reception desk.

Before taking the elevator, he detoured via the Men's restroom. No-one would have noticed any outward difference when he exited, unless they closely examined the toilet's trash can. The discarded fake skin, more usually used in a Broadway theatre, told how the twenty-centimetre-long commando knife strapped to the underside of his forearm had evaded discovery. It was now in the place he had been trained to hide it, held by two elastic straps inside his right calf muscle. The forearm scar was real, as was the twenty-five-centimetre pin still in his arm, and it had come from Helmand province. *The most successful lies are the ones closest to the truth,* he reminded himself as the lift announced its arrival on the eighty-sixth floor.

'Marc, so good of you to return at short notice. That was quite a thing last time, huh?' An effusive Brad Towner flashed his ready smile as he shook Ben's hand and backslapped him into his office.

'Please, take a seat. I've asked a couple of my guys to join us, as they're in the same game as you, so to speak.' Towner was getting high on the vicarious danger of the encounter and its likely conclusion. As high as he had got from four lines of Columbian and those two Thai whores last week. *Said they were twins – who gives a shit, all look the damn same. I made them sweat for their dollar. Or, more accurately, their thousand dollars, but who's counting?*

Shelia, his PA, showed the two casually and identically dressed men into Brad Towner's office then left.

The alarms that rang this time were in Ben's mind.

'Guys, come in. Marc, can I introduce Vincent Stabilo, Vinny, my head of security and his associate, Raul Fergani.'

The casual dress enhanced, rather than hid, their healthy occupation with keeping in shape, doubtless it had contributed to their survival in combat. The plastic smiles were a more recent, private sector development. Vinny went to Ben's left and Raul to his right – just out of reach.

Vinny smiled and stuck out his hand. 'Great to meet you, Marc.'

But Ben was exploring exit strategies and not handshakes, until he felt cold metal on the back of his neck.

'Yep, it's suppressed. So, if you don't do exactly as we tell you, you're dead, and not even the nice lady sitting just outside of this office will hear or know anything happened. Now, sit down, Mr. Whatever-the-fuck-your-name-is.'

'We heard from Mr. Towner about your amazing diversionary tactic which allowed you time to plant that little device two days ago. That was cool, and now you're back to download?'

The words hit Ben like a runaway train, but before another word was thought or uttered, Raul kicked him hard behind his knees, ramming him down into the chair, and Vinny quickly secured his wrists to the chair's arms with cable-ties. Raul walked round to join the two other men in front of Ben.

'OK, Mr. Fake-Name, you know the drill. We're gonna waterboard you, burn you with an oxy-lance, and pull out your fingernails. That's when you're gonna give us wrong names which you'll plead with us are the right names. We'll discover they're wrong, which is when you enter a world of unbelievable pain, then you'll tell us everything. So, be smart, save yourself some indescribable agony.' Raul Fergani's lips curled away from his teeth in a snarl.

'You mentioned a drill. You shouldn't use a drill with waterboarding. Don't you know it's dangerous to mix water and electricity?'

Ben was strapped into the chair and couldn't turn his head any quicker as Raul hit him hard across the bridge of his nose with the butt of his pistol. The room swam, and he was in danger of losing consciousness. Intense pain and a strong flow of tangy copper-tasting blood gushed down his throat. The convulsive cough sprayed a mouthful of thick blood over every casually dressed person in front of him.

'Jeezz, what the!' All three involuntarily jumped back. Blood gushed from Ben's nose and mouth as he tried repeatedly to raise his head.

'Ssshh,' implored a worried Towner, whose voyeuristic adventure was getting out of his control.

Ben's attempt at a shout was silenced in its infancy, courtesy of another swingeing and vicious arc from the butt of Raul's gun. He immediately lost consciousness, and Towner's intercom buzzed. It was Shelia, his PA.

'It's OK, Shelia. Mr. Barrault's had some sort of fit, and he's fallen over. I'll get Vinny and Raul to get him to hospital. Give me a minute.'

Towner clicked into enraged mode again. 'What the fuck happened to the plan of: restrain – sedate – discreetly exit, using the excuse of him passing out? Even though it's a Saturday, we can't walk him through the office looking like a truck hit him, for chrissakes.'

Brad Towner knew he had traded subtlety for ruthless barbarity when he gave his specification to Vinny. He said he wanted someone who could get the toughest guy to plead for his Mommy in the shortest time possible. Vinny had delivered as ordered, but it came with a health-warning for Raul Fergani – a man who evidently loved his job too much.

'Sorry, Mr. Towner, you're right, this wasn't the plan,' Vinny assured his boss while casting angry glances at his oblivious colleague. 'But while he's out cold, we can clean him up. We'll say he passed out, hit his head, and we're taking him to hospital. It'll be fine.'

'It better goddam well be fine. I'm paying you a small fortune for this, and so far you're not delivering. Get him outta here and find out everything he knows, and quickly.' This had not been Brad Towner's intention. He had hoped to be the first to call Thomas Liang with the names of the others. Fergani's sadistic obsession had set back his plans.

*

The pain reached deep into Ben's semi-conscious mind. He could feel someone cleaning his face irrespective of the discomfort caused. He exaggerated his drowsiness to distract himself from the pain; difficult when every part of his head hurt, and a rough male hand was scrubbing his injuries.

After they had cleaned off the worst of the blood, he let Stabilo and Fergani lift him out of the chair. He feigned unconsciousness as they draped each of his arms over their shoulders, effortlessly supporting him so that his feet bore hardly any weight. Like two seconds carrying an unconscious boxer out of the ring. He hung there limply, trying to clear his head as he finalised his next move.

Towner had calmed down slightly. 'OK, get him out of here without attracting any more goddam attention to him, or you.'

He pointed at each of his two and, he had just decided, ex-security operatives.

'Yes, Mr. Towner,' replied a contrite Vincent Stabilo, pulling out a military grade walkie-talkie. 'We're coming down now. Bring the car to the B1 level.'

Even though it was a Saturday, CBAC's business was 24/7, so there would always be a skeleton staff working on a rota basis. CEO's offices at companies like CBAC do not always want their visitors to be on public display. Except for a very concerned looking Shelia, their journey to the elevator avoided any open office spaces.

They were almost at the elevator bank when Ben began Act One of his escape plan.

'Sick, going to be sick,' his mumbled words were deliberately barely audible.

'Oh jeezz, you asshole, Fergani. He's gonna be sick because you concussed him. You didn't need to hit him again. You take him to the John, let him chuck. I'll secure an empty elevator.'

Ben wasn't faking everything. His head really did feel like it was splitting open with the pain, as he hung himself from Raul's shoulders like a limp, wet sail. His head was hanging down, partly deliberate deception, partly unavoidable physical consequence of Raul's brutality.

From his view of the floor, his mood improved when he saw Vincent Stabilo's feet turn away and the sound of his footsteps receding as he walked towards the elevator lobby. Ben estimated he now had three minutes maximum. He affected an even greater inertia with sound effects. Act One in Ben's plan worked on the theory it would be almost impossible to pass two men of athletic builds through a standard-width toilet door at the same time. Particularly when one was unbalanced and supporting most of the other's weight. That would lead to one party to become very distracted, and the other free to act.

Draping his right arm, plus an exaggerated amount of his weight to emphasise his lack of consciousness, over Raul's shoulder, Ben drew the sadist even closer to him. As they squeezed through the toilet door, Ben, head hanging down in feigned submission, dropped his left arm lower. Increasing the weight transfer to Raul, his arm nearly touching the floor, allowing him to reach the tungsten steel blade strapped to his right calf.

He rode above the ringing in his ears to listen for the click of the door closing behind them. There it was, just as he had scripted it.

Raul hefted him towards the bright-white line of ceramic sinks, not realising that had he the time – which he did not – he would have admired the artistry of his own death. Ben performed Raul's execution with a precise and murderous purpose. Raul only knew something was wrong, after it was already wrong.

The instant of Ben's weightlessness was fractionally before he drove his legs, straightened from the waist, and powered the keenly-tipped, tungsten steel shaft through skin, muscle, and abdomen to penetrate Raul's heart. Blood pressure drop is so immediate that the brain loses functionality, resulting in the often-reported look of surprise on a victim's face. As indeed it was now, when Ben's powerful upward thrust impaled his torturer on a steel lance.

Ben held the inert Raul a couple of centimetres from his face. The latter's wide eyes stared blankly into Ben's.

'My name is Sergeant Benjamin Raymond Mason, First Battalion, Parachute Regiment. It is not "Mr. Fake-Name", and you should remember that.'

A fast-spreading carpet of deep crimson posed a stark contrast to the glossy white tiles, as he noiselessly lowered his would-be executioner to the floor.

Leaning heavily on the sink, barely conscious, he let the taps run. Ben and the man in the mirror stared at each other; neither recognised the other. Ben's reflection presented an irregular triangle of blood instead of a face. Its apex on the bridge of his nose, the baseline was his jawline, and everything in between shimmered deep red. The macabre image was balanced by a contusion from Raul's second blow, which had created a semi-sphere of trauma above his left ear, now the riverhead of a steady flow of blood.

Ben ran the taps and plunged his head into the cold water, letting it wrap around his head and calm the furnace of body and mind. He closed his eyes and welcomed the sensation of the cooling blanket as it recharged his senses. The only clear thought was that they had run out of time.

He started to prioritise his actions, arranging them in an order which would save as many lives as possible. Careful to avoid the expanding red pool forming around his motionless assailant, he searched Raul's pockets to find a Glock pistol, a mobile phone, and a military grade walkie-talkie. He pointed the phone towards Raul's face, and moved it until the screen brightened, face-ID kicked in, and he disarmed the screen security function. Putting the phone in his pocket then, silently he made for the door.

With the gun in one hand, he pulled the door slowly inwards, tuning his ringing ears for any protesting squeak from the hinges. None came; only the distant sound of Vinny talking into a radio, not close, but close enough. Vinny was animated, speaking quickly about what had happened, annoyed with Raul. By now he would have secured an empty elevator, holding it for Raul, expecting him to come round the corner supporting a semi-conscious Ben at any moment. Ben guessed Vinny was not a patient man, so he had to move.

With the Glock poised, he opened the door fully and scanned the limited field of vision. No-one to be seen or heard, just the distant Vinny, less animated now, still giving instructions.

It was a Saturday, so the floor was virtually deserted, but Ben knew he was too injured to tackle eighty-six floors of concrete stairs. He would have to find another way as he stepped out and into the lobby. His vision blurred and he swayed, expecting Vinny to come sprinting around the corner any second. Still feeling faint, he set off through the labyrinth of small internal corridors towards the centre of the huge building. Stealing softly on his toes, he made his way along the vacant inner passages, still with the gun at the ready. Past a refrigerated vending machine humming obliviously, moving quietly away from a filing room in which two people were having a pointless discussion about file numbering. Far behind him he heard a panicked loud, male voice shout, followed shortly after by a woman's scream. Presumably, she'd doubted her colleague and had gone to see for herself.

Someone else, or was it Vinny himself, had decided this event should be marked by the fire alarm. Possibly a legacy nervousness from last week's hoax evacuation. Ben had just made the bare concrete lobby of the Facilities Elevator, but unhelpfully it was home to two alarm bells whose clanging reverberations echoed inside the bare concrete chamber and his throbbing head. His mind was dense with pain and refused to clear. *What was the number that Mike Pearson told me to use? Hell, it was only two days ago.*

As the bells continued, they rocked his body; he shook his head and was quickly reminded that pain had no limits. *The number was an important date, but what was the date? That was followed by a #, but what was the number?*

Ben heard footsteps running along the corridors towards him. Doors crashed open nearby, shouted commands, surprised innocents screaming muted by the intervening doors. He held the gun ready. More shouting, then a door banging echoed loudly open along a passageway near him, setting off painful explosions in his head. Men's voices were raised, shouting to one another. Stabilo and his guys. *They're checking room-to-room, what was that damn number?*

Of course, 1776, America's most celebrated anniversary, what else?

He quickly punched in the numbers followed by #. He could hear the sonorous hum of the lift's huge cables on the other side of the battered elevator doors. The raised voices were closing in, so close he could almost make out individual words. The lift crawled slowly towards him, so did the voices, as time crawled slower still. The lift emitted a bored clunk, as the lethargic doors crunched along their interminably slow journey to fully open.

He was punching the B2 button as he stumbled into the elevator, willing the doors to close quicker, the voices now only one unlocked door away. The elevator's doors ambled along their disinterested return journey as he crouched in the centre of the lift floor, the gun in a two-handed grip. His blurred sight was aiming along the barrel at what would be head-height of the next person to come through the door, the door that was swimming in and out of focus.

Ben felt faint but fought the urge to lie down, lie down and sleep. The shouting grew louder, the excited voices ran closer, he was panting as the gap in the doors drew smaller and his head throbbed more. The doors' apathetic reunion completed in a dull clunk, and the elevator jolted and began its measured descent. He collapsed onto the floor.

He couldn't move. The Northern Lights flashed inside his head as small detonations of pain sent spasms across his head and into his aching neck while he ticked off his mental survival To-Do list: Exit by stealing a car from the basement carpark, alert the others, get back to the plane and as far away as quickly as possible. He thought he had known before, but he certainly knew now that the Five were completely ruthless in pursuit of their objectives. *Who and when would the next ambush be? Next retrieval?*

Monte Carlo, Hilda and Christophe. The realisation made him sit up so quickly it sent a herd of pain-laden needles stampeding across his head and chase down his neck. He fought away the pain. *Shit, they'll blow them away; what's the time in Monte Carlo? Eight pm, they'll be at dinner. I've got to warn them.*

The escalator's battered doors opened onto a rectangular grey concrete chamber twenty feet below street level, accompanied by the shrill, reverberating fire alarm. He checked his and Raul's mobile – no signal. He had to get to street level to call.

As he followed the signs pointing the way to the basement car park, he didn't have to wait long before the tyres of the Tribeca Linen Service minivan squealed on the painted floor to announce its hurried exit, climbing the ramp from the floor below. Ben stepped out from the concrete pillar as it drew around the corner, holding the gun steady on the driver's head. Act Two of his plan was realised when the driver wisely brought the van to an immediate halt.

'Good decision, my friend. Now, keep your hands where I can see them and step out of the vehicle. Turn round and take off your cap and jacket.'

Even better, thought Ben, *a logoed- baseball cap to cover the damage.*

Ben knew precisely where, and how hard, to hit the short but broad driver. He had done it many times before, just hard enough, behind his ear with the butt of the handgun. *Enough to buy me two or three minutes,* he calculated, as he put on the man's jacket and cap. Climbing into the minivan, he pulled down the cap, started the engine, and drove up two levels.

Welcome afternoon sunlight beckoned on the far side of the underground car park's exit barrier. The familiarity of the logoed minivan, plus his cursory, if cheeky, thumbs-up to cover his face, and he was waved through the barrier. Gunning the engine for the last stretch of the exit ramp, he was out.

After two blocks, and risking the attention of a traffic officer, he pulled in to the left-hand side as soon as he could, bumping the low kerb and drawing the two phones from his pocket. His had a full signal and he dialled Hilda. It rang out to voicemail. *She must be on silent as they're in the restaurant.*

Ben left a short and clear message: 'Cover's blown. They know everything. Get out asap. I'll warn the others but get out now.'

Trying hard to remain positive and focused, he called Christophe, silently praying they did not both have their phones on silent. But same result. 'Shit'! he exclaimed out loud, slamming his palm against the steering wheel. 'At least leave them on vibrate if you have to go silent, for chrissakes.'

He pulled out Raul's phone, tapping the screen to wake it, then he froze.

With the screen security function disarmed, the phone went straight to the start-up screen. Raul's wallpaper picture was of a tattoo – a tattoo of a beautiful bluebird on a woman's tanned right shoulder. Ben had the same one on his left shoulder; he and his wife had matching tattoos inked into their shoulders in Cambodia a few years ago, and this was a photograph of hers. He knew it was hers, as he had studied it in minute detail a million times until she died in a car crash in the upper reaches of the Amazon River, miles from where she was supposed to have been. He sat, open-mouthed and motionless as the pain in his head was exceeded by the turmoil in his mind. The sharp tap on his window made him jump.

The first thing Ben registered were the gold letters, NYPD, melted into the badge set against the familiar dark blue livery of a New York traffic cop's uniform. Just below were half a dozen service ribbons and his precinct number decorating his lapel.

'Red Zone, buddy. Can't stop here, I'll have to ticket you,' barked the cop.

Ben pointed his head to the floor, started the engine in an instant, engaged drive, and was already moving to curtail any further conversation. He was on autopilot, staring wide-eyed but not registering anything, a mind too crowded to process anything more. He just drove in a haze, he didn't know where. He drove south and turned into a smaller one-way street running east, then pulled into a vacant bay on the left. His head was attached to his body through a causeway of pain and confusion.

Feeling very alone, he rested his head against the steering wheel and closed his eyes for a beat. He slowed his breathing and pulled out Raul's phone. He hadn't imagined it; the skin tone and texture were unmistakeable. He stroked his fingertips softly across the screen. It was Sam, it was her shoulder, it was her tattoo, he was one hundred per cent certain. He zoomed in, examining each pixel. He noticed some small dots – red dots. Sam had no blemishes, not there, not around her bluebird, not while she was alive. He was looking at her spilt blood. He was confused and in pain, but now he had a third emotion – doubt.

Securing Raul's phone in his pocket he used his own mobile to re-dial Christophe and Hilda's numbers, with the same lonely and crushing result. He hastily sent a message to all the phones in the group they had created – hoping that even if they had their phones to silent, they might hear a text alert.

An unfamiliar panic formed at the fringes of his emotions. His head throbbed from Raul's treatment, but it was worse when he shook it. *Positive action, that's what I need, but what? What should I do next?* His overloaded mind processed slowly: Stephanie was safe, she was at the RDV point. Next retrieval, Andy. He dialled Andy Taylor's mobile number. No reply, just eternal ringing; not even a voicemail facility. Next? Ingrid. Call Ingrid. Slightly clearer now, he dialled Ingrid's mobile.

'Ja?' He almost didn't recognise her hesitant response.

'Ingrid. It's Ben. You must get hold of the Grill Room restaurant. You must warn Christophe and Hilda that they know everything. I was ambushed when I went to retrieve the data from the New York PDC, and they'll do the same to all of us. I heard it directly from them; they know everything. You've got to get away. Anywhere, somewhere far away and untraceable to you. I think they're coming for all of us now.'

'But how? How have they found out?'

'I don't know, but I do know they won't stop until we're all dead.'

Ben stopped, a sharp movement at the edge of the door mirror's reflection distracting his numbed mind. His instincts shouted loudly as in the mirror he saw the black Chevrolet Suburban turn into his side street.

On the passenger seat, Raul's walkie-talkie emitted a static squelch then announced, 'We've got him. I can see the van. We're on Bridge Street and he's just ahead of us, on the left. Towner's instructions are no prisoners.' It was Vinny Stabilo talking. Ben realised they must be talking to another vehicle behind them.

He watched them in the door mirror as they came up behind him at a measured pace – not too fast – hoping to maintain the element of surprise.

The radio squelched. 'Nice and easy, pull up level with him.'

The driver was pulling alongside. Ben was already crouched and turned towards them in anticipation, the dead Raul's powerful handgun held steady in a double-handed grip, pointing through the right-hand edge of the front passenger's window. As the Suburban's cab drew level, even before it had fully stopped, he unleashed a storm of nine-millimetre annihilation from Raul's gun into the front row, hitting the driver and front seat passenger with the next rapid burst. Retaliation preceding attack had taken them by surprise.

He had the minivan accelerating away as a hail of bullets from semi-automatic weapons from the other vehicle ripped into the side and the back of the minivan. Instinctively flinching, he went quickly through the gears, taking the engine to its maximum before crashing into the next gear. The fast-approaching traffic lights shone a beckoning green.

Ben's foot was already flat to the steel floor as the lights changed to red with thirty yards to go. He pushed his foot harder. Bullets clanged against the rear panels. Outnumbered and low on ammo, his options were limited. The heavy minivan hurtled flat out across the junction, clipping the rear fender of a south-bound yellow cab, sending it into a tyre-squealing blur of sideways motion. He corrected from the impact and flew head-long into the street on the other side, towards the next intersection and its red traffic lights, less than two hundred yards ahead.

One of the sweetest sounds ever heard, he reflected later, was the sound of unstoppable force meeting an immovable object. Particularly if one of them is a black Suburban carrying the remainder of Vincent Stabilo's crew. In what remained of the minivan's cracked door mirror, he saw smoke, carnage, and his salvation in the multi-car wreckage behind him.

Another of the city's numerous underground car parks provided temporary sanctuary. Descending the short ramp, he found an empty bay at the far end and sank his aching head onto his bloodied hands. *How the fuck did they find me?* Then he saw Raul's phone next to him. 'You idiot, Ben, you bloody idiot,' he shouted, as he threw Raul's phone through the open driver's window to shatter against the bare concrete wall. He was happy with his own memories; he had no room for any others.

Bright New York sun drilled through his eyes and into the back of his skull as he gunned the minivan up the steep exit ramp. He winced at the throbbing inside his head as he concentrated on his phone.

'Steph, are you at the rendezvous point?'

'Yes, but what's happened? I can hear police sirens all over the place, where are you?' Panic buffeted Stephanie's voice.

'I'm on my way to you now. It was a trap, an ambush. I'll be with you in ten minutes, we'll be at the plane in under an hour, so phone the plane, tell them to be ready to take off as soon as we get there. I'm driving a white Tribeca Linen Service van. When you've done that, find a pharmacy and buy everything you think we'll need to clean, stitch, and bandage, plus I need a clean shirt.'

'What?' Stephanie's shriek jarred inside his head. Flinching, he snatched the phone away from his ear. 'What's happened?'

'I'll tell you when I get there. Now, can you get those things please? And call Hilda. We can't go back to Hong Kong; they know everything. We've got to change our plans, and the safest place for us now is away from here and in Zurich. Get Hilda to tell the plane crew to file a flight plan there.'

*

'Shit.' Stephanie's face said as much as her word when she opened the minivan's door. 'I'm driving, you're in no state to. Move over and take this.' She handed him two bags filled with medical supplies and clothes. 'Christ, what happened to you?' She knew it sounded stupid, but the compassion in her voice asked the real question.

'They knew I was coming. We must warn the others.'

They pulled into the reserved parking lot at Teterboro airfield and Stephanie parked the stolen minivan out of sight. 'You still look like a train crash, but I'll do some more on the plane.'

Ben placed a hand on her arm. 'One of the men I've just killed had a photo of my wife on his phone. He had a photo of her tattoo, possibly taken just after she was killed. How the hell did that happen?' Keeping his eyes open hurt, but he kept them open. He had to, even if it hurt Stephanie too.

Initially, Stephanie's mouth moved but no words came out. 'I don't know, Ben,' she managed after a while. 'The Five seem capable of anything.' Stephanie spoke with the same hesitation that Ingrid had when he had told her he was being blackmailed.

Ben certainly looked and walked like he'd been in a train crash, but no-one says anything in a private plane reception when they know it's your Gulfstream that's just started its engines for you.

Chapter Thirty-Six

Ingrid's perfect French was as useful as her forceful manner with the polite lady who answered the Grill Room's phone. It was early evening in Monte Carlo, and Ingrid would not wait *un moment, Madame,* as she forced the point that this was a matter of the highest importance. The result, unfortunately, was the same. Mademoiselle Hilda Kaerle and her dinner guest had already left.

Again, she tried calling mobiles; again, with the same result. Time difference was not a consideration as she tried Stephanie's and Ben's phones. The result was a desolate echo of her earlier attempts. Even though Ben had already sent a brutally clear text to the group, to ease her feeling of complete helplessness, she also sent her own message to the group. Then she sat down in a beautiful, grand, and empty mansion overlooking the Zurich See and cried.

*

Had these events taken place a few hours earlier, she would have encountered a carefree Hilda and Christophe being shown to their table overlooking a shimmering Mediterranean.

'Was the signal on the veranda strong enough to retrieve all of it?' Hilda asked Christophe.

'Yes, it looks good. Danny said the app compresses everything, so while I pretended to take a selfie of us, it took less than a minute to capture. Don't know what's on it, but we can take a look when we get back.'

'Great, then we can send it over to Danny. I suppose now we just need to pretend we're enjoying dinner.' Hilda's eyes taunted. They were level with the rim of her glass as she extended it towards Christophe. Their on-off affair had variously aroused and tired them at different times in the last ten years. Both were independent spirits needing their own space but enjoying each other's company, and bodies.

Christophe smiled. 'All of a sudden, I'm not very hungry. Do you want to skip dessert?'

'To get the download to Danny? Yes, that's worth missing dessert.' Hilda's freckles tumbled into the dimples now creasing her cheeks.

Their young waiter, Jean-Marc, had been paying close attention to them. 'Madame, Monsieur, would you like me to order you a taxi?'

'*Non, merci.* We can walk from here,' Hilda replied. Thanking the beaming Jean-Marc, they made their way out into the Principality's balmy evening.

Jean-Marc could hardly wait to call the mobile number the stranger had given him. He had been promised the other five hundred Euros if he saw anyone using a phone suspiciously in the Grill Room. Easy money, as far as he was concerned.

A cloudless sky was the perfect canvas for the sun's legacy. Deeper hues above them washed lighter to the horizon, far away, out to where the sea met the sky. Nature had overlaid a narrow spectrum of purples on top of crimson melding into light mauve.

'Anything stupid, and I'll shoot her in the kneecap, then you in the face.' Neither Hilda nor Christophe had heard the men until they pressed in close to them, one discreetly holding a gun into Christophe's lower back. 'Don't be a dead hero. Be smart and get in the back.'

It hurt, but it didn't hurt that much as Hilda cried out in pain when the powerful hand gripped her elbow. The owner of the hand knew the greatest concentration of nerves was just above the joint, and he squeezed hard there. Hilda felt the pain, but not as much as her cry made out. She was painting a picture for her assailant.

'Ow, don't. You're really hurting me.' She offered almost zero resistance, stumbled a bit, and cried out again.

'Ouch, that really hurts. Please, please, stop.' Finishing off with a pathetic sob and an uncharacteristically submissive body shape, she made eye contact with Christophe, to tell him she understood and that she wasn't scared. They had been reading each other for so long, neither needed to add anything; they knew.

Hilda saw Christophe's faked and futile protestations draw a sharp jab in his back from a powerful looking handgun, directing them through the car's rear doors. Her assailant looked out from bottomless eyes to look into Hilda's. He started tunnelling into her mind, into her spirit, as he pulled even harder on the black plastic ties. She cried out in genuine pain as he pulled harder than he needed to; no doubt he wanted to see if extreme pain would break down her defences, allow him into Hilda's real self.

She hastily built barricades and stood behind them as the strong plastic ties bit into her wrists. He continued to stare deep into her eyes as he stood on the false ground she had built in front of her barricades, which said, 'I'm weak and scared.' With a last vicious tug on the cable ties, he gave a guttural shrug and jammed a sack of rough cloth over her head. Hilda knew she could not hold back his evil forever.

'Why are you doing this? We don't have any money. Please, what do you want?' Hilda pleaded. Even Christophe was surprised by the desperation in her voice as Hilda, head now hanging down, sobbed and softly sniffed.

'Shut the fuck up.' The malice was real, the tone bitter and cruel, a voice anchored in misery because it had known nothing else; it came from the one in front of her.

Hilda shook her head, clearing her mind. These men had to be working for the Five, but how had they found them, and what did this mean for the others? Her mind spun with all the possibilities before her muddled thoughts started to fall into some order. She and Christophe in the Grill Room to retrieve the data from Mueller's PDC to convict the Five, and suddenly they were kidnapped? This was not a coincidence; changing tack was required. She guessed Christophe's thoughts as they each raced to catch up and come to terms with their situation.

Through the isolating darkness of their hoods, the one who seemed to be the leader commanded, 'No more talking until we get there.'

Christophe was quick. 'I know I can't talk, but am I allowed to think? Because I think in future, I will seize my opportunities when they present themselves.'

He had just got the last word out when the man behind him hit him hard with his gun. Hilda flinched at the sickening whump of metal on the bone of Christophe's skull; he slumped, groaning, to one side. Not unconscious, but only just.

Hilda couldn't help herself. 'Stop it, please stop it.'

Hilda never saw the fist that came fast out of the darkness, but she felt its full weight as it crashed hard into her face. It snapped her head backwards, and she felt sick as salty blood filled her nose and mouth. She coughed up the fluids seeping down her throat, her eyes furiously watering as the hood's rough fabric burned her right cheek. Disoriented, with eyes tightly closed, she saw a galaxy of stars crazily spinning around the edges of her vision.

The man behind gave a sarcastic laugh, and revenge set its foundations. 'He said no more talking, are you deaf or what?'

Her cheek throbbed in time with her pulse, and she felt the unnatural heat inside it push the swelling out further so that it rubbed against the hood. She dropped her head to one side, moving the soreness away from the material. Her face felt raw and sore, and the hood now felt hot and suffocating. She shook her head; it helped a little. Hatred became her latest ally, and it helped to quell the panic rising inside her.

She knew she had to distract herself, recalling moments in the past when she had wanted to give up but had never done so: the last ten kilometres of her first marathon; the middle day of the Marathon De Sable. The distraction helped.

Hilda started to compose herself, calmer now, to concentrate on where they were going. She felt her phone buzz in her pocket. She remembered that in the restaurant they had put them on silent. Seconds later, Christophe's phone emitted a barely audible hum and vibrated. In the darkness she felt a slight movement from Christophe, a signal; he had also heard. Her intuition was confirmed when, a few seconds later, both phones emitted a familiar ping to signal the arrival of a group text. A barely audible 'Hmm' spoke volumes.

'Get their bloody phones,' the leader shouted, as rough hands hastily searched for their mobiles. 'Take out the SIMs, snap them, and throw the phones out.'

Hilda felt the rush of warm evening air as the rear windows slid open. She heard brittle plastic and Perspex smash against stone before the windows sealed them in again. A hint of jasmine briefly interrupted the odour of male sweat and her fear. Another avenue of salvation closed.

Hilda knew Christophe's thoughts would be in tune with hers; in the past it had happened at different times. They had taken turns to be the unrequited lover, and she understood why he had invited being hit; he was communicating with her. He was sending her a message, and she knew what it was. Their kidnappers were working for the Five, which meant they probably knew about the PDCs, so there was no longer any pretence. War had been declared, and she knew Christophe would have come to the same conclusion: this was their final chapter.

She sobbed, and this time it was for real, as she leant into him and whispered, 'I know.'

'Shut up, bitch, or you'll get another one.' The kidnapper in the back seat jabbed her hard with the barrel of his gun.

Hilda leaned back into the darkness. Her neck and shoulders ached with tension, her head pounded, but she closed her eyes and slowly, ever so slowly, she breathed in Christophe. She smelled their uncompleted life. She smelled the smile in his eyes and the sensation of his fingers on her flesh. She smelled the memories of their lovemaking. She smelled his easy manner, his laughter, and the smile that crinkled his face. She thought she could smell the salt in his tears through her hood, although she could not be certain, as hers were flowing freely down her cheeks. While she would gladly give her life for his, she knew he would not give her the chance.

I've got to distract myself. What was it Ben said? He would distract himself with positive action. Hilda repeated the mantra in her throbbing head, ignoring the impossibility of the situation. She would work out where they were and how to escape.

She turned her attention to the car, how fast were they going, how it was moving, what type of road were they on. They weren't going fast, they drove in a low gear for a few hundred metres at most, then a sharp bend, the gradient eased her back in the seat. The engine was straining, driving uphill, another short straight, another curve, another uphill. They must be headed due north, the steepest route out of Monte Carlo. That would eventually take them into the hills and the mountains beyond. Wooded and sparsely travelled, few people and fewer houses. Only two roads went up there. *If I'm right,* she thought, *we'll come to the Autoroute soon, where we can go east or west along that, or further into the mountains beyond.*

Her question was answered a few minutes later. They weren't driving fast but she could hear fast traffic nearby. Hilda recognised the sound of the Autoroute and now knew, to within a few hundred metres, where they were. The sound of the traffic disappeared, then reappeared on their right – the underpass. She now knew their location to within a few metres.

Hilda decided to celebrate by emitting a series of deliberately pathetic whimpers to continue painting an impression of vulnerability with her captors. She knew the road well, so well that she counted down the metres to where the tarmac changed, the tyres went from humming a melody to a discordant thudding sound as they approached and went past the Monte Carlo Golf Club. The local Marie had ensured they used top grade tarmac up to the golf club and then resorted to the cheaper stuff after that.

They were climbing again, and she counted the hairpins. They had to be climbing up Mount Angel. Ten, eleven, twelve hairpins, they were halfway up, and then they slowed, turning to the left onto an unmade road. Even though the car was a big four-by-four, it struggled with the terrain, and they came to a dusty rest after three or four minutes.

'Show Time,' Hilda muttered to herself.

'The woman first,' said the leader, signalling for Hilda to be dragged roughly from the car. 'You can take off their hoods. I don't know why we bothered with them anyway.'

The announcement confirmed her fears that they would never be allowed to leave. Strangely she was strengthened by knowing what she was up against, and even more so when the hood's rough material scraped her bruised cheek as they pulled it off. She gratefully drew the cool mountain air into her lungs, soothing the hot swelling on her cheek.

Hilda looked directly into her captor's eyes. He stood with her hood in his hands, and they both understood what removing the hoods meant. She had feared this would be the outcome when they were abducted, but her mindset had sought the positive. *No option now but to put on the performance of my life,* she decided, *as that may now have a very short tenure.*

She alternately sobbed, cried, and pleaded, with fake tears forming a confluence with the real tears staining her face, finally sinking into a child's pose on the sandy ground between the car and a small, old wooden farmhouse. They were in a large, sloping clearing, on the higher level of which stood a small, weathered house. It leaned in various directions but mainly towards the front, following gravity's calling. A dull light glowed from the only window at the front and through the open doorway, which was reached using a few old wooden steps and crossing the rickety and narrow wooden porch.

Hilda continued her performance, sobbing and hunched down on her knees. Head and shoulders bent forward. The epitome of a loser surrendering.

'Please let me go. I don't know anything. My daughter will be worried if I don't come home.'

When they didn't immediately pick her up or beat her, she knew she had put doubt in their minds. The pause didn't last long, but the hands lifting her were not as rough as the ones that had viciously punched her and dragged her out of the car.

She was pushed, sobbing and pleading, into the small shack. There was no tenderness for Christophe either, as two of them dragged his half-conscious body up the steps and into the dingy front room.

Hilda knelt submissively on the floor, still drilling away at the man's vulnerability, pleading to phone the daughter she did not have, interspersed with convincing sobbing. After a while she gave a shrug of feigned resignation, affirmed with a mumbled, 'OK, I'll tell you, but please can I go to the toilet? Please, the toilet, I'm scared.'

Looking pleadingly at the man towering above her, she didn't need to say anything as her bruised, tear-stained face and dishevelled hair painted a self-evident picture. He stepped even closer, pulled his left arm and hand over his right shoulder, torquing his body to deliver a powerful backhanded blow. Hilda looked into his eyes – an emotionless abyss. She braced as he leaned down towards her, turning his shoulders more.

The leader walked into the room. 'Hold it! We need her conscious, so take her to the bloody toilet to shut her up. Keep the door open and don't let her out of your sight. We need her alive enough to talk, so don't get too handy with her.'

She slumped down onto the dusty floor, her sweat-beaded forehead resting on the bare floorboards. Relief circulated slowly through her, and she breathed for the first time in some minutes. The sadist pulled her up by her hair and directed her trance-like shuffle towards a door at the rear of the room. It opened onto a small kitchen with an old-fashioned walk-in pantry. To the right was a well-worn but sturdy doorway, leading to the primitive toilet. The floor was hard-packed bare earth, and the only light came from a small grill high up on the thin wooden outside wall. Time, neglect and the weather had treated the walls poorly, with gaps visible between most of the thin planks, letting in the very last of the day's dwindling light. Hilda continued painting a picture, leaning heavily on her captor, reinforcing her pathetic state.

She disengaged and turned towards her captor. 'How can I? Look.' She offered up her hands and mimicking the impossibility with her hands tied at the wrists, throwing in a few deep sobs for good measure.

He sceptically examined her tiny prison. Seemingly satisfied, he nodded in approval and stepped forward to cut the cable tie. Hilda raised her hands in expectation as his left hand shot out and grabbed her tightly around her throat. She couldn't breathe, as his huge hand closed almost all the way around her neck. He started to squeeze as he pushed her against the flimsy wall, leaning into her. Her eyes bulged and she struggled for breath, raising her tied hands, clawing hopelessly at his forearm.

He was too strong. He pushed himself into her, holding her off the ground, and he raised his knife. His face a few centimetres from hers, she could see the scars of his previous battles, smell his desire as he raised the knife, waving it in front of her eyes, tapping its point against the bridge of her nose. The uppermost edge was horribly serrated, glinting in the diffused light. He snarled as he spoke.

'You fuck with me, Princess, and I will slice you open.'

He lowered the knife to her right breast, now heaving under her futile exertion, only her toes in contact with the ground. He traced small circles through the blouse, around the faint impression of her nipple under the thin cotton, before sliding the blade's tip into the gap of her blouse, tugging upwards against a fastened button.

Hilda's defences teetered as she looked into his dead eyes. No connection, no humanity, eyes that wanted to penetrate her as he smiled crookedly and pushed himself closer, hard against her. Scything the knife upwards with a flick, he cleaved off three buttons, opening up her blouse and leaving a shallow cut in the milky flesh of her breast. A trickle of blood seeped out, dark ruby contrasting against soft pale skin, following the curve of her breast downwards and taking her captor's eyes with it. She felt his arousal, saw the excitement in his eyes.

She felt violated and terrorised; the pain was intense, sharp, and stinging, but as nothing compared with the pain in her imagination. She wanted to cry, just to curl up and cry. Her resolve at breaking point, her body trembled with fear, she went limp and cried.

With one more flick of the scalpel-sharp blade, he slashed the cable ties and pushed her hard against the back wall. Hilda collapsed onto the floor, in a state of shock, sobbing uncontrollably.

'And I'm just outside the door. So if you wanna go, you better go.'

Hilda needed no help in acting as scared as she felt at that moment. Fighting the internal turmoil, her trembling hands untied, she shook so much she could hardly close the door latch. She was no longer acting, but she forced her hatred to be stronger than the fear.

*

In the front room, Christophe was regaining his senses after the clubbing he had received in the car. Somewhere towards the back of the small house, he could hear Hilda sobbing, he could hear the sadist making her plead, and he drew upon anger and fury to commit himself to his plan. Through bleary eyes and ringing ears, Christophe could see the leader's gun trained on him while the other one positioned a chair behind him. Even though he had expected it, being kicked hard behind the knees, collapsing him into the chair, knocked the wind out of him.

'Have a seat, Christophe.' The leader of the kidnappers laughed lustily. 'Yep, we know your name, but we want to know all the names, so start talking. If you've given us enough by the time the yummy Hilda comes back, then we may let her live. Although be careful what you wish for, as living may not be her best option. I'll leave that up to the deranged one behind you. He'll decide what to do with her.'

Christophe tried to spring to his feet, but the one behind was expecting it. With better leverage, he smashed the gun into his temple and held Christophe easily. 'Tie him into the chair. We need him restrained and paying attention when Hilda returns.'

The anger pushed him through the pain. His mind was clear, and he was reconciled with his plan. The one behind tied his elbows into the old wooden chair's arms, but not too tight as his wrists were still tied together.

'First, tie his feet, then his wrists to the arms of the chair,' instructed Leader.

He did as he was ordered with Christophe's feet and then came round to stand in front of him to separate his wrists to re-tie them to the chair.

Hilda cried out, a genuine, terrorised cry. Christophe directed the fury away from his mind and into his body. Anger coursed through him, waiting for the instant the ties holding his wrists would be cut. Then he exploded upwards, headbutting the kidnapper hard on the bridge of his nose and seized the knife tightly by the blade.

He'd prepared himself for the pain, he knew it would be intense. He knew he'd bleed quickly as his palms and fingers clamped hard around the serrated-edge knife. The pain was still unbearable, travelling up the inside of his arms, through veins now severed in his fingers. But the surprise of the suicidal move allowed him to wrench it free from the shocked kidnapper, and he quickly turned the blade in his bloodied hands. Surprise and gravity were key weapons as he lunged onto him and drove the blade deep into the assailant's chest as he fell on top of him.

Christophe knew a long time ago that his plan would mean Leader would shoot him, and at that close range Leader couldn't miss. He knew what was coming and twisted as the rounds hit him and the mercenary. He was dying, but not dead. As the shots rang out, he twisted, with the chair still attached to his feet, dragged the inert corpse on top of him. Bullets tore into both the dead and the barely alive.

Hilda's scream energised him; willpower pushed him through the invited pain. Christophe, in one last supreme effort, kicked from the floor and swept Leader's feet from under him. The man stumbled onto the long knife he was holding upright.

Christophe was dead by the time Leader landed, but the combined momentum was just enough for the sharp blade to pierce Leader's thigh. The last four, panicked rounds, didn't alter the ending. They merely drew an audible line under the tragedy.

Chapter Thirty-Seven

At that very moment, a thousand kilometres north of the small wooden house, two masked men slipped silently into a grand and quiet mansion on the outskirts of Frankfurt. In the still night air, with suppressed handguns, they shot Uwe Mueller twice in his heart and once in his head.

*

At the same moment, Andy Taylor was doing his rounds, checking that his cleaning crews were doing their jobs on the forty-fourth floor of One Cabot Square in Canary Wharf, London. He had no idea the hidden CCTV cameras in Bianca Sabitini's office watched him as he connected to Bluetooth and downloaded the PDC's data onto his phone.

*

At around the same time, Inspector Remy sent a message to Ben's mobile.

'Just in case you thought we had forgotten you... we did get a positive match with a couple of the bullets and lifted some good prints from the gun. Hope you haven't forgotten our arrangement? Look forward to hearing from you. R'

Chapter Thirty-Eight

The sounds of agony and death echoed loudly inside the small house. Gunfire and screams bounced off the bare wooden floors and walls, drawing Hilda's jailer away from his post outside her tiny prison. Christophe and Hilda's telepathy in the car had warned her to expect something, but even so, she did not want to hear her lover trying to escape because she knew the outcome.

Hilda knew he would seize any opportunity, something that would give her a chance, her only one and given its cost, one which she could not waste. Even before her jailor had run away, she had prepared herself, standing and waiting, her back pressed against the thin outside wall. Arms spread out against the thin planking, her knee and leg raised in mid-air, ready to swing her heel hard into the wall's thin planks. Allowing a few seconds for the commotion in the front room to call her jailor, she began. Less than six blows with her heel and she had opened a hole big enough to wriggle through. Crawling on her hands and knees through the opening, she was up quickly and heading for the darkening purple haven of the treeline.

The ground at the back of the house sloped up steeply into the mountainside, dotted with brittle bushes and trees, all struggling to survive amongst the rocks. She might be faster than some of her captors if she ran downhill, but she would definitely be faster than all of them if she ran uphill. They were powerful, but too heavy, and they wouldn't expect her to choose the hardest route.

She set off uphill at a good pace, her soul relishing the action. The dim light grew even dimmer as she entered the treeline and welcomed the steep gradient, scrambling on all fours up the rocky slope in semi-darkness. The rock and stone cut her hands and legs with every contact; the unyielding, brittle branches of the pine trees reached out to whip at her face and body. She hardly noticed them, focussing instead on Christophe's smile and how he would be encouraging her. She remembered her first Iron Man – why did they call it that when women also competed? She remembered their discussions during her arduous training regime, and his craggy features breaking into a smile when running alongside her for the last few kilometres. She remembered his embrace when she had crossed the finish line.

No heroic, last gasp collapse, just his respect as she stood tall and proud, relishing competing with the best. 'It's something they can never take away from you,' she remembered her dead lover's words in her head, and she broke into a run, sprinting through branches up the steep slope of screed and rocks.

She was powered up it by the memory of her best friend; her lover; her... *Oh, why the fuck didn't you propose to me when you had the chance, you bloody idiot?* she almost screamed. The adrenalin surge lifted her higher and further. She was covered in sweat, scratches and cuts. She didn't care, she would never give up. She would track each and every one of them down and make them pay.

*

Sticky, glutinous blood oozed from the spirals of cloth that Leader had used to stem the flow from his punctured thigh. Twisting a leg from Christophe's smashed chair through the material, the flow became a trickle until it stopped, and he secured it with his belt. Not deep enough to be life-threatening, he decided, but it would require stitches. He also discovered Hilda's escape.

'I can take care of myself. You've got to find her before she gets too far; there's too many places to run and hide on the mountain. Remember, we don't get the bonus unless we find her and get the information. Christ knows what the Chinaman would say if he knew about this. I'll take the car and go up the mountain; you go down it, take the flashlight from the car, and only shoot if you have to, but for chrissakes do not kill her. Bleeding is fine, provided she can still talk.'

Hilda's jailor set off down the mountain and into the helter-skelter of shadows dancing from his flashlight. Sitting in a shallow pool of three men's blood, Leader surveyed the scene.

'What a cluster,' he mumbled as, straight-legged, he pulled himself up on a chair. Holstering his gun and, using the door for support, he limped his painful way across the dusty ground to the car.

A veteran of many conflicts, Leader had studied human behaviour in the hunter Vs. hunted equation. People act individually, almost rationally until they are panicked, then they make hasty decisions using the wrong criteria. Leader hoped this was the case with Hilda, as he sat in the stationary SUV, performing mental arithmetic in his head. Did he have enough money already? Was this last job really worth it?

He could drive down the mountain now, away from all this, away from all the killing – he hated it now – back to Sophie, his caring and trusting new partner who thought he was a fascinating 'security advisor' and whom he had promised that this would be his last job. They had more than enough. Not money any tax authority knew about, as his job didn't work like that, but they had enough for a comfortable quiet life somewhere in the sun.

The Chinaman was starting to worry him. He was becoming too cavalier, and all the caution of the early years had been replaced with rash bravado. But forty grand added to his Panama account, plus a bonus of sixty if he got her to talk! He was still relatively young, and that was one year's tax-free high living where they were aiming to retire to. *Make this the last one then,* he decided, then started the SUV and headed down the dusty track to the road and from there up to the summit of Mount Angel.

He pushed the big SUV hard along the unmade track, sending a sharp stabbing pain through his thigh. He promised himself not to be so gentle with Miss Kaerle when he found her. On the tarmac road, he could cover the few kilometres of hairpins to the summit in no time and without meeting another car. No-one would be using this road at this time of night.

The small car park at the summit provided sightseers with a dramatic backdrop for their selfies during the day. Tonight, though, there was only a luminescent moon and no sightseers. The approach to Mount Angel's summit from the Monte Carlo side was not for the faint-hearted. The final section was a straight and steep fifty metres of crumbling tarmac which drilled a gap through the overhanging escarpment. Vertical, dramatic, and loved by free climbers, the escarpment's only gap for many kilometres in either direction through which everything had to pass to reach the summit, was a tarmacked take-off ramp rising at forty degrees straight through the middle of the overhang. An ancient route which had seen the death of many a pack horse, it was now a famous tourist attraction in its own right, as it required some driving skill and nerve to climb it.

Climbing above the treeline, the higher altitude thinned out the vegetation as the tall, dense, pines of the lower slopes gave way to smaller trees and bushes. Hilda had settled into the rhythm of a long-distance runner, helped by the moon's monochrome wash over the white dusty ground making navigating a route slightly easier. Running more and stumbling less, although her palms and knees were already cut and bleeding, she stopped every now and then to listen for pursuers. She heard nothing – only her own blood pumping, while her memory reached into recent history to clutch something less ethereal. Hilda knew if she ran uphill at a pace which really tested her, none of her pursuers would be able to catch up, let alone make up her five-minute head-start. The shots and cries from the front room meant that Christophe must be dead, sacrificing himself for her, and she hoped at least one of the kidnappers. The thought produced a burst as she hurdled a thorn bush.

Her quiet confidence was quickly overtaken by anxiety as the sound of a big engine powering a vehicle uphill interrupted her calculations. She was nearly at the summit – maybe only a semi-vertical hundred metres away – when the car's headlights cut through the night, penetrating the blackness of Mount Angel's higher reaches. The shadows zigged and zagged a mazy dance as they jumped from darkness into light before plunging back into darkness as the heavy four-by-four wound its way through the hairpins towards the summit. The car's lights twisted away from her, then towards her, as the road snaked through the sharp curves, always climbing and climbing fast.

Hilda quickly realised the driver's objective. She remembered how the steep road passed through the overhanging escarpment, and that everything had to funnel through that sheer, narrow gap. The ideal ambush point. She was up and running in an instant, straight up the mountain's fall-line, in a desperate race to get to the pinch-point before the car. The moon's light was enough, just, but she took a risk with every sprinted stride. Loose stones spat out from under her rapid-moving feet, hands crawling at the mountain like a leopard climbing a tree, heart thumping as she raced uphill against the car's mechanical progress. It was faster than her but on a longer route. She was climbing vertically quicker than the car, but now the altitude and energy began to work against her, her heart beating dangerously fast.

*

The powerful four-by-four had no problems in reaching the top, circling around and coming back down the slope, stopping halfway. Leader decided his vantage point would be at the base of the slope, where the rocks provided cover and a good field of fire for anything approaching the summit.

His leg ached, and the recent activity had weakened the tourniquet's effect as the dark cloud on his chinos spread. He parked the car and limped down the steep road, favouring his good leg, to take up his vantage point. Leaning heavily on the large boulder, placing his gun and a flashlight on top of it. He knew it would have been impossible for any normal person to cover this much difficult ground in the time since Hilda had escaped.

*

Hilda, sweating, bleeding, and heart beating nearly out of her chest, watched his progress from above. She made the gap only seconds before the car's headlights swept round towards her. As Leader circled around at the top, she was now looking down upon him and his car. Exhausted, she lay panting on the stony ground, behind a clutch of small bushes, and looked up at the

251

stars as the sweat coursed off her body. The still night air made a cool blanket of her torn blouse as she closed her eyes and willed her heart rate to slow.

She froze when she heard the car door open. He was ten metres from her. Daring to look, she peered through the sparse bushes to see leader drag his injured leg down the slope to prop himself against a rock formation. She saw him place a gun and a flashlight on top of the rock, then he leant heavily it. Grabbing his trouser leg, he hoisted it up to his other leg, emitting an audible groan.

Looks like your handiwork, Christophe, she said to herself. *I wonder what condition the other two are in. I expect you took at least one with you. Thank You.*

Lying still in the cool air helped her heart return to normal as she looked down from her hiding place. She weighed up the odds. *Leader doesn't know I'm above him; in fact, he's positive I'm below him which is why he's set himself where he has. He's injured but he's armed, and he is a trained killer. He can't know for certain I ran up the mountain as opposed to any other direction, so I have the advantage of surprise. If he finds out where I am, he could shoot at me, but he can't run after me. Doing nothing is not an option,* she decided. Then she noticed the car door was open.

The car was ten metres away. The distance from the car to the man, twenty metres in a straight line downhill.

Several cerebral rehearsals later and she was ready. Picking up a golf ball-sized stone, weighing it in her hand she launched it high over his head, away down the rocky, bush-strewn slope. The man's head snapped in the direction of the stone's clattering descent, and Hilda stepped softly across the rocky ground and out onto the road. Keeping the car between her and the man, moving stealthily, she reached the car's open door without a sound.

Viewed from her hiding place, the car's internal courtesy lights had appeared to spread a warm inviting glow. Now her anxiety transformed that warm glow into bright beacons heralding her presence. She battled to stop the panic overwhelming her. The man, still with his back to her and staring downhill towards her stony distraction, was twenty metres away and in a straight line with the car. Hilda could see his body language shouting that the injured leg was causing him problems. The difficulty he had shifting into a position half leaning against the boulder in front of him was evident even in the dim light.

She couldn't risk opening the door any further. She had to squeeze in and gradually transfer her weight, sliding across the leather seat until firmly grasping the automatic gear shift. Directly downhill from her, Leader had his back to her as he leaned his weight further onto the rock.

Hilda offered up her most thankful prayer when she saw he'd exited the car too quickly to take the keys with him nor engage the parking brake. Offering up a short prayer she inhaled, held her breath, and pressed the disengage button on the gear shift. With a dull click, she slid the stick into Neutral. The mechanical whisper would not normally be audible, but through Hilda's ears on the quiet mountain, it sounded like a hammer hitting a metal dustbin lid. The car rolled forward, picking up speed as gravity quickly overcame inertia. Drawn to the fall-line of the steep slope, the big car rolled faster and faster towards him.

She saw him cock his head with the clunk of the gearbox disengaging. Now the sound of tyres crunching over crumbing tarmac had turned his shoulders. The lack of any engine noise took him too many precious seconds to work out what was happening. Hilda crouched behind the wheel, peering through the lowest part of the windscreen, as two metric tonnes of metal gathered speed, rolling inexorably towards Leader. He saw her head move, he raised his gun and fired, three shots in quick succession simultaneously shattering the windscreen and his chances of survival. She saw futility dawn when he concentrated his efforts to limping out of its path. The car came quicker and quicker. With the engine off, Hilda could not steer or brake. She peered through the crazed glass of the shattered windscreen and prayed as Leader, dragging his injured leg, staggered hastily in slow motion.

Crouching, Hilda braced her feet against the floor and turned her shoulder into the steering wheel to hear a supressed thud as the ex-kidnapper absorbed two tonnes of energy between vehicle and boulder. The heavy car rocked on its suspension before coming to rest, and silence once again settled over the summit.

Tentatively stepping out from the stationary car, any lingering doubts evaporated at the sight of his body impaled in a grotesque pose against the rock. Blood trickled slowly from his mouth and nostrils, thick black molasses in the moon's turbid light, as the warm night air aided coagulation. Leader stared up in wide-eyed surprise at the last night sky he ever saw.

She felt sick, and very soon was, as the shock created chemical mayhem inside her.

Feeling a light-headed cathartic release, she sat cross-legged on Mount Angel's warm tarmac in the middle of the night and waited for her body and mind to return to something near normal. Which they were both gradually doing as she searched his pockets. Staring at the gun and phone in her hand, she flinched when the phone pinged to announce an incoming message: *'Heard shots? U get her?'*

Still seated on the warm road, Hilda Kaerle calmly replied.

'Yes, she doesn't have long, have to move fast, where R U?' She didn't have to wait long.

'Bonus time! Chinaman will B plsd. Am at bottom near golf club. Can U collect me?'

'C U in 5.'

Wondering why she felt so calm and virtuous was a luxury to be savoured on another day. Right now, though, she was dining on the delicacy of revenge served cold. She felt neither fear nor remorse as she reversed the car and turned to descend the mountain through its sequence of rhythmic hairpins. Her would-be rapist, her ex-jailor, the man who had instilled such fear into her only an hour ago, was at the bottom of this road, expecting to see this car. She had already killed, she had a gun, and she had the element of surprise. Energy coursed through her, fuelling and filling her with confidence as she committed to murder again, in the name of righteous revenge. And she felt good about that.

Counting down the hairpins – had to be about sixteen or seventeen of them – the terrain flattened out lower down. To make it more convincing, she drove faster, impersonating how Leader would have driven, with the headlights deliberately on full to make it more difficult for her next victim to see into his future.

Only one more bend and we'll be at the golf club, she thought, as doubt crept into the lower defences of her mind.

Then she saw him, directly ahead of her, holding up one hand to shield against the car's headlights, a gun in his hand, hanging loosely by his side. Fifty metres to go; forty, hold your speed and your nerve; thirty, slow down a little. Twenty metres, he started to move towards the passenger side. Hilda knew timing was crucial. She was within ten metres when she stamped hard on the accelerator, lining up her ex-tormentor dead-centre. The engine quickly climbed, big and powerful, as the car leapt forward.

Hilda again saw the exact moment when realisation dawned. She relished him taking the same number of fatal seconds to process the danger as the Leader had, as the big car hit him hard. Acceleration impaled him onto the car, and Hilda pressed her foot harder to the floor as he was lifted onto the bonnet, up to the shattered windscreen. Fear coalesced with bewilderment was how Hilda recalled it later. Her ex-jailor's expression painted a startled portrait when it recognised the driver a millisecond before his face smashed into the windscreen.

Hilda braked hard and he flew from the car's bonnet onto the road. His head hitting the tarmac sounded like a coconut dropped from high, and he lay unmoving on the road. Hilda approached tentatively, holding the gun unfamiliarly in front of her with both hands. Prodding with her foot, testing for any signs of life, she moved round to where she could see his face. Closed eyes presaged a blank expression, masked by the horrific damage of the collision. She had to be certain she had avenged Christophe. Placing one hand on the road, she kneeled to check his breathing.

His crazed eyes flared open, and his bloodied hand snatched at hers. Automatic reflexes kicked in, the gun barked, and an orange flame spat revenge into his grotesque head.

Hilda's shoulders slumped, not in defeat, but in the victory of a weight being removed from her. She arched her neck and back, raised her arms above her head and stretched up to the stars, then sank to her knees and cried in relief.

*

Christophe was wiry as opposed to muscular, which made loading him into the car easier. Many years ago, Christophe and Hilda had chosen their burial place, on a walking and lovemaking holiday in the Swiss National Park. On a mountain they christened 'Our Mountain' they had made a pact over a picnic lunch, a bottle of wine followed by some of their most memorable lovemaking. The mountain, in the south-eastern corner of Switzerland, was about six hours' drive away. It would give them plenty of time to chat and reminisce as she put a match to the old newspapers stuffed under the shack's front porch. Tinder-dry, the whole place was ablaze by the time she passed the golf club and dialled Ingrid's number.

Chapter Thirty-Nine

Renate Siebert sat in shock as she re-read the front page for the third time. 'Uwe Mueller, CEO of Euro Bank, executed.'

Her office enjoyed one of the best views in Frankfurt, on one of the highest floors in the city's tallest building, looking over the River Main and the business sector of the historic city. Renate was a partner at Zandvliet Gross, the city's leading private-client law firm, and the Mueller family was one of her most prestigious clients. Renate looked out to the stunning view, not seeing anything, and shook her head again.

She buzzed her assistant. 'Ralph, call a Partners' meeting as soon as possible please, and I remember Uwe sending us a strange request a week ago. Something we had to do in the event of his passing in mysterious circumstances. That needs to be circulated to the Partners before the meeting. Thank you.'

Re-reading the newspaper's front page, and even allowing for journalists sensationalising everything, she found herself agreeing with the theory of an execution, a professional assassination. But motive? The Head of Euro Bank would attract respect from most and envy from others, but not to the extent you would be shot three times in bed in your own home. Whatever lay behind this, her firm still had to execute its deceased client's instructions to the letter of the law, provided they were within the law.

Renate connected her tablet to the room's multi-screen projectors and, passing through several layers into the firm's secure servers, she came to Uwe's latest instruction, which for the first time she opened in front of them all.

'Dear Renate, if you're reading this, then I am dead, probably murdered, and you must be suspicious as to the cause of my death. I suspect you may be reading this relatively soon after I sent it to you. If that is so, then I made the correct decision in sending it to you when I did.

My instruction is quite simple. I wish you to forward this and its attachment to Frau Ingrid Oppenheimer. Her email address is Ingrid@cui-oppenheimer.ch I also instruct that you personally speak with Ingrid to confirm safe receipt of the email and its attachment. Thank you for all you have done for my family. Uwe.'

*

An hour later, in a beautiful, grand and empty mansion overlooking the Zurich See, Ingrid Oppenheimer finished her phone call with Renate Siebert and opened the attachment to an email she had just received.

'Dear Ingrid, I am so sorry. I can never apologise enough for my actions which, by now, you will be aware of. Greed pierced me with its barbed claws many years ago, and I am truly sorry for Claus. That was something I desperately did not want to happen.

With good reason I expect you to despise both me and my apologies, but I cannot change anything, especially not now. It will never make amends for my actions, but I can give you something far more meaningful than my remorse, I can give you proof of the unquestionable guilt of the three remaining members of the Five.

Follow this link and it will take you to a secure site, an FTTP site. It contains fifty-two videos of our conference calls over the last couple of years. You will use these wisely, I know. Again, I never meant it to be like this.

Yours, Uwe Mueller.'

She had never wanted Claus to join the Five. Long ago she had liked Uwe, but she had never trusted Liang, Towner, or Sabitini. She only went along with it because Claus believed he could change them. The irony was suffocating, and the unnecessary waste and futility crushed breath out of her. She reread the email which proved she had been right all along, willing time to reverse.

*

'Where did you learn to do this?' Ben asked Stephanie as she carefully applied the last of twelve sutures to his head. He was lying, fully reclined, in one of the Gulfstream's leather seats.

'YouTube. Seriously. I looked it up while you were showering. It's a lot easier than I thought, but the real medical skill is in managing the pain and avoiding infection. I couldn't be too specific with the pharmacist, and he could only give me over-the-counter products. But taken together, they're quite strong.'

'Whatever the cocktail, it's working. I can hardly feel anything.'

'On-line-doctor.com says you can't rush the swelling and bruising, so it's a hidden blessing we're inside a metal tube at forty-five thousand feet for seven hours. Gives you a chance to rest and not try anything crazy.'

One hour into their flight to Zurich, and they discovered how chartering a Gulfstream delivers many unexpected benefits. One was zero reaction from Emma, their previously engaging and smiling flight attendant, when she saw Ben's face. She looked petrified, mumbling, 'Please let me know if I can do anything. Otherwise, I shall leave you alone to rest.' She was obviously shocked but was diplomatic enough not to say anything.

'Flying away from Towner at over six hundred miles an hour, with a crew who're doing their best to avoid us, was worth whatever Hilda negotiated.' Ben avoided mentioning that he had directly or indirectly caused the death of at least half a dozen people on US soil. Irrespective of a self-defence plea, it was an advantage that the US authorities had no proof he was ever there.

'Yes, we're better off being as far away from them as possible. I have no idea what time it is in any country at the moment, but we need to get together as many of the group as we can.' Stephanie drew the keyboard towards her as she fired up the plasma screen and connected to the on-board WiFi.

Ten minutes later and the big screen projected Ingrid, Danny, and Francois, with Hilda on a mobile phone from her car journey to Christophe's burial place. While Ben waited for them all to connect, he checked his phone for messages.

The first was from Calvert. *'My dear Ben, the good news needs to be very good for Danny Mullen's sake – treason carries very long sentences… look forward to hearing from you very soon. AC.'*

Ben almost laughed out loud at how far out of the loop Calvert was. His employers obviously didn't deem him important enough to let him know that pretence had been abandoned and both sides had now declared war. Trying to tighten a noose around his and Danny's necks, while everything had turned to shit, was almost funny. But not quite.

The plane's conference facilities were state-of-the-art, high definition, with surround sound. And all at forty-five thousand feet. Ben got them rolling, saying he would explain about his face later and asked if anyone had any news about Andy Taylor.

'I called him a dozen times, went round his gaff, called his office – they haven't seen him since the day before yesterday. I put in a security system for him a while back, right, so I know his alarm and entry codes.' Danny sheepishly continued, 'I got into his gaff, but he hasn't been there for a day or so. And from the state he left it in, he wasn't intending on being away for more than a few hours.'

Hilda interrupted their thoughts. 'I'm sorry to hear about your friend, Danny, but I'll be in the mountains soon and I'll lose any signal. So while I can, I need to tell you about Christophe.' Hilda recounted her and Christophe's kidnap, and how she had twice avenged his murder. A stunned silence fell over them. Ingrid was visibly shocked and held her hand over her mouth for most of the time.

'Whoever says we shouldn't take the law into our own hands hasn't been through what I have.' Hilda was adamant. 'I'm glad I did what I did, and I'd do it again. Whatever the consequences.'

Ingrid broke the silence. 'Oh Hilda, this is terrible. I've known you since you were born, and I know how much Christophe meant to you. I'm so sorry. Before we lose you, I have a very important development I must tell you about.' She composed herself.

'I've just received video films of the last fifty-two video conferences that the Five held.' She inhaled deeply and paused, as much to let the news sink in for herself as for the others.

'They're from Uwe Mueller, via his lawyers. He obviously didn't trust Liang, or the rest of the Five, because he had been secretly filming their video conference calls for the past year. He got around their hi-tech security by simply hiding an old camcorder in a bookshelf behind him.'

'Ingrid, this is dynamite!' Ben's excitement overrode his pain. 'Can't wait to see them, but why did Mueller's lawyers send them to you?'

'The Partner who deals with Uwe called me. You may not have heard, but Uwe was shot and killed at home, in his bed, early yesterday. Some weeks ago, Uwe instructed his lawyers that if anything suspicious happened to him, they were to send me an email which he had prepared some weeks ago. So, they did. These video films will have everything, their crimes, their personal financial structures unravelled, their unguarded discussions. It's far more incriminating than anything we could have captured.'

Ingrid held a handkerchief to her eyes and breathed deeply. Although they could guess what she expected to see and hear, an audible excitement ran through the group at the news.

'I've only read Uwe's email and an attachment. I haven't gone into the site, because a warning flashes up saying it will only allow one, single-user, account to be set up. If more than one person accesses it, the site will collapse. I don't know what to do, and I don't want to destroy all that evidence.'

'This is fantastic. It means we can really nail these bastards.' Stephanie looked triumphant. 'Mamma, I can remote-onto your computer from here and handle all that now.' Stephanie took a few minutes to talk Ingrid through how to hand over control of her computer to her. 'In a second, a message will pop up on your screen; it's from me. Just click *Accept* and I'll do the rest.'

A few minutes later, the six of them watched in stunned silence as Stephanie remotely connected to Ingrid's PC in Zurich and played one of Uwe's recordings. It was of a video conference meeting the Five had held two weeks earlier. The camera hidden in Mueller's bookcase looked over his shoulder, filming the large monitor on his desk showing the four of them, one in each quarter, with Thomas Liang concluding their agreement to sanction a hit squad to blow-up the Sonne Berg Hotel, burying Claus beneath it.

Each of them had their own thoughts and took some time to digest what they had seen, as a sombre silence settled over them.

'Ingrid, I'm so sorry, but from the little I know about Claus, if he were here, he'd already be in the IMF's offices showing them this. It blows the whole thing wide open.' Ben restrained his excitement. 'Fifty-one other videos like this and the IMF, Interpol, police forces worldwide, will bury what's left of the Five.'

'That's why Uwe risked his life to send them to me. Such a waste, but what's done is done. Ben, what on earth happened to your face? It looks so painful. We'll get you met at Zurich Airport by an ambulance. There's a private clinic we use, I'll alert them. How painful is it?'

The shocked silence continued as Ben relayed the events in Towner's office, as if describing a film.

'Steph's patched me up good, and I've taken a cocktail of meds which has taken the edge off it. They've numbed me, but I'm awake enough to be very confused. I need someone to explain how the man I killed in Towner's office had a picture on his phone of my wife? More exactly, a photo of a tattoo on my dead wife's shoulder? I think she may have been dead when he took it, so he could have been Sam's killer. And I think it was taken in the Amazon jungle while she was on business for the World Health Organisation.'

Ben paused, his energy had pushed the meds to one side.

'I need to know what the connection is between the Five, Claus, this guy, Raul, and all of you.' As he cast his arm around. 'And my wife.' Ben lay back in his chair, visibly drained. And waited.

The silence stretched out. Had they been in one room, they would have exchanged glances, but they weren't.

'I'll tell you how they're connected, Ben. If anyone deserves to know, it's you.' Stephanie's voice was clear. Ben hoped no-one noticed his relief, and that it had been Stephanie who spoke.

On the screen, Ingrid nodded in resignation while Stephanie continued. 'Ben, let me play you a recording Claus made of a disagreement between him and Thomas Liang. Then I'll explain what happened.' She took a minute to find the recording.

262

Liang's distinctive voice played.

'Give us exclusive access to the World Bank infrastructure deals or those two die.'

Stephanie paused the replay. 'Ben, we didn't know then, but we do know now, the two people Liang refers to are Sam and her colleague, Marco.' Stephanie continued to play the recording.

'It's the World Bank, Thomas! Even if I wanted to, and I don't because I won't give in to your blackmailing, you know that's not a decision that can be made by anything less than a dozen people. And these are real people, they're not pieces in a game, you can't play God with their lives.'

'We can and we do, Claus. Their lives are in your hands.'

'No, they're not, you're just camouflaging sadistic greed by making me your excuse. You're probably going to kill them no matter what I do. Saying that their lives are in my hands doesn't justify your actions.'

'Very well.' Liang shrugged. 'I suggest you keep an eye on the South American papers in the next week or so. My regards to your family, please tell them I'm thinking of them.' The monotone hum of a disconnected line played as the line went dead.

Stephanie turned towards Ben. 'You already know that the Five tried to force Papa to join them, and that once he discovered more about them, he tried to change them by saying that if they didn't, he'd go to the authorities. They threatened to kill Mamma and me, our family, his friends. Papa refused to be blackmailed.' Stephanie paused.

'Go on,' Ben encouraged.

'Most of that you already know. What you don't know is why Liang and the Five wanted to kill Sam.' Stephanie paused for a beat. 'One of the Five's subsidiaries – a lithium miner in Brazil – was dumping cadmium into the Amazon, killing dozens of babies and small children every week. Your wife discovered this and had gathered enough evidence to expose them. Unconnected to Sam, the Five threatened Papa that if he didn't give them the World Bank deals, they would kill her and Marco. By then, Papa knew the Five were ruthless; they'd killed everyone who ever stood in their way and that they'd probably kill Sam, Marco, and anyone else anyway. He tried to warn the WHO, but it was already too late.

I'm sorry, but Raul and Vinny killed Sam and Marco.' Stephanie did not avoid eye contact as Ben let the revelations sink in.

'There was nothing Papa could have done, but he still felt responsible. That's why he organised us, and his bank, GMB, to become a haven for families of people murdered by the Five. He had people look into their families, then he resolved to offer everyone contracts, employment or some form of benefit with GMB; to provide whatever it took for you and the others to pick up their lives while he tried to fight the Five. That is why you're here, that's what happened to Sam, and I cannot begin to tell you how many times I wanted to tell you, how bad I feel about not telling you before.

'We thought you were just going to be given a well-paid job at GMB; that somehow you'd recover and it would give you an opportunity to put your life back together. We had no idea you'd be in the Sonne Berg, nor that you'd save Papa from the attack, and that meant we had to take you with us to the chalet. We had no idea the chalet would be attacked and that you would become so involved. The deeper your involvement, the more difficult it became to tell you about Sam. We didn't know how you'd react; you might go crazy and get yourself killed. We were undecided, so we thought it best not to say anything, hoping we could get the Five and it would all end, and then we could tell you.' She held eye contact with him even as tears ran down her cheeks.

Ben now had more pieces than anyone else and he decided it was time to tell them, then the door to the plane's conference room burst open, nearly ripped from its hinges with the force of the kick.

'Nobody fucking move, nobody disconnects, and most importantly, all you lot,' the man holding the gun pointed with his chin towards the screen, 'you hold your hands up in the air where I can see that you're not tapping out an alert to anyone on your keyboard.'

He had one thick forearm wrapped around the throat of Emma, their flight attendant; in his other hand he held a gun, which he pressed against her temple. 'If I have even the slightest suspicion that someone's fucking with me, I'll send a hollow-point bullet through her very frightened head, and then I'll start on these two.' He pointed with his chin again towards Ben and Stephanie.

Chapter Forty

Earlier that morning in London, after signing his overnight crews' timesheets, a contented Andy Taylor clocked off and started to think about the weekend. Big weekend this, final round before the dance-offs, and they'd be doing it to the tango. Suited him perfectly, as accordions and violins began to play in his mind. Programme said, 'expressing themes of love, loss, and urban life'. *Right up my strasse,* he whispered to no-one, because no one was there.

Now his phone held the data he'd downloaded from that little white box in Bianca Sabitini's office, he was a thousand quid better off. *What the fuck's in there?* he asked himself. *Mason's smart, and his little mate Mullen didn't fight too hard against the grand I asked for, so he's gotta be making loads more. Should've asked for two, but a deal's a deal, flash git or not.*

He carried his twenty-five stone easily, lighter on his toes than someone half his weight. Even so, his soft footsteps echoed in the emptiness of the Canary Wharf car park several levels underground. Each space coveted and expensive, Andy loved this privilege; his parking space came with the job and made him smile inwardly every time he saw his lovingly restored 1970 Ford Capri rubbing shoulders with supercars and trucks twice the size. His inward smile quickly changed when he saw the size of the gun the swarthy stranger pointed at his head. That's when he heard the Range Rover behind him.

'Don't even think about it.' It was the last he could recall before the intense and brief pain in his head as he was hit from behind, twice.

'Enough, Maksym, enough.' A thick accent penetrated his dulled senses.

Andy Taylor knew he was a fat bastard. He didn't care, but he didn't need this wanker continually shouting it at him. Andy's handcuffs secured him to the door handle because he was too big to be tied anywhere else.

The four men had struggled to get him into the car, as he was twice as heavy as any two of his captors. Rendering him semi-conscious had been the only way they could do it, and now they were driving across Rainham marshes. Andy knew it was the marshes because, blindfolded or not, he had been born and had lived near here all his life. He recognised every turn they had made since the three of them attacked him fifteen minutes ago in Canary Wharf. He also knew why people were brought to the marshes – they were brought here to disappear. No-one would ever know how many had been buried or fed to the pigs here, so he knew he wouldn't be making the dance-offs. Ever. *No point in being nice to anyone then,* he reasoned.

'Oi, fat bastard, who you retrieve data for?' snarled the man in broken English sitting next to him.

'Mate, you can't even talk proper English, so go fuck yourself.' His words brought on a burst of verbal abuse, accompanied by the unproductive blows to Andy Taylor's head, arms, and body. If you weigh over one hundred and sixty kilos, even a big car becomes a difficult place for people to hit you properly.

'Leave him, Maksym, we'll be there soon. You can work on him then,' said the one called Bohdan.

'Yeah, Maksym, do as your boyfriend tells you, you fucking pussy. Not smart enough to think for yourself, eh?' Another shower of punches, another tirade of abuse, eliciting only taunting laughter from Andy Taylor.

'Fuck me, you really do punch like a girl, don't you? Do you shag like one as well?'

Maksym now had to be restrained from climbing on top of Andy, swinging wild, ineffective punches in the confined space.

'Maksym!' shouted Bohdan from the front, followed by a tirade in Belarussian.

Andy recognised the language from one of his cleaning crews. *That's a coincidence,* he thought.

He had got under their skin and that felt good. Soon they would be wherever it was they were going – Rainham marshes wasn't that big – and then they would torture him. In the end, they would kill him whether he told the truth, a lie, or nothing at all. *They've given me no option,* he logically concluded. *So, I'll do this little wanker Maksym along the way,* he equally logically concluded.

Loose clinker crunched under the Range Rover's broad tyres as it turned in a tight circle and drew to halt. More Belarussian discussion. Andy prepared himself as they got out of the car and came round to open his door. Blindfolded or not, the bright arc lights in the yard, or wherever they were, painted fuzzy silhouettes as Bohdan cut the cable-tie securing his handcuffs to the door handle. Two others stood left and right of him with their hands under his huge arms. They shoved him forwards, Maksym walking in front of him.

In a light and quick action, Andy stepped forward, raising his arms over Maksym's head, and wrapped the handcuff chain across the front of Maksym's throat. Placing his hands on the back of Maksym's neck, he fell forwards onto the ground, smashing his captor's face into the gravel and pinning him underneath his huge frame. When they hit the ground, Andy raised himself, put his knee in the back of Maksym's neck and pulled back hard against the chain.

Maksym gurgled as one hundred and sixty kilos of no-option, unwavering pressure strangled him. His captors repeatedly punched, kicked, and tried to wrestle an immovable Andy Taylor, but to little avail. He was almost unconscious from their punches, and Maksym was almost dead as Bohdan's gun fired. Andy Taylor's huge body flinched and momentarily loosened his hold. Then he tightened it for the last time.

Another shot rang out, then another.

Maksym died a second before Andy did, which was just after Bohdan's other rounds found their mark.

Andy Taylor rolled over in the soft mud of Rainham marshes, near where he had been born and lived all his life, a tango rhythm still in his mind. And if you didn't know better, you would say he was smiling.

Chapter Forty-One

Ben glued himself to the Gulfstream's upholstery, held his hands where the hijackers could see them, and fought the urge to react. He quickly checked the others on the video conference screen; thankfully none of them had moved, but Danny was looking straight at him. He felt like saying *"I have no fucking idea either"* out loud; he could see Danny was thinking the same and gave an imperceptible sideways head movement. Danny imperceptible nodded.

There were two hijackers, heavily armed and equipped, both dressed in their unofficial uniform of chinos and sports shirts tailored to speak of time spent in the gym. The one who had so loudly announced their entrance was eager to let everyone know he was the more senior and, in between issuing orders, had not taken his eyes off Ben. He was the taller of the two, broad and lithe, his cruel eyes set deep into a Mediterranean complexion with two thin red lines for lips stretched tight across his mouth in a fixed, imitation smile. And from a mouth that hadn't smiled since childhood. Ben calmly returned the look, feeling the dried blood of his wounds cracking; there was something about the man that didn't fit; *too confident, too challenging* thought Ben. For now, though, it looked like he enjoyed his job of experienced combat soldier and was pressing a gun hard against Emma's head.

Emma was crying for her unborn child; she was crying for Jill, her wife and the mother of her unborn child, who did not even know she was going to be a mother. The tall leader did not hide his pleasure at Ben's surprise.

They're armed, I'm not, thought Ben, *and they've just heard everything we discussed.* This was the reason for Emma's change of character. These guys had been on the plane for some time. They must have got on while the Gulfstream was parked at Teterboro Airport and waited for Ben and Stephanie to return.

Ben raised his hands slightly. Stephanie looked at him, he could see in her eyes she was drifting away. Her mouth, opening and closing like a fish gasping for air. He pushed his arms higher, looking at her with a stern stare.

Emma, their previously affable flight attendant, was petrified. Red, swollen eyes evidenced the horror of the last few hours. The same eyes swivelled almost out of their sockets towards the gun being pressed hard into her temple as she incoherently sobbed to be released. The second hijacker moved decisively to stand behind Ben and Stephanie, his gun held in a comfortable manner, a natural extension of his arm while his eyes took in everything.

'Sit,' the taller one commanded, as he shoved Emma onto the couch next to Stephanie.

Emma's hands instinctively went to her flat stomach, cradling a bump that wouldn't exist for months., Stephanie recognised the action, placing an arm around Emma's shoulders she pulled her close.

'You.' He pointed at Ben. 'Sergeant Hotshot. We know all about your handiwork in New York, so if you try anything, Tommo here will shoot her first. OK?' He nodded towards Stephanie as he spoke. 'We don't want to add to the tally, do we?'

'Thanks for letting us listen to your call,' the lead hijacker effected pantomime gratitude. 'You've saved us a load of bother, and saved yourselves a world of pain. It's everything we ever wanted. All the questions we were going to ask you, all neatly answered in advance. Sweet. By the way, in case you're wondering about the pilots, there's three of us. The other one, we'll call him Punchy, is secured inside the flight deck and will shoot both pilots if anything in here doesn't go according to plan. By a stroke of good fortune, Punchy is qualified to fly just about everything, and he'll fly this if anything were to happen to those two pilots. Say hello to Punchy everyone.' And with that they felt the plane waggle its wings in an aviation 'Hello' at nearly five hundred miles an hour. 'He's watching us on CCTV, so don't do anything to make him nervous, eh.'

Ben assessed the danger and his options. His gun was out of reach, but firing a gun loaded with regular ammunition – as his was – in a pressurised cabin, usually ends badly for everyone. These two appeared to be a step up on the likes of Raul. He believed them when they'd said they had hollow-point rounds in their handguns; that meant they could fire them and, provided they hit a body, there was no danger of puncturing the fuselage.

The remaining three of the Five had again evidenced their reach by tracking them down, planting their hijackers on board, and now they knew everything.

'You, Oppenheimer's widow. I want the link to that site, and the password.'

Ingrid was hurt and flustered. She stared blankly for so long that Ben wondered if she had the sound muted. 'What? I don't know how. I don't understand these things,' she replied hesitantly.

An irritated wave from the hijacker silenced Ingrid. 'You, Oppenheimer's daughter, you just created the account in that site. You get me the videos. Give me the link, the User ID, and the password.'

'No,' replied a committed Stephanie. 'Because you'll kill me as soon as I do.'

'I'll kill you all if you don't, so give me the fucking link.' The leader flicked his head from side to side, flexing his neck.

'She can't. That's the whole point of Uwe's fail-safe.' Ben almost had to shout to match the leader's volume. Thoughts and options bounced around in his mind as he locked his stare onto the hijacker.

Ben melded plausibility with desperation. 'You just heard it for yourself. Uwe deliberately designed it that way for his own protection. He gave the single-user link to Ingrid; when she used that link to open the site *through her computer*, the site recorded her computer's IP address. The site can now only be opened from Ingrid's computer; you learned that at exactly the same time we did. If the site is accessed from anywhere other than Ingrid's computer, it'll crash the site and scatter fifty-two very incriminating videos all over the net. What do you think Thomas Liang will do to you when he discovers you released those to be virally circulated around the world? A quick death would be a blessing, don't you think?' For the first time, Ben saw uncertainty replace arrogance in the lead hijacker's anxious expression.

Ben noted how the leader habitually swapped his gun from one hand to the other, stretching his neck left and right as he did so. A slight sheen had formed on his forehead as he took his time to process the information. Ben sat, impassive, neutral. Leader hesitantly looked towards Tommo, who responded with a half nod, half shrug.

'If you're shitting me, Hotshot, I'll do you first. What the fuck is all this tech bullshit anyway, and what's an IP address?' Confusion replacing confidence was evidenced by a furrowed brow as he spat the question. The wave of control he had sailed in on was draining away, to be replaced by doubt, the left hand-right hand, gun holding habit increased.

Ben now spoke in a more measured tone. 'You can Google it from here; IP address is an Internet Protocol address. It's the unique identifying signal of a computer through which it accesses the internet.' He tried to relax his chest. 'It's a call-sign electronically tattooed onto that bit of kit; it never changes. Ask your buddy here,' Ben jerked his thumb towards Tommo, the other hijacker. 'Or ask Punchy.' Ben poured on confidence like a gambler bluffing with a nothing hand. It was all he had left; he'd gambled everything else.

The leader waited a beat, then picked up the cabin's internal telephone and jabbed at one of the buttons. Ben knew he was talking to Punchy, but he didn't need to explain much. Punchy would have been watching on the CCTV.

Ben realised he hadn't breathed in a full minute, carefully exhaling without making it obvious, not daring to look at Stephanie or the others on the screen. He knew he could lie convincingly; he was not sure the others could.

After a minute Ben realised their combined IT knowledge wasn't enough to challenge him because they hadn't shot him. He rechecked his posture, trying to effect confidence without cockiness as he planned what he would do in response to each of the hijacker's next actions.

He knew they were unsure about his IP address ruse. Like all the best lies, it contained a measure of truth. He had altered the balance, now he needed to press his advantage further.

'When you accepted this job from Liang, neither he nor you knew about Uwe's home movies, did you?'

The leader whispered something into the phone and hung up.

Sensing his uncertainty, Ben pushed him. 'Thomas Liang's instructions were to kill us when you'd got what you wanted from us, weren't they?' he probed confidently. 'Then probably kill the crew, turn off the locator beam, land the plane somewhere where it could disappear, no way of linking you to the crime. But now, thanks to Uwe's videos, you've had to take the risk of revealing yourself to three people on a video call so that they don't go viral with fifty-two incriminating videos when Steph and I mysteriously disappear. Since we got on this plane, Uwe's videos have changed the game for everyone, haven't they?'

The leader hadn't said anything in a full minute, so Ben increased the pressure. 'Liang doesn't know about the videos yet, because you've only just found out yourself. You now know that getting control of the videos isn't straightforward; you need Ingrid's computer at least. So, now you can't carry out his order to kill us until you've spoken with him to tell him about Uwe's videos and to ask what you should do next. If you make the wrong decision and lose the videos, he'll kill you.'

The frequency with which their captor swapped his gun from one hand to the other and stretched his neck increased. Ben sensed he was now in control of the leader's plan.

'You!' he shouted angrily at Stephanie.

'Stop shouting, you fucking noisy Italian.' Stephanie's shout surprised most. But not everyone.

'What are you talking about? I'm not Italian,' the leader shrieked, grabbing Stephanie by her hair, making her scream, making Ingrid scream louder. 'You're all fucking with me. You don't want to do that.' He shook with rage. 'You'll see what happens when you fuck with me.'

As he held Stephanie's face a few centimetres from his own, his teeth bared in a snarl. Tommo had pre-empted Ben's intentions, holding his gun in a double-handed grip, aimed between Ben's eyes, while his own eyes said, 'Don't.' Everyone added their own noise to the pandemonium.

'Shut the fuck up. Everyone.' The manic expression and his gun against Stephanie's head held everyone's attention. 'Or someone's gonna get hurt.' His gun never moved away from Stephanie, the other hijacker's gun aim steady on Ben's chest.

Ben sat back down; Ingrid held a handkerchief against her mouth; Francois continued to stare; Stephanie's sobs abated; Danny said nothing, but his eyes moved constantly.

The cabin's phone beeped twice, and everyone turned to look at it. Leader picked up the handset. Although he was guarded, Ben heard, 'Is he connected now?' after which the leader raised his eyebrows to look directly into the CCTV camera in the cabin.

Ben now knew Thomas Liang was looking at them at that moment, and a wave of killing lust washed over him. Leader's body language changed, he stood upright, raised his chin, and made Stephanie cry out when he lifted her higher. The conversation was conducted mainly by the person on the other end of the line. Leader's contribution was to receive instructions, repeating, 'Yes, yes, OK, understood.' After he hung up, Leader continued to look deferentially towards the CCTV camera.

'Let's try again, shall we? Old Mrs. Oppenheimer, some associates of ours will visit you shortly, and you will give them your computer.' He turned to Stephanie. 'Miss Oppenheimer, you're coming with me when we land, and you'll give me everything I need to access that video site through your mum's computer. Meanwhile, we'll hang onto you for insurance, just to make sure everyone behaves.'

Ingrid was first. 'I won't give you anything until I know my daughter's safe.'

'You will, because I'll cut off little bits of her until you do.' This drew a hysterical reaction again from Ingrid.

'You won't let us walk away, not now we've seen your faces.' Stephanie surprised herself with how calm she was as she stared at the CCTV camera.

The hijacker sighed. 'You all need to start taking this more seriously.'

Throwing Stephanie back onto the chair, he grabbed the sobbing Emma.

It was partly the sound the gun made; it was partly the red dome from Emma's head that was painted instantly onto the bulkhead behind her. But the speed of the lead hijacker's decision was what mostly took everyone by surprise. That and his crazed eyes after the kill, indiscriminatingly executing Emma even before he had finished speaking.

The conference room's audio distorted with the range of reactions. Ingrid pleaded loudly, hysteria competing with sobbing to finish her short sentences; Danny repeated, 'Shit, shit, shit' over and over, as if in a trance; Francois sat still, his eyes wide and wild, his jaw clenched tight. Stephanie was hyper-ventilating, wheezing a high-pitched whimper in time with her quickened breathing. Ben said nothing. His knuckles were white with the force exerted to hold onto the chair's arms.

Leader stood like a circus ringmaster, commanding everything around him. 'I told you not to fuck with me. Now, Miss I'm-A-Fucking-Heroine Oppenheimer, do you see what you've gone and made me do?'

Deliberation and emphasis were heavy on each word as his voice boomed louder. Stephanie screamed as he rammed his gun into her left leg, his whole weight going through the dark metal, boring into her knee. His knuckles whitened and his finger tensed around the trigger. A cruel smile grew from his red-lined eyes, not from inflicting pain but from regaining control. 'When we land, and we've got your mum's computer, you're going to get me into that site, aren't you?'

'Go fuck yourself.'

Ben recognised the look in Stephanie's eyes. He had seen that look in soldiers' eyes, the look that says, 'I don't give a toss what the odds are.' That was the point at which Ben knew Stephanie would never do what the hijackers wanted.

Ingrid's cries echoed from every surface of the cabin.

'Steph, it's OK. Videos aren't worth a copy-cat killing.' Danny's unmistakeable Cockney tones cut clearly through the chaos. 'Give 'em what they want. It's alright.'

'At last. The voice of reason.' Leader's smile proclaimed his victory and he turned enquiringly to Stephanie. 'Well? Are you going to follow your Cockney friend's good advice? Or do I start with the left kneecap, or would you prefer the right?' He now stroked the gun against the inside of Stephanie's thighs.

Ben's eyes flicked to the other hijacker, but it was no use; Tommo had always had Ben in his sights and his gun hadn't wavered.

Stephanie's shoulders sagged as she leant forward, and her auburn hair fell forming a curtain from which came a barely audible, 'OK.' Then, pushing back her hair, she slowly sat upright. 'You only need Mamma's computer, you don't need her. I'll give you the user ID and password when we've landed and I know she's safe. Not before.'

The leader instinctively looked up to the CCTV camera. Then he walked to the cabin telephone and raised the handset to his ear and listened, nodding continually. His eyes twitched back and forth across the cabin and the three motionless figures on the screen, coming to rest on Ben. He guessed he had been given his instructions by Liang, and Ben knew which part he played in those.

Ben made eye contact with Stephanie while they waited, mouthing 'OK?'

'Oi, Hotshot, shut it.' Tommo was close enough to Ben to shove him hard in his back to make his point.

Ben didn't take his eyes off Stephanie. Given that she was sitting a few metres from a wall covered in Emma's head, he was surprised when she responded with an affirmative nod and a calm, confident expression. He nodded back, a movement so small it went unnoticed. He added her reaction to his thoughts.

Leader continued holding the phone to his ear. Making the excuse of stretching his head and neck, Ben turned to look at the others on the large plasma screen. Ingrid's handkerchief still covered half her face; she was still in shock, and he could hear each breath. As with many people for whom video calls are not a part of everyday life, she stared at the screen and not into the camera, making it look like she wasn't looking at you.

Francois was the same; impassive, statue-like, tense-jawed, and also staring at his screen, not the camera. Danny, though, was looking straight at his camera, straight at Ben, and his eyebrows twitched inquisitively when he saw Ben looking straight at him. He remained motionless, staring straight at the camera, straight into Ben's eyes, whose own were wide open. It took Ben a while to notice that Danny's eyes looked up, then down, up, down, up, down. Danny was nodding without moving his head.

Ben gave an imperceptibly small smile, which was returned in like fashion with two blinks. Ben also added that to his thoughts, although at the moment he wasn't sure what to make of them.

The lead hijacker stood tall again; it was obvious he was talking directly with Liang. His body language changed, he'd become more tense, if that were possible, he was saying little and nodding a lot. Leader's eyes swept towards Ben again, an expression of surprise when he realised Ben was staring at him. It was like a sniper, sweeping the field of fire for his target, only to discover his target was already sighting him down the barrel of his own rifle. Ben was now sure of what Liang had just ordered his hit-man to do, he stared him down. The call lasted a few more words, then Liang ended it.

'Strap them into the seats,' Leader snapped. 'We'll be landing into Zurich in three hours, and we'll hold on to you two until we've got the computer and we're sure we've got the only copies of those videos.'

Then, pointing at Ingrid, he went on, 'Oppenheimer widow, our friends are nearly with you, so just do as they say and I hope that everyone understands that if anything doesn't go according to our plans, we will kill both of these?' And he waved his gun between Ben and Stephanie. Robotic nods answered his question.

'A word of caution to anyone feeling brave and foolish.' He looked directly into the camera as he spoke, then bent down in front of Ben and strapped a thick black belt to his leg, just above the ankle. It had a fist-sized bulge on the outside. 'We call this the Good Boy belt, and it's a fiendish little bastard. Really simple; it can only be unlocked electronically from this here tablet, not even powered bolt-croppers can get through the chromium tungsten steel bands before it goes off. And it's got some really cool electronics. Let me show you. Each one's got its own

SIM card, just like a mobile phone, which sends and receives a GPRS signal to this little box of tricks.'

So that the others could see, he held up a mid-sized tablet projecting a map screen, showing two dots. 'From this little box, and because it only needs a 2G signal, I can see the Good Boy belt wherever it is on about eighty-five per cent of planet earth. Now that's cool, but let me tell you what's really cool. From anywhere on planet earth, I can detonate the one hundred and fifty grams of high explosive it carries.' A malicious smile stretched his mouth and creased his eyes until he resembled a demonic gargoyle. 'Don't you just love tech stuff?' He fell backwards, laughing at Ben's disguised fury. Ingrid's handkerchief resumed its default position.

'I wonder how much you'd laugh if we went one-on-one. Because I don't think you're anything without your gun, your Good Boy gadgets, or your back-up over there.' Ben nodded towards the other hijacker.

'Yeah, yeah, yeah. Whatever, Hotshot. You should be careful what you wish for, and in the meantime, you just be a Good Boy.' He continued to laugh at his own jokes as he turned to strap a similar device to Stephanie's lower leg.

Chapter Forty-Two

The unnatural package strapped around his leg delivered on its design to be unmovable; it was sturdy and solid, out of the same school as the cable ties. Ben had tensed his arms before they were tied, bulking his muscles so there would be slack when he relaxed them, but even so the cables were still too well tied to do anything. Stephanie was similarly restrained.

Silently thanking the intervention of Uwe's videos, Ben allowed himself a wry smile. Without those, they would have already been tortured, shot, and dumped into the ocean forty-five thousand feet below. Opportunities would present themselves when they disembarked, he assured himself. If they didn't, he would create one, or as many as it took. The hijackers had been sloppy, they hadn't searched him or his carry-on luggage containing Raul's gun, but whether he could get to it was a different matter. He closed his eyes. It was important to rebuild energy when you could, and he knew he would be needing a lot of it soon.

He knew that Liang would be eager to find out exactly how much Uwe's videos incriminated him. To do that, he'd need to put Stephanie, with her User ID and passwords for Uwe's website, in front of Ingrid's computer as soon as possible. Then Liang would want to ensure he had the only copies; after which he would want to tie up any loose ends. Ben knew he, Stephanie, and the others were all loose ends. They had to change that.

Ben looked at Stephanie sitting opposite. She was calm, composed, and had been looking straight at him. *She's either the best bluffer ever, or she doesn't know how much more shit is about to fall on us,* thought Ben. If body language is a window into the mind, her mind was in good health.

She sat upright and relaxed, held her head up, unblinking eyes reflecting Ben's, and she smiled. She smiled like someone who knew an answer others didn't. Ben returned the smile, not fully understanding but secretly thankful it was he who faced the bulkhead behind Stephanie, the one with Emma's remains slowly coagulating against it. He closed his eyes and tried to rest.

Chapter Forty-Three

Early morning rain drew diagonal lines down the Gulfstream's windows as the plane descended out of a leaden sky. Heavy air buffeted the plane's path into Zurich International Airport, body-checking the medium-sized plane, keeping the pilots concentrating on their task. There was the familiar drag and a high-pitched whistle as the landing gear was lowered, and the clunk when it locked into place. Ben had experienced the sensations a thousand times. What was different this time were the two men seated across the aisle, guns held casually in their laps, as they touched down lightly onto a damp runway.

As they taxied around the apron, even though Ben's view was obscured by steady rain, he knew they'd be avoiding officialdom in any guise and would have organised a private hangar. The view from a plane's window was not something Ben had ever paid much attention to on previous landings into Zurich. Now though, he viewed it eagerly, hoping in vain for something, anything, as the main terminal buildings slipped away behind him, and they headed to a cluster of smaller buildings in a corner of the airfield.

He sensed no anxiety in his captors as they sat relaxed and ready. All it would take was one cursory, official, glance inside the plane, with Emma's bulkhead telling the story of how her young life had ended. The fact no effort had been made to clean the crime scene left little to the imagination as to how they planned to deal with the evidence. It solidified Ben's plans, and his resolve.

The static sound of rain drumming on the fuselage gradually receded as they pulled inside the aircraft hangar, empty apart from them, and big enough to take half a dozen planes. One engine whined loudly as they rotated under the bright interior floodlights, the painted pale green floor the colour of a spring meadow reflecting them upwards.

The sleek jet rocked back on its landing gear after they had turned in a full circle and halted. Ben looked out at three large black SUVs, lined up like a child's toys, bumper to bumper, a damp rectangle beneath each as the last of the morning's rain dripped from the shiny black bodywork, forming glossy frames on the painted floor. Men in chino and polo-shirt uniforms stood, like statues, in classic bodyguard poses next to each vehicle. From their build and body language, Ben knew they were another of the Five's kill squads.

'I'm sure I don't need to remind you, I can track you anywhere on this.' Holding up the small tablet to emphasise his point, the leader told them because he liked what it did for him.

'Wherever you are, I can detonate it by selecting the Fire button from this menu.' He turned the screen so they could see a drop-down menu with the self-evidently titled option, Fire. 'That's why they call it the Good Boy belt, because that's exactly what you and your friends will be, or you both die from acute blood loss trauma from your missing limb.'

The lead hijacker's gloating was interrupted by two bodyguards entering the cabin. Again, no-one was in a hurry, as if kidnap, extortion, and murder were everyday events.

'She goes in the first car; you know what we need. He comes with me in the second. They've both got the bracelets on, and I've got the control. OK, you know where you're going.'

Ben watched as the ex-soldier advanced towards him. They'd never met, but each recognised themselves in the other. He noted Ben's injuries and how the blood had dried around Stephanie's sutures; he had more red and deep purple covering his face than any other colour.

'I bet that'd hurt if someone were to smack you.' It wasn't a question, merely good advice as he flicked open a knife and cut the ties round Ben's ankles. 'Nothing silly, Hotshot.'

He warily cut the ties securing Ben's forearms to his chair, stepping back a pace when he had done so.

Ben massaged his forearms, taking his time, then looked up from his chair at the four armed men. There would come a time, but it wasn't now.

'Never done anything silly in my life, mate,' he answered. As he stood up, he pleasingly noticing he was an inch taller than all, of them apart from the leader, who had carefully watched Ben throughout.

'Wrists,' ordered his captor.

Ben obliged, holding out his wrists, but pumped up his chest and spread his forearms wide as he did so. Pressing his palms together and tensing his wrists would create slack after the cables were tied. Ben dropped his arms in front of him, holding his forearms together to test. He could feel the slack; it wasn't much, but it was a start.

'Let's go.'

As he was shoved forward, Ben looked back. 'See you later, Steph.'

'You bet.' Accompanied by a sharp, confident nod.

The hangar's corrugated metal roof and walls amplified the sound of the rain as it echoing off its hard surfaces. White noise. It was the only sound in the hangar, and Ben used the space to plan. Four identikit bodyguards formed a tight ring around the base of the short steps, expressionless behind unnecessary dark glasses. One of them steered Ben towards the second SUV; he compliantly strolled with him towards the left-hand rear door, the one behind the driver; another chink of light at the end of the tunnel. A short piece of nylon rope secured the cable-tie handcuffs, but not his hands, to the driver's seat headrest. His hands and body pulled forward meant Ben couldn't wear a seat belt and more light appeared from the end of the tunnel.

He watched as they guided Stephanie down the plane's steps, no cable ties, no four-square reception committee waiting at the bottom, just two of the new mercenaries to chaperone and drive her. *They don't see her as a threat, and they're right, it won't take them long to get what they need.* And he knew what came after that. He fought panic; it wouldn't help, and he knew time was short.

*

The convoy set off, the lead hijacker from the plane sitting next to him in the back, watching him, his gun held lazily and pointing at Ben. No-one could see in through the heavily tinted windows. Tommo from the plane sat in the front, his gun now holstered.

He faced forward with the sun-visor lowered, and slid open the mirror to study Ben in its reflection. The driver was one of the new additions.

'Tell me, Hotshot, you regular British Army? A common squaddie?' the leader enquired mockingly. 'Or were you something more? You did a number on our boys in New York, so I'm guessing something more. British Special Forces maybe?'

'You could stop the car, untie me, and I'll be happy to show you, but I don't think you've got the balls, mate.'

Leader straightened, irritated. 'If you're a good boy, then I might just grant you your wish when we get there. In the meantime, shut the fuck up.' Leader didn't settle back into his seat as he had before.

Ben tutted loudly and shook his head in a disappointed taunt. In the visor's mirror, he saw Tommo raise his eyebrows. *Was it in interest, surprise, or amusement?* Either way, he was distracted by leader being challenged and didn't notice as Ben ever so slowly started to pull more of the nylon rope through the gap in between his wrists, using the slack in his cable ties. It was a tight squeeze, and the friction against the inside of his wrists rubbed them raw. He pulled a little harder.

Ben laughed. 'No. You won't stop the car, will you? You won't stop the car to untie me and go one-on-one because you're only capable of shooting defenceless women. Aren't you?'

'It's called getting results, Hotshot. Which is what I hear Raul and Vinny got with your missus.' Leader's faked indifference lacked confidence; it hung in the air after they'd all sensed it.

Ben teetered. Violent emotions cascaded through him, but he knew he couldn't give in. Instead, he laughed. 'Stop the car, untie me, and we'll see who gets the result. But you won't because you're a scared bully.'

Ben saw from both men's reactions that his jab, with the full weight of public embarrassment inside the car, had found its mark; Leader was taking a beating in front of two subordinates. Ben saw Tommo's expression in the mirror, and Tommo wasn't looking at Ben any more. He was looking to see how his leader responded, while Ben continued to work the cable further through the ties, towards where he could slip it outside a wrist.

Leader's eyes were louder than any spoken reply. He was now too preoccupied with the accurately landed verbal punches to notice Ben pulling more of the nylon through his wrist ties.

Dried blood on his face cracked like baked earth as Ben smiled, turning his bruised and bloodied face towards the leader, disguising a grimace, as he unobtrusively pulled more nylon through. Ben sensed he was on the right track and continued to twist the knife.

'You shot that girl because you'd lost control of Liang's plan and, not for the first time, you didn't know what to do. You shot her to make it look like you're *really hard*, *really* in control, but you're neither. You're an unbalanced loser, merely copying the actions of real leaders that you aspire to be like, but know you never will be, so you cover the gaps with false bravado. Inflicting pain is easier for you because you're emotionally undeveloped and not because you're hard. Liang can see the difference. Of course he doesn't care who you kill, but he does care about surrounding himself with capable people whom he can trust to keep their heads. He sees straight through you. He knows you're fragile, and that's why he's already decided to have you killed when this is over.'

Leader wouldn't have reacted if some of it wasn't true, but he knew most of it was. He came quickly and with more weight than Ben expected. He roared and drew back his lips in a savage snarl as he swung back his gun arm to smash Ben's skull; feeling secure in opening up his defences because Ben was restrained. But Ben wasn't, moments earlier Ben had freed himself, he'd slipped the nylon rope past the cable tie outside his left wrist.

His wrists were still tied together, but free from the headrest he was as ready and as balanced as he could be when seated. In an instant, he twisted his shoulders and crashed his double fists straight into the oncoming attacker's jaw as he lunged. Ben's preparation, the surprise, plus the man's momentum when his face met a perfectly timed ball of muscle and bone, were enough to temporarily concuss the ex-leader.

Tommo's seatbelt slowed him down and he took too long to pull his gun from its holster. Leader had collapsed onto Ben's lap and gave no resistance as Ben ripped the gun from him and fired from underneath his groggy body. He only needed to fire once; the hollow point round's effect was immediate, tearing through Tommo's chest, exploding inside him, instantaneously.

Ben pushed Leader back into his seat. He was starting to come round, but Ben didn't have the luxury of time to savour his assailant's surprise.

'For Sam, and for Emma.' Ben dispatched another hollow point round, this time into Leader's chest, holding eye contact with his victim until the lights went out. He wanted to ensure that Ben was the last sight and thought that Leader would ever have.

The driver swerved in shock and swore. Ben quickly held the gun to the man's cheek, resting it there, making sure the driver fully experienced the acrid smell of burnt gunpowder and felt the lethality of the cold steel.

'I don't need to kill you, but I will if you make me.' Ben's breathing was slow and quiet.

The driver's breathing was fast and audible, his eyes darting between the rear-view mirror and the bloodied bodies of his ex-colleagues. *'Tied, restrained and in less than five seconds'* bounced around in his head. *'Less than five bloody seconds.'* The driver's thoughts could be heard in the little squeaks emitting from his over-tight grip on the steering wheel; twisting them back and forth as he subconsciously flicked his tongue at tiny beads of perspiration on his top lip.

Decision made; the SUV gained speed quickly as the driver floored the accelerator. More than one hundred kilometres an hour, and they were in danger of overtaking Stephanie's SUV – the one they were supposed to be following. 'Fuck you, Hotshot. You shoot me and you'll die as well.'

Ben placed the gun's muzzle as close as he dared to the driver's right ear and pulled the trigger, sending the round through the car's roof, deafening the driver with acoustic trauma, and completely disorienting him. The tiny squeaks from gripping the wheel were louder and more frequent, top-lip perspiration ran freely.

He shouted in the man's other ear, 'Now slow the fuck down, or the next one's through your head.' It had the desired effect. They started to decelerate just as the radio squawked into life.

'Two. What the hell are you doing?' It was the SUV behind them.

Ben tapped the muzzle hard against the driver's inflamed cheek. 'Handle it… if you want to live.'

In the car's rear-view mirror, Ben could see the driver making some main-life decisions before he pressed the Speak button on the walkie-talkie. 'Yeah sorry, just getting a feel for these wheels. All good now.'

'Asshole.'

Ben breathed for what felt like the first time in ages as he gathered himself for the next stage of his plan. 'I'll stick to my side of the bargain. I won't kill you, provided you tell me everything.'

'Liang will follow me to the end of the earth if I tell you anything.'

''You won't make the end of this road if you don't. Tell me, what was the next stage of the plan? Torture me just to be absolutely sure you've got everything, then kill me? Then do the same to Stephanie?'

'They'll kill me if they find out what's happened.'

'I'll take that as a yes,' said Ben in a flat, direct tone. 'You're in the shit whichever way you look at it, but I've got no reason to kill you provided I get to Stephanie before they do anything to her.' Mentioning her name brought on a small surge of emotion, though he knew he had to keep it in check. 'I'm not a psychotic nutter like these guys, but I am prepared to kill you if you don't do exactly as I say. OK?'

The driver paused to consider Ben's offer. They were on a highway constructed from individual concrete sections whose metronomic beat thrummed throughout the car, while the windscreen wipers kept time with a lighter beat.

Ben's heart tapped a pacier percussion somewhere in between as he wondered how he would control the car if he had to shoot the driver.

'I have a counteroffer for you.' The driver had made his decision. 'Let me go, and I'll show you how to track your girlfriend and remove those Good Boy bracelets using Rafael's tablet.' The driver resembled a small boy negotiating a treat for doing his homework.

It was now's Ben's turn to consider. 'OK, I can live with that. Now, as far as the other two cars are concerned, what was the plan from here?'

'The plan is that we detach from the other two cars, take you to a disused industrial unit, just north of the main station. It's an old goods yard that Liang's company owns. Rafael, the guy in the back with you, he's a proper nutter. He wanted to do all kinds of shit, but Liang just said to find out everything you know, then kill you. Sorry, pal, you know how it is.'

'Not sure I do. *Pal*. But that's all changed now. Are they taking Stephanie to the same place?'

'No. She's going somewhere near the lake. I don't know exactly where, honestly, but I know it was right on the lake, because Liang said to set her adrift in a small boat when they'd, you know, finished with her. He's got into the habit recently of sending messages.' Ben could see from the driver's eyes that his fear wasn't faked.

Ben struggled to control his anger, to maintain focus. He wanted to blow the driver's head off. A rage was building inside him. He took time before speaking.

'When do we separate from them?' He was back in control.

'After the next junction. They take the tunnel into the city; we stay on for one more junction, then turn off.'

'OK. Stick with their plan. Keep a good distance from Stephanie's car, hand me the walkie-talkie, and try to act like you're not facing imminent death. Because you are if I find out you're lying.'

The driver did as he was told.

Ben found the knife he knew Rafael would have been carrying and cut his cable ties. 'That's the best day's work you've ever done, my friend. We've passed the tunnel junction now and we're on our own, so take us to Liang's disused warehouse. I'll tell you where to pull over.'

*

He dragged the driver into Liang's disused industrial unit after he had hit him with the butt of his gun and used the nylon rope to tie his hands to his feet. Liang's men had chosen the unit well. No-one went there, so he knew the driver wouldn't be discovered or able to free himself for many hours. *A moot point,* thought Ben, *as Stephanie didn't have many hours.*

The dead Rafael's tablet was intuitive to use: a basic GPRS tracker located the bracelets as two green dots on the superimposed map, from which you could zoom in or out. Stephanie wasn't too far away, five kilometres at the most. But would he be in time? The driver had shown him how to remove his bracelet before Ben incapacitated him. Now he rolled the inert driver onto his back and searched his pockets – Suisse Francs, phone, another gun, and a short-bladed filleting knife attached to his calf.

Ben spat on the inert man's fingertips, wiped them on the man's shirt, and unlocked his phone at the third attempt, replacing the fingerprint on the phone with his own. He pocketed the cash and strapped the knife to his calf, tucked the other gun into his belt, and fixed the tablet on the dashboard where he could see it, distracting himself with action to keep the anxiety at bay. The SUV's wheels spun furiously against the loose surface as he dialled Danny's number from memory. He knew he did not have long.

Chapter Forty-Four

The shortest distance between two points... His route weaved a path through derelict and seldom-used industrial units towards Stephanie's blinking green dot. The other green dot, Ben's Good Boy bracelet, was on the seat next to him, complete with its one hundred and fifty grams of high explosive. He'd been extra careful when making the selection from the various drop-down menus, double and triple checking to make certain he wasn't setting something in motion as he released the electronic lock.

'Unknown caller' Appeared on his screen. Danny was hesitant, his non-committal 'Uh-huh' was the most he was willing to risk.

'Dan, it's me, Ben. Where are you?'

'Oh mate, thank Christ. It's panic stations here.'

Ben heard Ingrid's panicked voice and Francois' deep tones questioning in the background. 'Is Steph with you? Are you both OK?' More shrieking in the background. 'Ben, I'm putting you on speaker, hold on.'

'Dan, I'm OK, I'm free and I'm on my way to get Stephanie. I had to take care of a few more of Liang's boys, the psycho and his sidekick from the plane. I've nicked one of their cars, driving it now, following the tracker in that gadget on Steph's leg. As far as I can make out, they're right next to the lake, about half a click below the ferry terminal. The map shows some derelict buildings there that Liang owns. I've got the tablet that controls these bracelets, so I've disarmed and removed mine. I hope I can get there in time.' He was immersed in his reality, but Ingrid's cry reminded him he could have been more tactful.

Francois' deep tones were calmer but still anxious. 'Ben, where are you at the moment? Do you know how many men he has there, and are you armed? I'll get Remy to mobilise an armed response team, and I can be there in less than fifteen minutes. Wait for me.'

'I'm not waiting. The margin of Steph's survival is now measured in seconds, not minutes. Remy's team will have rules to follow. I don't.' Ben heard Ingrid inhale deeply, no-one else said anything.

'Danny, I'm turning on the app on this phone that allows you to track me. Follow that and give it to Francois. Meanwhile, I need you to get those voice-synthesised videos of Calvert and the others at the St. Gallen ready to send to me. I'm here now, I gotta go.' Ben abruptly ended the call.

The straight line of the broken concrete path, strewn with rusting machinery and weeds, tempted him. It was an appealingly direct route to the warehouse containing Stephanie's green dot, through invitingly open gates, right up to the disused and isolated building. He could see the rear of a black SUV parked next to an old loading bay, just inside the open entrance. His instincts steadied his emotions, pulling him away from the temptation of the straight line and its two hundred metres of a coverless, open field of fire. Instead, he kept driving, past the gates, outside the rusted perimeter fence, and further away from Stephanie. A short distance ahead he could see the road turned at the edge of the property and the line of sight was broken by a dozen abandoned ship's containers, stacked two high, and bolted together. Once, long ago, converted into a site office, it was now home to wildlife and scrub plants.

A stiff breeze carried the cries of seabirds circling the lake on the other side of Stephanie's prison, blowing earnestly towards him and mixing with the irregular tempo of a corrugated iron sheet flapping against the side of the building. Trying to free itself from the one remaining bolt tethering it, like a petulant child pulling away from a parent in a store.

Ben checked the car for anything useful – two flash-bangs and two fragmentation grenades were not a bad haul, considering. He jammed his Good Boy bracelet into the gap between the petrol tank and the chassis, locked the car, and packed his weapons as best he could in his pockets. One hundred metres between him and Stephanie's blinking green dot on the tablet. Part of him wanted to sprint across the open ground, to kick down the door without breaking stride, and put a round, dead centre, between the eyes of every one of them. He harnessed the intent. The energy would be useful, but he needed a more subtle plan.

The wind hurried untamed around the stack of containers. The butt of his gun tapped against the pressed steel sides as he held close to them, setting off an echo inside the empty vessel as crisp paint flakes arched away from the dents and scars telling its robust maritime history. Ben peered cautiously around the corner, looking towards Stephanie's building. No windows on this side, no doors either, as he blinked watering eyes against the strengthening wind.

Then he heard the unmistakeable cry of agony. A lonely, plaintive and painful plead being carried on the wind. The cry that tails off into an uncontrollable and desperate sob, involuntarily triggering Ben to sprint in a dead straight line towards it. Leaping over rubble and abandoned ironwork, he raced across the ground, knees and heart pumping harder as he tensed every muscle, every sinew, in his desperate charge.

His head pounded, his heart was beating out of his chest, and his knees almost gave way as he collapsed against the side of the old wharfage. His training quickly took hold and he crouched, holding the gun in front of him, poised and ready for whatever came around the side of the building. Nothing did, though, only the invisible wind inventing ghostly words in his head, and his mind. He let his heart slow while his lungs raced to repay their debt.

Chapter Forty-Five

Unperturbed by human presence, rats ran along the rusted rail-tracks set long ago into the damp concrete of the disused warehouse next to the Zurich See. The stink of small dead animals and produce long since departed left a putrid legacy. A light zephyr of marine diesel and rotting marine life from the lake prowled the empty spaces of her mind. Its pernicious fingers probed the senses; it was rancid and Stephanie felt sick, but it wasn't the smell. She felt sick and very alone as she knelt on the cold, wet floor of the old warehouse. She was scared. Scared of death, but more scared of what was going to happen before then. For the first time ever she couldn't see a way out.

I'll be fine, she kept telling herself by way of distraction from the impending pain. *They've got what they wanted, they won't want to hurt me if they've got what they wanted.* But she knew.

They had driven her straight here from the plane, brought Ingrid's laptop to her, and Stephanie had accessed Uwe's video site and handed them everything – the address, the single User ID and Password.

Liang was connected to every step, he had controlled the whole process and seen everything. An IT boffin somewhere confirmed the single user ID security aspect of the site, so Liang was now the only person on the planet with access to the videos – all that priceless and damning evidence. That's when he was supposed to have set her free, but he hadn't, and now he wanted more. He instructed them to find out everything she knew even if that was nothing.

Stephanie sobbed in impotent terror. She'd never felt fear this deep, never even thought it could exist. It flowed through her core, through her bones, through her veins. She did know more, of course she did, but they would kill the others in an instant if she told them. She had no option; she couldn't say anything. She knew the agony would come soon. It would last for a long time; it would last forever for her; and would grow inside her until it overwhelmed and killed her.

The reddish-brown stains of the corroded chain spoke of its history over many years. It was an unsympathetic material to tie someone's hands with, and it crushed painfully into her wrists. Not as unsympathetic as the Good Boy, though. They had come prepared. Using a secondary tablet, they had unlocked and removed the bracelet from her ankle and secured it around her neck. It wasn't tight; that wasn't the point. It was its presence that caused wave after wave of nausea to course through her. Salt from her tears reddened the skin under the pitiless choker, and they hadn't even started yet.

The rusted pulley above her yielded little resistance as many metres of corroded chain were pulled through it. It was a discordant prelude to pain's imminent arrival when, with the chain's slack spent, Stephanie's arms were dragged aloft. She was hoisted bodily and painfully off the cold concrete floor, hanging from the rusted chain clamping her wrists. Securing the chain heralded an unwelcome silence and the promise of pain's arrival. Suspended by her arms, she swung slowly, bodily exposed and helpless, as her two captors set to work with the loose end of the chain.

Stephanie went to her most recent memories of Papa, of Mamma, of Ben. Her spirits lifted when she remembered how good it had felt to fight back; when she had driven like a woman-possessed through Canary Wharf; when Hilda had avenged Christophe in the hills above Monaco; when Ben had taken down so many of them in New York. Then she cried out in unimaginable agony as the chain smashed through skin, muscle, and tendons to break a bone in her leg. Now she was back in a derelict Zurich warehouse just before a sadist tortured her to death.

There was a rhythm, the build-up emphasised as if in a theatre. The rusted chain was dragged back across the concrete floor, a jangle as the sadist gathered up measured loops around thick muscular hands, then the whoosh as the arc of impending pain flew through the damp air. Then the agony, the horribly deep inner agony as the heavy blunt metal links smashed bones in her feet, then in her shin. Left, then right, then left again, as she swayed slowly while the chain crushed her hands. More of the same rhythm. She knew a bone in her lower leg was broken; the dull ache and an inability to stop sobbing assured her of that. Not that there was any doubt, but if there was, the fear-driven acid bile gushing up her throat confirmed it.

She cried loud and uncontrollably, mentally crawling over broken glass to the sunny uplands of her childhood. She cried out for her Papa, for her Mamma. She remembered her parents when she and Adrian, her brother, were young and on holiday at the coast. The sun always shone, she was safe and they were always happy.

Then she screamed. She screamed louder than she had ever done before, because the pain was greater than anything she had experienced before. She stared into her parents' eyes, into her beautiful mother's emerald eyes, her dead father's caring, smiling eyes, and she smiled for an instant before collapsing into convulsions of uncontrollable sobbing. The pain was overpowering. Working their way up from her lower legs, breaking a bone, then moving up, breaking another bone, then moving higher again.

It was different to any pain she had ever experienced before – this pain was intensely lonely. All previous pain had been for a reason, falling off a horse, playing sport, or youthful adventures; you were never lonely with those, and partly you controlled how long they lasted. Now she was completely alone, she couldn't control it, and she knew it would never end. Waves of dark loneliness and uncertainty multiplied the pain.

The one who took pleasure was swinging the heavy chain hard. Each time, before the chain transferred its vicious energy to her soft flesh, he looked into her eyes. Each time he dragged back the chain, he ran his eyes over her body. Defiance was her only defence as his eyes roamed freely over her vulnerability and he paused to fantasise. Crying out in agony was involuntary – she couldn't stop herself anymore as her mind was dragged brutally to a place she never knew existed. Neither of the two men had spoken a word, they hadn't asked her a single question. She was dreading that when they did, she would tell them everything, because at the moment, she wanted so much to die.

Chapter Forty-Six

He checked the tablet's small screen. He could zoom in tight, as he was now only twenty metres from Stephanie. Then he heard police sirens. 'Oh shit' ran unchallenged through his mind as he stood still to concentrate on their sound. They were getting louder. Gradually they faded, passing along the main road as they faded further.

He checked he hadn't dropped anything – knife, flash-bangs, grenades, gun – and made his way around to the lake side of the building. The wind was stronger as he rounded the corner, blowing back up the lake towards Zurich, and rattling the metal sheets against their fittings. There was a trap door ten metres ahead frantically trying to escape its frame as the wind bounced it back and forth. He stepped up to it and gripped the cold, worn metal handle. It turned easily. If it made a noise, he couldn't hear it as the wind shouted down everything other than its own power, barging its way past him as he slowly opened the door and dragged him over the iron step. He had to lean against the door to close it, making sure the lock latched itself inside the frame.

It was dank and rancid inside the old building, almost musty, but gradually he adjusted to the dim light. The warehouse was an old processing plant, a legacy of more prosperous times with only the remains of machinery. Scavengers having taken what they could use or sell, the building now patiently awaited redevelopment.

Then he heard it: the clank and scrape of a chain being dragged across a concrete floor. He was on his toes quickly, hurrying softly towards the sound, less than ten metres away, round an iron staircase supporting the upper levels and two large, rusting cylinders. The chain stopped; he stopped; there was a whooshing noise, then a sickening thud as the chain's cruel energy penetrated something soft.

Then Stephanie's scream.

His brain shut down and raw emotion took over. Stephanie's sobbing plea for mercy delivered fury, just as the chain recommenced its brutal drag. Ben hurtled around the cylinder, flat out, fuelled by anger, rigid arm in front of him and aimed his gun between the startled man's eyes. He fired twice, quickly. Chainman was dead before the second round burst through his furrowed forehead.

Ben's instincts spun him round, towards the sound behind him. Chainman's accomplice snapped upright in shock, the chair he'd been sitting on flew backwards, and he made a move towards the gun on the table in front of him.

'Go on, give me the excuse I'm looking for, you perverted fuck.'

The man's hand hovered over the gun on the table, deciding his unwritten future. Ben had his gun in a double grip, his unblinking stare drilling through Stephanie's torturer as he stepped towards him. He was back in a zone that was once his life. He didn't have to think any more; he'd made his decisions and handed over control to his reflexes; their reaction time was faster than thinking.

As Stephanie cried out, Ben's eyes flicked towards the sound, and the torturer made his decision. A milli-second later, the soft-nosed bullet exploded inside his skull.

Uncontrollable sobs shook Stephanie's cold and beaten body, sagging against Ben as he loosened the chain. He wrapped his arms around her.

'I knew you'd come. I knew you would. I gave them the videos because it doesn't matter anymore.' Exhaustion and relief overwhelmed her. 'I didn't tell them. They don't know what we've done. I didn't tell them.'

Ben didn't understand. 'It's OK, Steph, it's OK. They're gone now, they can't hurt you anymore. It's over now.'

With one hand under her knees, the other under her shoulders, he swept her up and carried her to where two camp beds and sleeping bags were arranged around a primus stove and collapsible stools. Ben recognised the set-up, classic military; they had been expecting to be here for a few days.

Stephanie exclaimed loudly when Ben laid her down.

'Sorry, Steph. It's hard but try to relax. Go with it just for a minute. These guys will have med kits with them, I'll get them.' He tipped the men's kit bags upside down, spilling their contents across the concrete floor.

'Yes!' Ben exclaimed. 'Twenty-five mil morphine syrettes, one now and one for later. Keep the packet, the hospital will need to record what you've taken.'

Ben snapped off the head of the auto-injector sachet to reveal the small needle and jabbed it into Stephanie's thigh, squeezing the sachet as he did so.

'We should call Ingrid, she'll want to know you're safe.'

Ben dialled Danny using his other hand, putting it on speaker, then tucked the packet into Stephanie's pocket. He decided to postpone straightening her legs until the morphine had knocked her out.

'Ben?' Danny's urgent tone came from the phone's speaker.

'I've got Steph. She's hurt but safe. She'll be fine.'

Ingrid's wail of relief bounced off the old warehouse's corroded metal walls.

'She can speak for herself.' Stephanie propped herself up on an elbow. 'Is Mamma OK? Is she there?'

'Yes, yes, I'm here, Stephanie. I'm absolutely fine, but are you OK? What did they do to you?'

Stephanie cried. A different cry now; one of relief as much as pain. 'Oh Mamma, I was so scared, I was certain they were going to kill me. I would be dead if it wasn't for Ben. They've broken some bones, but nothing that won't heal. It hurt like hell but the morphine's kicking in now.'

She stared at the two dead torturers. 'I don't know how he found me, but I think a minute longer and…' Her voice, which was already showing the effects of the drug, trailed off.

Ben disarmed and removed the Good Boy bracelet from her neck while she was speaking. He walked to the back of the loading bay before throwing it over the SUV. He still didn't trust the technology not to misfire.

'Thank you again, Ben.' Ingrid's relief was evident.

'We're hanging up now, because I want to get out of here before any of their friends or the Police come to investigate. Ingrid, Stephanie needs a doctor and a hospital, but the Five will have those covered. She can't risk even a private one, unless we can take over the whole place. Can you sort that?'

'I'm sure we can. I'm so grateful to you for saving Stephanie. Thank you. Francois said he is tracking your phone and should be with you in five minutes. I'll let him know which clinic when I've arranged it. We'll see you there.'

'I can hear a car approaching.' Ben hung up.

It was coming fast, and Ben knew it was too soon to be Francois. It could only be the remainder of the Kill Squad who had met the plane.

The morphine had kicked in as Ben pulled up the sleeping-bags to cover her as best he could. Grabbing the gun from the table, he sprinted up the old iron staircase, sending a shower of tiny dark-brown dots of rust tinkling down, covering his tracks and forming a speckled carpet over everything. A spider's web of corroded steel gantries spread out across the higher level, supported by a network of cross members spanning the level below. Old-fashioned Swiss over-engineering that would take a bomb to demolish. *Let's hope so,* Ben thought. He stopped just below the very highest level and knelt on a gantry of steel mesh, directly above the loading bay. He had his plan.

A heavy metal guitar riff clanged loudly against the metal insides of the old warehouse. Disorientated by the discordant guitar and drum number, Ben hunched his shoulders and gripped his gun, his eyes flicking back and forth in search of an explanation. Until he realised someone was ringing the dead torturer's mobile phone lying on the metal table forty feet below him.

The ringing stopped. Ben heard the car's engine beat change. He closed his eyes and listened; their car had slowed, barely ticking over as they cautiously circled the building. They had called their colleagues, but with no reply they now knew not all was as it should be.

Ben couldn't see them, but he could hear them. He heard the click of a car door softly closing. They had dropped off one at the back, probably coming through the same door that Ben had used fifteen minutes earlier. The engine pitch changed again, the sound coming from a different direction. They were slowly coming round to the loading bay, trapping him in a pincer movement.

He reviewed his options: outnumbered, outgunned, and an injured Stephanie to defend. His heart was making more noise than their car as he laid out his arsenal in front of him. His training hadn't wandered far; it could have been yesterday, as all the familiar disciplines flooded back and took control.

His first weapon: from below, he was in darkness. Second weapon: they didn't know if he was still here, although they would soon discover he had been here. Third: he had a better field of vision than anyone below him; he could see most of the ground floor, including where they would probably park, next to the other SUV.

He looked down to see them do exactly that, as they pulled into the loading bay. Ben had a bird's eye view of them as the front doors opened and two men stepped out, backs to the car, guns at the ready, each scanning a semi-circle in front of them. He knew the third one was now inside because of the change in pressure when he had struggled to open the same door as Ben had.

If he let them split up and search the building, they would discover two dead colleagues and the seriously injured Stephanie, who would be their hostage again. He needed to group them together, where he could see them. Below him would be ideal, but none of them were below him now. In fact, none of them were even in sight.

Ben started to question whether his plan to find higher ground had been a good one. He was a long way from them, a long way from Stephanie. Holding back the beginnings of panic, trying to think clearly, he went over his training. *What do I have? Grenades, two guns, flash-bangs, and a tablet.* A light went on in his head. Within a second, he primed a flash-bang and dropped it to land twenty-five metres below, right in between the two SUV's. Knowing what to expect, Ben closed his eyes and pressed his hands into his ears. Even so, the impact was considerable as a shower of rust was shaken loose from the roof as the booming noise echoed around the building. It was quickly followed by three loud voices shouting to each other from below.

He resumed his kneeling position, peering through the mesh gantry as two of them reappeared through the smoke. They'd come back to investigate, guns at the ready, each warily scanning half a circle, with their backs to each other. Both looked up, trying to pierce the darkness above, distracted by the noise of birds previously nesting amongst the girders, now panicking and flying into metalwork and each other.

Neither could see Ben, their puppeteer, motionless and far above them; they were unwilling players on his stage, in his production to bring them together into his kill zone. The two puppets were confused when the smoke cleared and there was no evidence as to what had caused the explosion.

Ben tapped the tablet to wake up the sleeping system and went into the Fire menu. He had two green dots to choose from. One was beneath him, which would definitely take care of the two below him, but it would still leave the third man, and he would be calling for reinforcements by then. Not good. The other green dot was one hundred metres away, wedged next to his car's petrol tank. He selected that one and pressed the Fire option on the small screen. The desired effect. A modest bang, followed instantaneously by a loud boom and a whoosh, as sixty litres of fuel in the abandoned SUV instantly ignited.

The two men ran to the loading bay to view the explosion. They were now out of sight. A few seconds later, the third man followed, running underneath Ben to join them. He was also now out of sight.

The puppeteer gave a taut smile; he had herded them together.

'What the fuck was that? Has to be that Hotshot guy.'

'Do you think it was a Good Boy?'

'Could have been, but why over there, and how was it triggered?'

'He could have triggered it when he was trying to take it off.'

Three reasonable explanations, thought Ben from his eyrie, *but none of them correct.* He held two fragmentation grenades over the side of the gantry's rail. They were primed, so all he had to do was release them, then he had three-and-a-half seconds until they exploded. He tried to calculate the distance to the floor, then the speed of a falling grenade, then convert it into seconds.

Abandoning his calculations, he removed the pins and dropped them as soon as he saw the boot of the first enemy come into view twenty-five metres below him. While they were falling, he grabbed the tablet, hit the Fire option for the remaining green dot, also below him, covered his ears, closed his eyes, and prayed.

The hard surfaces and cavernous old metal structure magnified the sound, but the impact was devastating; one hundred and fifty grams of high explosive in the Good Boy he'd removed from Stephanie, and two fragmentation grenades. When you're outnumbered and outgunned, there is no such thing as too much.

Both their cars blazed, and the intense heat rose directly in a scorching column up to his nesting place. The distinct smell of spent flammables scoured his nasal passages and made his eyes water. Smoke and falling debris were everywhere as he sprang up and raced down the iron stairs, prayers being offered and promises to deities being made for no harm to Stephanie.

Descending into dense smoke, he tumbled down the ladder, feathers fluttering down in a thick snowfall from where the percussion had destroyed anything stupid enough to remain after the flash-bangs. Ben was covering the ground quickly now, gun held forwards, through swirling smoke, towards the burning cars.

Enemy one: a confirmed kill, limbs detached. Enemy two: ditto. A bloody trail telegraphed Enemy three's whereabouts. Ben caught up with him dragging himself across the damp concrete, kicking him hard in what remained of his leg and flipping the screaming casualty onto his back.

'Maybe you'll live, maybe you won't, I don't give a shit. But you'll live long enough to tell Liang that I have something he wants. Something that when he knows what it is, he'll want very badly. When they come for you, tell Mr. Liang that Ben Mason will be calling him to discuss a trade. You got that?'

The traumatised and bloodied man could barely manage a nod, but he did, just.

Ben ran back to where he had left Stephanie. *Surely she would have been far enough away from the explosions?* he reassured himself. Trauma multiplied by trauma from the noise of the flash-bangs, grenades, and explosives; unavoidable, but that was discomfort as opposed to injury.

She wasn't there. The sleeping bags had been tossed to one side, but no Stephanie. The one who came through the back door must have taken her somewhere.

The sound of debris being crunched by a footstep came from behind him, and he spun, crouching, and aimed all in one practised motion as he glimpsed the gun aimed at his head.

Stephanie stumbled forward with a gun in her hand, incoherently mumbling. 'What happened?'

He caught her before she fell, removed the firearm from her weak grip, and tucked it into his waistband. 'They're definitely all gone now, Steph, definitely.' He lifted her up and walked towards the loading bay.

*

The driver flashed his headlights as it raced across the open ground of the disused site. It slowed to a halt just in front of them, and a concerned Francois jumped out of one side while an ex-colleague, as Francois later referred to him, leapt from the other.

'She's out on morphine. I gave her twenty-five mil IV. They've broken some bones but she's strong, so I don't expect it to slow her down much,' Ben added with a smile. 'Could you take her? I might drop her.'

Francois stepped forward to carry his goddaughter.

With a practised eye, he took in the scene: the two SUVs burned furiously, another one did the same a hundred metres away, while the last of the smoke swirled and feathers fluttered on the wind, with two dismembered corpses nearby.

'Four confirmed kills and one barely alive,' announced the ex-colleague as he reappeared from inside.

'The live one's my messenger, taking a message back to Liang,' Ben called over his shoulder.

'Are you OK?' Francois' customary economy.

'We need to end this. We can't afford another stunt like this, or London, or New York, or Hilda's Monte Carlo nightmare, the plane, or anywhere for that matter. We have to finish it with Liang once and for all. Meanwhile, I suggest we get out of here before the Police arrive.'

In the distance, the faint strains of police sirens carried on the wind.

'Agreed.' And Francois turned with Ben to walk back to his car.

Chapter Forty-Seven

'Two metatarsals left foot, three right. Spiral fractures of both fibula – fortunately for Stephanie, those are soft bone fractures – and a cracked left tibula.' The sympathetic, but matter of fact diagnosis by Stephan Virchow, the orthopaedic consultant, came from under a mess of unkempt, shock-white hair. The rangy medic used hand gestures and shoulder shrugs to apologetically describe every aspect of Stephanie's injuries. He looked over, as opposed to through, his half-frame glasses, wearing them like a theatrical prop, to be used as a distraction, something he fiddled with, while preparing the answer to a difficult question. And there had been many this morning, ever since Hilda had arranged to take sole occupancy of the ten-bed, private hospital facility, generously compensating the owner-consultants for temporarily moving surgery and medical procedures to another clinic.

'Thankfully the tissue damage is more in the bruised category than a hematoma, but it is acute and widespread. She's young and in good health, so they shouldn't present a long-term concern. The immediate concern is the cracked fibula; that'll cause severe discomfort, and she will not be able to weight-bear for at least three weeks. Rest is the best medication, and keeping it still, straight, and as high as possible, to aid venous flow.'

'It doesn't feel that bad, not as painful as you're describing.' Stephanie sceptically joined the conversation.

'That'll be the legacy effect of the morphine, plus codeine we gave you before you went into the MRI scanner. The morphine will soon wear off and then it'll feel different.'

Stephanie's look disagreed as she sank back into the bed. 'But I could get about in a wheelchair provided I keep my leg up?'

'Miss Oppenheimer, you have been exposed to severe trauma. My strong professional advice is that you rest for at least seventy-two hours. Let's see how the bruising and swelling progress, then perform another MRI scan. Until then, I don't think we should be discussing wheelchairs or going anywhere.' Mr. Virchow had developed a tactful bedside manner during his career, but even so he was surprised by a patient with these injuries mounting such a strong challenge.

Stephanie feigned being too tired to engage in a more forthright discussion. She had already worked out that Virchow wouldn't be in the clinic forever.

'Thank you, Herr Virchow, we really appreciate your discretion in this matter. I know I don't have to explain the implications and seriousness of recent events, nor that of Claus' murder.' Ingrid's composure slumped from elegance to sorrow in one sentence when she mentioned Claus' name.

'Frau Oppenheimer, it is my pleasure, and I will return tomorrow morning to check on your daughter. I am on call, if required.' And as if to emphasise that he could do no more, he added, 'But I doubt that will be necessary.' Politely bowing to Ingrid then nodding to the others, he turned and left the room.

*

'You've all met Danny, haven't you?' Ben looked enquiringly at Ingrid, Hilda, and Francois, now gathered around Stephanie's bed. Collective nods said they had, so Ben continued.

'Good. Given events in New York, the plane, and the lakeside warehouse, we've less time than we thought. Liang has more men, weaponry, and better funding than we do, but we know our objectives so we just need a plan for how to achieve them. Unfortunately, now that he has sole control of the videos – which he'll have destroyed by now – our options are reduced.'

'Not exactly old son.' Danny's distinctive Cockney lilt interrupted, his angular features restraining a pinched grin.

'What does that mean?' Ben shared everyone's confusion.

'Well, you see, I accessed the site before Liang did and created a duplicate in another name, right? Believe it or not, we've got copies of all fifty-two beautiful, life-sentence-guaranteeing videos.' Danny's grin was at breaking point.

'How the hell did—?' Ben couldn't finish before Stephanie's enthusiasm cut straight across the room.

'Danny Mullen, I goddam love you.' She sat up and smiled through obvious pain. 'I knew you'd got it; I just knew it. You and your fucking noisy Maserati.' To everyone's confusion, Danny and Stephanie laughed loudly together, a tension-releasing, vocal-chord blast of pleasure.

Ingrid looked disapprovingly in an approving way.

'You guys need to let us in on your secret, because we have no idea what you're on about.' Ben remembered on the plane picking up a vibe from them, without understanding why.

'Danny, you're the hero, you tell them.' Stephanie smiled and winced simultaneously.

'Princess Stephanie 'ere gave me everything I needed. Remember before that nutter on the plane burst in, Steph remoted onto Ingrid's PC, right? When Ingrid read out the PC address, I made a note of it – couldn't help meself, force of habit.' Trademark Danny grin. 'Then Ingrid gave us her password, and I copied that an' all, so I just followed Steph as she remotely accessed Ingrid's PC. If you can imagine, I'm right behind 'er as she's walking down the virtual road to set up that site what Uwe gave us.' Danny gave the smile of the child who had deliberately not bet on the horse his dad told him to, had bet on another, and it had come in at twenty-to-one.

'That's smart, Danny, but tell them how you read my mind and worked out the password for Uwe's site.' Stephanie was reliving Danny's story as if she'd heard it a thousand times.

'Now that's where Steph should take all the credit. First time we met was when Ben brought 'er into the pub, and the first words she ever 'eard me say were...' Danny and Stephanie looked at each other as they chorused in Cockney unison, '..."it's Italian for fucking noisy Maserati".' Then they both laughed.

'So, when you two was on the plane, and out of the blue she screams at that psycho, "you fucking noisy Italian", it was so not-right, that I knew she'd said it for a reason. And when the psycho started blowing flight attendants 'eads off, I didn't know how much time we 'ad left, so I gambled. I went back into Uwe's site – a bit nervous, right? And typed, "Maserati". Honestly, I was close to crapping me self when I hit Enter, then did a little jig when it let me in. I've saved it under a different name; thereby creating two versions of the site, each containing fifty-two videos. If Liang's destroyed his site, which by now he probably has, that means we now have the only remaining copies of those lovely incriminating vids.'

'You're an absolute legend, Dan.' Ben turned to Stephanie. 'But how did you know Danny had done that? He couldn't have told you, because you were on the plane with me and the hijackers.'

'If you remember, after he shot poor Emma, the guy was shouting and swearing at me, telling me to give him the password, and waving his gun around like a phallus substitute when Danny interrupted him, saying "Steph, it's OK. Videos aren't worth a copy-cat killing." That's about the only way to say "Steph – OK – Videos – Copy", without actually saying it. That's when I knew; I didn't know, that's when I so hoped that Danny was sending a message back to me. At least, I hoped he was.' Stephanie gave a relieved laugh.

When they'd been on the plane, Ben had realised that Danny was trying to tell him something, and he remembered Danny nodding with his eyes without moving his head.

'So, that's why you knew you could safely give Liang's goons the video password to Uwe's site, because you knew Dan had already created another site. Amazing. You're both bloody legends.' Ben clapped in approval.

Francois still needed convincing. 'I thought Ben said it would collapse unless it was done through Ingrid's computer?'

'Golden Boy lied, Francois. Simple as that. Like most things, Ben made it up as he went along. All that IP address stuff is technically true, but what he said about only Ingrid's computer being able to access Uwe's site was total bollocks. And Golden Boy put it out there, knowing I'd spot it.' Danny's matter-of-fact explanation quietened them all as they reflected on the scale of Ben's gamble and how close they had come to disaster.

'Liang is a powerful nutter, and he may discover what you've done, Danny. For your own safety you've got to circulate to all of us the address, password, etc. in case anything happens...' Ben didn't need to finish the sentence.

'Will do.' Danny gave a thumbs-up with a nervous grin.

'OK, we're looking better all the time, but the videos are just like a nuclear weapon; they only work as a deterrent. If we use them, they may prove fatal to the Five, but we'll have written our own death sentences. We need to buy time, quickly, we need a very clever plan, and I think I know what that is.'

Chapter Forty-Eight

'We've got to turn them against each other, to kill each other, or they'll kill all of us.' Ben looked into the five faces staring back at him: a broad canvas from agreement to uncertainty. 'We're six amateurs and they're a small army, but as the Army taught me "All warfare is based on deception", so we've got to deceive them.

'When we left that lakeside warehouse, I sent Liang a message through one of his wounded henchmen, to say we had something he wants and that we were willing to trade. I'm hoping we can lure him out. If not, we may need to explore a more permanent solution with them. The trouble with that plan is, they would not be around to cancel the contracts they've already put out on us.' Ben studied each of them.

'What do we have that is so valuable to Liang, and how do we cancel those contracts?' Stephanie expressed what they all thought.

'I asked Danny to create another video. It's a deepfake that plays so well to Liang's insecurities he'll believe it's true. What you're about to see is augmented reality. It never actually happened, but through the lens of Liang's paranoia he'll believe it did. Dan, you ready?' Ben looked to his friend, who nodded in return and tapped commands into his laptop.

Danny turned the screen so Stephanie, propped up on her pillows, could see, and the others crowded around as he played the video.

'That's Calvert,' observed Francois, as the tall and distinctive features of the Charges d'Affaires to Britain's Embassy in Berne could be seen striding confidently across the St. Gallen Hotel's sunlit terrace. His hand and facial features were outstretched in a faux welcome to the two similarly faux-smiling people who stood to greet him, the ubiquitous Panama hat in his other hand.

'That's Towner. God, I detested that man. And Bianca Sabatini, so transparent.' Ingrid did not trust herself to say any more.

Danny turned up the volume. The stage was the St Gallen Hotel terrace, the two men and a woman were the players upon it, and Danny's Implied Voice Synthesisation controlled the narrative.

Calvert: *The Panama bank and the Uzbek Bank have confirmed everything is in place. Everything is set up as we discussed.*

Sabitini: *Good, I've done a bit of digging, and Liang's so liquid at the moment he has trouble getting rid of it. He can easily afford a hundred million. Whether he will, I'm still not sure.*

Towner: *Liang's just a bully and nowhere near as smart as he thinks he is. When he sees the evidence, he'll crap himself, especially as he won't know who the hell is blackmailing him. Nothing less than he deserves, and when we've got him on the run, we can take him for another hit in a month, and then another after that. We'll bleed the Chinese fucker dry.*

Calvert: *We're not in any rush here. We have common cause to hate him, but don't forget, one hundred million is a huge amount in one blackmail hit. Let's do the first one, make sure the whole chain operates smoothly, then we can think about the next hit.*

Sabitini: *Remind me again, why do we need the Uzbeks?*

Calvert: *Uzbekistan is just a smokescreen. Nothing more. The money doesn't actually go there, it just looks like it does, and Uzbekistan is so corrupt that anyone attempting a forensic audit there will get absolutely nowhere. When the funds from Liang's secret bank accounts are cleared through Panama, they'll be split three ways, transferred to our three accounts as agreed, then the whole structure will elegantly collapse itself. Like sealing off a mineshaft. No-one will ever be able to discover anything.*

Towner: *Sounds good to me, I had it checked out, I'm cool with it. I say let's hit the button and wipe the smile of his fat face.'*

Calvert, Sabitini, and Towner then chink their glasses in a self-congratulatory toast, smiling and laughing like old friends at a reunion. Danny closed his laptop.

'That's amazingly real for a conversation that never happened.' Francois' nature was to be sceptical of everything.

'The audio's fake, the video's real. Those three did meet on the St. Gallen terrace exactly as you saw, and they had a conversation, but it wasn't the conversation you heard. They discussed a variety of topics which gave Danny's app a good database of words and phonetic variations to manipulate. Danny's Voice Synthesiser app captures someone speaking, analyses the voice-patterns, converts it into digital form, and then into text. I wrote the script, Danny entered that into his app, reversed the process, and hey presto, they all spoke the words I wrote for them.'

'But I saw their mouths moving in sync with the words.' Francois still needed some convincing.

'Yeah, human brain's beautiful, init?' Danny picked up the explanation. 'They ain't in sync, that's your brain's conditioning thinking they're in sync, right? Ever since whenever, your brain has seen people's mouths move and words come out. Provided there's no lag in timing, you're now conditioned to make them appear to say those words, even if they're not. Gotta love the human mind, eh, Francois?' Francois mulled over Danny and Ben's explanations.

'It sounds very realistic. If I close my eyes and listen, that is Calvert, Towner, and Sabitini speaking.' Ingrid's endorsement encouraged them, as she was the only one to have had spent time with the three subjects. 'How do you see this playing out, Ben?'

'Liang will believe that I have something real, because I could so easily have killed his goon in the same way as I did the others. Instead, I'm taking a huge risk coming to visit him on my own, and his paranoia will pique his interest. He'll be suspicious, but he'll be curious enough to sample what we've got. If he's not interested, we'll know soon enough as he'll try to have me killed. But I suspect he'll want to trade when I show him a sample of the video.'

'How will you show him that sample without being killed?' Stephanie's pained expression was not just from her injuries.

'Francois is driving me there now.'

Chapter Forty-Nine

The two black arms swept in parallel. A hectic, synchronised ballet alternately bowing to each wing, sweeping the windscreen to reveal a view of the mountain road ahead before fresh moisture clung to the glass. It wasn't rain; it was water vapour imprisoned in the cloud, awaiting a warmer surface to set it free, to release it into liquid form. Francois' car provided the vapour's escape as they descended through the misty morning into the bright valley. Automatic sensors slowed the ballet as the moisture reduced, and the black arms paused.

Ben looked up at the cloud's underbelly, suspended above Zurich, gently swaying to the west, sliding slowly up and over the hills ringing the old city. The lake stretched away beneath them, a shimmering mirror of the cloud's complexion, grey morphed into a pale sunlight as the cloud tumbled over the hilltops.

'Liang's offices are at the far end of Stockerstrasse, next to the Schweizer Banque building.'

'Yes, I know the one.' Francois' eyes scanned the rear-view mirror while his expression searched for the right words. 'I don't like this; it's too high risk and not even a plan. It's just shaking a tree to see what happens. And you have no Plan B, no contingency, no back-up.'

'You're my back-up, Francois.' Ben gave him a wry smile, trying to avoid a deep conversation; the smile was not returned. 'My plan is a non-plan. I know the beginning and I know what I need to achieve, so I'll play what's in front of me and adapt as circumstances change, because we don't have time to cover every eventuality. Don't worry, Liang won't do anything after he sees the St. Gallen video. He'll want it too much to risk losing it.'

'That's not a plan, that's just extreme risk-taking, making it up as you go along. I still don't like it, nor do the others, we...'

Ben cut him off. 'Francois, the others haven't seen the world that you and I have. They don't see the dangers you and I see. And you may need to explain it to them if it's needed; we've just run out of options. Simple as that. We're in Liang's end game, we were lucky to escape the last end-game. In an ideal world I wouldn't plan it like this, but we were blown out of the ideal world a long time ago. Liang will have destroyed Uwe's videos by now. He'll believe those were the only copies, and now we six are the only remaining loose ends. The longer we wait to do something only gives his hired killers more time to find Ingrid, Stephanie, and Hilda.' Ben deliberately chose names which would hit Francois the hardest.

'I know. You're right.' Francois said quietly. 'But please be careful.'

'Drop me on Gotthard Strasse. I'll get a better feel for surveillance if I'm on foot.' Ben checked the mechanism on his Glock, sliding it forwards and back several times before tucking it into his belt, then pulling his jacket over it.

As Francois' eyes scanned for anything out of the ordinary, he gripped the wheel more tightly than he had on the twisting descent from the hills. He edged the car towards the pavement, driving slowly alongside it for fifty metres, hoping to draw out anyone expecting their arrival.

'I'll find a parking space and take up a position near Liang's offices. A couple of my ex-colleagues will already be around there. One will cover the back of the building, another the underground car park. You got your gun? Spare mag, knife?' Francois' expression told Ben he would be right behind him.

'I do, but I've also got something far more powerful. I've got Liang's paranoia and insecurities batting for us, so we can't lose.' Ben half smiled as he punched Francois' arm and stepped out onto the pavement.

Immediately he felt exposed. Every pedestrian looked like a hit man with a contract to fulfil, and he was suspicious of everyone. He tried to walk but his legs had turned to wood. With an awkward gait, he made the corner of Stockerstrasse, imagining snipers in every window, drive-by machine gunners in each passing car, even the trams carried knife-wielding assassins. He forced himself into a jaunty bounce, exuding a positive body language but probably looking like an over-eager car salesman.

Ben arrived at number 29. A short set of steps was topped by two pairs of blast-resistant, sliding glass doors, one pair behind the other, creating a mid-chamber of transparent vulnerability. The second set of doors wouldn't open till the first closed, and they were manually operated by the ex-military lookalike standing at ease behind the second set. Ben knew there was no need to be shy now as he announced himself into the intercom.

'Ben Mason to see Thomas Liang. He's expecting me.' Ben stood and made eye contact with the ex-military doorman inside the lobby. The look that a boxer gives his opponent when the referee holds their gloved wrists before the bell.

A hard stare returned from the doorman, a delayed reaction of a few seconds, then recognition. He spoke animatedly into his lapel, holding his finger to his ear, and looked towards the grand reception desk for instruction. Ben named the three receptionists Calmness, Headless, and Clueless, as he stood motionless, waiting outside the four thick glass doors. Statue-like, apart from a small trickle of sweat tumbling slowly down his spine, his heart pounded and every nerve tingled from the expected impact of the high calibre round. He could only stand, outwardly calm and still, which is what he did while his gaze never broke connection with the now less-composed military doorman. *You'll have to shoot me while I stare into your soul,* Ben said to himself. *I won't make it easy for you.*

No high calibre round tore through his vital organs nor exploded in his head as, after a minute, the doors slid silently open. He walked naturally into the mid-chamber and waited. Externally a paragon of composure; internally a battle to overcome his fear. He heard the outer doors behind slide smoothly closed as the second set opened in front of him. As Ben stepped into the lobby, he sensed the doorman step back ever so slightly and place his hand on his hip. *Hardly a concealed weapon now,* thought Ben, as he smiled and motioned the doorman to follow, walking up to the receptionist he had named Calmness.

'I'm going to take my phone out of my pocket. I will press play, and you,' he pointed at Calmness, 'will use your camera to film a ten-second sample of a video. You will then send that to Thomas Liang, or even play it to him via that camera that's poorly hidden in the painting behind you.' He indicated a 3D mess of paint and rubble, hung in a huge frame behind the reception area.

'Mr. Liang is not in this office today, Mr.—?'

'Yes, he is,' Ben cut Calmness short. 'He's watching us now through that camera, because you called him when I announced myself. The choice is yours. If I walk out now, I'll play the video to the people in the video who don't yet know how badly it incriminates them. When they see it, they'll do anything to stop Liang from seeing it, offer me billions, and probably put a hit on Mr. Liang. As Mr. Liang will blame you for that, do you want to check again to see if Mr. Liang is actually in the building?' Direct action energised him as he dominated Clueless.

'Please, Mr. Mason, take a seat and I will enquire.' Clueless decided to check Mr. Liang's whereabouts while Ben found himself a seat and waited, amused at the doorman's inability to decide what he should do. Ben made it harder for him by not taking his eyes off him. Eventually the doorman turned to gaze out into the street.

Less than a minute later, Calmness walked to where Ben was seated. 'I have my phone, Mr. Mason, can you play that video please?'

'So, Liang is in the building after all?' Ben smiled kindly. This wasn't the receptionist's fight. 'Funny that, eh?'

As Ben swiped the video forward and pressed play, Towner's distinct American accent bounced around the marble and glass cube of the lobby. His words sounded even more convincing off the harsh surfaces.

'Liang's nowhere near as smart as he thinks he is, when he sees the evidence, he'll crap himself, especially as he won't know who the hell is blackmailing him. Nothing less than he deserves and when we've got him on the run, we can take him for another hundred mil in a few months and then another hundred after that, We'll bleed the Chinese fucker dry'.'

'Tell Liang I'll wait here for exactly one minute. Then I'll sell it to the man who's talking in that video. You know who he is, don't you?' Ben could see Calmness was miles out of his depth, nearly stumbling in his haste to return to the security of the reception counter.

Ben calmly crossed his legs and, while straightening one trouser leg, drew his gun from behind him, resting it on his thigh. It wasn't a snatched movement; but it wasn't slow, taking the doorman by surprise. Ben could see his thoughts as they ran through the man's head. He locked eyes again with the doorman and shook his head. Eventually the doorman nodded, spread his fingers, and held his hands clasped behind his back, away from his gun, it wasn't his fight either and Ben came with a reputation.

He checked his watch, outwardly calm, inwardly fighting to control the fear. Twenty seconds gone, he sat back and forced a small smile just to make himself feel better. He wanted to check his watch, his insides screamed at him to check his watch, his heartbeat said check your bloody watch, but he resisted the temptation. The bead of sweat sliding down his spine had been joined by several others, he checked his watch with all the nonchalance he could garner. Fifty long seconds had gone; ten even longer ones to go.

He counted eleven seconds, rose easily, eyes still locked on the doorman. *Liang's had his chance.*

Ben walked across the lobby towards the glass doors, right hand clasped around the Glock now placed back into his pocket, out of the double glass exit, obligingly opened for him by the increasingly nervous doorman. Ben had one foot on the top step, his heart beating a big drum in his head, when he saw Francois on the other side of the road, walking quickly towards him. Francois had a gun poorly disguised under a newspaper, but it was a gun.

Recognising a kindred military spirit, he knew Francois sensed danger, hence his sprint towards Ben, just before the panicked and sudden shout from behind him. Ben spun in a flash, levelling the gun onto the man's chest. It was Calmness.

'Mr Liang says he is free to see you now.' Calmness was anything but, clasping his hands to his chest and screwing his eyes shut when he saw the gun pointing at him.

Ben thought the receptionist did well not to leave the contents of his stomach on the steps. Curiously, it made him feel better.

He marched back into the lobby. 'Come on then, let's go.'

Calmness couldn't get Ben into the private elevator quickly enough, shakily hovering his electronic master key over the tab of the upper-most floor, before quickly retreating. Ben knew he couldn't afford to relax; he knew Liang would be watching him through any number of concealed cameras.

A melody chimed to announce his arrival on the eighth floor – one of Zurich's highest – as the doors glided open. As expected, he was greeted by two of Liang's security. He raised one arm while the other opened up his jacket, and he nodded towards the butt of his gun sticking out of his waistband. One of them carefully lifted it while his associate held a gun aimed at Ben's chest. They disarmed him as Thomas Liang rounded the corner.

'Ah ha, the legendary Ben Mason.' Ben could see Liang was not completely comfortable looking up to someone twenty centimetres taller. 'You intrigue me, Mister Mason. You can't be completely stupid but, here you are, appearing to be completely stupid.'

'You don't intrigue me in the slightest.' Ben's matter-of-fact delivery cut Liang short as he strode purposefully, bumping Liang's shoulder as he swept past, through the open door and into the office behind. Liang's security hastily followed.

'You're also the last person I ever want to conduct polite chit-chat with, so let me educate you as to why I'm not completely stupid. I'm going to play you a fascinating short film.' Ben's tone was weighed heavily with distaste as he pulled out his phone and played the full St. Gallen video, doctored through Danny's voice synthesising app.

Ben studied Liang as he watched the video. He had to be shocked; three of his closest associates colluding together to destroy him, one hundred million blackmailing dollars at a time. That had to hit home.

'Stop, go back,' Liang commanded. 'Go back where he calls me Chinese fucker.'

Ben could see Liang was affected by the video; it wasn't the money, it was power. They were no longer afraid of him.

He pretended otherwise but it had hit him. Ben was even more pleased with his scriptwriting when Liang snorted derisively at his colleagues' view of him.

'Uzbekistan? Ha. I taught them all how to launder through Uzbekistan, through Belarus, through Slovakia, all places.' Liang was totally absorbed and becoming agitated as the video played on. He did a very good impersonation of someone shrugging it off, but Ben sensed he had bitten.

'How did you get this?' Liang spat his enquiry.

'Claus.' Truth no longer mattered, and Ben needed to press all the buttons he could.

'Ha.' Liang snorted in time with his breathing. 'Smart. Why would I buy this video now I've seen it?' The folds of skin around Liang's eyes recessed them even further. 'I don't need this video to justify the revenge I will take. I'm hardly likely to take it to the Police, am I?' Liang's laugh was quite natural and his round and short body shook with laughter. Turning to the bodyguard who had accompanied Ben into the room. 'Take him away and deal with him.'

The bodyguard drew his gun easily – his hand had been resting on the butt – and pointed it at Ben's heart.

'Put it away, mate.' Ben had expected this could happen, so he was ready. Fighting hard to project complete confidence, he smiled and shook his head sympathetically, forcing a chuckle from somewhere.

'Oh my, you just don't get it do you. I'm not here to *sell* you the video,' Ben's composure halted Liang. 'You're going to pay me NOT to send it to Towner, Sabitini, and Calvert.' A light began to cut through the fog of Liang's arrogance. 'This video is attached to an email addressed to Towner, Sabitini, Calvert, and you, which, if you don't give us what we want, will be sent to them in two minutes. When your three colleagues open the email and watch the video, they'll see you are on the address list, and they'll realise you know about their plot.

'They will then know that you'll do whatever is necessary to kill them, and each will know their only chance of survival will be to kill you first, then to buy out the contract you took out on them.

You can buy a lot of hit men if you're a multi-billionaire, so you'll all spend as much of your illegal billions as it takes to protect yourselves. But, as there's three of them and only one of you, the odds are with them.'

The dim light in Liang's mind was now a set of floodlights.

'What do you want?' he snapped. 'And how do I know you won't also sell it to them afterwards?'

'I want our freedom,' Ben replied. 'I want all contracts on us cancelled immediately, never to be reinstated. I want you to handle Towner and Sabitini however you need to, so that they don't go rogue and do their own thing. If anything ever happens to any of us, or our families, then the video, along with an explanation, will be released anonymously to the Police because, by then, I expect each of these three will have suffered inexplicable fatal accidents. The Police will have your motive, opportunity, and means for those murders.' Action helped Ben drive home his proposal.

'OK, but you haven't answered the question. What's stopping you from selling it to Towner, Sabitini, and Calvert anyway?'

'If I did, then they'd kill you, and that's the paradox: we need you to stay alive, and you need us to stay alive. The ultimate survival symbiosis. We've put measures in place – let's call it insurance – so that if any of us six dies unnaturally, then the video is anonymously delivered to the Police. I'm sure you'll make similar arrangements. It's a mutual poison-pill. If I sell it to your three colleagues then they would kill you, which would trigger your insurance, and a contract will be taken out on us.'

Liang was nodding by the time Ben concluded. He knew Ben had correctly guessed how he would react.

'And you think you can trust me?' Liang couldn't help himself. He had to see where the other side's tolerance would stretch to.

'Of course not, but I don't need to. You'll be signing your own death certificate if you try to screw us. It's a mutual stranglehold, and you have,' Ben made a point of looking at his watch, 'to make a decision in thirty seconds or that email will be sent, and I can't stop it.'

Ben didn't blink as he looked straight through Liang. He knew Liang would tell his bodyguard behind him to shoot as soon as he decided not to go with their plan. He slowly let the knife slide down the inside of his jacket sleeve. They'd been sloppy when they'd searched him; he'd given up his gun early, and they had not bothered to search him beyond that. Probably they were grateful to have avoided a conflict with someone who had already killed a dozen of their colleagues.

'Less than ten seconds,' Ben announced confidently. The bass drum was beating in his head, the knife was inside his palm. Liang was close enough and would be too slow to stop Ben stabbing him in his carotid artery. At least the others would be safe and Sam, his wife, would be avenged.

Liang stood motionless. *Is he calculating the odds?* Ben wondered. *Or does he take pleasure in experiencing extreme human emotions?* Ben surrendered himself to a place where instincts had control; it was familiar to him. He smiled to disguise the tense and coiled muscle of his right arm. He could kill Liang before the bodyguard could kill him. Three. Two. One.

'OK, we've got a deal.' When Liang spoke, Ben tried not to look relieved. Liang also looked anxious.

'Good decision, Liang. Now I need to stop that email.' Ben typed a meaningless txt and sent it to Francois, as tension flowed out of the room.

Liang held up his hand to Ben. 'I pay well for men with your skills, Mason.' A questioning intonation suffixed Liang's audacity. 'Here, take my card.'

Ben slapped it away with contempt. 'Go fuck yourself, Liang.'

'Suit yourself, but if you change your mind...' Liang again left his comment hanging in the air.

'I won't.' And turning towards the bodyguard, Ben held out his hand. 'Gun.' The man waited for Liang's shrug before handing it over.

'And don't forget, you need to call off any contracts you have on us, and do it now.' Stepping into the lift, Ben turned and faced Liang. 'Do it now, Liang or bear the consequences.'

As the lift doors began to close, Liang stepped forward and flicked his business card into the lift. 'This was never your fight,

Mason, you just wrong time wrong place. It was always business, nothing personal.'

Interesting, he still doesn't know Sam was my wife. This is going to be so sweet when it happens, thought Ben. And it felt good.

As the lift doors closed, Ben allowed himself a controlled exhale, resisting the urge to react; he knew the lift had its own CCTV. *I don't trust Liang not to pull something, it's in his DNA,* he whispered to himself as he checked the Glock – full mag and one in the breach.

Liang's card taunted him from the marble floor of the lift. He was tempted to grind his foot into the card, the vicarious pleasure of stamping on Liang's name, then he noticed Liang's personal mobile number. He bent down and picked up the card as he sensed more jigsaw pieces slotting into place, early signs of a plan coming together. Slipping it into his pocket he walked out of the lift with his gun levelled at the doorman, marching straight towards the frightened man.

'Gun,' he commanded loudly of the confused employee. 'Give me your gun. Now,' Ben repeated with even more authority. Numb, the man obliged, and Ben again hid his relief as he removed the magazine, double-worked the slide mechanism to expel the round already in the chamber, and handed it back.

'No offence, I've just got this thing about people shooting me in the back.' Ben walked smartly out of the glass doors.

Chapter Fifty

Thomas Liang snorted derisively at the CCTV monitor when he saw his ground-floor security meekly surrender his gun to Ben. 'He's fired,' he muttered. No expletives now, he wanted to save his energy, much of which was being consumed by planning his next move. Mason's video of his treacherous colleagues' plot to blackmail him had changed everything.

He studied the phone. He'd never noticed how heavy it felt, how sticky it was in his hand. His fingers trembled as he made an encrypted call to an untraceable number.

'Da,' came the short reply.

'Do you recall the "library" I sent you?'

'Da,' the untraceable number replied after a pause.

'I need you to make the necessary arrangements, because I need numbers two, three, and six taken care of.'

Silence.

'Simultaneously,' added Liang.

Silence.

'Did you hear what—'

'I heard. I'm thinking,' the untraceable number interrupted. 'You are sure? Numbers two, three, and six? All at the same time?' the number enquired hesitantly.

'Yes. Two, three, six. All at the same time. But not yet; I will tell you when. Make all the necessary arrangements and be ready to go when I tell you. That will be in a day or so.' Tension squeezed every one of Thomas Liang's words. 'How much?'

'Five million.'

'Agreed.'

'Each.'

Five seconds of silence lasts longer than five seconds.

'Agreed.' Thomas Liang flexed his neck from side to side and punched the intercom button on the phone. 'Get me on the next flight to Hong Kong.'

Chapter Fifty-One

Ben recognised the back of Francois' head. He was standing on the pavement in front of Liang's building, watching a delivery van as it drove towards the lake, holding a gun inside a newspaper. It looked ridiculous. Francois turned when he heard the glass doors slide open.

'You're alive, the clean-up squad just took a call and vanished, and you sent me a nonsense text. So I presume your non-plan went according to plan?' It was obvious Francois was unaccustomed to smiling, but the thought was there.

'You can never be certain with a psycho like Liang, but if he's already called off his men, then I think we got the result we wanted. Come on, let's get back, the clock's ticking.' They walked back down Stockerstrasse with an easier rhythm than fifteen minutes earlier.

*

'Liang's in deep with Towner and Sabitini, so I doubt he'll do anything to them immediately. He'll wait to see if we take the video to them, and he'll know if we have because he'll notice people will be trying to kill him. When that doesn't happen, he'll realise we haven't given them the video, and he will unwind himself as far as he can from them before killing them. Calvert is not a partner; he's just the hired help, so I'd say he doesn't have long.' They were gathered in the private clinic's orangery. Ben had already relayed to them his conversation with Liang.

'Liang didn't suspect the video was dodgy then?' Danny enquired.

'No, and he called off the hit squad that was waiting for me in front of the building, so that speaks volumes. He expects everyone to behave just like him, duplicitous and out for themselves, because he would probably try to do something similar in their position.'

'I still feel uneasy about giving him a faked video if that causes him to kill those three. I'm not against them dying, and we're not the executioner, but we've appointed ourselves their judge and jury. There's a due process, an order in life, and if we stray from that, well...' Ingrid did not finish her sentence.

'You're right, Ingrid, but there comes a point where intervention in the order of life is necessary to preserve that order.' That was as much as anyone had ever heard Francois say at one time.

'Francois is right, Mamma, but I love you for the way you think.'

'We've got them fighting each other, which massively alters the odds, but let's be clear. We've only bought ourselves time with this ceasefire, and the war will never end all the time Liang exists. Liang will now eliminate Calvert, Towner, and Sabitini; they'll all suffer terrible "accidents". It'll be front-page news – certainly for the latter two – and we're the only people on the planet who know that Liang did it. That's when it becomes even more essential for him to take care of us. This ceasefire, for us, will last a week at the most, during which time we need to work out how to finish it once and for all. Our survival depends on it.' By now, they all knew Ben, and they knew what this meant.

'I certainly want him dead, and I'm happy to do the killing.' Stephanie propped herself up on her elbows, the tension in her neck and shoulders exacerbating her fervour. 'I'm only here because Ben saved me. Otherwise, I'd be as dead as Papa.' Stephanie remained uncomfortably poised and in pain until Hilda nodded.

Ben made eye contact with everyone, Ingrid in particular. 'We still have a copy of Uwe's fifty-two videos, and that's our ultimate nuclear deterrent. For now, no-one's trying to kill us. And, Danny, we need to call upon your skills once more.'

'Yes, and while you plan our next steps, Ben, I have to organise Claus' funeral.' Ingrid dabbed at her eye with a small tissue. 'Hardly a normal event, but after all this, I will ensure we celebrate his life and not mourn his passing.' Stephanie put an arm around her mother and rested her head on hers.

Chapter Fifty-Two

Three days later, Ingrid gathered the six of them in the tall-ceilinged drawing room of the Oppenheimer summer home before the formalities of the funeral. It was the Omega to the Alpha of the meeting they had held in the reverential calm of St. Johann's church ten days earlier.

Christophe was the only one missing from the original seven, but many of them were now quite different people – Hilda and Stephanie in particular, whom Ben had custody of in a wheelchair, her leg supported and heavily strapped. Hilda was treated with great care and deference when anyone spoke with her.

Ingrid addressed them. 'I'm sure Claus is applauding us from somewhere. Maybe he's in the same cloud as Uwe's videos.' The quip instantaneously drew grateful, authentic laughter. 'I know Claus would have been incredibly appreciative of each and every one of you, thank you all so much. You have requited my dear husband's memory, but now we have a couple of hundred friends, family, and of course the world's media to deal with over the next few hours. God give us strength, and a glass of champagne – hopefully.' Again polite laughter as Ingrid ushered her guests through the doors to the terrace and lawn beyond.

Gliding between her guests she made her way to Ben, touching him lightly on the sleeve.

'Ben, I decided it would be wrong to mention any one person's contribution over the last couple of weeks, and I'm sorry I couldn't mention you, but you're the anomaly. We are Claus' family, or have known him all our lives, whereas you've only known him for a couple of weeks. I wanted to let you know we recognise what you've risked, and that we will be indebted to you forever. You will always be a part of this family, and we'd like you to stay here as our guest for as long as you want. I hope Stephanie has already made that clear to you?' Ingrid Oppenheimer used tact and diplomacy as an artist uses paints on a palette, creating hues of alliances and relationships with subtle brushstrokes. Then, step back and the strokes blend into a single engaging picture, what appeared to be random daubs blur harmoniously together – like nature herself.

What an invaluable asset to Claus in their dealings with the rich and powerful, thought Ben, as he enjoyed the attention of both Oppenheimer females.

'Stephanie mentioned your offer. I'll stay, at least until she's able to walk. Let's see what the future brings, eh?'

*

A cloudless, pale blue sky provided the heavenly mantle for Claus' last formal function on earth. Bright and sunny, although the breeze coming off the Zurich See posed a reminder autumn was gathering. The sun dappled avenue of tall plane trees, peeling bark mottling their trunks, stood to attention as the cortege cruised reverentially between them.

A chill wind from the mountains to the south carried small raindrops to tinkle softly against the cold, black paintwork of the funeral cortege's vehicles. The trees cast early autumn leaves in homage as eager humanity overflowed from the small church to the relay-screens set up on the surrounding lawns and paths. Ingrid, radiating elegance, insisted she link arms with Ben as he guided Stephanie's wheelchair, inferring a subliminal message to the congregation.

Ben and Stephanie were unperturbed. Each had their own way of trying to deal with the recent past. Grief moves at its own pace, slowly re-grinding the same raw and scarred emotions. A never-ending rotation of pain, introspection, and remorse, taking different routes through the what-if's and self-blame, but always reaching the same conclusion.

Ingrid had not understated the number of people who would be attending. There were many – maybe as many as four or five hundred; it was difficult to tell, as the human pool spilled from its religious epicentre. Rich and famous rubbing shoulders with tradespeople; Government ministers and the globally powerful with GMB's most junior employees.

Ben knew that Liang, Towner, and Sabitini's firms would have sent representatives. He wondered where they were and how much they knew of the last two weeks' happenings. He pushed those thoughts away so as not to sully his memory, short but impactful, of a man he would like to have known better.

Was it a sixth sense that made Ingrid squeeze his hand at that moment? He didn't know, but returned her easy smile as Stephanie leaned forward in her seat to look at him, having walked slowly into her place on crutches. Two generations of incredible women framed in elegant and proud remembrance; he was in awe of them both. Appreciating the reassurance, Stephanie returned his smile.

In contrast to the rank of the average attendee, the service was unfussy and simple. The strong and composed Oppenheimer ladies narrated their own eulogies which, had you never known Claus, triangulated to a point where stood an extraordinary human being. Few dry eyes when recalling the tender moments was balanced by relieved laughter at the humorous ones, and a standing ovation at the conclusion. Certainly not old-church, judging by the surprise on Father Knepper's face, but this wasn't a day for anything other than uninhibited celebration of an amazing life expunged before its natural conclusion.

A more intimate group was invited back to the Oppenheimer manor and, after the polite non-overstaying of welcomes had been performed, they drifted off promising to stay in touch. As the crowd thinned and the purging effect of every funeral's line-being-drawn-under-something was felt, Francois beckoned Ben to one side.

'Do you still have the gun?' Francois' eye contact was more intense than normal, even allowing for the lethal topic.

'Yes, It's in my room upstairs. Why?'

'It may be nothing, but the man you wounded on the Verbier chairlift is in Switzerland.' Ever to the point, Francois' brow furrowed at this announcement.

'How do you know it's him?'

'We know Calvert was bluffing about grabbing the webcam footage from the Medran lift. As you realised, that was just to squeeze you for information. We've got the footage, and it shows the mercenary you shot getting off the chairlift at the top. He is obviously in a lot of pain – you must have got him in the hip or the top of the leg, judging by the way he tumbles off and just leaves his dead colleague on the chair to go back to the bottom. This guy is wanted by just about every intelligence agency worldwide, which is how Interpol's facial recognition system picked him up coming in from France. A complete fluke, he crossed with the usual traffic near Geneva Airport. But our friend happened to glance at one of the cameras and technology did the rest.'

Ben felt uneasy. 'Liang's not stupid. He knows it's not in his interest to order a hit on us. He doesn't want anything to happen to us, not yet at least. If it does, we could deliver the St. Gallen video to the Police, or to Sabitini, Calvert, and Towner. If they're still alive by then.'

'Agreed, and from our sources we know Liang has cancelled the contracts on you. We believe that this particular guy, working on his own, has gone rogue, seeking personal revenge because you shot him and he'll walk with a limp for the rest of his life. After Verbier, he immediately left the country and was operated on in a private clinic in Istanbul. Then he went to ground, presumable to convalesce, and has now reappeared, here in Zurich. We'd be fools not to consider it a serious threat.'

Francois enforced the point, 'Remy is looking for him now, but you need to be extra careful, Ben, no unnecessary risks. You can legally carry a firearm in Switzerland; do so for the time being. At least until we can track down this guy. Ingrid says you're staying here, which is good, as it's safer than the St. Gallen Hotel. We will resolve this as fast as possible.'

*

The emotional roller-coaster didn't want to release Ben. After promising Francois he would be careful, he went to find Stephanie. She was sitting with Hilda, side by side in one of the tall bay windows where the low window seat, with its sweeping view down to the Zurich See, doubled as an ideal venue for private conversation.

Do we learn by nurture, or is it in our nature, he wondered, *how you know when you are the subject of other people's conversation?* Knowing smiles and nothing is said, because it didn't need to be.

'Hi Hilda, you alright?' Hilda nodded and smiled in response. Ben turned to Stephanie. 'How's the leg?'

'Bearable if I don't put weight on it, but I'm going stir crazy to be honest. I know everyone means well, but it's much the same conversation repeated every time. I need some air, can you take me out in the wheelchair? There are public footpaths beyond our garden, and we could take the dogs.'

'You sure you're up to it?' Ben enquired.

'Completely. You'll be doing the pushing, I'll be sitting. I just need to change my mental scenery.'

'OK, I'll get my coat and see you by the boot room in five.' Ben acknowledged it was impossible for him to refuse as Stephanie pulled him away from the last of the guests paying their respects to the Oppenheimer family. It was mid-afternoon, and the remaining few dozen were slowly drifting away. He sprinted up the stairs to his room and retrieved his coat, removing the gun from its hiding place and weighing it in his hand. He hoped he'd never need to use it again. *Wishful thinking,* he muttered, as he checked the magazine, placed the gun in his pocket, and jogged to meet Stephanie.

The Oppenheimers' two dogs went crazy when Stephanie freed them from their caged kennels. Irrespective of whether it was relief at being set free or happy to see Stephanie, the dogs were as excitable as any he had ever seen.

Stephanie sat in the wheelchair and held the dogs on their retractable leads while Ben navigated the tarmac path through the manor's gardens and out into the public paths overlooking the lake. Stephanie's lower leg, in its plastic surgical boot, pointed their way like the figurehead on an old schooner, as they set off in the crisp late afternoon air towards the lake.

'I still can't believe it when I look back. The Five, the Sonne Berg, the chalet, being chased and shot at in London, Monaco's exploits, Hong Kong, Gina, back to New York, then the plane and the…'

Ben recognised the pattern and jumped in before Stephanie's thoughts wandered too far.

'It never does any good to dwell on the bad stuff. Never look back; move on and look for positives. You've got to think about Ingrid. She's amazing and strong, but grief demands repayment, and it sets the terms.'

'You're right. It's difficult, though. So much happened in such a short time.'

They had walked out of the grounds and onto the paths criss-crossing among the few trees, sloping down to the huge lake. The dogs were grateful to be allowed to run free, chasing and barking in a mock fight. Ben was out of breath on the uphill sections.

'You sure you're warm enough?' He could see where the autumn mist had attached itself to strands of her hair, like a spider's web in an early morning dew, escaping from under her beanie.

'It's this breeze, it's chillier than I thought.'

'Well, I'm boiling.' Ben stopped and applied the wheelchair's brake. 'Take my coat, I'm overheating.' Ben placed his winter coat backwards over her shoulders, pulling it up to her chin.

Stephanie reached for his hand as he did so; Ben paused as they studied each other properly for the first time.

'Thanks for everything, Ben, we could never have come this far without you. I didn't realise before what it took to face death, to hold your nerve, and to overcome it. I'm not sure we can go back to what we were before. We owe you so much.'

'It wasn't just me, you know. Everyone's done their bit, you've done more than most.'

'Yes. But you know what I mean.' Neither had broken eye contact.

'I do.'

They rolled on and towards autumn's advent, seasonal change foretold in the browning of a leaf's edge and the hint of their breath's visibility as the light faded.

Ben stopped, came round to face Stephanie, and squatted down to look at her, holding her hand. 'There is something I need to tell you. It's about what you told me on the plane, about the Five and Sam's death...'

'Oh Ben, I'm so sorry. We thought it would be more dangerous for you to know.'

Ben held up his hand. 'I know.'

He wanted to wait for the man on his phone to pass out of earshot and was irritated when the man walked close to them, too close, then turned. He wore his collar up, chattering into the phone pressed against his ear, his other hand thrust into his pocket.

Then Ben noticed. The man was walking with a limp.

Time stood still, then it crept forward in slow motion as Ben registered the man's limp. He recognised the eyes in the same moment; the same eyes he'd seen on the chairlift emerging out of the Verbier gloom seven nights ago. Claus' killer was five steps away, and he was holding a gun. Ben was crouched in front of the wheelchair, Stephanie motionless and seated, and the man knew he had them cold.

The wheelchair was on a slope, Ben's gun was in the pocket of his coat draped over the seated Stephanie above him, as the man theatrically raised the gun, ever so slowly, to point between Ben's eyes. Posing with his head held high, arm pointing straight down, shoulders turned sideways as if in a duel. Ben didn't see anything other than the eyes he knew from the chairlift and a cruel smile, as limping man took careful aim at Ben.

'No!' Stephanie screamed, as she pushed herself up with her good leg, twisting herself towards Ben. He saw the determined look in her eyes as she struggled to get out of the chair and fell on him in a tangle of uncoordinated limbs.

Ben wrapped his arms around her, grappling to find the pocket in his coat wrapped around her shoulders. She pressed herself against him, her back to the man, as Ben groped for the pocket. His fingers felt the gun's outline through the thick material, and he slid his hand towards the pocket's opening as Stephanie remained clamped to him.

'No!' Stephanie screamed again as she pressed harder against him.

Ben knew he would never have time to get Stephanie clear, remove the gun, and shoot. In that time, limping man could empty his entire magazine. His mouth felt dry.

'It's easy to fire at someone from behind, Mason, like playing a war game on a computer. It's different when you're facing them, close up, like this. This is proper killing, when you look into their eyes, a window into their soul, see them as a live human being.' Limping-man snarled his monotone as the tip of Ben's finger brushed against cold metal, slowly working his hand towards the grip.

Limping-man continued. 'That's why most people can't pull the trigger when they're this close.'

They stared unblinkingly into each other's eyes, and the man smiled as he pointed the gun at Ben. Ben could see his limp made him unsteady in the breezy conditions.

The man fired, and Ben instantly felt the fiery pain in his hand an instant before Stephanie shook with the bullet's impact as she collapsed into Ben. Their combined instability knocked them over, the wheelchair and the dogs' leads chaotically tangled between them. Ben fought to overcome the pain in his hand. His other hand now held the gun, still stuck in the pocket as he gripped Stephanie. The man stepped closer and stood over them, the gun pointing at Ben's chest. Ben heard the supersonic crack as the bullet tore easily through the fabric of his coat.

One eightieth of a second later, that bullet tore just as easily through the gunman's coat. It did not begin its destructive mushrooming, tearing through his vital organs and arteries, until it crashed into the ribs framing the man's chest cavity. By the time the nine-millimetre harbinger of death had transferred all its energy, the gunman was dead, half a second after Ben had fired the gun from inside his pocket, still unable to free his hand.

'Steph, Steph. Talk to me.' A burgundy shadow grew beneath the material of her coat. A small darker dot in the centre signposted the bullet's entry point, having passed through the back of Ben's left hand. 'Talk to me, talk to me.'

He held her head, beseeching her to wake as he blinked away tears. Her eyes remained closed as he cried out her name through unconscious anguish. He felt empty and desolate when fury in its ugly glory arrived at his open door, and he invited it in. Francois was with him now. His voice raised — Ben couldn't hear him – he was emptying the gun into the life-vacated body of the gunman, shouting and swearing until it was spent, and him with it. Then he sank to his knees.

'She's still breathing. The bullet's still in her but her pulse is strong, so it's missed the vital organs. We've got to get her to hospital quickly. Pick her up while I phone for an ambulance.' Francois' direct and economic instructions fired Ben into action as he scooped Stephanie up. One hand under shoulders, the other under her knees, Ben tipped her into his chest so he could study her face.

'You stupid, beautiful idiot, you knew exactly what you were doing. You better bloody live.' He staggered as fast as his burning legs would carry him, back up the slope towards the Oppenheimer manor, through the late afternoon mist, blood and agony coursing through the wound in his hand.

'Ambulance will be here in two minutes. Can you manage?' Francois was back next to him, one hand under Ben's arm.

'I'm fine.' Ben was focussed on getting up the incline to the house as fast as possible.

'You're bleeding.'

'Yes, he shot me through the hand. It was on Stephanie's back, that's what's inside her now.'

'Come here, I'll take her.'

'I said I'm fine.' Ben broke into a jog, as much to prove a point as to shorten the time until Stephanie was in medical hands. His lungs screamed at him, his legs were on fire, so was his hand, but still he increased his pace. His focus was clear: save Stephanie, kill Liang.

A leaden sky blanketed the hillside, casting the manor into a gloomy half-light through which the flashing blue lights of the ambulance bounced off every surface. The rear doors of the private ambulance were flung open as two paramedics jumped down onto the gravel drive.

'Rear entry, right shoulder, small round, her pulse is strong. I've seen shock like this before, get her an oxy mask and a morphine shot. She's had morphine before with no adverse reaction,' gasped Ben, as he held her out towards the medics.

'Right, we've got her,' replied one of the paramedics. 'Your hand.' He pointed at Ben's left hand. 'Have you been shot?'

'No. It's hers, I got it from carrying her.' Ben didn't have time for hospitals. He knew Liang would soon hear about limping-man and his unsuccessful attempt. 'You need to get her to hospital as quickly as possible.'

Ben ushered the paramedics back into the ambulance and slammed the doors, banging on them with his good hand, the other tucked under his armpit. As the ambulance pulled away, lights flashing and siren bleeping, he felt the intense pain shooting through his hand, up his arm and into his head, as his chemical reaction subsided. He felt dizzy with the exertion as Hilda and Ingrid ran shrieking from the house, Danny following a few paces behind. Francois had told them, and he now held his best friend's widow in a tight embrace and tried to calm her.

'She's going to be fine, Ingrid. Shock knocked her out, but I think the bullet's missed any major organs. She's young and fit. She'll be fine.' Ben knew Francois was hoping, not diagnosing. He also knew that Francois couldn't bring himself to believe this had happened. Claus' only remaining child could be killed on the day of his funeral; it was too much to bear.

Danny put Ben's good arm over his shoulder, and Hilda put her hand under the other as they hobbled their way back to the house. Ben recognised one of Francois' ex-colleagues standing inside the entrance hall. Francois was speaking to him. 'Take Ingrid to the hospital immediately, stay with her, go everywhere with her, and do not let her out of your sight. I'll be there as soon as I can, and call me when the doctors give any diagnosis.'

The ex-colleague nodded.

Francois turned to Ingrid. 'You go with him to the hospital; he'll take care of you. We have some things to organise here.' He placed a comforting hand on Ingrid's shoulder.

He could see she was in shock, but there was nothing he could do about that at the moment. Ingrid walked numbly out of the door and into the night.

Chapter Fifty-Three

'You should've gone to hospital.' Francois pointed at Ben's bloodied, ugly hand.

'We don't have the time, Francois. We know Liang didn't sanction this, but when he hears about his ex-hit man going rogue, he'll know we'll be after him. So we have to accelerate our plan and retaliate before he learns about limping-man's attempt.'

'Agreed, but do you have a plan? Or even a non-plan?'

'It's incomplete, but I do have a plan. First, we've got to keep Stephanie and limping-man out of the news for at least twenty-four hours, or it'll alert Liang. Second, does anyone know where the Oppenheimers keep their painkillers? I need a big box of them and some super-glue.'

'I do, and I've called Dr. Virchow, the consultant who looked after Stephanie. I've told him everything, and he's on his way here to treat you.'

'Thanks, Hilda.' Ben struggled to concentrate as the gunshot wound sent bolts of pain up his arm and into his chest.

'Twenty-four hours is doable. Any longer with a gunshot wound and it gets tricky. I know Inspector Remy's made your life difficult, but basically he's a good policeman, and he'd do it for Ingrid and the right reasons. I'll speak with him.' Francois was dialling Remy's number as he walked away, passing Hilda bearing super-glue and bandages.

'Hilda, how quickly can you get me a cell phone and somehow register it in the name of Andrew Calvert?'

'Half an hour, no more.'

'Good, we can collect it on the way to the airport, as I need to be on the next flight to Hong Kong.' Ben poured glue into the hole in his hand, dripping blood into the kitchen sink. His statement stopped the room.

'Hong Kong? Why Hong Kong?' Even as Danny asked his question, he realised he knew the answer.

'He's going there to impersonate Calvert, so he can get close to Liang.' It was a statement from Francois, not a question.

Ben raised his eyebrows. 'Yes, Francois. Spot on.' Ben stared hard at each of them. 'We've got to put an end to this. The only way I'll get close enough to Liang is to become someone who Liang wants to meet. Since we showed Liang the faked video of Calvert, Towner, and Liang plotting, he'd welcome any of them into his spider's web. But especially Calvert.'

'Why especially Calvert?' It was Danny's turn to not follow Ben.

'Because he can kill Calvert without worrying about repercussions. Whereas Towner and Sabitini will already have arranged *insurance* should anything mysterious happen to them.' It was Francois' turn to answer for Ben.

'Spot on again, Francois. And to help him do that, I'm going to give Liang a perfect excuse to invite Calvert to his Peak Apartments penthouse, in Hong Kong.'

'Ben, I've arranged a Pay-As-You-Go mobile which you can collect at the airport. By the time you collect it, I'll have it registered in Calvert's name and loaded it with credit.'

'Great, Hilda, can you send the phone number to Danny? Thanks.' Ben went on, 'Danny, this'll really test your creativity. Using your voice synthesis app, I need you to create another fake video of Calvert. But for it to fool Liang, I need it to be a selfie video. Can you do that?'

Danny's face pinched in concentration. 'Yeah, should be able to. I think I've got a few close-ups of Calvert from the St. Galen CCTV grabs. I can zoom in and crop it, which'll make it blurry, right, but the sound should be convincing.'

'Nice one. Now, can you make Calvert say the following...' Ben grabbed a pen and, using the back of an envelope, he wrote Calvert's most famous script ever, the one he would never know he had ever delivered. The one that wrote his own death sentence.

'Then when you've made the fake video, can you send it in Calvert's name from my new cell phone to Thomas Liang's private mobile? It'll be the middle of the night in Hong Kong, so he'll view it when he wakes up. Here's Liang's private mobile number.'

He Ben handed Danny the business card Liang had thrown into the lift when Ben left their last meeting.

'I'm on it.'

'You're on the next, and only, Hong Kong flight, Ben. Swiss Air, seat four F, departs twenty-two-forty this evening, arrives just under twelve hours later into HKIA at seventeen-thirty local time tomorrow.'

'Fantastic, Hilda, thank you.' Then he laid back as the painkillers kicked in.

Chapter Fifty-Four

The strong inclination of Switzerland's authorities was not to disturb the status quo any further than it was already. After Francois' conversation with him, Inspector Remy's influence meant Ben's self-defence shooting of limping-man was not challenged. Especially as the victim was a known terrorist whom the Swiss were embarrassed not to have detected and stopped at their border.

Remy's boss agreed to classify everything connected to Claus, including limping-man's death, as 'National Security'. That allowed him to exercise emergency powers preventing the hospital and the Police from recording or reporting Stephanie's gunshot wound. Remy had bought them their twenty-four hours.

*

'Was she really driving that Audi all the time around Canary Wharf? You didn't drive at all?' Danny's head wobbled energetically as he questioned his friend.

'She was driving the whole time. She's a seriously good driver, really good. I thought she'd be a lot of talk, but she gave it everything. Drifting a four-wheel-drive car is a lot harder than a two-wheel one, but she handled it brilliantly, hand brake-turns into corners, the lot. Don't think you or I would have done much better.'

'Respect that. Do you remember when I first met her in the boozer, she was talking about the merits of different Maserati engines for chrissake. No chick's ever done that to me before.'

Danny was driving Ben to Zurich Airport for his late evening flight to Hong Kong. The others had left to join Ingrid in the hospital, where Stephanie was still unconscious and unresponsive. Danny knew Ben had twelve hours on a plane which he would spend thinking about Stephanie.

'You're going to do this, aren't you?' Danny couldn't hide his nervousness.

337

'Yes, Dan. I am. Don't worry, mate, it'll be fine. You'll weave your magic and fake another voice synthesised video from Calvert. You'll send it to Thomas Liang, supposedly from my new phone, and he's going to be completely taken in by it.' Ben held his new phone aloft like a prop in amateur theatre. 'We're playing to his fears. When he sees that video, he'll be so keen for an audience with my Andrew Calvert that he'll demand Calvert come to his penthouse. He'll lower his defence shields for Calvert to come through his security, to take the lift up to his floor, because he wants to kill him. He'll welcome Calvert in, and will want it so badly that he won't notice it's not Calvert; not until it's too late. What could possibly go wrong?' Ben laughed as he wrapped his arms around and crushed an unconvinced Danny Mullen.

'I'll text as soon as we hear anything about Stephanie.'

'Thanks, mate. Check with Francois and Hilda about my shopping list, will you?'

'Shopping list. Right.' Danny gave an uncertain wave, unsure what else to say as Ben was swallowed into the procession of Zurich International Airport's travellers late on a Monday evening.

*

Thomas Liang nearly deleted the suspect message without opening it; *Unknown Number* flashed up, and he was just about to delete it when he saw Calvert's name in the text. Now, though, he was glad he had been curious enough to find out why his soon-to-be-ex puppet was playing at espionage.

He played the video. It was typical Andrew Calvert, conspicuous as ever in hallmark Panama hat, cream linen suit, and blue shirt. The drawled, ever-so-properly pronounced vowels grated on Thomas Liang's verbal heritage; his phonetic DNA was Chinese, the polar opposite mouth-shape required to speak non-Chinese languages. He re-played the video again.

'*Mr. Liang, I've discovered a plot against you by Towner and Sabitini. They said they'll kill me if I tell you. In return for your protection, I will tell you what and when they are planning. I believe execution of their plan is imminent, so I am on my way* to Hong Kong now. If you do not guarantee my safety, I will disappear, and no-one will be able to find me. If you guarantee my safety, I will come to your HK apartment tomorrow night. I've destroyed my old cell phones; I'm sending you this from my new number. I am bringing you something of great value for which I want to be paid. Andrew Calvert.'

'You always were a weak and greedy fool Calvert,' Thomas Liang said out loud. 'But your fly has just invited itself into my spider's web. So, every cloud, Calvert. Every cloud...'

He made an encrypted phone call to an untraceable number.

'Da' came the short reply.

'I want you to execute the plan for number two and three tomorrow. Number six is coming here. I will take care of him.'

'Price doesn't change.' Flat Slavic tones brooked no discussion.

'I've already paid.' And Liang hung up.

*

Ben's hand throbbed; it was a dull, deep in the middle of his bones ache. The cortisone injections Dr. Virchow had given him twelve hours earlier were wearing off. He woke quickly; the memory of Stephanie throwing herself into the line of fire was as effective as any stimulant. Thirty minutes from beginning final descent into Hong Kong International Airport on a cloudy and humid Tuesday afternoon, his mind started to place the jigsaw pieces together. He turned on his new mobile, searching for a network, but they were still too high; it would pick up one when it was available. Hilda would have ensured he'd have no connection issues, as he ran through his playbook once more.

He smiled at the placard displaying 'Andrew Calvert'. *Nice one Hilda* he muttered under his breath and held up a finger in recognition.

'Hello, Mr. Calvert, this way please. I see you have no luggage, so we use fast-track through VIP, the car is just outside.' The deferential driver led the way through customs and immigration with consummate ease.

Ben kept pace, both with the driver and with his new, temporary, identity. He mused on whether it had been Hilda or Francois' idea to use Calvert's name in case Liang's men were watching the arrivals area. They certainly couldn't use Ben Mason, he knew.

Sitting innocently on the back seat of the car was a suit carrier and a hat box. Ben thanked the driver as he held the door open for him.

'I collect your packages as instructed, Mr. Calvert. I hope all OK?' The driver courteously enquired.

'I'm sure they'll be just fine, thank you. Peak Apartments now, please.'

Ben unpacked the suit carrier as the comfortable car ran along the Lantau Highway, speeding towards the shimmering evening lights of Hong Kong and Kowloon beyond. He tingled in anticipation when he saw the Peak come into view as they crossed the Tsing Ma Bridge over the open waters of the channel beneath them, dark and still; they reflected Ben's demeanour.

Undressing with some difficulty on the back seat, redressing with equal difficulty, the driver discretely pointed the rear-view mirror to the floor as Ben changed clothes and rehearsed his moves. With the driver's mirror turned away, Ben checked inside the Panama hat. The snub-nosed, three-inch, thirty-eight calibre revolver inside its dome was held in place by two Velcro straps. He checked that all of the six chambers in the revolving cylinder were loaded, then flicked through the stack of one-thousand Hong Kong-dollar bills, held securely within the large money-clip. Roughly fifty – a deliberately vulgar amount of cash which would make it an even more effective distraction.

In Ben's ordered mind he envisaged every eventuality and developed a solution to each, while hoping for a text to say Stephanie was OK. His anxiety drove a curious urgency, but he couldn't resist sending a brief text to Danny as the sleek black limousine slowed to a halt in front of Peak Heights Apartments.

'I'll be about two hours; it could be less. You OK to wait for me?' Ben said to the driver.

'Yes, Mr. Calvert. I'll be here when you need me.'

*

The car door was opened for Ben by a member of the Concierge's desk, respectfully bowing, as Mr. Andrew Calvert, Charges D'Affaires for the British Embassy in Berne, Switzerland, alighted. The usual six foot three inches tall Calvert, wearing the usual tailored cream linen suit with hardly a crease in the material, highly polished brown brogues and a cornflower blue open-necked shirt, strode confidently and loudly to the front desk to announce himself. His usual blue handkerchief was tucked into his breast pocket for good measure.

'Calvert,' Ben boomed. 'Andrew Calvert. Here to see Thomas Liang. My card.' Ben bowed fractionally and handed the business card Calvert had given him all those days ago to the receptionist, who received it in the customary double-handed fashion and bowed slightly lower than Ben.

'Please, Mister Calvert, would you follow me?'

The receptionist led the way to the Penthouse suite's private elevator, in front of which stood a metal detector archway. The wealthy residents of Peak Heights were taking no chances. *Nor should they,* thought Ben, *there are bad people everywhere.*

The receptionist pointed to the archway. 'Please, Mr. Calvert.'

Ben stepped forward, and with Calvert's usual arrogance announced, 'Of course, but I should warn you some parts of me are made of steel.'

He emphasised the last word with a clenched fist and a pantomime smile to the receptionist as he placed his phone in the tray next to the archway. Then, in a carefree manner, he tossed his Panama and money clip into the tray beside the archway. The clip was heavier, the fifty thousand dollars within it deliberately arranged so they spilled from the brim of the Panama hat, in which it was never intended to stay, and onto the floor. Given certain stimulants, human nature can be very predictable, and the reaction to the equivalent of many months' wages in cash being carelessly tossed onto the floor was one of them. A perfect distraction, the receptionist and archway operator dived down to help retrieve the discarded money.

Calvert faked remorse. 'How clumsy of me, I do apologise. Never was any good at cricket.' He accompanied the quip with an unnecessarily loud guffaw.

'Is no problem, Mr. Calvert, please.' And the receptionist again directed Ben through the archway.

'It'll beep, I'm warning you.' This was soon proved true as the detector emitted a loud, repetitive beep. Ben stepped back, removed his linen jacket, and rolled up his left sleeve to reveal a twenty-centimetre-long scar plus accompanying puncture marks.

'Don't say I didn't warn you.' Again this was accompanied by the trademark Calvert laugh at too high a volume.

The archway operator picked up a hand-held wand detector. 'Please.' Motioning Ben to hold his arms out from his sides, he glided it thoroughly over his body, emitting a beep only when it hovered over his forearm scar. Satisfied, he flicked a switch and beckoned Ben through the powered-down archway, turning it back on when he was through.

'Please.' The operator pointed with an outstretched palm towards the tray containing his re-constituted money clip, and of course his harmless Panama hat.

'Many thanks, old boy,' Ben boomed as he smiled a Calvert smile and donned his hat with a settling tap on its dome, then headed off to the penthouse lift.

Ben stood, Panama in place, with his back to the lift's camera and his head facing slightly downwards, as if lost in a meaningful contemplation, while he whistled a jaunty sea shanty. He advanced his mental rehearsal: *I am Andrew Calvert, I'm loud and arrogant.* He occupied himself with thoughts of positive action to keep fear and doubt at bay.

The lift doors slid soundless apart, opening onto a small lobby in which stood a purposely positioned security guard. He was powerfully built, ex-military, competent looking, with searching eyes and holding a metal detector wand. Ben didn't care about the security guard; he was pleased he could not see any CCTV cameras.

This is the real thing, Ben, he said to himself. *No second chances if you get this wrong.*

'Don't trust Chummy downstairs, eh?' Calvert boomed in Ben's best impersonation of his alter ego. 'Already been through that down there.'

Ben jerked his thumb back towards the lift as he repeated the exercise of placing phone, money clip, and Panama hat onto an antique table next to him. He stretched out his arms and offered an indulgent, but slightly impatient smile as he took in every detail of the penthouse's entrance lobby proper, just beyond him.

While the security guard waved his wand over him, Ben could see the main reception area at the end of a thirty-metre-long main corridor, beyond which was a huge wall of glass leading onto an equally large terrace, thirty-two floors above the highest point on Hong Kong. Vertical bolts of gossamer thin, soft, white fabric hung from the ceiling in front of the glass preventing him from seeing beyond the terrace balcony, although he knew it pointed towards the harbour more than a mile below them.

'This one's got a metal pin in it, old boy,' Calvert helpfully announced, holding up his left arm, as they repeated the same revelatory procedure as on the ground floor. The security guard was either not satisfied or he didn't like Calvert, as he insisted on a full pat-down search with physical contact. Wordlessly he nodded with his chin to Ben, who picked up his phone and money clip while resetting his Panama hat.

'This way.' The curt instruction.

'Of course, dear boy. After you.' Calvert was back to his booming best.

The main reception room was huge; there was no other way to describe it. Three levels tall, two of which were galleried landings looking down from two sides of the square onto the floor where Ben now stood, and that was the size of a tennis court. It was like a Moorish courtyard, but indoors on the thirty-second floor, an ostentatious display of wealth. Echoing down from above him came the sound of Liang shouting at someone on a call. He was one, or possibly two, floors above him.

Perfect, Ben thought to himself. *Viewed from above, I am Andrew Calvert. A white oval hat of rigid straw, atop cream shoulders, a glimpse of my blue shirt, and an ever-so-English, public school accent.*

'Is that you, Andrew?' Liang called from two floors above, his voice echoing around the vast atrium. He was expecting Calvert, so Ben gave him what he was expecting.

Ben raised and replaced his hat without looking up. 'The one and only,' he bellowed in his best Calvert voice hearing it echo off the atrium's hard surfaces.

'Great to see you. Be with you in a minute.' Liang disappeared back to shout at someone else on a call, back to wherever it was he'd come from.

Ben didn't want to know, as that would involve looking up. He was in the lion's den, and now his emotions started to simmer. He had to control and direct it, use its energy positively and maintain focus. He distracted himself with examining pieces of Royal jade in a display case. The stone was smoother than anything he'd felt before, frictionless and bone dry, and his fingers slid over the surfaces as they would over wet soap. Time slowed to a crawl, almost stationary; seconds took minutes, and minutes took an eternity to pass. He strolled slowly around the room, hands clasped behind back, looking to all intents and purposes like a tourist in a museum, except tourists seldom need to hold back the wall of fear and anxiety which Ben was.

'Andrew, so sorry. You know, one of those calls which drag on for ever. Please come.' Liang's politeness was transparently insincere, impersonated and on permanent loan from someone else, drawn when required from a lexicon of characteristics Liang did not naturally possess.

Ben walked into the middle of the room, to where the spiral staircase began its sweeping ascent. Broad, deep glass steps fanned out from a polished chrome column as thick as a man's chest. *Scale was everything in Liang's life,* thought Ben, as he began his climb.

He tried to imitate how a cocky Calvert, bringing this valuable news to Liang, would step. Not too fast, slower than a jog but not much; imitation athletic was how Ben saw it. He settled into a rhythm, fractionally tilting his head downwards, hands swinging more from the elbow than the shoulder, as he rehearsed his plan and went over the eventualities.

Two security guards; were there any others?

All the while, Liang narrated for him. 'So glad you could come, Andrew. I've arranged extra security, so don't worry, I'll make sure they can't get to you. I'll fix this permanently for you.'

344

Ben was past the first floor now, breathing more heavily but maintaining his rhythm. He knew the pinch point would come in ten seconds, so prepared himself.

'You out of breath, Andrew? You've hardly said a word.'

Ben increased his pace, jogging slightly faster now, on the balls of his feet and humming his jaunty sea shanty, pumping his arms. He took the last half circle two steps at a time, landing on the top step with a leap, and put his hands on his knees.

'So, Andrew, what are Towner and Sabitini planning, and how shall we fuck them?' His wife's killer, was only a metre from him now.

Ben removed his hat and held the gun in his hand before he'd completely straightened to his full height. 'Well, Thomas, *old boy,* I'd say that you're the one who's going to get fucked.'

The normally self-assured Liang rocked on his heels. 'Mason.' It was all he could squeeze out and then, with a heavy shove from Ben, he collapsed into the armchair behind him. 'What? How did you?'

Ben had the snub-nosed thirty-eight in one hand, while the index finger of the other hand pressed onto Liang's pursed lips. 'Not a sound now, Thomas. Don't want to alert anyone, do we?'

Liang's eyes darted back and forth, reflecting his mind's current activity. 'The video was a fake, wasn't it? Which means there is no plot against me.'

Ben enjoyed smiling at Liang for the first time ever.

'That means the video of those three planning to blackmail me was also fake, wasn't it?'

Ben was pleased that he wouldn't have to explain much to Liang. He wanted to savour the moment, but that was a risky luxury.

'No more questions, you can work it out for yourself if you want to. You knew that hit man of yours had gone rogue and was coming after me, didn't you?' Ben had prepared himself for this moment. Even with Liang's fleshy visage and deep-set eyes, he saw the recognition.

'It was nothing to do with me.' They were the only words he uttered before Ben's fist slammed hard into his face, smashing his nose, and splitting his top lip with his teeth. Ben had promised himself not to take any pleasure from this inevitable event, but that proved impossible. Liang sprawled on the floor, coughing and choking on blood and harsh, physical reality for probably the first time in his life.

'Bollocks. You knew and you didn't do anything to stop him, because you could claim innocence and it suited you to test our resolve. I told you in Zurich that you would have to bear the consequences, and that is why I am here.'

Liang was on all fours, wheezing in shock and struggling to breathe.

'I'll tell you what's going to happen now. You obviously didn't take me seriously enough at our first meeting, so now we're raising the stakes. You're going to sit at your computer and you're going to type as I dictate. If you try to hit a panic button or send an alarm signal, I will kill you. If you don't do as I say, I will kill you. Is that clear?' Ben was completely calm and focussed, his voice said so.

'Is that clear?' Ben raised his calm voice.

'Yes, but I have money, loads of it. I can give it to you.' Liang had correctly read the danger signals.

'Forget the money for now. First of all, how many staff do you have on at the moment?'

'What?' A confused Liang struggled to raise his head from the floor, mumbling through split lips and broken teeth.

'I said how many staff are here at the moment? How many Thomas?' Ben repeated. loudly.

'Two; there's two. The two security guys.' Liang fell back onto the floor, breathing noisily.

'Tell them to go out for ten minutes, no more, because you don't want to be disturbed. When they return, they are to come up here to collect a package from you. And make sure the phone is on loudspeaker so I can hear.'

Liang was like a rabbit in a car's headlights as Ben pointed towards a phone on his desk. Liang climbed with difficulty to his feet and stumbled to the desk and dialled his two security guards, instructing them exactly as Ben had told him to.

When Ben waved him back to his sofa, Liang appeared grateful to be out of range from Ben's fists.

'Now show me this money, Thomas. And as I said, if you try anything, I'll happily kill you.' Ben grabbed him roughly by his collar and pulled him to his feet.

Liang stumbled towards an original Monet of water lilies in rose-tinted evening sunlight that hung on the wall behind his desk. He tilted it from the bottom right-hand corner, pivoting it by a few centimetres. It clicked then pulled away from the wall on a hinge, revealing a safe almost as big as the painting. The blue LEDs of the digital keypad glowed obediently.

'If this is rigged to set off an alarm when a certain code is used, even if that's a silent alarm, I will kill you. Do you understand?'

Liang nodded dumbly. He didn't care; it was only money after all. He correctly entered the six-digit code and twisted the handle, pulling open the steel door to reveal several neat stacks of bills plus an assortment of bearer bonds, jewellery, and documents. Ben presumed the latter were not for completely legal purposes.

'OK, take out everything and put it on the desk.'

Liang was very happy to oblige. This was a lot of money, twenty million or more, but it wouldn't cause even a flicker of the needle measuring his overall wealth.

'Now, sit at your keyboard, log in to your most frequently used social media account, and do as I say. Andrew Calvert's new mobile phone has just sent you a text with a link to an FTTP site. Access it, open it, and copy it into your social media account.'

Ben waited, refining his plan while Thomas Liang followed his instructions. 'OK, now you go sit over there and don't say or do anything.'

On his phone, Ben texted a message to a stored number. *'Send it now.'*

A few seconds later, Danny sent an email from an untraceable account to Bianca Sabitini, Brad Towner, Andrew Calvert, and Thomas Liang. It was titled 'Blackmailing Thomas Liang' and contained Danny's doctored earlier video of the CCTV grab from the St. Gallen Hotel terrace. It clearly showed Sabitini, Towner, and Calvert plotting to blackmail Liang. The other recipients saw the title and opened it immediately.

Thomas Liang looked at the large pile of cash and valuables on his desk. 'You've got your money, now walk away. It's what you should have done right at the beginning, but you chose to stay and fight for the Oppenheimers' lost cause.' Even through broken teeth and split lips, Liang spat contemptuous arrogance.

'I chose to hunt and kill you and the rest of the Five, because years ago I found out the Five killed my wife. I was going to kill Claus first, until I discovered he was not one of the Five. That's why I let him think he was recruiting me; it was my fast-track route to get to you, Sabitini and Towner.'

Liang was still processing the revelation when Ben's mention of Sam and his pent-up hatred delivered two punches: fast and hard into Liang's nose and mouth, one of the areas of the greatest concentration of nerves in the body. Liang gasped in shock as much as in pain.

'You murdered my wife. Her name was Samantha Forbes, your sick psychos Vinny and Raul forced her off a cliff in the Amazon forest because she discovered you'd murdered children and babies by pouring poison into their river.' Ben punched him again. This time was about power, not speed, and he followed through powerfully. 'Then you killed my friend Claus and tried hard to kill the woman I love. That's why I did all this.' Ben's next punch knocked Liang clean off his swivel chair, and he landed in a confused and frightened heap on the floor.

'You just don't get it, do you, Liang? People like you, think you can buy your way through life, behaving as you do, and be immune from the consequences.' Ben stopped, breathing heavily. He wanted to punch the man again but was distracted by his phone announcing a text. It was from Danny. *'She's out of surgery, in recovery, and TALKING!! Call me. Dan.'*

'Now, come back to your chair, Thomas, I want you to finish typing something.' While Thomas Liang stumbled his unsure way back to his desk, Ben dialled a number on his mobile.

Danny answered. 'Hi, mate.'

'Hi. How is she?'

'Good, she's going to be fine. The bullet missed the vital organs, although there was a bucket-load of internal bleeding they didn't spot. We nearly lost her twice and they had to resection some arteries, whatever that means, and she's had six pints of blood. All the bleeding's stopped now and she's in and out of sleep from the meds. Her vitals say she's good and will be fine. It was close, mate, too close, right?'

'Thanks, Dan.' Ben's reply was flat, unemotional.

'One other thing. I was sitting with her when she woke for a minute. Although she was in some pain and whacked-out by meds, first thing she wanted to know was how you were. She meant, how were you after she told you it wasn't a coincidence that Claus offered you a job at GMB because they all knew the Five murdered Sam.'

'You didn't tell her, did you?'

'Nah, 'course not. None of them have any idea.'

'Good, there's no point in telling them, not now. Thanks, Danny, you're a top man. I'll call you later, I've got a few things to tidy up here.' Ben's mind was clearer now than for a long time.

He turned calmly towards Liang. 'Sit here please, Thomas.' Ben patted the seat as Thomas nervously sat back down. Ben moved the keyboard a metre to the right. 'Are you comfortable enough?' Thomas Liang was totally confused.

'You look uncomfortable, Thomas. Here, let me get you a cushion.' Ben reached behind him and selected a cushion from the sofa. Liang's face was distorted from the punches, but even more so from his confusion.

Ben placed a comforting hand on the back of Thomas Liang's neck, placed the small revolver into the cushion under Liang's chin, and pulled the trigger.

Liang slumped down in the seat, staring at the ceiling. Ben went to the keyboard and finished off the last few words of Thomas Liang's last ever social media post, which included his suicide note, attached the link to Uwe's fifty-two incriminating videos, and sent it out.

Chapter Fifty-Five

The staircase did not allow for a silent approach, and Ben was interested to see that neither man was sprinting to meet his employer. When they were a few steps from the top, Ben met them with the snub-nosed thirty-eight in his hand.

'Thanks, guys. I'm Andrew Calvert, as you know. Very slowly, please remove any weapons and place them on the floor. Then you have a choice to make. You can take whatever you want from that pile of many millions in cash, bearer bonds, diamonds, or whatever, and no-one will know. I certainly do not intend to be talking to the Police, so I won't be giving any descriptions. But Thomas Liang is dead, and the Police will obviously question you. You will say Andrew Calvert came to see Mr. Liang. You know it was Calvert because Mr. Liang told you it was, and ground floor reception announced him. Mr. Liang told you not to disturb his meeting with Mr. Calvert, so you did as your boss instructed and left the building. When you came back, you discovered Mr. Liang was dead and Calvert was nowhere to be seen.

'Or you can leave all that cash there and wait for the Police to arrive, by which time I will have shot you. Your choice.'

The confused men looked at each other. Ben was betting they had identical thoughts. They looked at him. 'Don't you want any of it?'

'No. I didn't do it for that. I did it because he deserved it.'

It took the two men less than a minute to clear the pile, leaving the unfamiliar bearer bonds on Liang's desk.

'So, we're cool, yeah?' the other one asked Ben.

'Yep, we're cool. We each have our own reasons. I suggest you leave now and hide that cash somewhere with no connection to you, because the Police will search your homes thoroughly. Then come back here and call the Police. Provided you stick to the story I described, don't go flashing that money around, and say as little as possible, you'll be set for life. Leave your guns on the floor, for now, just until I've gone. Nothing personal, OK?' Ben kept a relaxed hold on the revolver, but he didn't need to. They had far more important things to attend to, and hurriedly left, leaving behind the bearer bonds.

Familiar with bearer bonds, Ben picked them up and examined them.

Then Andrew Calvert, Panama still classically in place and bearer bonds tucked into his inside pockets, waltzed breezily through Peak Height's ground floor reception, whistling a jaunty sea shanty, and into his waiting limousine.

Chapter Fifty-Six

Bianca Sabitini was empty; she sat staring at the monitor in total shock. She had just watched the video for the second time. She knew it wasn't real, but she also knew that didn't matter. What mattered was that Thomas Liang was on the address list, he would think it was real, and by now would have put in place an unstoppable chain of events.

Bianca Sabitini was dumbfounded. She knew it was deepfake, a very good one. She knew that conversation had never happened, but she had just watched herself appear to agree with that pompous sycophant Andrew Calvert and Brad Towner to blackmail the most dangerous man in the world. She knew how Thomas would react, and she had never been so scared. She had only one option.

Opening her phone, she selected an unidentified number.

'Bohdan?'

'Who wants to know?'

'It's Bianca Sabitini, and I have another job for you. In fact, I have two jobs for you. One is in Hong Kong, the other is in New York. I need it concluded within twenty-four hours.'

'The price will be high for twenty-four hours.'

'Is one million pounds high enough?'

'Twenty-four hours it is. You know which account to send it to. Text me the details.'

*

Brad Towner also watched the video twice; just to be sure. He did not have to think for long as he examined every inch of the happy Towner family photograph on his desk and punched a few buttons on his intercom.

'Salvatore.' He was Towner's new Head of Security after Vinny's demise. 'Do you wanna be rich?

'Sorry, Mr Towner?'

'I said, Salvatore-Do-You-Want-To-Be-Rich?'

'Yes, Mr Towner.'

'Then come into my office now, and I'll explain how you can earn a million in cash.'

Chapter Fifty-Seven

Two of the world's largest social media sites crashed later that day under the weight of the demand to watch the fifty-two videos. In the next twenty-four hours, over one hundred million people viewed at least one file, many viewed more than four, and several million downloaded copies.

The next day, with world markets in free-fall, the IMF called an emergency meeting of all Central Banks, the G20 Governments, the World Bank, and a dozen of the world's systemically important financial institutions, to stop the world crashing into financial-fuelled turmoil.

*

Ben gently laid his hands on Stephanie's shoulders as she sat in her wheelchair. She reached up a hand to place on his, as Ingrid handed him the tall lilies. He crouched down on the cemetery's damp grass and placed them into the vase on Claus' grave, arranging them so each petal could be kissed by the warm sun.

Hilda, Danny, and Francois stood close by. The late summer sun made one of its last appearances of such strength for the year. It would be back, though.

About the Author

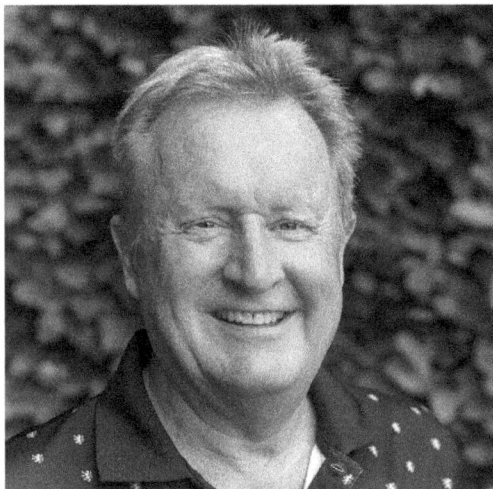

Author photograph by Simon Barratt

After forty years in the reinsurance industry, the retirement void was easily filled by John's family, friends and *hobbies*. Then came Covid imprisonment......

A need to scratch the literary itch combined with a sense of commenting on the damage we inflict upon humankind when enough, for some, obviously isn't enough.

John hopes to return to his pursuits and will be donating all profit from sales of copies of this book to charity, primarily, but not exclusively, to the one he works for:

- Nourish Community Foodbank, https://www.nourishcommunity foodbank.org.uk/

Milton Keynes UK
Ingram Content Group UK Ltd.
UKHW031454231024
450082UK00001B/144

9 781836 150152